Love
and the
Forbidden City

A Time Travel Romance Duology
Book One

Bijou Li

Bijou Li

Love and the Forbidden City

Published by Pearl Books

Pearl Books

Bijou Li

Love and the Forbidden City

Glossary

Although the following information can be found in the book, it's presented here as a quick reference for the readers.

List of main characters

Kangxi: The fourth emperor of the Qing dynasty, who ruled over China from 1661 to 1722.

Kangxi's sons who appear or are mentioned in the story:

Yinjen: The fourth prince and the fifth Qing Emperor Yongzheng. In the story he's referred to by his title Prince Yong.

Yinjeng: The fourteenth prince, sometimes referred to as Prince Fourteen, or Prince Jeng in the story. In history, he was forced to change his name to *Yinti* after his brother took the throne, because their names sounded similar.

Hongli: Prince Yong's son, and the future Emperor Qianlong.

Yinreng: The second prince, Crown Prince or *Taizi*.

Yinzhi: The third prince.

Yinsi: The eighth prince.

Titles / Terms of the Qing dynasty

Qinwang: Prince of the First Rank. Duke.

Junwang: Prince of the Second Rank. Duke.
Beile: Prince of the Third Rank.
Beizi: Prince of the Fourth Rank.
Nucai: Servant or slave. The term originated from Manchu language.
Gong-gong: A respectful way of addressing a eunuch.
Momo: An elderly palace maid.
Guniang: Girl, young lady.
Fujin: Wife or concubine of a Manchu aristocrat.
Fujun: Husband

Miscellaneous terms

qipao: (pronounced *chi-pao*) *Qi* means banner, and *pao* means gown. Thus, qipao means gown of the Manchu, which were better known as the banner people. Originally, the women's Manchu gowns were loose-fitting and long-sleeved, and the tight-fitting shape did not emerge until the 1920s.
changshan: A traditional Chinese dress worn by men, also originating from Manchu culture. Also called *changpao*, or long robe.
dudou: A traditional Chinese halter top, normally worn by both men and women as an undergarment. *Du* means belly, *dou* means wrap.
queue: Hairstyle of the Manchu men in the Qing dynasty. The front of the head is shaved, and the hair in the back braided.
pipa: Chinese string instrument.
zheng: Chinese zither, string instrument.

hutong: A narrow street or an alley in Beijing.
Siheyuan: A community of four buildings and a courtyard in Beijing.

Unless specified, the months are given in terms of the Gregorian calendar.
The months in the lunar calendar are approximately a month behind the Gregorian calendar. For example, lunar November would be Gregorian December.
Besides numbers, a traditional way of describing the Chinese lunar month is to use seasonal phenomena, including blossoms. A variety of choices can be used to for a single month, I particularly like the following:

January – *Willow*
February – *Apricot*
March – *Peach*
April – *Wheat*
May – *Pomegranate*
June – *Lotus*
July – *Orchid*
August – *Sweet olive*
September – *Chrysanthemum*
October – *Dew*
November – *Hidden dragon*
December – *Ice*

PORLOGUE

☯

December 1725

SNOW BURIED THE entire Imperial Mausoleum complex—the spirit way, spirit pavilions and chambers, towers and bridges, stone animals and the juniper trees. The only life perceived in the whiteness of the Imperial Graveyard was the sound of a lute being played by a frail woman, and the snoring of a drunken man in front of a grand tombstone.

The woman stopped playing, adjusted the drunken man's cloak, then patted him on the shoulder.

"Prince, wake up!"

The man stirred. "Leave me alone."

"Please, Prince. It's cold. Let's go home."

The man's eyes snapped open and he stared at the woman as she repeated her plea. "Home? I have no home," he mumbled.

"There, there. You have to take care of yourself. You'll get sick if you—" The woman burst out in tears.

"What does it matter if I get sick? What's the point of taking care of myself? I'm already as good as dead!"

"Please! Don't say that!"

"Leave me alone!" the man shouted.

A couple of guards rushed from a nearby stone chamber.

"What's going on here? Quiet! You're disturbing the spirit of the late emperor."

The man stood up, hand on his sword. "How dare you talk to me like this? Don't you know who I am?"

The guard rolled his eyes. "Yes, Prince Jeng. I know who you are. You're the fourteenth son of the late Emperor Kangxi, the brother of the current Emperor Yongzheng, the *previous* general of the Imperial Army, and the current guardian of the royal tombs." And then he burst into laughter, the other guard joining him.

Humiliated, Prince Jeng drew the sword from his waist and advanced towards the guards.

"No, Prince, don't. Please calm down!" the woman entreated.

The rage in the man's eyes terrified the two guards, and they backed up a few steps. "You'd better behave. We can confiscate your sword if we want!"

The prince moved forward, pointing his sword at them. "Come take it if you dare!"

Of course, they wouldn't dare. Prince Jeng had seen the fear in their eyes whenever he practiced his sword in front of them. Before they retreated into their shelter, one of them shouted out a warning. "Just you wait. We'll report your misconduct to the emperor! You could be demoted to a resident of the tombs!"

But Prince Jeng was undaunted by the threat and laughed instead. "Then you'd be doing me a favor."

The woman left with tears in her eyes. But the prince remained.

He sobered up after the confrontation with the guards. Dropping his sword on the ground, he bent to brush away the snow that covered the grand tombstone.

Great Qing Emperor Kangxi.

He stared at the engraving for a moment, then suddenly his legs gave way and he dropped on his knees and sobbed. "I'm sorry, Father Emperor. It's my fault. I came home too late!" He pounded his fists on the tombstone as sobs racked his body. "What's the point of still being alive?" After he exhausted himself crying, he picked up his sword, put it against his neck, closed his eyes, and took a deep breath.

But before he could do what he intended, he heard a voice singing, "*Life is death / if you live like a ghost. / Tears are nothing / but grief thrown to the winds. Amend the past / if you can't forget!*"

"Who's that?" He looked up.

In the whiteness of the snow, a figure in a black robe and black cap emerged. White hair fluttered out of the cap, and white brows and a white goatee danced in the wind.

"What's a Taoist priest doing here in the sacred resting place of a Buddhist soul?" the guards yelled as they came out.

The priest laughed. "Taoist, Buddhist, Christian, as if it matters to the dead. My humble name is Wang, and I came to pay my respects to Emperor Kangxi, a great ruler who embraced all religions."

"Go away, go away!" The guards blocked the way of the intruder.

Intrigued by the poem the priest had recited, Prince Jeng intervened. "Let him stay!"

Priest Wang bowed to Prince Jeng and headed directly towards Kangxi's tombstone. He took out an enormous incense stick from the sack he carried on his back, lit it on a burning candle, and knelt in front of the tomb. He chanted inaudible words until the stick was burned to half, and then stuck it into the ground. When he got up, he wobbled a bit as if losing balance. But before Prince Jeng could steady him, he stood on his own.

"Thank you, Prince." The old man bowed before he turned to move away.

"Wait!" Prince Jeng grabbed his arm. "What is the meaning of your song? How does one amend the past?"

The priest laughed. "Oh, it is but a silly song. Please drop by my humble dwelling. The Temple of Light and Shadow is only a short distance from here."

"Get out of here! He isn't allowed to leave the Imperial Graveyard. Understood?" one of the guards yelled.

The priest gave the prince a sympathetic look and vanished into the whiteness. His song echoed in the open plain. *"The past and the future are in unity / Yin and Yang are two halves of the same circle / Today was tomorrow and tomorrow will be yesterday / Morning and night are illusions of Light and Shadow!"*

THE WHITENESS TURNED gradually to gray, and then to darkness. Lanterns swayed in the fierce north wind, and the fires in them extinguished one by one. Prince Jeng leaned on the wall of a small stone house and stared at the lanterns hanging on the walls of another building nearby. The shouts of drinking games, the clinking of wine cups, and the jingling of coins drifted from the buildings. Prince Jeng wrinkled his nose at the smell of alcohol in the night air. The night was chilly, and he badly wanted a drink—but no, not tonight. He resisted the urge to touch the wine gourd at his foot, which he had brought out in case a guard sneaked up on him so as not to rouse any suspicion.

A gush of wind attacked him, and he shivered with cold. The sobriety that surrounded him was sharp to the point of painful. For the last three years, he had only been sober for very short intervals. He had preferred feeling numb to anger, grief, or hopelessness. But after the visit from that Taoist monk, he'd gained the wish for staying sober, so he could think and reflect. Once again, he was consumed with the grief of his father's death and the regret that he had not stayed with him at the moment of his death. He was obsessed with anger that his brother had stolen away the throne that had been intended for him. He was overwhelmed with sadness over the loss of his mother, half-brothers, and friends. Hatred surged inside him for the man who was responsible for their deaths. Even through his numbness, he wished for a way to amend, if not to avenge.

He wished he had insisted on staying at the palace instead of returning to the western borders. His last conversation with his father remained vivid in his memory, despite his daily torpor, and now it replayed through his mind.

The emperor had coughed as he drank his medicine, and Jeng gently patted his back. "Father, let me stay in the palace, please!"

The emperor stopped coughing and asked with a wheezing breath, "Why?"

"So I can help you and take care of you."

"Nonsense. I'm fine and I have plenty of people taking care of me."

"But—"

"No buts," said the frail emperor. "Your duty is to ensure the Dzungars don't invade our land again. That's the best thing you can do to help me, and to protect the Qing Empire."

He nodded, his vision blurry with tears.

"Oh, Father Emperor!" he muttered now as tears streamed down his cheeks. He should've insisted on staying, or at the very least he should have hidden in the palace, so he could've prevented the atrocity that had followed. Part of him had wished the emperor would get well, and he couldn't disobey his father. He had been raised to obey his father's wishes.

Shouts and coarse laughter filled the quiet night. The imperial soldiers who had arrived during the day were drinking and carousing with the guards. Tomorrow, Jeng was to be transported back to Jing City. The guards had congratulated him without sincerity, and he doubted he would have his freedom back any time soon. His brother had become increasingly cruel since he'd ascended the throne three years ago. He had persecuted most of their half siblings, and he hadn't given him, his full sibling, an easy time at all. Rage filled Jeng as he remembered the new emperor's refusal to send an imperial doctor to see his ailing wife, and later ordered him to move her from the grave he had preferred to a spot the emperor designated. During countless sleepless nights, he often wondered whether they shared the same blood at all.

These thoughts cleared his head. He was certain that his brother wouldn't show any leniency towards him. Once he returned to Jing City, he would be imprisoned, perhaps even executed.

The last lantern flickered and died, and the noises in the guards' quarters were hushed. No, he wouldn't be tricked. He would escape while he had the chance. It was pitch-dark around him now. Wolves howled on the other side of the gates and walls.

He quickly returned to his house, securing his sword and putting on a cloak. He ran towards the gate and started climbing. A pair of Tibetan mastiffs chained to the post by the gate barked at him. Soon, he heard a door creaking in the guards' quarters, and the light of a lantern illuminated a patch of snow. He quickened his pace but the gate was slippery from the frost and had no handholds for him to grab on to, and he lost his footing a few times. Guards and soldiers rushed towards him and arrows flew through the air, some hitting the gate. But he kept climbing, hoping that the drunken men couldn't aim well in the dark. When Jeng neared the top, an arrow scraped his shoulder and he yelped in pain. The blow caused him to lose his grip on the gate and he fell to the ground. The guards were next to him now, and he jumped up, drawing his sword in one swift movement.

"Try'na escape, huh?" one of the guards slurred as he stumbled towards Jeng.

He wasted no time with words, simply swung his sword arm with a flash of speed and the nearest guard's head dropped to the ground.

The other three men cowered away from him, their legs trembling.

"Who dares to have a match with General Invincible?" Jeng called out the challenge.

None of them moved for a moment, but then one of them let out a cry and dashed forward. The other two snapped out of their stupor and followed the first, brave guard. Jeng relished the fight. He had missed the thrill of it, the feel of the sword in his grip as it slashed through the air. The three guards weren't a match for him, and even if the amount tripled, he could easily slice through their necks. He lost himself in the fight, in the desire to win in a battle, and prolonged the fight like a cat with mice. Then suddenly he remembered his goal. He had to get out before dawn. More guards would arrive by then, which would be extremely inconvenient for him. If he failed this attempt, he wouldn't get a second chance at escape. His brother the emperor would be glad to have one more reason to kill him, and Jeng would die a disappointed ghost.

He slashed swiftly, incapacitating them instead of killing them. He clambered up the gate, and finally made it over to the other side. He jumped down, landing sprightly on his feet, then set off running, forcing himself not to look back for fear that some monster was chasing him.

The plain was vast and there was nothing ahead of him except darkness. He ran like a madman, without a clear sense of direction. His legs felt heavy—it had been years since he had had such physical exertion. Blood dripped from his smarting shoulder. He knew he ought to stop and bandage it, but he couldn't risk stopping until he was far enough away. Finally, he collapsed from exhaustion.

The sound of panting woke him. Slowly, he opened his eyes, blinking blearily until his vision adjusted to the darkness. There were lanterns around him. Tiny, greenish lanterns that looked like fireflies, except they weren't flickering, and they were more intense. They froze in the air in pairs. Little by little, he could make out the shape around each pair of lanterns—gray against the night, like large dogs. They stared at him without blinking, and he swallowed hard. He'd seen wolves before, but never on his own. To win the battle, he couldn't show the wolves his fear. His eyes flicked from one wolf to the other, counting silently. There were six wolves with bared teeth. He glanced at the wound on his shoulder. The scent of the blood must have drawn the wolves to him. They were assessing him, deciding whether or not to attack.

Wolves were coursing predators, he knew that. They hunted best when they chased a running prey. He resisted the urge to run. Wolves were also patient hunters and wouldn't make a move until they spotted their prey's weakness. If he chose to stay still, then they would probably keep waiting. But he couldn't afford to linger. Dead or alive, he had to get to the Taoist temple by dawn. His mind was on his sword as he vigilantly watched the beasts around him. He'd have to draw his sword swiftly, quicker than the predators could sink their teeth into his neck.

With a speed that startled himself, his sword was in his right hand, his left arm raised high to shield his neck from the ferocious animals. The wolves growled at him, and before he knew it, one was clutching at his back, and another biting on his boots. He frantically waved the sword to keep the rest at bay as he tried to find a good aim at the one on his foot. He twisted his sword arm, stabbing his blade into the belly of the beast. The wolf

18

collapsed on the ground, blood spilling from its open gut, but its death caused the other wolf to go into a frenzy. It let go of his shoulder and bit into his right arm, causing him to drop his sword. He stifled his cry of pain and crouched to pick up his sword with his other arm. Another beast came at him, but he was able to kill it before it could get the kill strike in. The wolf on his back wouldn't let go of his arm, and blood was soaking through his sleeves. He had to stop the beast before he lost his arm, but he couldn't aim a blow at it without turning his head, and he couldn't turn his head without risking more severe injuries from the other wolves. He could perhaps fling the beast to the front, but it was heavy and larger even than the mastiffs. He was afraid that in doing so, he himself would be dragged to the ground instead, and that would be the end of him. No, he decided, he must concentrate on driving the other two away first. He advanced an inch forward, dragging the wolf with him, and waved the sword at the two that seemed younger and milder in temper. While the two young wolves stood still, the one on him jumped at his neck. He dodged and managed to keep some distance from it, then quickly aimed his sword at the animal's neck. A jet of blood shot into the air, spilling on the snowy ground and on his gown. As he advanced towards the two youngsters, they turned tail and fled. He waited until they were out of sight, then he fell on the bloody, snowy ground, gasping for air.

Dawn was beginning to break. He started from the ground, put his sword back into the sheath and looked around him. There was no sight of the Imperial

Mausoleum, and not far from where he stood, a patch of green fields, and a mountain on the other side. On top of the mountain, he saw a yellow, upturned roof of a temple. He quickened his pace.

CHAPTER 1

❻

July 2015

I LEANED AGAINST a balustrade on a hilltop, looking at the morning sun climbing up the horizon and casting a surreal, orange light onto the multitude of sweeping yellow roofs and red walls in front of me. "It's beautiful!" I murmured.

"Magnificent," the man standing next to me echoed. There was a sadness in his voice that made me turn to look at him. He was tall and had a striking profile—straight nose and high cheekbones. I squeezed his arm to comfort him. When he kissed me, I closed my eyes and wished the delicious moment would last forever. But it didn't. Soon, I heard someone calling me from a distance, "Julie! Julie Bird! Wake up!"

My eyes fluttered open. There was a silk canopy embroidered with dragons above me and antique furniture strategically placed all around the sunlit room. I turned my head, and the face of a handsome young man greeted me. He had his head propped up on his elbow and was smiling. He didn't seem like the same man I had seen in my dream, whose face I couldn't recall, and for a moment I was puzzled. Then I smiled as I remembered I was on a business trip with Peter, and we were staying at the Palace Hotel in Beijing.

"Good morning, my fair boss!" Peter greeted me with a grin.

"Oh, stop it," I chided, closing my eyes. "Don't remind me of work. And don't call me boss when we're alone."

"All right, my love," Peter said and leaned over to kiss my lips.

It was a sweet kiss that really set me on fire. But it also reminded of my dream. I pushed Peter away. "We're late!"

"Late for what?" Peter asked, frowning at me.

"We're supposed to be in Jingshan Park to see the sunrise."

"Oh," Peter rolled his eyes. "You aren't serious about that, are you? The sun rises at five here in summer."

"And I can't even get up before seven." I sighed. Sunrise at the Palace Museum was breathtaking, but I could only see it in my dreams. Who was that man in my dream?

"We could go see the sunset. It's not much different, is it?" Peter suggested.

I considered it. Then I shook my head.

"Oh, cheer up," said Peter. "I'll give you something better than the sunrise." He kissed me again, his talented lips moving to my earlobe and my neck, sending shivers down my spine and making me forget my earlier moroseness completely.

I was the accountant manager of YouClo, a clothing company based in the U.S., but its factories and most of its market were in China. I frequently had to travel to Beijing to meet with the branch accountants to monitor accounts and sales. I liked the opportunity because my father lived here and I loved the city. I normally traveled alone, and I had hesitated when Peter begged me to take him with me, but now I was glad I did.

"Thank you, Peter, for coming along," I said when we were resting after our love-making.

"You're welcome," he said. "You know, I could come with you on every trip if you transfer me to your office."

My head cooled a bit at the remark. Peter was an accounting clerk and had expressed his interest in the position of assistant accountant for months.

"Are you using me for career advancement? I thought you loved me," I teased him.

"I do, but I'm tired of being an accounts receivable clerk. It's been two years." Peter pouted.

"Already? Well, I was a staff accountant for nearly five years," I said, squeezing his shoulder. "You have to be patient, my pet, and getting a college degree will help, too."

"You don't trust me." Peter stared at me, his pretty eyes too big and cute for an adult.

"Why would I bring you on the trip if I didn't trust you?" I grabbed his face so he faced me.

"I'm your boy toy. You only need me for the night."

I rolled my eyes. "Oh, not this again."

"See? You'll never say the L-word to me!" Peter sulked.

"It's just too soon, my treasure. We've only been seeing each other for . . . how long? Three months? Give me some time, okay?"

Peter wouldn't stop sulking. I didn't know what to do. Sighing, I reached into my purse on the nightstand and pulled out some hundred-yuan bills. "Here, go shopping later."

Peter smiled. "Really? What about the meeting?"

"You don't have to come with me."

Peter took the money and placed a kiss on my cheek. "What're we going to do after your meeting?"

"My dad wants me to have dinner with him and his family tonight. Do you want to come along?"

"Sure." He shrugged. "But after that?"

I paused to think. Beijing's nightlife wasn't boring, but not exactly exciting, either. Peter took up the hotel guidebook on the nightstand and flipped through the pages.

"Well, we could go to a Kung Fu show, an acrobatic show, a magic show, a Peking opera, or a—"

"Magic show!" I interrupted him. I had loved magic shows since I was a little girl and had once aspired to become a magician. I had taken online lessons and performed at parties, but that was it. My stage fright prevented me from performing in front of large audiences. And after becoming an accountant, I had completely abandoned my hobby.

"I knew it," Peter grunted. "But why? You already know how each trick is done."

I pinched his cheek. "I don't watch for the tricks, I watch the magician's skills. Like watching a skater doing her triple loop—you know what the technique is, but you want to see how well *she* does it."

Peter thought for a moment, clearly not getting it. He laughed. "You're so old fashioned, my love."

"You might as well omit the *fashioned* part, my pet." I sighed.

Realizing his blunder, Peter apologized with another kiss.

I wanted to linger in bed, but responsibility got the better of me. I had a meeting with the branch accountants at nine.

"I'm going to shower, want to join me?"

"No. You go ahead. I want to rest a while longer." Peter yawned lazily.

In the shower, I thought about Peter's complaint. Why couldn't I tell him I loved him? I definitely liked him. We had been inseparable for three months, although he wasn't exactly my type. He was a bit too feminine. God knows how I got hooked on him. I often had the feeling that he had seduced me, and that he wanted to use me for career advancement, but the concern vanished as soon as he looked at me with those big, clear eyes of his, and worse, when he whispered the sweetest words, or the dirtiest words, to me. And honestly, I was flattered that a younger man wanted to seduce me. Even so, I had resisted him for nearly a year, but he had been persistent. He kept showing up at the right time and right place. Whenever I was working overtime, he would be there. He volunteered to attend conferences with me and be my translator when we had to meet with Cantonese business partners.

Minutes later, as I dried my hair, I looked into my own reflection in the mirror and reminded myself that I was thirty-three years old. Ten years older than Peter. He couldn't possibly be serious about me. This was just a fling. Although a bit feminine, he was cute, at least in the eyes of Asian girls. I knew it from the girls who stared at him when we went out together. Although I wouldn't call myself ugly, I knew I wasn't comparable to the young Asian women with delicate features. I looked more Anglo than Asian—my nose was too long, forehead too high and cheekbones too broad. And I was five foot six, an inch taller than Peter. Even though I didn't look much older than him, I still felt like a cougar when we went out.

"Are you done?" Peter materialized in the shower, startling me.

The sight of his naked body, although smaller than I preferred, stirred the heat in my core again. But I resisted the temptation. I couldn't be late for my meeting.

"Yep. It's all yours, sweetie." I kissed him lightly on the cheek and closed the bathroom door behind me. *Foolish old woman, you're feeling insecure. You should feel lucky instead. Maybe he's after money or career advancement, but what does it matter if money and power make you attractive?* Okay, tonight, I told myself, when we returned to the Emperor Suite after the magic show, I would say it.

I was still promising that to myself when Peter's cellphone rang. I ignored it and went to the closet picking out a sleeveless cotton dress and a suit jacket hanging on the rack. As I was putting on the dress, the hotel phone rang.

"Hello?

"May I speak to Mr. Peter Yang, please?" a man said in standard Mandarin on the other end of the line.

"He's in the shower. Would you like to leave a message? I'm his girlfriend." I blushed at the word. It was the first time I acknowledged the fact to anyone.

"Sure, thanks. I'm calling from the front desk at Central Park Holiday Inn. It's about his room reservation for today."

"What're you talking about?" I frowned. Peter had told me we were going to stay here for the next two nights. He hadn't said anything about switching hotels.

"Mr. Yang called about ten minutes ago and reserved a room with us. He had wanted to check in before noon. I said no. But I checked with my supervisor and he told me it would be fine. He can check in at eleven. Could you please let him know that?"

Still puzzled, I said, "Sure. I wasn't aware he was looking for a different place. How many days will we be staying there?"

"Oh, it was only for today. He said he would be checking out before four."

"For half a day?" I tried to make sense of it. "What kind of room is it, a single? A double?"

"A romantic suite. "

"Romantic suite?" I frowned. What was Peter up to?

"Yes. It comes with a Jacuzzi."

"That sounds good. Sure, I'll let him know. And what's the room number?"

What was the meaning of all that? I thought confusedly after I had hung up. Was Peter trying to surprise me with a treat? But why? I didn't care for Jacuzzis. This Emperor's Suite was already above my expectations, with all the nonsense royal standards—a dragon bed that felt like a pavilion and a phoenix tub the size of a goldfish pond. Besides, it wasn't my birthday or anything. And he was not a generous boy. The only gift he had ever bought me was a birthday card. He had always given me the same reason—I had everything I needed, and anything from him would seem pitiful to me. I knew it was an excuse but didn't really mind—that was the tradeoff of having a younger man for lover, especially when he was so attractive.

This romantic suite thing didn't make sense to me!

Maybe it was his way to get what he wanted—a promotion. I had refused him earlier, and he wasn't happy about it. But it seemed he was pretty determined. Pleased with the answer, I smiled. A promotion wouldn't really be a problem once he finished his AA degree in accounting. But I was afraid that once he got his promotion, he wouldn't stay to work for me for long. I had learned from experience that men usually quit after getting the experience they needed, since they didn't feel comfortable taking orders from a woman.

But why would he want to reserve a room in the morning? My business meeting wouldn't end until afternoon. Was he planning to stay in that room instead of going shopping, and if he was, what was he going to do there?

I couldn't stop my curiosity and reached for Peter's cell phone while he was blow drying his hair. My hand trembled as I looked through his phone. I had never spied on Peter's personal life before. Not because I trusted him, but because I had wanted to leave our relationship open. Peter had made a couple of phone calls to a person name Liyuan Zhang the day before. I had no idea who the person was, and neither could I tell whether it was a guy or a girl. The sound of the hairdryer stopped, and I quickly put the phone back in place.

When Peter came out of the bathroom with the towel wrapped around his waist, I opened my mouth to tell him about the phone call but decided not to. If Peter wanted to surprise me, then I didn't want to ruin it.

Instead, I asked casually, "Where are you going for shopping, my toy?"

"Actually, I'm going to meet up with an old friend," he said nonchalantly as he pulled on his t-shirt.

"Really? I didn't know you havd friends here in Beijing. A guy or a girl?" I asked in a joking tone, watching him closely.

"A guy," he said without turning to face me. "He's a high-school classmate and works here."

"Oh? What does he do?"

"He, uh, I'm not quite sure. I believe he works for some cell phone company."

"I see, so you're going to hang out with him?"

"Yep. Mainly just lunch and catching up."

Maybe the guy's name was Liyuan Zhang, and the suite was reserved for the two to chat. I thought. But that was a bit luxurious—and why a romantic suite with a Jacuzzi? I opened my mouth to ask, but again I paused and said, "Um, sounds good. Will you be back at two?"

"I'll try. It depends on his schedule."

"Great, don't forget to reserve tickets for the magic show. I'm looking forward to it," I whispered into his ear.

I HAD NO idea how I got through the traffic to the Accounting Division of YouClo in downtown Beijing in my rental car. Mr. Lin, the YouClo accountant manager, and his staff accountants received me with civility, and I forced myself to put my private affairs in check. In front of a roomful of people in business attire, I managed to concentrate on the presentations and discussions and go through the business meeting at ease. But once I started auditing alone in a room, my mind easily drifted away from the computer screen. I kept wondering what Peter was doing at the Holiday Inn.

I was relieved when it was finally time for lunch. I told Mr. Lin that I wasn't feeling well and would like to skip the afternoon. It was the first time in my career that I ever skipped work, and I felt terrible. But Mr. Lin gladly told me not to worry and to take my time to recover. I drove straight to the Holiday Inn in Central Park.

"Just what am I going to do?" I asked myself as I maneuvered through the horrid traffic of downtown Beijing. "What if I catch him in bed with a slut? It isn't going to do any good, is it?"

But I couldn't convince myself that I didn't care what Peter was doing. I had to find out the truth.

I went straight to the elevator and pressed the button for the twelfth floor, where the room Peter had reserved was on. My heart beat frantically as the elevator took me up, and I stepped out onto the twelfth floor with shaky legs. I had never done anything so bizarre in my life. I took a deep breath before ringing the doorbell. No one answered it. I knocked on the door and still no answer. Then I went to the hotel lobby, showed the front desk my Visa card, which Peter had probably used to reserve the room since he was an authorized user, and demanded a key. The clerk hesitated for a moment, but after confirming the credit card information, she handed me a key.

Clothes were strewn on the bed and on the floor. Among them were the shirt and jeans that Peter had worn this morning. The other items included a lacy top, a denim skirt full of holes, and a bra. They must've belonged to Liyuan Zhang, who was no doubt a girl. Peter had lied to me. I felt my temperature rising and looked around the room for the doors and exits. Then I became aware of the noises coming from a half-open door—the humming of Jacuzzi motor mingled with groans of humans. Holding my breath, I went towards it. On the other side of the door was a covered balcony that was just large enough to contain a Jacuzzi. Two naked bodies were soaked in bubbling water, one on top of the other. I stood frozen in place. It was Peter's torso—there was no mistaking it, except it wasn't beautiful anymore, but disgusting. I wanted to scream, but instead I let tears stream down my cheeks. I had expected this but still couldn't believe it was true.

Suddenly, I heard a woman's shriek. "Somebody's watching us behind the door!"

Peter turned around and muttered, "Oh shit! Julie, what're you doing here?"

"What does it look like I'm doing? I'm here to see whether the whore is worth my money," I said sarcastically.

"I'm sorry, Julie. It's not what you think," Peter said, still holding the woman as if protecting her.

The woman, who was quite young, shouted, "Why are you apologizing, you wimp? She called me a whore! Tell her I'm your fiancée!"

CHAPTER 2

IF I HAD a choice, I wouldn't have chosen to come to Beijing in July, because it was the hottest month over here, and the busiest. But when I was driving down Expressway S32 into the suburban area, I found myself in the middle of a vast plain covered by blue sky and surrounded by green hills. The crowds that plagued the city were nowhere in sight. I temporarily forgot my misery in the open space and looked forward to my destination. The Eastern Qing Tombs—the Imperial Mausoleum complex of the Qing dynasty located in northeast of Beijing—was about an hour's drive on the highway, according to the advertisement. I had never been remotely interested in the place and had never planned to visit it, but after I had left the Holiday Inn, I didn't want to go back to the Palace Hotel, and it was too early for dinner at my dad's house. So, I drove aimlessly out of Beijing. A moment later, I saw the billboard advertising the Burial Chamber of Empress Dowager Cixi and got on the highway.

I admired the blue sky and silver clouds for a moment longer, and even started to hum a tune to assure myself I was fine and that Peter was just a worthless piece of junk. But pretty soon the attraction of the scenery started to wane, and I sank back into the dark corner of my mind and started to mope. I had been such a fool. The young woman in the Jacuzzi had been his girlfriend in China since high school, and they were planning to get married soon. Liyuan Zhang lived in Guangzhou and had flown to Beijing to meet him. He had asked for my forgiveness, but I told him to have his things moved out of the hotel by evening. I stopped sulking when I saw a yellow rooftop and red walls among the blue hills in a distance and exited the highway as soon as the sign that indicated my destination popped up.

"EVERYONE, MAY I have your attention please?" The tour guide pointed to an old blanket in a glass case. "This is the most valuable item in the tomb. It is woven with gold threads."

A murmur rose through the crowd and everyone moved towards the display to take a good look at one of the few remaining burial items of Cixi, the last empress of the Qing dynasty and one of the two female rulers in Chinese history. The blanket had been sewn with tens of thousands of pearls and gemstones, but they were all stolen by tomb raiders in the early twentieth century. The tomb itself had been extravagantly built. Dragons made of gold wrapped around the pillars, the ceilings and walls were carved with gold pieces, and even the Buddhist scripts were written in gold. But all the original gold had been lost during the numerous tomb raids in the past. The restoration looked fabulous but was only an imitation of the original.

I wasn't particularly impressed with anything I saw, but I was lost in awe and sadness. These pieces of antiques only reinforced the popular belief that Cixi was a corrupted, ruthless ruler whose luxurious lifestyle was built upon the misery of the peasants. Few remembered her as an ambitious daughter of a Manchurian general who had been offered to the emperor and had refused to succumb to the fate of a forgotten concubine. She had gained the favor of the emperor not only by sexual appeal, but also through her wit and political aptitude. Her strong will was a great complement to the weak-minded Emperor Xianfeng. Her ruthless acts were only fractions of crimes that most of the male rulers in history had committed, yet unlike those rulers, she had been condemned for her wrongdoings and her merits conveniently forgotten.

"Was Eunuch Li really Cixi's lover?" a woman with a Southern accent asked the tourist guide.

The guide laughed. "Well, that's the rumor. Nobody knows for sure. But it's certainly possible."

I glanced over at the tomb of the empress. It was hard to be a ruler, and harder to be a female ruler. Even in her old age, Cixi had had countless lovers, although of course, no one had been truly in love with her. She had power, money, and prestige, but she had no love.

That reminded me of my own distress—I hadn't had any true love, either. A boy in the eighth grade had clung to me for a year, seeking my affection, and I had treated him like a little brother. But then he suddenly grew up and stayed away from me. In high school and college, I preferred reading and practicing magic tricks alone to hanging out with friends. After I became an accountant, I was too busy getting to the top to commit to any serious relationships, although I had dated sporadically. And once I had climbed to the top, men seemed to stay away from me, except Peter. Tears threatened to well in my eyes as I again remembered Peter's beautiful face, but I forced my tears back. He's not worth it! I reminded myself. And yet it was hard not to remember him, since he was whispering passionate words into my ear not that long ago. How deceptive!

As I stepped outside of Cixi's burial chamber, I found myself in the center of the Imperial Mausoleum complex—an immense graveyard of the Qing emperors and their consorts. Even under the bright sunshine and among the green mountains, the place felt bleak. Buried inside those magnificent structures around me had been the most powerful men and women, but now they were nothing but dust. I felt at a loss. Up until now I had considered myself successful—I was making a six-figure income, and I was on the top of my career ladder. But I had a sudden revelation that I couldn't take any of my possessions with me when I died.

No, I don't care for money and power. All I want is to be knocked over by true love once in my life. I would give anything for that. All my money, even my life. It doesn't even have to last long. A few months or a few days would be enough.

I lingered in the Eastern Qing Tombs for the rest of the afternoon and visited tombs of various emperors and empresses. It was near sunset when I made my way out of the Imperial Graveyard. The exhaustive tour pretty much distracted me from my misery, and I was feeling light-hearted when I got back to the highway. When I spotted the sign that said *Honey Peach Tasting,* I was instantly lured towards it. It took me about an hour among the farm roads before I got to the orchard, but it was worth it. Honey peaches were a major attraction in Beijing and most of them came from these farms. They were sweeter and juicier than any peach I'd had in my life. After gorging on two of them, each about half a pound, I bought another ten pounds before hitting the road again.

It was getting dark, and pretty soon I got lost in the peach fields. My GPS was not getting any signal at that point, but I didn't mind and kept driving. I'd called and canceled my dinner plans with my father and wasn't in a hurry to get anywhere. It felt nice getting lost in the wild, and I was certain my signal would be back soon. After about fifteen minutes of aimless driving, I came to a fork in the road, when I finally saw a sign. *To S32* pointed to the right. I slowed down for a moment, looked to my right and then my left. But on both sides were endless fields and nothing more. "You've got to trust the sign," I muttered to myself and turned to the right.

I soon lost myself in driving. Some sign would surely turn up again. But instead of signs, I now kept seeing mountains. The road became narrower and bumpier as I drove. This couldn't be right. I must have made a mistake at the fork earlier. I slowed down. It was getting dark, and I started to panic. I grabbed my cell phone, hoping to call my dad and ask for help, but there was no signal. I kept driving, hoping it would end soon.

Suddenly, such an overwhelming sadness surged in me and tears streamed down my face. I was not a sentimental person and would usually be overcome by anger instead of sorrow. But at the moment, I was lonely, scared, and disappointed. I thought about Peter's betrayal and couldn't control my tears. As I wiped the wetness from my cheeks, I saw a large grouping of rocks in the middle of the road. I grabbed the steering wheel with both hands and slammed down on the brakes, screeching to halt before the rock. After measuring the space on either side of the rock, I came to the conclusion that the only way I could get through was to push the rocks away from the road.

I opened my car door and stepped out. I had barely neared the rocks when a man jumped out from behind the rocks and knocked me to the ground. I screamed as he grabbed my arms and held a knife to my throat. Highway robbery! I had heard about it but had never run into any before. He was shorter than me and his arms were quite thin, but I had no knowledge of self-defense and the blade terrified me.

"Give me your purse," the man threatened. His breath reeked of garlic. "Money is all I want. And there's no use shouting, no one else will hear you."

"Okay," I said, trying to keep the tremble out of my voice. "If money is all you want, you can have it. Just let me get to my car to get it."

"Go ahead, I'm not holding your feet," the man said, still clutching my hands.

With my hands pressed to my back and a knife at my throat, I led the man to the passenger side of my car. My purse was visible on the seat.

"How much do you have in it?" the man asked. "And don't trick me."

"Five thousand yuans in cash," I said. It was more than half a month's salary for most of the city dwellers in Beijing, and I hoped that the robber would be satisfied.

But he wasn't. He kicked the back of my hip with his knee. "Come on, you must have more than that!"

"That's all I've got," I said. My throat went dry, but my fear lessened after the initial shock. "You can take the purse and sell it, it's worth about a thousand. Just leave me the cellphone, please."

"So you can call the police?" the man asked as he pushed me against the car with one hand and opened the car door with the other. "No, I'm going to take everything."

"Oh please," I begged. "I need my phone. I can't do my job without it. I promise I won't call the police, just leave me the phone, you can have the car if you want, but I need the phone, please!"

Of course, I thought, it wasn't too crazy a proposal. My rental car would be covered under the insurance, but the data on my phone couldn't be recovered.

The man took out the phone, looked at it, and sneered. "Pathetic. Everywhere I go I see people carrying their phones around like an extra hand." Without blinking, he threw the phone down the ravine behind us.

"No!" I screamed in a fit of rage. My phone wasn't expensive, but it had been closer to me than any person. "What kind of sick man are you?"

I forgot my fear and a surge of energy pulsed through me. I lifted my foot and stomped down on the man's canvas shoe with my sharp heels with as much strength as I could muster. He yelped in pain, loosening his grip on me. I took the opportunity to swing myself against him. I pushed him to the ground, then ran from him as fast as I could manage in my heels. I hadn't gone far when I heard the man shouting after me. I glanced over my shoulder and saw his small frame catching up to me. Before I could go further, he caught me and pushed me into the brush on the side of the road.

"You wild bitch!" the man cursed as he tied my hands to my back with his belt. "I wasn't gonna do this to you, but you just earned it!"

I shrieked as he tore my shirt open, and kicked his legs when he pulled down my tights. There wasn't much else I could do.

Disgusted and desperate, I screamed, "Unless you kill me, you scum, I'll make sure you get executed for this!"

"Stop talking or I'll cut out your tongue!" the man threatened me with a menacing glare.

I squeezed my eyes shut as the man opened his fly. I felt him wrench my legs apart and his hand brushing over my underwear. I braced myself for what was to come, biting down on the inside of my cheek to keep myself from giving him the satisfaction of my cries, when he suddenly stopped. I heard another man's voice, rumbling and deep. "Let go of her!"

I opened my eyes. A long, chilling blade shone in the dim moonlight. It was pointed at the nape of the criminal's neck. A tall man in a cloak was holding it. I couldn't see his face clearly, but the outline of a square chin was unmistakable. His head was half shaven, and a long braid dangled behind his back. On his neck he wore a pendant the size of a dollar coin. His cloak fluttered in the night breeze. I was so shocked at seeing this apparition that I forgot my immediate danger. The robber must have felt the same since he froze momentarily.

Only momentarily, though, for soon he said, "Hey brother, we're all in the same boat, I'll give you a share, no need to fight amongst ourselves."

"I don't want your filthy share," the man with the sword said calmly but firmly. "Let go of her now or I will cut off your head!"

The man put up his hands, "Okay, take it easy." He got up and pulled on his pants. Before he left, he bent over to my side to reach for the handbag he had thrown on the ground.

"Leave it!" the swordsman's rumbling voice vibrated in the quietness of the night.

"Come on," the robber hesitated, still clutching the bag. "I won't take everything. I'll—" Before he could finish his sentence, the man's sword sliced through the rock next to him and sparks rose like fireworks.

I gasped at the sight, and the robber dropped my handbag instantly and vanished into darkness.

Still lying paralyzed on the ground, I was left facing the man with the sword, too shocked to feel shame about the state I was in. The man had put his sword back in its sheath by his waist and took off his cloak. Oh no, I squeezed my eyes tightly and shivered all over again. *What does he want?*

I felt the touch of soft velvet against my bare skin, and followed by that, the calm breathing of a man near my ear.

I opened my eyes and saw the face—pale, square, and handsome. It was the face of integrity and equanimity, a kind face without a smile, but filled with resignation between the thick brows.

"Are you all right?" The same low, rumbling voice sounded soothing and warm at the moment.

"I'm all right," I croaked. I attempted to get up but failed.

"My hands are tied," I said.

He turned me to my side and untied me, then he helped me up. My arms were numb, and shocks of pain shot through them. I groaned.

"Wait," the man said, rubbing my arms as he gently moved them.

Perhaps it was induced by his gentle touch, or simply by his trustworthy presence, but the tears that I had been holding earlier all burst out into a deluge of sobs. And it clearly startled the man. He hesitated as he cuddled me in his arms. He waited until I calmed down, and asked, "Do you have any company, guniang?"

Guniang? The man had a peculiar way of speaking. He sounded like a character out of a historical TV drama. It took me a second to remember that guniang meant something similar to Miss. "No, I'm alone."

"Out alone so late? What're you doing?" The man's face turned stern and he looked at me with disapproval.

"I was driving. I got lost." I buttoned up my shirt and returned the cloak to the man.

"I see."

"What about you?" I was a bit wary. By the look of him, he could be another highwayman.

"Oh, I'm, uh, I'm a traveler myself," he said, and there was a sudden air of urgency around him. "Excuse me, I must go on."

Then he just leapt out of the brush and went on his way.

"Wait," I called to the vanishing shadow. "Thank you!"

Upon hearing that, he returned. "Can you walk fast?"

"Uh, why?"

"It's not safe to leave you alone here. But I'm in a hurry. Perhaps you can follow me until we reach a village?"

"Sure, that'll be nice." I gathered my purse and stood up. "But I have a car, and I can give you a ride. Where are you going?"

"Jing City."

"Jing City?" I repeated the archaic term. "You mean Beijing? That's where I'm going."

When my car came into sight, the swordsman stood where he was. "That's a strange-looking carriage. Where are the horses?"

"Horses?" I blinked.

"How are you going to move it without horses?" the man asked.

"Oh," I laughed, taking it as a joke. The man had a sense of humor despite his somber appearance. "I have a key and it'll turn on the horsepower."

The man got in the car, a bit circumspectly, watching me turn on the engine with my key. He didn't speak, but from his expression, I could tell he was truly amazed, even startled by the sound of the engine. I glanced over the man, amazed in turn by his reaction.

"You've never been in a car before?" I thought it was a bit unusual. Twenty years ago, when I first came to China, many people hadn't seen or ridden in a car, but we were in the twenty-first century now. The streets of Beijing had more cars than people.

The man shook his head as the car started to move, his face full of amazement. "It must be some kind of sorcery. Are you a Taoist nun? What temple are you from?"

I laughed. He was probably a monk from a nearby temple, I thought after taking another glance at him, or a hermit who had shut himself out from civilization. Lately, many people chose to abandon city luxuries and live in old ways. I'd read about a man shutting himself in a cottage in the mountain, wearing only handmade gowns and shoes, growing his own vegetables and soybeans, and reading ancient texts by candlelight. I finally understood why the man was wearing a cloak over a changshan, carrying a sword, and speaking with old phrases such as Jing City for Beijing.

"No, I'm not from a temple. Are you?" I asked.

The man, however, did not answer me. He stared straight ahead into the darkness, making it clear that he did not intend to engage in further small talk.

We finally got to the main road, and the lights from houses suddenly flooded the plains.

I had never been so glad when I saw the road sign ahead. *Beijing 5km.*

"We're almost there," I said with relief. "Now, where do you want to get off?"

As we approached the city, I looked at my passenger again and noticed that his equanimity was gone.

"Why are there so many lights?" He leaned forward, his head touching the front windshield.

"Oh, I know," I said. "Un-green, right? Wasting electricity really. But I must say, hermit brother, I've never seen a more cheerful sight than this in my life."

"What name is the town ahead?" He stared into the city ahead, lit by the brilliant billboards and neon lights.

"Beijing, I mean Jing City!" I said cheerfully, hoping he would smile.

"That's Jing City?" the man asked incredulously. "It can't be. Where is the palace?"

"You mean the Palace Museum? It's over there." I pointed to the neon lights against the vast darkness that separated the old palace from the clamors of the city, clearly delineating the outlines of the Heaven Gate and the Meridian Gate.

The man followed the direction of my finger. He was silent for a moment before he spoke again. "What's going on over there? Why are there so many lanterns? New Years' celebration already?"

"No special occasions. It's just the way it is every day."

The traffic on the road got heavier, and the stranger looked anxious whenever cars sped by.

"What happened to all the horse-drawn carriages?"

"Horse-drawn carriages?" I thought for a moment. "You won't see them until you get to the city. They're for tourists, and only during the day. At least that was what I was told."

"Tourists?"

I sighed. What cave had this man come from?

When we passed the first high rise, the man spoke again. "What year is it?"

I paused. "2015. Have you really been away so long that you lost track of time?"

He looked puzzled and ignored my comment. "Who is the emperor?"

"Uh? Oh, you mean the president? Xi Jinping."

He looked shocked. "What happened to Emperor Kangxi?"

"Kangxi of the Qing dynasty? Er," I paused, eyeing the man to see whether he was joking. "He died, a long time ago."

The man closed his eyes and sighed. "How long?"

"I'm not sure exactly when he died, but it must've been over three hundred years ago."

"Three hundred years?" The man gasped. His face turned a ghastly white under the bright lights of the highway. After a long moment, he said, "I need to go back to where we met. Let me out."

"Now?" I cried. "Can't you wait till tomorrow? We're already back in the city!"

"No, I must go now. I'm three hundred years late, I can't wait any longer." He reached for the handle.

I didn't understand what he meant, but I saw the determination on his face. "All right, calm down. I'll take you back," I said, and got off the highway. "What do you mean you're three hundred years late?" I asked the stranger once we were heading back to where we had come from.

"I'm not at liberty to answer your question."

"Oh, okay, then." I did not press for an answer, but I conjured one up instead. Could it be that the man had been a hermit for more than three hundred years? Had he practiced some sort of Kung Fu that rendered him longevity and eternal youth? Or was he a ghost who had died three hundred years ago? A chill ran down my spine. We had left the outskirts of Beijing, and all around us were the black shadows of mountains. It felt eerie, and the beacons flickering in the shadowy mountains did not help. Perhaps, I thought, I could simply drop my passenger off on roadside and let him find his way? But I couldn't do that. Ghost or not, he had saved me earlier. Besides, although he was pale, his breath was warm. There was no way he could be a ghost.

I hit the brake next to the spot where we had met, and the stranger stepped out of the car eagerly. "I'm most grateful for your help, guniang. So long!" He paused before closing the door.

"Same here!" I said, waiting to see him off.

He looked around and lingered at the same spot. Then he asked me through the window, "You don't happen to know the Temple of Light and Shadow, do you?"

I shook my head. "I'm sorry. I'm not from around here."

"No problem. I'll find it."

"Good luck!" I called and watched as he disappeared into the darkness.

I made a U-turn on the road but hesitated as I drove on slowly. From the windows and the rear mirror, all I saw was monotonous blackness around me, and not a light or a shadow that would indicate a house, not to mention a temple. In fact, I didn't remember seeing any temples along the way at all. And there was something unsettling in the man's manner. He didn't seem to have known his way, and he didn't even seem to know where—or *when*—he was. Could he have been lost? I couldn't leave him alone like that, not after what he had done for me.

I parked my car on the road and caught up with the man.

"Wait, sir," I said. "I'll go with you."

"That's not necessary."

"I can be of some use to you," I said, turning on the small flashlight on my keychain.

"A lantern?" The man stared curiously at my hand.

"Ay, and a small one." I laughed, moving the tiny flashlight close to his eyes for him to see it.

He squinted. "This is amazing! So tiny and yet so bright!"

You've never seen it before? I swallowed my question. How long had he shut himself out from the world?

We were about a mile away from the place where I had been attacked. An empty wasteland stretched into the darkness, weedy and uneven. His paces quickened as he headed towards the weeds. There was a pit behind the weeds, and with the help of my flashlight, a few pieces of broken furniture and some junk revealed themselves—a broken chest of drawers, an old mattress, a washer, and a bicycle.

The man stopped at the top of the pit and looked around him.

"Is there where you live?" I asked timidly.

"No." He shook his head. "But it's where I'm from."

"What?" I frowned. "I thought you were from a temple."

"Yes. The Temple of Light and Shadow. It's on the top of the hill in the back."

I looked up, but didn't see any hills in darkness, then I studied the man's face in the glow of the flashlight, and was struck by the thought that the man might have been a nut and he might have run away from a madhouse.

I was thinking of a good excuse to leave him, when he spoke. "Three hundred years ago."

He must have seen the doubt on my face, or it might have been my silence.

He sighed. "I know I must sound crazy to you. Don't worry, guniang, you're free to go. Just please don't tell anyone about me."

I looked at him, and my feet glued themselves to the ground. The sincerity in his face, and the gentleness of his voice made me ashamed of my earlier selfish thoughts.

"No," I said adamantly. "I want to help you to find the temple."

He paused, then said, "Thank you. But it's quite unnecessary."

Before I could process his words, he had jumped down to the bottom of the pit and landed on top of a space free of garbage. He weaved through the junk and went all the way to the back.

"Please leave, guniang, and thank you again!" his deep voice rumbled in the night.

I lingered a moment longer, seeing no movement down below. The man might be meditating or fallen asleep. Feeling drowsy, I stumbled towards my car.

CHAPTER 3

❧

I WOKE AS a streak of sunlight hit my eyelids. When I opened my eyes, I realized I was sleeping in my car, in the same spot where I had parked last night.

My first thought was about the mysterious man. Was he still in the pit?

I shivered as I stepped out of my car. The morning air was chilly in the mountains.

The pit was clearly an illegal trash dump. It looked smaller than it had appeared to be in the dark, with all its contents visible. The chest of drawers had two drawers missing. The bicycle had only one wheel and the washer had lost its lid. A few black garbage bags were scattered around the debris. A black mass on the mattress next to the chest of drawers suggested the presence of a man.

"Hello? Is anyone down there? Hello? Hello?" I called out after not seeing any movement.

Not a stir. Not a sound. I waited and called again—still no response. Finally, I lost my patience, and began to look for a way down. The slope wasn't steep, but I was wearing high-heeled sandals. I was about to take them off when I saw indentations on the wall of the pit, clearly made for stepping.

I followed the steps down, wondering what on earth the pit was for. Then it occurred to me that the man could have been homeless—crazy but harmless—and this pit could be his home.

I went to the sleeping man on the mattress. He was snoring softly. I crouched and stared at his face. It was still pale under the sunlight, but strikingly handsome—a defiant chin and aquiline nose. There was a scar on his chin near his neck, like a claw mark, that I hadn't noticed the night before. He was clutching his cloak tightly, shielding himself from the cold morning air. The man was large, even when curled into a ball. His pendant had fallen on the mattress. Looking closer, I saw it was a yin-yang emblem made of two stones, one white and one black. The stones were framed in a bronze shell etched with some markings. He slept so soundly, as if he hadn't slept for years, and his chest rose and fell with the sound of his snores. I put my finger close to him to feel his breath. It was warm, in fact, a bit too warm. My finger moved gingerly to his cheek, but I quickly withdrew it. He was burning hot to the touch!

I patted his arm gently. "Hey, wake up, you're burning up!"

He stirred but did not move.

I shook him and he let out a groan. It wasn't until I touched his right arm that he started.

His eyes fluttered open and he stared at me for a moment without any signs of recognition. Then he said, "Oh, guniang, You're still here."

"Yes, and so are you."

He closed his eyes and sighed.

"Hey, you can't fall asleep again," I said and grabbed his shoulder.

He groaned again, and I saw a dark stain on his sleeve. I turned my hand and saw blood. "You're hurt!"

The man didn't respond, so I took the liberty to open his shirt. A bloodstained bandage covered his shoulder and most of his arm. Even under the bandage, I could see the swollen tissue. I flinched as I imagined the pain he had to be in.

"Heavens, what happened to you? Were you in a fight?" I whispered.

"Sort of. It's nothing. Don't worry about it," he said weakly.

"What do you mean, nothing? We have to get you to a hospital!"

"Hospital? What is that?"

"Hospital. It's where you see doctors. Healers. Your fever must be from the wound. You've probably got an infection. Get up! Let's go!"

He wouldn't move. "I'm not going anywhere. I have to find the temple first."

"But you'll lose your arm or die if you don't see a doctor."

"So be it."

Is this man nuts? Should I just leave him here to die? I couldn't. I tried to think of something to say, but from the look on his face I knew there was no way I could convince the stubborn man to come with me.

"Fine," I said as I stood up. "Let's look for the temple together."

He stood up and walked past the chest of drawers. A narrow path was hidden behind it, and I followed him through. The path went up and stopped on the top of a hill. The man looked anxiously around for the sight of the temple. But there was no manmade structure, only a flat piece of land with protruding rocks.

"Is it the right place?" I asked.

He hesitated. "To tell you the truth, I'm not sure. I've only visited it once, and it was three hundred years ago. It's probably gone."

I wanted to suggest that we leave, but he kept scanning the area, as if hoping to find evidence of the temple's existence. Suddenly, he froze, his eyes fixed on a rock. "The gourd rock! I remember seeing it. It was right by the temple."

The rock did indeed look like a gourd with a thin waist, and more precisely, it looked like an hourglass. He went next to it and put his palm on it, then he sighed. "The temple is gone for sure."

When we got back to the pit, he looked exhausted.

"You have to lie down and rest," I said to him. I climbed out of the pit to get the First Aid kit in my car. There were bandages and antibiotic ointment in it.

I returned a moment later with the box in my hand and also a blanket I had found in the trunk of my car. When I insisted on changing the bandage for him, he consented passively. My stomach clenched as I saw what was hidden under the bandage. He had multiple wounds—a deep gash on his shoulder and many punctures on his arm. His arm and shoulder were badly swollen, and patches of his skin were starting to turn purple from the bruising.

I cleaned his wounds using the iodine and cotton balls from the First Aid kit. When I had run out of bandages, I rushed back to my car, returning a few moments later with a towel to cover the rest of his wounds.

"Are you a *Jianghu* doctor?" he asked with a weak smile.

I rolled my eyes at the derogative term used to refer to quacks. "I guess anyone could be, with the medical supplies so readily available nowadays."

"You're not a doctor? Then what do you do?"

A bit flattered by his interest on my life, I said quickly, "I'm an accountant."

"What's an accountant?"

After my brief explanation, he nodded. "I see. You take care of the accounts. Are you good at the abacus?"

I stared at him to see whether he was joking. "Not at all. But I'm good with the computer."

"Computer?" He frowned, the line between his brows deepening.

I threw up my hands. "I'll explain later. Why don't you tell me what you do? Are you at the liberty of doing so?"

He paused for a moment. "I used to be a general."

That was all he said. We fell silent, and I didn't press him further. After a while, he started snoring faintly. I sat quietly by his side and trying not to jostle him.

I leaned back against the chest of drawers behind me, thinking about what I was going to do. So much had happened in the past twelve hours that I had forgotten my breakup with Peter. It seemed to have happened years ago. Then I remembered that I was supposed to return to YouClo to continue the audit. I had to call Mr. Lin and reschedule, but I couldn't because that scum had thrown away my cellphone. Well, there was nothing I could do about it right now. I would wait until the man woke up, and hopefully he would let me know where he was really from, so I could take him home. With that on my mind, I dozed off.

I was awakened by the sound of whispering. The man was muttering something in his sleep, and I forced myself to pay attention.

"I'm sorry, Huang Ahmah! I'm too late, too late! Forgive me! No, brother! You must not kill him! Don't! Mother!"

Then he started and was silent.

I stared at the handsome, pale face. *Who is he? Where is he from? Who's killing whom?*

A familiar tune nearby interrupted my thoughts, and I recognized it as the ringing of my cellphone. It wasn't far from me.

I looked around and saw the gleam of silver inside a bush. I smiled, gently moving away from the man as I stood up.

When I returned, the man was sitting upright.

"Let me take you home," I said.

"I have no home," he mumbled.

So I was right. He was homeless.

"But I must return to my time."

"How?" I asked curiously. "The temple you mentioned, it's gone, isn't it?"

He nodded sadly. "I must find a way."

I was trying to make sense of his words when he spoke in an urgent voice. "I appreciate your help, guniang, but there's nothing else you can do. Please leave me!"

Reluctantly, I went back to my car. I started the engine and drove away, but I only drove for a mile before I stopped. I couldn't abandon the man. I thought about calling the police—they might be able to send him home—but I couldn't bring myself to do it. He was certainly mysterious, but he didn't really look like a lunatic to me. Instead, I made a U-turn and headed back towards the pit. I had to convince him to come with me.

He was still sitting in the same spot I had left him in.

I squatted down and took his hand. "Let's go get something to eat."

"Thank you, guniang, but I—"

"I know, you have to go home. That can wait, can't it? You're already three hundred years late. One more hour, one more day, won't matter, will it?"

WE EACH HAD a peach as I drove. I got off the highway as soon as I saw a town. We stopped at a noodle shop where I ordered beef noodle soup for each of us. The man was famished, finishing the bowl of soup in two gulps. I took pity on him and ordered him another bowl. Before leaving the restaurant, I asked the cashier to point me in the direction of the nearest hospital, and she directed me to Peach Town Medical Center a few blocks away.

The man didn't object when I told him that we were going to see a doctor first. Soon, I saw a gray bungalow with the medical center's sign. It was more like a clinic. I had only gone to a hospitable once in Beijing and had heard bad things about small town doctors. I hesitated as I approached the building. The man had been quiet since he got into the car, and as I glanced at him, I saw that he had fallen asleep again. Worried about his infection, I turned into the parking lot.

I woke my passenger and helped him out of the car. He stumbled a bit, his steps sluggish. An old man sat on a bench outside, smoking. When he saw us, he got up and opened the clinic's door. There wasn't a front desk clerk, but a robust middle-aged woman in a white gown showed up shortly. She helped me and the patient to a cot.

"What happened? Was he in a fight?"

"I think so. I don't know exactly what happened," I said. "Are you a nurse?"

"No, I'm Dr. Wu," the woman said proudly and a bit defiantly.

"I'm sorry," I said. "Doctor, could you please treat him?"

"Of course," the doctor said as she started examining the patient.

"Tsk, tsk, tsk." She shook her head. "Pretty bad. Is he a martial artist?"

The doctor's comment sparked some curiosity in me. I looked at the man. With his peculiar braid, archaic clothing, and his sword, he looked exactly like a character in a costume drama. He must've been one of those Kung Fu monks in a temple. What was the name of the temple he was looking for? Light and Shadow?

The doctor shook her head and said, "I don't understand these martial arts fanatics. Why use real weapons? This wound looks like it was made from a very sharp point, shot straight into his bone. An arrow or a spear, maybe. But I think it was an arrow." She applied antiseptic to his wound, and the man, who had lost consciousness momentarily, groaned as he opened his eyes.

"Tell me, which Kung Fu school are you from?" Dr. Wu asked.

The man stared at her, confusion clear in his bleary eyes.

"Now let me see what's on his hand. Uh, a canine bite, no doubt. I need to administer a tetanus shot, just in case."

As she prepared the syringe, the doctor sighed. "Nowadays there are too many pets wandering around in the rural areas."

"Why is that?" I asked.

"Oh, isn't it obvious? City folks get tired of their pets and abandon them."

I shuddered. I didn't own any pets, but I loved dogs and cats and couldn't imagine such cruelty.

Dr. Wu rolled up her patient's sleeve, but before she could inject the needle into his arm, he knocked it from her hands and sat up abruptly.

"Hey, easy, easy!" the doctor said as she picked up the syringe from the floor. "It's just a needle! Not an arrow! Why are men so afraid of it?"

I was quite shocked by the man's behavior as well. I couldn't believe the hero who had saved me was so afraid of getting an injection.

"It's okay. It won't hurt," I said gently and patted the big man's arm.

"What is it?" he croaked, eyeing the syringe warily.

"Huh? Never seen a syringe before?" The doctor looked surprised.

Since I had become used to the man's ignorance of modern equipment, I explained, "It's medicine. It gets injected through the needle. It'll treat your wound."

"No." He shook his head like a petulant child.

"Aya." The doctor shook her head. "What's wrong with you? Did your master teach you to reject everything modern?"

His lips formed a tight line and he refused to let the doctor touch him.

The doctor sighed. "Well, I can give you pills, but it'll take longer to heal the infection. A shot will clear the infection in a day."

I pleaded with the stubborn man. "Please, it'll save your life. Don't you want to go home sooner?"

Just as I had thought, my words worked. The man reluctantly let the doctor stab the needle into his arm. Dr. Wu made use of his sudden compliance and followed the tetanus shot up with a shot of antibiotics. The guy was a true hero because although I saw tears rushing to his eyes, he didn't so much as groan.

After the doctor had bandaged his wounds, she prescribed a bottle of antiseptic liquid, a tube of antibiotic cream, cotton, and bandages.

"Cleanse it once every day. A quick shower is okay, but don't soak the wound. And don't let him practice any martial arts until he's fully healed." She shook her head as she packed the medicine supplies. "These young people don't care about their lives."

Before she handed me the packet, she made me fill in a form and pay for the visit.

"What's your name?" I asked the man.

"Yin-jeng," the man said after a moment's pause.

"Yin-jeng?" I frowned. I couldn't figure out how to write it. My Chinese wasn't sophisticated enough, although I had been learning it since grade school. Embarrassed, I thrust the pen into the man's hand.

"What is it?" He took the pen and examined it curiously.

"It's a pen," I said, aware that the doctor and the old man who had opened the door for us were staring at us.

"Pen? Without brushes?" Jeng held it gingerly, as if holding a brush-pen. Then he wrote two huge characters firmly on the form, so firmly that the paper tore.

I studied the beautifully written characters. While I recognized the first character, I had never seen the second one before—it was complicated with many strokes.

"How unusual. That's pronounced Jeng?" Dr. Wu asked.

I was thankful to know that I wasn't the only person who didn't recognize the character.

"What does it mean?" I asked.

He shrugged. "It means upright."

I nodded. The man might be a weirdo, but I had no doubt of his honesty.

Before we left the clinic, I asked the doctor, "Is there a temple named Light and Shadow around here?"

"Temple of Light and Shadow?" The doctor shook her head. "Never heard of it. I've lived here in Peach Town for thirty years. Do you know anything about it, Mr. Liu?"

The old man exhaled a cloud of smoke. "What?"

The doctor shouted the name again into the old man's ear.

The old man nodded slowly and started to mumble through the gaps of his teeth. It took me a few seconds to make out what he was saying. "Yes, yes. I know. I visited it when I was a child. But it was demolished in the seventies, during the Cultural Revolution."

CHAPTER 4

❡

JENG FELL IN and out of sleep on the highway, but once we were inside Beijing, he started to become restless. He looked out of the car window with bewilderment on his face, his eyes wide, as if he was in a trance.

His eyes were like saucers when he saw the skyscrapers that crowded the city. "Why are there so many magnificent fortresses? Is the empire in danger of invasion?"

I stifled my urge to laugh. "These aren't built for military purposes. Some are commercial buildings, others are condominiums. The tallest is the China World Trade Center."

He asked me what commercial buildings and condominiums were, but it seemed as if he struggled to process the information. He understood what department stores were for, but he asked me why markets were indoors, and he found it incomprehensible that

66

businessmen and traders had become so powerful. He was utterly shocked by the amount of condominium communities we passed. "How many commoners are living in the city nowadays?"

I shrugged. "Tens of millions."

My amusement at Jeng's reactions to the city he had probably left for too long faded. I dreaded going back to the Palace Hotel. I thought about finding a different place, but I didn't want to waste the night's reservation—it was incredibly pricy. Having been brought up by a single parent and supporting myself since college, I was frugal. I never reserved hotels that cost more than fifty dollars a night. When Peter had told me what the hotel cost, I'd thought he was joking.

"A thousand dollars a night! That's insane!" I had complained.

"Yes, but it's the best in town and it has everything. A spa, a balcony, and a dragon bed."

Before his parents divorced, Peter's family had been well off, so he had a penchant for luxury.

I got out of the car in front of the lobby and gave the valet my key, then I opened the door and helped Jeng out.

Jeng's feet glued to the driveway of the hotel when he got out of the car.

"Come on, let's go," I said, eager to get to my room for a shower and a nap.

But Jeng stood unmoved as he glanced at the entrance of the hotel. "Whose palace is this?"

I laughed. "It isn't a real palace. It's a hotel."

"Hotel?"

"Yes." Seeing that the word didn't ring a bell to him, I added, "An inn."

"An inn?" He looked genuinely impressed. "Grandest inn I've ever seen!"

I shook my head, wondering again how long he had been a hermit. Then I held the glass door for him just in case he'd forgotten how to open a door.

His height and costume attracted the attention of a crowd in the lobby. When two girls came over and asked to take a picture, Jeng agreed. Seeing his own instant image in the cellphone, he gasped in surprise.

"Are you a magician?" he asked the girl.

The girl giggled.

I resisted my urge to laugh. By now I was more or less used the man's clueless behavior. *Who is he?* I'd have to find out later. As we waited for the elevator, Jeng looked around at the lobby with amusement in his eyes, like a child visiting Disneyland for the first time.

"What are those candles made of? They're so shiny," he commented, staring up at the chandeliers in the hotel lobby as we waited for the elevator.

"They're electric lights," I said. "And they're made of glass."

Jeng jolted when the elevator moved, but to his credit he stayed calm. "We're rising?"

"Yes, our room is on the thirtieth floor."

When we reached the door to my room, Jeng's eyes lit up as he saw the plaque that said, "Emperor's Suite."

"The emperor lives here?"

"Well, that's what they want you to think," I said, without any of the excitement I had felt two nights before. Now, the sheer luxury of the room was depressing. Jeng, however, was obviously taken by the ridiculous royal furniture.

"What a comfortable recliner!" he exclaimed as he went over to the chaise lounge made of carved rosewood in the center of the living room. "How beautiful. Mother was looking for something like it."

"Oh really?" After putting the peaches in the fridge, I dropped onto the sofa facing the couch. "It looks nice, but I can hardly sit in it for long."

"A dragon bed!" I soon heard the cry as he wandered into the bedroom.

I had grimaced when I first saw the dragon bed— a bed for an emperor. Everything including the canopy and the duvet was made of golden silk and embroidered with dragons and phoenixes, symbols of the emperor and empress. It looked exactly like the images I had seen in movies, except it was real. It was so sumptuous that I was reluctant to sit on it. If I hadn't been worn out by sex the other night, I doubted I could've fallen asleep in it.

When Jeng emerged from the bedroom, he looked very solemn.

"Tell me, guniang, who lives here? Is it a vacation house for the emperor? And who is this Emperor Xi?"

I sighed. I was simply too tired to answer these silly questions.

"Jeng," I said, yawning as I sank further into the sofa. "Can we talk about it later? My eyes can't stay open another second. You aren't looking well, either. Dr. Wu said you had to rest. Let's both take a shower and then we can talk over dinner. And please, call me Julie or Miss, not guniang." My eyes closed, exhaustion sweeping over me.

It was evening when I woke. Through the satin curtain, the setting sun cast an orange hue over the room. The sound of even snoring fell on my ears. At first I thought it was Peter, but soon I remembered the events of the past day. I sat up, catching sight of the colossal body of a man on the couch opposite me. I went closer to check on him. He was sleeping peacefully, and his forehead was no longer burning. Relieved, I tiptoed into the bathroom so as not to wake him.

What I really wanted was a bath, but I knew if I took one, I would keep thinking about Peter. We had made love in this very tub. Already, I couldn't stop myself from remembering the way he'd caressed me and kissed me. I had the sudden urge to get my cellphone and call him. I could forgive him and pretend that nothing had happened. I'd take him back if he left that scrawny girl in that denim skirt full of holes. But no, I stopped myself. I couldn't swallow my dignity. How could he have lied to me all along? Was I really nothing but a cougar to him? True, I was a lot older than Liyuan Zhang, but I was still an attractive woman. Years ago, a modeling scout had approached me on the streets of San Francisco and offered me a job. The only reason I wasn't dating when

Peter came along was not because I couldn't find a guy, but because I was too busy with my career.

Putting on the silk bathrobe provided by the hotel, I went out to the living room. Jeng had opened the curtain and was looking out the window, deep in thought.

"What're you looking at?" I asked as I sat down on the sofa.

"I'm looking at the palace."

For the first time since arriving at the hotel with Peter, I noticed that the view was fantastic. Beyond the high rises, the red, yellow and green squares of the palace museum peeked out. It looked other-worldly—a part of unchangeable history in the midst of the twenty-first century; a tranquil corner inside the bustling, modern city.

"It's beautiful, isn't it?" I sighed. "I went there once but didn't see much of it. Next time I'd really like to take my time to see every corner."

"Can you take me there?" Jeng asked without moving his eyes away from the scenery.

"Sure," I said. "In fact, I was planning to . . . Let's go tomorrow."

"No. I want to go now." He turned suddenly and gazed directly into my eyes.

I chuckled at his urgency. "Now? Oh, I don't think so. By the time we get there, they'll be closing."

"But I can't wait one more night."

"Yes, you can. We'll go to dinner, and then we'll sleep. When you wake it'll be tomorrow."

He looked disappointed and turned back towards the window. I waited patiently for him to finish sulking, until my stomach started rumbling. The beef noodle soup hadn't lasted very long.

"Let's get ready for dinner please," I said. "The hotel restaurant isn't bad. Oh, maybe after you take a bath, and get some normal clothes on."

He didn't respond. I tapped his shoulder to get his attention and he turned unwillingly. His eyes fell on the opening of my bathrobe and his face flushed. He averted his gaze. "Please be discreet, guniang—Miss. We're strangers."

I was taken aback for a moment. I smiled uncomfortably. "I'm not indiscreet. I'm in a bathrobe, not naked!"

Jeng shook his head. "Not that different. Please put on some proper clothes."

I scoffed in annoyance. Who was he to give me orders? I liked the soft silk of the bathrobe against my skin and intended to wear it as long as I stayed in the hotel room.

"Sorry," I said. "I'm not going to change. If you don't like it, don't look at me."

Jeng's eyes widened in shock. "You speak without shame."

"Who're you to judge me like that?"

"I'm Prince Fourteen," he answered haughtily.

"Prince Fourteen? Who's that?" I inclined my head. "I've heard only of Louis the Fourteenth."

Jeng glared at me for a moment and sighed. "Never mind." He turned back to the window again and fell into a long silence.

My rude remark made me feel bad. The man might not be in his right mind, but he was harmless. "I'm sorry, Prince Fourteen, would you like to take a bath?"

"Yes," he nodded gratefully. "I would very much like a bath."

He went into the bathroom and came back a second later, naked from the waist up.

My jaw dropped at the beautiful, athletic torso in front of me. "Whoa, and who was talking about being indiscreet?"

"Pardon me," Jeng said with a crimson face.

"What's wrong?"

"I, uh, there is no water in the tub."

I sighed in annoyance as I went into the bathroom and turned on the faucet. Had this man really grown up in a temple?

Jeng was wide-eyed again. "Is there a stream inside the wall?"

I laughed. "Yes, Prince. Two streams, one hot and one cold. All you need to do is to turn these handles left or right and press it down when the tub is filled!"

"Marvelous!" he said, smiling ear to ear. "I must import this technology into the palace. Imagine how much work it'll save! No more carrying heavy buckets from the well!"

Although I had never seen anyone so impressed by a bathtub faucet, I could understand the man's appreciation. When I was still a teenager, my dad had taken me to the southwest of China, and we had lived on well water in a mountain inn. We had actually carried water in buckets, and it had been much harder than any workout in the gym.

"Can you tell me how it works?" Jeng asked me again, eager and expectant.

"Uh," I hesitated. "It's, uh, let me see. I know that there are pipes that channel the water from the ground level or a water tank somewhere, but I'm not sure about the actual mechanism."

Seeing his disappointment, I added quickly. "But I can probably find out if you really want to know."

"Will you? That'll be great!" He grabbed my shoulders in a fit of excitement. "Thank you!"

I giggled at his boyish excitement. We stood closely for another second, letting the water run. Aware of the steam rising from the tub, I felt the heat boiling inside me. Prince or no prince, sane or insane, this man was the hottest Chinese man I had seen in my life. If I stared at his beautiful body a moment longer I would be on fire. I turned and got out of the bathroom before it happened.

"Be careful not to soak your wound," I warned him before closing the door behind me.

As I waited for Jeng to finish bathing, I washed two peaches and ate one while foolishly looking up a video online that explained how plumbing worked. As soon as Jeng came out from the bathroom in his bathrobe, I let him have the other peach and told him what I had learned.

"According to the video, you need to install a pump into your well, and also some pipes that will channel water into your house."

But Jeng hardly paid attention to the video. He seemed mesmerized with the computer. "What is this? And how does this man get inside?"

He touched the screen gingerly.

I rolled my eyes. Of course, he hadn't seen a computer before. I thought for a moment of how to explain it simply. "It's just a picture of a man, except he talks and moves."

He nodded. "This world is amazing!"

It took him a moment to focus his attention on the video. "Huang Ahmah would no doubt love this. He and his science men would figure out how it works."

"Great," I said. "Now let's get something to eat."

He was going to put on his changshan again, but I stopped him. "We have to find you something appropriate to wear before we can dine anywhere."

After changing his bandages, I had him put on the pajamas provided by the hotel and took him to the shops on the first floor. After visiting a few shops, and after Jeng was convinced that he wouldn't be able to find a changshan here, he let me pick a polo shirt and a pair of jeans for him.

A moment later he came out dressed in the new outfit, walking gingerly towards me.

"You look so handsome," I said as he neared. The shirt was a bit tight, but it showed off his muscular shoulders. The jeans were just the right length. His legs were long and shapely! "Don't you like them?"

"Not really. I can hardly walk!" he said, a bit shyly.

"You'll get used to it." I tucked the shirt into the jeans and adjusted the collar for him. "We'll also do something about your hair later."

"What's wrong with my hair?" Jeng touched his little braid protectively.

"Your mouse tail is cute on a little child, but a bit funny on a big man like you, and it certainly doesn't match your new outfit," I said as I looked him over, trying to imagine how handsome he would look with a modern hairstyle.

"No one is going to cut my braid." Jeng backed away from me. "You can take my life but not my braid!"

I arched a brow. I had heard similar declarations from girlfriends in high school, but never from a man. I threw up my hands. "Okay, calm down. I won't touch your hair, I promise."

Perhaps I would get used to it. After all, it wasn't the worst hairstyle I had seen on men. And I preferred it much more than ponytails.

UNSURPRISINGLY, THE HOTEL restaurant was decorated in Qing palace style. The tablecloths and chair upholstery were made of yellow brocade. Lanterns hung from the wooden ceilings, and all the servers were dressed in Qing dynasty costumes. Jeng looked delighted for a moment, then he frowned. "How come the servants are hatless?"

"They aren't servants. They're employees!"

"I don't see the difference." He shook his head.

As soon as we sat down, two beautiful girls dressed in loose-fitting qipao came to set our table.

"Which court are you from?" Jeng asked them. "Hasn't your master trained you how to greet your guests properly?"

The two girls looked bewildered at his words.

I smiled sheepishly at them. "Sorry, don't mind him. He's just talking to himself."

The girls smiled and continued what they were doing.

"I'm not a lunatic," Jeng protested.

The waitresses had intended to stay by our side and serve dinner, but they were obviously uncomfortable under Jeng's criticizing eyes. I dismissed them as soon as the table was set.

I ordered Peking duck along with other famous dishes on the Palace Bouquet menu, and a bottle of Yunnan red wine. By the time they arrived, I was so hungry that I gobbled down two bowls of rice in a row along with some of the royal delicacies.

Jeng was apparently aghast by my table manners, but being starved himself, he didn't make any comments.

After my hunger had been satiated, I put down the chopsticks. "How do you like the duck?"

"Oh, it's quite good. In fact, it's much better than what our chef makes," Jeng said. "But it would be better if we had some wine to go with it."

"What do you mean? You don't like the wine you're drinking?" I pointed to his glass.

"What? This is wine? I thought it was some sort of appetizing juice. It's sour and biting, without even a hint of alcohol." He then poured himself another glass and drank it up like juice.

I ordered a bottle of Maotai, a strong liquor made of sorghum and wheat. Jeng took a sip and nodded. "Good! As good as Gujing wine."

"Gujing? I've never had it. Is it good?" I asked.

"Oh yeah. It's Huang Ahmah's favorite. You should try it!" He went to fill another cup, but I held my hand over it.

"No thanks. I can't drink anything too strong. And I'm a red wine girl." I held up my glass.

Jeng laughed. "I wouldn't call that wine."

"The Europeans would disagree," I said.

"What are Europeans?"

"Oh, they're, uh, foreigners."

"Foreigners!" Jeng was suddenly vigilant. "Huang Ahmah invited them to teach him mathematics. But what they really wanted was to teach us their religion. Anyway, I don't like foreigners. They want our land and they want to trade useless things with us. Huang Ahmah did not fully trust them. He said if we let our guard down, they would destroy the Great Qing."

"Well, the Europeans nearly destroyed China, but that was in the past," I said uneasily. "China is strong now. No one would dare to repeat history."

"What do you mean? Past? History? So, the foreigners really did ravish our land? When did it happen? And who was the emperor?"

"Let me think," I said, racking my brain for my knowledge of Chinese history. "I believe it started in Daoguang's reign, in the early 1800s, when the British brought opium to China in order to solve their problem of trade deficits. Pretty soon the whole country, including the imperial family, became addicted to the drug, so it became the Opium Wars. Anyway, during the war, the French and British stole lots of antiques and treasure from the palace and destroyed many important imperial structures."

"That's outrageous!" Jeng hit the table indignantly, attracting the attention of the adjacent diners.

The waitresses came right away. "Is everything all right?"

"Yes," I said embarrassedly. "I'm sorry but my friend is slightly drunk."

"I'm not drunk!" Jeng argued. But the waitresses nodded meekly and left.

Jeng finished his cup of rice wine in silence. "I hate foreigners!"

I paused. "Not all foreigners are evil. In fact, I'm half foreigner myself."

"A foreigner?" Jeng looked at me. "I thought you were a Manchu with your hazel eyes and straight nose."

"Manchu?" I smiled. People normally thought I was French, Italian or Middle Eastern, but this was the first time someone thought I was Manchu. "Well, I'm half white and half Chinese. But I might have Manchu in me, who knows? Manchu has been more or less assimilated into Han."

He fell silent for a second. Then he shook his head. "Unbelievable. Is your father a foreign priest then?"

I was confounded by that strange question. "No, he's Han Chinese, and my mom is British."

He blinked. "A foreign woman? I've never seen one. So, they're allowed to come to the empire now?"

I rolled my eyes. "Yes, my dear hermit. But my mom doesn't live here, and my parents met in the United States, not in China."

"United States?"

"You haven't heard of it?"

Jeng shook his head. "The Great Qing is the only country I know. It's already bigger than I can measure."

"Sounds like you're the frog that sits in the bottom of a well. You think the sky is as big as what you can see," I teased him. "And you still call it Great Qing. That dynasty ended a hundred years ago. How many years did you shut yourself in that temple?"

"I didn't live in any temple," Jeng said, his face turning red and his speech slurring.

"I thought you were from the temple of what's its name? Temple of Lights?"

"Light and Shadow. But I didn't live there. I only visited it briefly."

"Oh. So where do you live?"

The question seemed to cause him great pain. His jaw clenched, and he sighed. "I used to live in Xunjun Mansion."

"What mansion?"

He didn't answer my question, but simply went on mumbling. "It used to be Beizi Palace. But when my brother made me change my name, he changed the name of my house, too. I wonder what it's called now, after he stripped all my titles. It probably has no name."

I couldn't make sense of what he was talking about. "Do you still live there?"

"No, I used to live there. And then I moved to the cemetery."

"You moved to the cemetery? What do you mean?" I was feeling a bit drowsy, but the possibility of getting more information out of him sobered me up.

"I'm not a ghost," Jeng said in a hurry. "If that's what you're thinking. I simply lived in the cemetery, taking care of Huang Ahmah's grave."

"What are you talking about?" I frowned. "Who's this Mr. Huang that you keep mentioning?"

"Huang Ahmah is my father."

"Your father passed away, so you moved to the cemetery to stay with him? You're such a filial son," I said, guessing at the meaning of his words.

Jeng shook his head and sighed. "I'm not. If I were a filial son, then I would've gone home before Huang Ahmah died."

"I'm sorry." I put my hand on his arm.

"It's all right," he said. "I'll make it right. I'll figure out a way after I go back."

He was clearly tortured with guilt.

"Take it easy. I'm sure your father has forgiven you already."

He sighed and emptied his cup again. After I refilled his cup, Jeng emptied it again promptly without saying a word. The bottle of Maodai was almost gone.

This guy certainly has a drinking capacity, I thought. Maotai was a strong liquid and he was gulping it down like water.

"Even if he had, many people haven't. I owe them . . . so many lives."

"What're you talking about? What happened?"

Jeng didn't answer my questions. Instead, he seized my hand. "Guniang, please help me. I have to go back."

"Sure I'll help you," I said, feeling a bit concerned. "But where is your mansion? Is it far?"

"Oh no, I don't want to go there. I need to go to Father's palace. It's not far. It's very close. I could see it from the hotel room." He looked up dreamily. "But it's the wrong time."

"What do you mean?"

"I mean." Jeng's lips quivered before breaking into a fit of sobs. "I'm three hundred years late!"

I shook my head and sighed. What was I going to do with this wacko? I stared at Jeng, who was getting drunker and drunker by the second. Could it be that he was three-hundred-and-something years old? No, he looked no more than forty. But again, he could be a Taoist hermit who practiced the magic of eternal youth. I had heard plenty of stories about that. And this guy, with his ridiculous hairstyle, definitely looked as if he had been preserved from the Qing dynasty.

"How old are you?" I asked when he quieted down.

Jeng thought for a moment and said, "I am in the years that a man ought to establish himself."

Ancient speech again. I rolled my eyes. I had heard of the term 'establishing years' before but couldn't recall what it meant.

"Please," I pleaded. "Give me a straight answer. No riddles. What year were you born?"

"I was born in the twenty-seventh year of Kangxi."

Still not a straight answer, but at least I could find out more. I tapped on my cellphone and gasped. The twenty-seventh year of Kangxi was equivalent to 1688. My earlier suspicion seemed to be confirmed. "You are 327 years old?"

Jeng didn't respond to my incredulous look but went on muttering. "I was born the year of dragon, the only *dragon son* of Huang Ahmah, and Mother said that the moment I was born, she knew I would be the next emperor."

I chuckled incredulously. "Yeah. I know the ancients called emperors dragons. Good thing I was born the year of rabbit, and my parents didn't expect much from me."

Jeng ignored my comment. "But my brothers weren't happy about it. Especially the fourth brother. He was jealous. I know he hated me. I always felt the hatred in his eyes."

"How many brothers do you have?"

"About three dozen. I'm the fourteenth."

"Three dozen?" My jaw dropped open. "Your father was quite a prolific man. What's his name again? Huang Ahmah? Was he a land owner of some sort?"

"How dare you? Huang Ahmah was Emperor Kangxi," Jeng answered with a bit of indignation, as if I had insulted him.

It took me a moment to process his words. "You mean *the* Kangxi, the longest-reigning monarch in Chinese history? Who officially had twenty-four sons and twelve daughters, and sixty wives? Hey, wake up!"

I looked at Jeng, whose head had fallen onto the table. He had started to snore. Was this guy really insane? And how could he possibly be the son of Kangxi, an emperor who had died some three hundred years ago*?* Huang Ahmah, yes, I had heard of the term in historical dramas, it was a Manchu word for . . . *Father Emperor.* No way! I wouldn't take the words of the drunken man seriously. I tried to dismiss it as a joke, but then I couldn't. The man's manner—gentlemanly and yet arrogant—suggested that he was of nobility. His speech was also full of court jargon of old times. My intensifying curiosity cleared the fog the wine had created in my mind.

I waited for a while before paying the bill, then I woke Jeng. Supporting him, we stumbled back to our hotel room.

CHAPTER 5

I GOT UP early the next morning. Since Jeng was still slumbering, I drove to YouClo and finished the audit. When I came back at noon, he was waiting impatiently for me and reminded me that I had promised to take him to the Forbidden City—the Palace Museum as we called it today.

I parked in the lot closest to the Palace Museum, which was about a quarter mile away. We walked towards Tiananmen, the south gate of the palace, along with crowds of tourists. Jeng looked nervous and excited at the same time, and followed me like a child in a zoo. As soon as the golden roofs of Tiananmen came in sight, he cried, "Ah! Gate of Heavenly Peace!" He was smiling, his eyes shining with tears as if seeing an old friend. I was glad that he at least recognized something in the city.

Tiananmen Square looked huge despite the thick crowds. Tourists gathered here and there, and tour guides spoke through megaphones.

"Why is it so busy here? Is there a peasant uprising? Or is the emperor going to make appearance?" Jeng asked apprehensively.

"Nothing unusual." I patted his arm to reassure him. "This is normal. It's crowded every day. Major tourist attraction of the city and of the nation!"

"Tourist attraction?" Jeng repeated.

"People from all over the world are here to visit the Imperial Palace of China," I explained patiently.

"Visit the palace? But it's forbidden," Jeng said warily and slowed down.

"It no longer is," I said, taking the big man's hand and dragging him with me.

But he stopped at the entrance of the gate tunnel, refused to move.

"What's wrong?" I was embarrassed because he was blocking the way of the tourists following us.

"This isn't right," Jeng mumbled. "How can they allow all the commoners to enter the palace?"

"Oh, come on!" I snapped in annoyance. "It's no longer a palace. It's a museum now. Do you want to see it or not?"

He moved reluctantly.

Between Tiananmen and the Meridian Gate, the main entrance of the Forbidden City was a long walk towards an even larger square. Tourists marched in like a deluge, flooding the courtyard before they continued towards the Gate of Supreme Harmony. Some were resting at patio tables under sun shades. Jeng watched the people around him in amazement.

"This is madness!" Again, he stood unmoving under the scorching sun.

Tired after the hour's walk, I sat down at a table and gestured that Jeng should join me.

A family of three sat at the table next to us. The child was sucking an ice pop while the adults ate ice cream. Sweat dripped down my forehead. The heat was excruciating. I told Jeng to stay seated at the table and went to the shop nearby where I bought two pineapple-flavored ice pops. I had liked them when I was a child, and it would counteract the heat. I gave one to the big man, who, after taking a cautious lick, uttered an appreciative "UM" and widened his eyes.

"Good, I'm glad you like it." I said, marveling at the power of the ice pop.

"It's my favorite summer dessert! I used to have it every day. But this one tastes so much better than the ones our dessert chef made. It's softer and tastes better. What flavor is this?"

"It's pineapple. Don't tell me you haven't heard of it?"

"I have indeed!" His eyes widened even more. "It's a rare fruit and I've had it but on a few occasions. So, it's made of pineapple?"

"No, just the flavor," I said, smiling at his childlike delight. "You have your own dessert chef in your mansion?"

"Actually, he's Mother's. He made the most amazing watermelon sorbet. Mother loved it. I wish she could try this. She loved pineapple—" He stopped talking suddenly, looking sad.

"Where is she?" I couldn't help my curiosity.

"She passed away, shortly after Father."

"I'm sorry." I watched him finishing the popsicle and sucking the stick.

After crossing the Meridian Gate, we were officially inside the Imperial Palace. Across the courtyard was the tallest building of the palace complex and the political center of the palace—the Hall of Supreme Harmony.

"For generations, emperors received their subordinates here at the very courtyard," a tour guide announced through his megaphone. "The government officials who were granted entrance to petition the emperor would line up at the Meridian Gate at four in the morning."

"And how long would they have to wait to see the emperor?" someone in the crowd asked.

"It wasn't uncommon for them to wait for hours, even days, to see the emperor. Sometimes the emperor wouldn't even show up all day. The officials had to suffer rain and heat, hunger and exhaustion, just to hear the words of the Son of Heaven."

"How do you know this is usual of the emperors?" a voice challenged the tour guide. To my horror, it was Jeng. He had moved away from me and stood removed from the crowd. "You didn't live here, did you?"

The tour guide seemed flustered by the unexpected question but quickly regained his momentum. "I've studied the historical records."

"Those were just rumors. Emperor Kangxi had never let his subordinates wait for him for over two hours. He gave priority to the elderly so they wouldn't suffer much. On rainy days, he received them in covered areas, such as the balcony outside."

"Sounds like you knew His Majesty well. Let me see, perhaps you were one of his sons. You certainly have your queue, but where is your court robe?" the guide said sarcastically, and the crowd erupted in laughter.

"Indeed, I am!" Jeng said, undaunted by the mockery.

The crowd laughed even louder.

Worrying that Jeng would make a greater spectacle of himself, I went to him, taking his arm and guiding him away. "Let's go, please. I would like to see the gardens!"

As soon I dragged him out of Hall of Supreme Harmony, I looked around to see where we should go next, preferably away from the crowds. As I searched for a quiet corner, Jeng broke free of me and walked towards a poster with the portrait of an emperor. It was the advertisement for a current exhibition of Wuying Dian—the Palace Art Museum—which was a few steps away. I followed him, hoping he wouldn't be interested in it, but he paused in front of it.

"Do you want to go see it?" I asked.

He didn't respond to my question, but I saw him clenching his fists.

"What's wrong?" I looked at the poster. "Do you know him?"

"Of course," he said through gritted teeth. "He's my brother."

I resisted the urge to roll my eyes. "Let's go."

"No! I want to see what they say about him."

We walked back towards the Meridian Gate and turned west. It was an exhibition of twenty-four of the emperors who had lived in the palace. To my relief, there weren't that many tourists inside.

I had trouble telling the Qing rulers apart, especially when they all wore the same red sailor hat and the same golden dragon gown. But Jeng looked at the pictures as if they were portraits of his ancestors. He bowed to the pictures of Nurhaci and Hong Taiji—the founding fathers of the Qing dynasty—and to Shunzhi, father of Kangxi. Then he dropped to his knees in front of the portrait of Kangxi and kowtowed. "Father Emperor," he murmured. "Your unworthy son is here."

"What are you doing?" I whispered, embarrassed at the tourists who were eyeing us from afar. "This is a museum, not a temple. You're not supposed to pray here!"

Jeng ignored me. He continued kneeling on the ground, praying silently with his palms closed in front of him. He muttered words of respect and perhaps regret, and tears streamed down his cheeks. I had never seen anyone who showed such respect and devotion to a ruler. Could he really be Kangxi's son?

Jeng stood up just before a flock of chattering tourists led by a tour guide entered the peaceful hall. "Everyone, here are the portraits of the Qing emperors. Here is Shunzhi, that's Kangxi, Yongzheng, and Qianlong—"

I tried to pull Jeng away from the group but he wouldn't move.

"Kangxi was the fourth emperor of the Qing dynasty. He was the longest ruling, the most prolific, and the best emperor in Chinese history. And, of course, he's a celebrity even today. Hundreds of films and television shows have been made about him in the past twenty years. Who hasn't seen a movie about Kangxi?" he asked his group, and sure enough no one raised a hand.

The guide went on to the next picture—the same picture on the poster.

"In my opinion, the greatest emperor of the Qing dynasty was not Kangxi, but his son Yongzheng. Although he only ruled for fourteen years, Yongzheng's contribution to the country was huge. His various tax reforms lightened the burden of the farmers and resulted in population increase. He centralized power, reviewed every single petition instead of letting members of the parliament make decisions, even though doing so meant a compromise of his health. In the Palace of Heavenly Purity there was a couplet written by Yongzheng. It says: "I want to rule the kingdom, not be served by it." It shows that he was the servant of his subjects, and not the other way around."

In the midst of murmurs of admiration for the emperor, I heard the voice that I had dreaded hearing. "You misunderstand the couplet. It shows his thirst for power."

The guide's smiled vanished for a moment, and it looked as if he wanted to argue with Jeng, but he composed himself and said, "Ah, a Qing dynasty specialist. Why don't you tell us about Yongzheng?"

"Gladly," Jeng said before I could stop him. "Emperor Kangxi had twenty sons who survived to adulthood. He had favored the fourteenth son Yinjeng, who was also his general. In the sixty-first year of Kangxi, when Prince Fourteen was away fighting at the frontier, the emperor suddenly died, and to everyone's surprise, the throne was passed to the fourth son—the man whose picture you're seeing now. You call him a great emperor, but do you know that he seized the throne by forging the will of his father?"

The guide shrugged. "We've all heard of the story. But it's just a rumor, no one had any proof of that."

"It isn't a rumor! It's the truth!" Jeng shouted, and all eyes turned to us.

What is he doing?

I groaned under my breath and stared at the ground, hoping to find a hole to hide in.

Jeng, on the other hand, wasn't affected by all the curious faces around him at all, instead he seemed to be satisfied with all the attention. "It was Emperor Kangxi's will to pass the throne to Prince Fourteen, which was why he made him the Frontier General and gave him full control of the army! He would never have considered letting Yongzheng be his successor, not when he knew what a spiteful and evil creature he was!"

The tour guide was taken aback by Jeng's statement, but only for a second. "Whether he was spiteful or evil is not for us to say. Although Yongzheng is portrayed as being merciless and moody, historians can be partial. We don't know for sure what Yongzheng was like."

"I'll tell you what he was like! As a child he was quick to anger, throwing tantrums whenever he couldn't get what he wanted right away. As an adult he was pitiless to whoever disobeyed him. And sure enough, as soon as he seized the throne he wasted no time killing all parliament members that opposed him, sentencing two of his half-brothers to death, and his only full brother to lifelong confinement in the Imperial Graveyard. He never respected his own mother, and even ordered her to commit suicide once he gained the throne!"

He stopped abruptly as if choked by anger.

His knowledge and passion had everyone listening to him in awe. When he finished, the people around them murmured and some even asked Jeng whether he was indeed an expert on the Qing dynasty. The guide wasn't pleased with Jeng's speech at all. "Well, again, we don't know any of that for sure. If it all were true, Yongzheng must have had his reasons, and might have done them for a greater good. For sure his brothers were jealous of him, and if he hadn't killed them, he might have ended up being killed instead."

I could feel the rage coming off Jeng. He marched towards the man, his face contorted in a snarl, his hands curled into fists at his side. The guide sensed the danger and quickly led his group out of the hall before Jeng neared him. After the crowd left, Jeng stood on the spot, his nostrils flaring. Then suddenly he broke through the barrier and slammed his fist into the portrait.

I gasped in horror and covered my mouth. He was an idiot! I cast a nervous glance around, hoping no one else had seen him. But the loud thump had attracted the attention of at least two people around us, including a museum employee.

My mind raced as the uniformed woman walked towards us. Knowing that vandalism was a punishable crime and the painting might be a priceless piece of national treasure, I had to make up a good lie, so it would sound like an accident instead of intentional.

"What are you doing?" I shouted at Jeng as the woman approached us, not giving him a chance to speak. "Why don't you hit me instead? You good for nothing son of a bitch! Hit me! I'm not scared!"

The museum employee paused a moment then rushed forward. "What's happening here?"

I turned to her and clung to her arm, "Help me, please! My boyfriend is such a jealous hog! He thinks I'm in love with Yongzheng just because I like reading books and watching movies about him! Even if I admire the emperor, it doesn't mean I want to sleep with him, does it? And besides, he is dead!"

It took the woman a moment to understand what I was saying. "Did he punch the picture of Yongzheng because of that?"

"No, I did that because he's a bastard, and he deserves it!" Jeng yelled, his face flushed, his chest heaving with his heavy breaths.

"Look at him!" I squealed louder, trembling and crying out of genuine fear. "He's insane, isn't he? Tell him, sister, tell him he's being unreasonable!"

The woman obviously did not want to get involved in our private business. She rushed over to the painting to inspect it for any damage, but fortunately the foam board it had been mounted on was still intact. She waved her hand dismissively. "Please go outside to resolve your personal matters. And I think it would be best of you leave immediately, before I change my mind and file a police report against you for damaging national property."

We hurried out of the Wuying Dian in silence, walking aimlessly along the paths and following the crowds. What was I supposed to do with this deluded guy who thought he was Kangxi's son? Perhaps the only thing I could do was to take him to the police station.

"I beg for forgiveness," Jeng murmured. "I didn't mean to get you in trouble."

I looked at his distraught face and forgot my earlier annoyance with him. "Don't mention it. Just don't do it again. You have to control your rage in public."

He nodded. "But what does *boyfriend* mean?"

"Oh, that." I blushed. "It just means male friend."

"Just as I thought." The man smiled. "Then you're my girlfriend."

"Well," I chuckled. "Sure."

OUR NEXT STOP was the Palace of Heavenly Purity. It was the grandest building in the palace, with its double eaves, glazed tiles, marble platforms, and the long walkway in the front with white balustrades. A shrine-like structure on a raised platform dominated the center of the hall, a throne set within the shrine. Characters written in gold on the tablet above the throne caught my eye—Honest and Magnanimous.

"Most of the emperors in the Ming dynasty worked and lived here," a tour guide said. "But not in the Qing dynasty. Kangxi, for example, worked here but lived in Zhaoren Hall, the east annex of the building."

"Is that true?" I asked Jeng, who seemed to be very knowledgeable of Qing history.

Jeng nodded.

The tour guide moved on to the history of Zhaoren Hall. "It's the place where Emperor ZhongZhen of the Ming dynasty killed his own daughter Princess Zhaoren and committed suicide upon the invasion of the rebels."

"Can we see it?" one of the tourists asked.

"No, unfortunately it isn't open to the public yet."

"Too bad."

I looked over at Jeng and saw that he was just as disappointed as the tourist sounded. We followed the crowd into the courtyard that overlooked the golden roofs of the surrounding buildings.

"Come with me," Jeng whispered, his lips dangerously close to my ear.

He led me towards a narrow path between the walls of the yard and the main building. Hidden behind bushes was a gate, rusty and locked, and guarded by a pair of stone lions.

"This gate leads to Zhaoren Hall." His voice was still a whisper even though we were alone.

I swallowed hard. "But it's locked."

"I know." He grabbed the rusty, brick-sized lock and pulled and twisted it a few times, then let go of it.

I gasped as he jumped on the stone lion and grabbed the top of the wall. Before I could reprimand or protest, he was already on the other side of the wall.

Terror gripped me and I wondered what I was supposed to do. Then I heard Jeng's voice on the other side. "Hurry up. Climb over the wall. It isn't that hard."

"What? I'm not going to do it, you psycho." I turned on my heel. But before I took a step, my curiosity got the better of me.

Turning around, I clambered timidly on top of the lion and reached up, grabbing the wall above me. I lifted one leg and then the other, pulling myself onto the wall, my legs dangling in the air.

"Help me down, you idiot!" I hissed at Jeng, who was looking around at the overgrown and weedy yard.

He reached up and grabbed me under my shoulders, pulling me down. He panted as he dragged me along the weedy yard towards Emperor Kangxi's old dwelling. He slowed his pace when the dilapidated building with broken doors and windows came into a full view. The doors, windows and patio pillars were all painted red, but the paint had long faded. The green tiles of the eave had also lost their veneer.

Jeng stopped after moving a few feet ahead, reluctant to move further. When I looked at him, the sadness in his eyes shook me to my core.

"How did it come to this?" he murmured, dropping to his knees and bowing deeply.

This guy, I thought, shaking my head. Whether or not he really was Kangxi's son—and there was no way he could be, right?—there was no doubt that he was a pious worshipper of the long-dead emperor. I waited patiently for him to pay his respects. When he got up, we walked up to the patio. Through a seam on the carved door, I caught a glimpse of the interior. It was dusty but spacious, with an intricate architectural design on the ceiling. Antique tables and chairs huddled in a corner, and in the other corner behind the divider stood what appeared to be a cot.

"Kangxi couldn't possibly have slept there," I commented, breaking the silence.

"He did," Jeng answered. His eyes were moist now. "Father liked everything simple. Luxury is for the women, he often said. And a man must be able to get used to rough conditions. He sent me to battle to toughen me up. And for that I thank him."

The sun was setting on the horizon and silence fell between us and around as another group of tourists left the Palace of Heavenly Purity. A few crows flew across the courtyard to rest on the eave, and squawked once they were settled.

Jeng closed his eyes and let out a long sigh. "I still remember the last time I saw Father here. The same crows were crying on the same place. I can't believe three hundred years have passed."

I tilted my head and looked up at the crows. "Three hundred years? Really? They can't have been the same crows."

But Jeng didn't seem to have heard me. He sat down on the patio stairs and closed his eyes. "I should've stayed in Jing City. I should've insisted!"

He stopped talking as a tear rolled down his cheeks. For a moment, I didn't know how to react to it. He sounded insane, but he looked so sincere, so sad, and I couldn't help but feel his remorse and guilt. This man in front of me . . . could he really be Kangxi's son?

I sat down next to him, rummaging in my purse for a Kleenex, then wiped his face gently. The soft touch seemed to agitate him more. He clutched my hand and groaned in agony.

"He'd wished to pass me the throne, but I let my chance slip—not that I wanted to rule. But I could've prevented all the atrocities. Ah, I've failed him!"

"No, you didn't." I stroked his face gently with my free hand. I still wasn't sure whether the man was in his right mind, but his anguish seemed real to me. "You were a good general who protected his country, and you were a good son to your father. I'm sure he was proud of you."

He looked at me for a moment not saying a word, then he buried his face on my shoulder.

"Attention please!" a woman's voice came over the loudspeaker. "The Palace Museum will close in thirty minutes. Please make your exit promptly."

"Let's go." I patted his back.

We stood up. But instead of jumping over the wall and going back the way we came, Jeng led me towards the back of the house—a waste yard clustered with old roof tiles and broken wood planks.

He found a rusty door—this one had no lock—and started fiddling with the latch. It took a while before he managed to push the door open. After passing a few more doors, broken walls, piles of planks and bricks, we stepped into a dense forest. Leaves of huge cypress, locust, pine and elm brushed against us as we made our way through. It wasn't until we reached the end of the path that I saw a pond of emerald water enclosed with draping willows. Numerous pavilions lined the shore on the other side of the pond.

"The Imperial Garden!" I gasped, staring at the beauty around me. Tourists milled around, snapping photos of the pavilions with golden roofs and red walls, stone sculptures of dragons and lions, and towering ancient trees.

The natural scenery enthralled me. For reasons unknown to historians, trees weren't part of the landscape anywhere else in the palace. I fished my cellphone out of my pocket and started taking pictures. Jeng, however, didn't really seem to be pleased with what he saw. He kept saying things like, "I don't remember this bridge." And, "where is that pavilion?"

I sighed inwardly. *Sounds like he grew up here.*

Jeng seemed to have heard my thoughts. He swiftly took my hand and led me into a rock garden. "This is my favorite spot in the palace. When I was a child, I used to play hide-and-seek with my brothers and sisters."

I looked at the forest-like rocks and nodded. It was an ideal place for the game.

"My secret storage is here, too," he said. "Under one of the rocks."

I looked at the rocks that had been artfully arranged to resemble mountains. They must have been standing there for hundreds of years. Although they had different shapes, they looked identical at a glance. But Jeng seemed to know them each as unique. He looked them up and down to gauge their height and looked over the surroundings to measure the position of the rocks. Then he stopped in front of a cluster by a pine tree.

"It should be this one," he mumbled, looking at the tree. "The tree has certainly grown much bigger than I remembered."

"It's been three hundred years," I said jokingly. I appreciated the man's efforts to prove himself, although I wasn't going to be convinced.

Jeng didn't seem to have heard me. He examined the rocks carefully, as if looking for something. Then he pointed to a piece and said to me, "You see, there is a hollow behind this piece."

He tried to move the rock that was supposed to be the door of the secret storage but couldn't. "It's stuck."

His disappointment affected me. "Perhaps it isn't this one?"

"It is. I'm positive. The shape of the mountain resembled a bowed figure and I used to call it *old eunuch.*"

I looked at the rock mountain. It was true. Overall, it did look like a man with his head hanging low and back hunching.

"The hollow is right in the middle of his body," Jeng said. "I apologize for the cruel allusion. But I didn't think of it. It was actually the idea of my trusted eunuch."

Jeng lingered around the rocks a moment longer, pushing every piece. "The rock must've gotten stuck to the others, since no one has moved it for a long time."

"Let it be," I said. "You don't have to prove anything to me."

"Do you believe me then?"

I hesitated. "It's not important. I mean, whether I believe you or not."

"It is!" Jeng said adamantly. "I don't want you to think I'm a liar or a lunatic."

"But there's nothing you can do now. Let's get out of here. It's getting late."

I started to move away, and Jeng followed me silently. But a moment later he suddenly turned. "Wait here," he said to me.

Jeng ran towards the rocks and lifted his leg. He kicked the rock that he had been unsuccessful in moving. I covered my mouth. As his foot touched the rock, I heard a loud thump. The impact forced him back and he hit the rock hill behind him.

"Are you all right?" I ran to Jeng, who had managed to regain his balance and stood firmly on the ground like a Kung Fu master.

"Yes," he answered as he promptly approached the rock. He pushed at it again. It still looked immovable, but Jeng hit it with his left hand again and again, each blow seeming more desperate. Then he grabbed the rock with both his hands, took a deep breath, and tugged at it. Sweat dotted his brow. After a few more deep breaths and more tugging, the rock finally moved. And there, to my utter astonishment, was a hollow.

Jeng released the rock and doubled over, panting heavily.

Blood oozed from his hands, and I quickly extracted more Kleenex to dab at his wounds. "You didn't have to do this! Now your hands are injured!"

Jeng shook me off and stuck his left arm into the hollow, and after a moment's search, pulled out what looked like a forked stick, covered with a layer of mildew. At first, I thought it was a tree branch, but the wood seemed to be of quite good quality, faint, carved patterns adorned it.

After wiping the mildew off its surface and staring at it for a moment, he grinned. "I've totally forgotten about this!"

"What is it?" I asked curiously as he again stuck his hand into the hollow to search for more.

"My slingshot," he said, still smiling as he recalled the past. "The leather was gone. A cousin gave it to me when I was about ten and I loved it. I was trying to hit a bird but injured my fifteenth brother instead. My mom ordered me to throw it away, but I hid it here instead. Sometimes I snuck out and played with it in the garden. But I lost interest in it."

I had been determined not to believe him, but I wasn't sure anymore. Although his actions and behavior were impulsive, he was not a mad man. The gleam in his eyes and the nostalgia in his voice were all genuine, and he certainly knew the Imperial Palace inside out. Had he really lived here before? What else could explain his knowledge of the place and his ignorance of the outside world? But how could I possibly believe that he was from three hundred years ago? Time travel didn't exist!

While I struggled with my doubts, Jeng pocketed the stick and put the fallen rocks back to their places.

He took my hand in his. "Let's get out of here before we're accused of destroying national property again!"

JENG LED ME through a narrow alley into another unlocked yard. It was even more neglected than the previous yard—the paint on the roof and walls were faded, weeds poked out of the wooden slats on the porch. The broken sign under the eave read *Upper Study*.

"Shangshufang was the school for me and my brothers. I spent most of my childhood years here, ever since I was six," he said with a melancholy sigh. "Never knew I would miss it one day. I hated it then. We would get here at dawn and leave at dusk. Our days started with language classes—Manchu, Han, and Mongolian. In the afternoons, we practiced swords and archery. We had to study mathematics and astronomy, too. I loathed math."

"Me too!" I said, remembering how I'd suffered through my math classes in high school and college. Being a math professor, my dad had taught me math early in my life. I had done well in math but had never liked it. I had actually declared my major in math in college but changed to business after a nightmarish advanced calculus class.

"But Ahmah loved mathematics." Jeng shook his head. "And he always wished we would do well in it. He always complimented my third brother's competency on the subject. While I, I failed to live up to his expectations."

"Don't blame yourself," I said in attempt to comfort him. "Mathematics aren't for everyone." But deep down I commiserated with Jeng. I felt the same sense of failure whenever I visited my father's new family. Yanlu, my half-sister, was getting her Ph.D. in math at Tsinghua University. Father was obviously proud of her, and there were times I wished I hadn't changed my major.

"I agree!" Jeng smiled. "It's just too boring. The master tended to lull us into afternoon naps with his gentle voice and long computations."

I laughed.

"Hey!" a voice shouted from behind us. A uniformed guard materialized from behind the building. "This area is not open to public!"

"Says who?" Jeng responded.

The guard was quite taken aback at the rude remark. Apparently, no one had ever spoken to him that way. "Says the government!"

I pulled at Jeng's hand, trying to stop him from arguing further. But Jeng didn't budge.

"Who's the government?"

"What kind of question is that? Are you a trouble maker?" The guard glared at us, his beady eyes bulging. "Get out of here otherwise I'll have you two arrested!"

"Go ahead!" Jeng said, advancing at the man.

The guard was considerably shorter and smaller than Jeng, and I thought he would back up because of Jeng's size. But he didn't. Instead, he said, "It looks like you want to fight. Good. I've been looking forward to a fight."

As he spoke, he shrugged off the stiff jacket of his uniform and tossed it on the ground. His arms were surprisingly thick and muscular, and so was his chest and abdomen under his t-shirt. He took a deep breath, straightened his back and stuck out his chest, then raised his arms. His muscles seemed to inflate like balloons. At the same time, his face distorted into a menacing snarl, and I heard his bones crack. This guard must've been a Bruce Lee fan, and was imitating his strategies. Worry crept into my heart as he circled around Jeng, bouncing and swinging his fists, shouting like a monkey.

"Let's go," I urged Jeng. But he ignored me and stayed where he was, the picture of calm, looking at the guy with amusement.

Seeing that his moves and shouts didn't frighten his opponent, the guard became fierce. He lifted his legs and leapt towards Jeng. But apparently his kick wasn't as intimidating as it looked to me, and Jeng was able to dodge it with ease. His next moves were faster, but he was still unable to touch a single hair on Jeng. It wasn't until the man doubled his efforts, that Jeng started to defend himself with some simple techniques. He blocked the guard's fist with his arm, deflected the man's leg with his own, but he didn't attack him. From Jeng's confident and relaxed manner, I guessed that his Kung Fu skills must have been much better than the guard's, who was panting and sweating already. Suddenly, in the midst of the guy's maddening shouts and kicks, Jeng reached out in a flash of movement and grabbed his opponent's foot. The guard twisted, readying himself to kick with his other foot, but Jeng grabbed at that one as well.

It was the first time I'd seen a fight in real life. My palms were clammy with sweat, my pulse racing in a wild gallop. I didn't know how Jeng managed to avoid every single fist or kick the guard aimed at him, and I certainly had no idea how he conquered his opponent like a parent catching a misbehaving child. I saw no showy or intimidating presentation, only someone at ease in his craft and the art of winning.

The guard didn't wait to surrender. "I'm sorry, Master, please let me go!"

Jeng let go of him. "Kid, you have the potential to be great. But you need a good teacher. Where did you learn your Kung Fu?"

The guard looked embarrassed for a moment. "Actually, I spent a summer at a Shaolin Temple. But I guess that wasn't enough."

"You're too much into style. Your basic skills aren't solid enough. Your kicks look good but are weak, your punches are fast but have no strength. I suggest you practice on Zama steps, and hit sand bags."

"I'm doing that," the guard mumbled.

"Not enough. You might want to change sand to rocks and metal."

Jeng took my arm and walked away.

"Master, wait! What's your name?"

Jeng turned. "I'm not a master."

"Where did you learn your Kung Fu?" I looked at Jeng in admiration.

"In the palace," he said.

I nodded. "Of course."

Jeng wanted to linger in the palace after that, but we heard another announcement, urging people to leave. I didn't want any more trouble or excitement. My legs ached from the day's walk, so I begged Jeng to head for the nearest exit.

We had dinner at a restaurant near the palace, and after that Jeng wished to see Xunjun Mansion—his residence. We went to the Xunjun Mansion according to a tour map, but it turned out to be the house of a later duke. After asking around, we found the palace the fourteenth son of Kangxi had lived in, but sadly, most of the original buildings had been demolished, and what remained was nothing more than a broken wall and a few pine trees. Jeng stood in front of the pine trees in silence, then turned and walked away.

CHAPTER 6

WE RETURNED TO the Palace Hotel around nine in the evening. While Jeng took a shower, I searched online for the fourteenth son of Kangxi and soon found what I wanted on Wikipedia.

Prince Yinjeng, the fourteenth son of Kangxi, was born in 1688. The date of his death was unknown. I couldn't find any pictures of him but found out that Jeng indeed meant upright. The prince had three wives, four sons and five daughters. His father had conferred him the title of Frontier General when he was thirty-two and sent him on a mission to subdue the Dzungars who invaded Tibet. He had indeed been away while his father was dying, and thus might have lost his chance of succeeding the throne.

As soon as the fourth prince Yongzheng became the emperor, he sentenced many of his half-brothers to death, and others, including his full sibling Yinjeng, to confinement. Yinjeng was sent to the Imperial

Mausoleum to guard Kangxi's grave from 1723 to 1725. I paused for a moment as I recalled Jeng saying that he had moved to the cemetery. The hostility between the two brothers had started long before the death of Kangxi, who had favored his fourteenth son, and Yongzheng might have been jealous. Prince Yinjeng had joined the faction of Prince Eight, who hadn't bothered to hide his ambition for the throne.

Even after his brother had become the emperor, Prince Yinjeng refused to bow to him. Enraged, Yongzheng not only stripped Yinjeng of all his royal titles and confiscated his property, but also stopped his salary and condemned him and his family to poverty. He even ignored Yinjeng's request for an imperial doctor for his dying wife. What an evil man! The hatred I had seen in Jeng's eyes when he had hit the portrait of Yongzheng flashed through my mind. *Perhaps he's not a lunatic. Perhaps he is indeed Prince Yinjeng.* I was tempted to accept the possibility. After all, we had met not far from the imperial tombs.

The article went on to say that Yongzheng had decided to have his brother brought back to the Forbidden City and imprisoned inside Shouhuang Temple—a place to rest the souls of the past emperors—but Yinjeng had escaped the night before the trip. After that, his whereabouts were unknown. Imperial soldiers had searched miles around the cemetery, but couldn't locate him, although they had found evidence of a fierce fight between the prince and some wolves, including corpses of the animals and a fragment of his cloak. Some

112

historians believed he had been killed by the imperial soldiers during the escape, but others weren't sure. I stopped reading, remembering the bite wounds on Jeng's arm and shoulder. I went to the closet and found the laundry bag that contained his laundered clothing. A corner of the hem was missing. My hands went cold.

I was still dazed over the facts when the door of the bathroom opened and Jeng called out in his bathrobe, holding the hairdryer.

"Could you show me how to get the wind out of this?" He pressed the switches back and forth.

I sighed. "You have to plug it into the outlet first."

I showed him how to do it, but he had trouble maneuvering the dryer, so I took it from him and helped him out. The long strand of hair dried in no time, and he murmured a thanks as I started braiding his hair. He clearly wasn't skillful at that, either.

"You forgot how to braid your own hair, too?" I teased.

"I didn't have to do it," he said, shaking his head. "I had a maid do it for me."

"You had servants in confinement? That's not bad at all."

He paused at the remark, then a grin lit up his face. "You finally believe me!"

It took me a second to register the meaning of his response. He was right. I was beginning to believe he was Prince Yinjeng, who had escaped the Imperial Graveyard three hundred years ago.

"Not really." I brushed his hands away. "But I could pretend to be your maid for the time being."

As I braided his hair, I glanced at him in the mirror. My heart skipped a beat. He was so incredibly handsome. High cheekbones and narrow eyes were characteristics of Manchu ethnicity. Emperor Kangxi, Yongzheng, and Qianlong all had the same facial features, which only further proved that this man was of imperial descent.

As my mind wandered, our eyes met in the mirror and I blushed.

"Okay, done," I said as soon as I finished winding the band on the end of the braid. Then I caught sight of his injured arm. "Let me change the bandage for you."

As I turned to get the medicine box, his hand caught mine. My heart raced as I looked up at the tall man, his bright eyes boring into mine, his breathing as heavy as my own. He smelled of sandalwood soap. I hadn't realized the scent could be so sexy.

"Is there, uh, anything else you need?" I fought back the urge to falling into his arms and put my face against his firm, muscular chest.

He didn't say a word but smoothed my hair with his hand, then bent to kiss me. I thought I ought to resist, but I couldn't. I melted against the touch of his soft lips, and his ardent tongue further aroused me.

Am I really kissing Prince Yinjeng? I thought confusedly. *Did he really have three wives and nine children?* The fire in me dampened instantly. I put my palms against his abdomen and pushed him away weakly. He let go of me reluctantly, his hard breaths coursing over me.

I FOUND SOME red wine in the fridge and poured a glass for myself, thinking that the prince probably wouldn't care for it. I had accepted the possibility that he was a prince—how else could I make sense of him? His mannerisms, his knowledge, and his passion for the palace were all unusual. He was simply not from this world.

Jeng was enjoying a TV program after switching channels for a while. He was absolutely amazed by the "magic box" and his eyes had been glued to it since I had shown him how it worked. He had trouble appreciating modern dancing and singing programs and didn't understand the talk shows. Finally, he settled on the classic drama *Outlaws of the Marsh.*

"Can I have a drink, too?" he asked. "I really need it."

"Sure," I said. "But they don't have anything stronger here."

"I'll go for that," Jeng said, pointing to the red wine. "It isn't bad."

I laughed. "Isn't bad? It's a French vintage and it costs a thousand yuans per bottle." Peter had informed me that it came with the reservation, but I doubted it.

We sat next to each other on the couch in front of the TV. *Outlaws of the Marsh* was over, and *Empresses in the Palace* started. It was a show that had been adapted from an online novel a few years back and had become immensely popular internationally. Remembering that the emperor in the series was Yongzheng, I quickly reached for the remote control. "It's not interesting."

But I was too late. Jeng had caught sight of the Palace of Heavenly Purity and insisted on watching it. After he had figured out the identity of the emperor, there was no way I could even distract him.

After watching the show intensely for a moment, he asked "Who's this woman?"

"Oh, she's the main character of the show. Her name is Zhen Huan."

"I don't recall anyone of the name."

"Well, she's a fictional character, probably not in any historical records. It's TV."

He didn't really hear me because his attention was on another person on the screen—Consort Nian, the sister of the right-hand man of the emperor. She was a jealous woman and the villain in the drama. At the moment, Nian was ordering her eunuch to punish an innocent maid.

"This is ridiculous," Jeng said after clarifying the identity of Consort Nian with me. He turned off the TV. "Silan is the sweetest creature on earth, not at all a shrew like that woman!"

"Silan?" I was surprised to hear him calling the consort by her first name. "Sounds like you know her well."

He didn't mind my mocking tone. "We were friends before she married."

"Oh yeah, of course. She's your sister-in-law." I meant to be sarcastic, but it didn't come out that way.

"She died too young. Poor thing. None of her children survived, either." He sighed and emptied the glass of wine.

He sounded so genuinely sad that I began to feel sorry for the "evil" consort.

He filled his glass with more wine and drank it down in silence. I guessed he was moping over his previous life again.

"So, Prince, how many *fujins* do you have?" I asked, both teasing and testing him.

"Three."

"That's a lot. Nowadays no man can have more than one wife a time."

He shifted in his seat. "Well, actually I have the least wives among my brothers. Most of them have more than five. But to tell the truth, if I had a choice, I wouldn't have any. They tend to argue and complain all the time. But I didn't get to choose. It was Father Emperor's orders. I merely did my duty."

"Do you mean you've never loved any of them?"

"Well." He blushed. "I took care of them. Made sure they got what they wanted."

"Do you miss them?" I asked softly.

He was silent for a moment. "How can I not? They're my family." Then he asked me, "What about you? Do you miss your *fujun*?"

"I'm not married," I said.

"Why are you traveling by yourself?"

I explained my life to him, telling him I lived in another country, and was here on business. I left out the part about Peter.

Jeng had been sleeping on the sofa bed, but that night I insisted he take the dragon bed. I tossed and turned on the sofa bed, pondering over what to do with him. How could I help him return to the Qing dynasty?

CHAPTER 7

THE NEXT MORNING at breakfast, Jeng asked me to take him to Changchun Yuan—the Garden of Joyful Spring—saying that it was the place where Kangxi had passed away.

I searched the location online and found out that the place had been mostly ravished and destroyed by the Anglo-French force during the Second Opium War, along with the Summer Palace next to it. The location was now the campus of Peking University, about twelve miles northwest of Beijing city.

"Do you still want to see it? It looks like they managed to preserve some buildings." I showed Jeng the pictures of what remained of the garden—a lake and the broken walls of some temples.

Jeng's face was downcast. "He died in the Bookhouse of Clear Stream. Is it still there?"

"Um, it doesn't say here. But we'll find out."

119

Worried that it would be difficult to find parking near the campus, I decided to take the bus. After about half an hour's bus ride, we got off on Summer Palace Road, a tree-lined street in front of Beijing University. I had been here a few times years ago, when my dad taught here in a summer. The traffic had been light in the area back then, and the place had felt like a huge park. But now it was crowded with shops and vehicles. Because of its history, the west entrance of Peking University had the look of an imperial palace with its red iron gates, pillars, and curved eaves. A pair of fierce stone lions guarded the entrance on either side, and a security guard stood between the two stone lions. One of the three gates was open, letting the students in. A frail, middle-aged man wearing a baseball cap and black-rimmed glasses swept the fallen leaves in the entrance area. As soon as he saw us, his eyes fixed intensely on us, or rather, on Jeng, most likely because of his hairstyle.

When we tried to pass the gate, the security stopped us. "May I see your IDs please?"

I pulled out my passport and handed it to the guard without a word. He took it, copied down my info, and gave it back to me. He looked at Jeng, who obviously wasn't making any attempt to show him anything.

"Uh, I'm sorry but he left his wallet in the hotel," I lied.

"Then he can't come in."

"Could you please make an exception?" I begged, sensing that Jeng would make a fuss again. "He really wants to see the place!"

"Why? What's his motive?"

"Motive?" I tried to think of a good reason. But Jeng was obviously too old to be a student. "He's interested in Qing history."

The guard shook his head. "This is policy. We can't let anyone in without identification."

"But you have my identification, if anything went wrong you could find me," I reasoned with him.

The guard hesitated. "But you're a foreigner."

"Oh, come on!" I felt insulted. "Don't call me a foreigner. I'm half Chinese!"

While the two of us argued, Jeng pushed past us and disappeared behind the gate in no time.

"Hey, wait!" the guard shouted.

He grabbed my arm and spoke into his radio. "A suspicious person has entered the west gate, and he's heading towards the Changchun Yuan area. Can somebody go get him?"

"Oh please," I said. "He's not dangerous. Just give him some time and he'll be back. He just really needs to see the place."

The guard ignored me. After a few minutes, someone replied on the radio. "I found him, I tried to grab him, but this man is wily. It seems like he knows some Kung Fu. Please call the city police."

My heart constricted, and I shouted at the radio, "No, please, don't call the police! He will come out, I promise! All he wants is to see Changchun Yuan! The place where his father died! He's harmless! I guaranteed with my life!"

Fifteen minutes later, Jeng reappeared, followed by two guards. Crowds, including students and tourists, had gathered around here and there, watching the eccentric guy with a long braid and long legs. Jeng walked with a gait unusually heroic and arrogant. But when he got closer, I saw that his face was distraught.

"How was it?" I asked. "Did you find Bookhouse?"

He shook his head. "It's all gone. Not even the streams are here anymore."

Two more guards followed him, and they attempted to grab him as soon as they got the chance. But Jeng didn't give them much of a chance. Without even turning his head, he pushed them away from him. He grabbed the wrist of the guard who held my arm and squeezed it until the guard loosened his grip. Wasting no time, we fled the scene.

We passed the gate and ran for our lives. The old man sweeping the floor threw his broom into our way, shouting, "Wait!" Jeng jumped over it, dragging me after him. I almost stumbled but steadied myself. The man ran after us, his shouts echoing through the air. We ignored him and kept running.

Sirens sounded behind us and we pushed ourselves to run even faster. I had never run so hard in my entire life. I was wearing sneakers but running on the streets of Beijing was as challenging as running an obstacle course. People and vendors were everywhere.

Neither Jeng nor I was native to the city—at least not in the present time—and it was difficult to navigate. After I stumbled again, Jeng scooped me up in his arms. I protested and told him to let me go, but he ignored me and simply kept running. I had no choice but to circle his neck with my arms to keep me from falling and to bury my head in his chest so my head didn't bounce around too much.

Just as I started to enjoy being carried in his strong arms, Jeng slowed down and stopped.

"Are you okay?" I asked.

"I'm a bit tired." He put me down. "You aren't as light as you look."

I laughed. "Thanks for not saying I'm fat."

I barely had the time to take a breath before someone caught my hand from behind. "Got you!"

We both turned in surprise. It was the old man who had been sweeping up the leaves.

"Let her go!" Jeng cried out, grabbing the old man's wrist.

"P-Please, I'm not going to harm you," the man said, wheezing for breath. "I just want to give you this."

He thrust a piece of paper in Jeng's hand.

"What is it? Who are you?"

"I don't have time to explain. Read it later when you're safe. The police are coming. You have to run!"

Indeed, two police officers were pushing their way through the crowd towards us. "There they are!" one of them shouted. "Stop!"

Half a block away a huge crowd was gathering in the center of the street. We ran towards the crowd without any hesitation.

"What is it?" Jeng asked as we ran. "A riot?"

"I'm not sure. But it doesn't matter! Let's go!"

We pushed into the crowd, hiding within the sea of people. People mountain and people sea—for the first time in my life I appreciated the Chinese idiom.

"I've never seen so many people in my life," Jeng shouted above the noise of the crowd so I could hear him. "Not even on a battlefield."

"Really?" I shouted back. "Welcome to the new China!"

The event turned out to be a magic show by some magician from Shanghai and it delighted me.

"Tricks?" Jeng said when he finally understood my explanation. "I like tricks!"

We attempted to squeeze further to the front, but it was impossible. The wall made of human bodies was impenetrable. We were far from the front and I could only see the stage between the heads of the people in front of me. Jeng, however, claimed that he got a clear view because he was tall. For a second, I worried that the police would spot him, but the thick mass of people around me made me throw my worries to the wind.

We pushed through the crowd, finally making our way closer to the front. The magician was still talking when we got there, but soon the show started again. It was the trick of separating bodies.

"Oh no!" Jeng squeezed my hand when the saw went down to cut through the body of the pretty girl.

"Don't worry," I said. "It's all an illusion."

"I hope so!"

When the lid of the trunk was opened at the end, and the girl stood up without a trace of injury, the audience cheered. Jeng's eyes were wide. "But how is it possible?"

I knew roughly how it was done, but I didn't want to satisfy Jeng's curiosity, so I only shrugged.

The magician started another trick, and I was just getting into it when the man in front of him put his child on his shoulders.

"Hey! I can't see a thing!" I complained. The guy sent me a look of contempt, but he didn't move his child.

Without warning, Jeng held me up and put me on his shoulders. The sudden intimacy shocked me, and I wanted to get down at once. But my eyes fixed on the stage, which I could see clearly now, and elation bubbled up inside me at being taller than everyone around me. I rested my hands on Jeng's head and watched the magician perform.

EXHAUSTED FROM OUR earlier adventure, we dropped onto the couch as soon as we were back in our room.

"These tricks are very different from the ones performed in our time," Jeng commented.

"Of course," I said. I no longer had the urge to roll my eyes. "These are all modern. I imagine three hundred years ago tricks were simpler. What tricks have you seen anyway?"

"I've seen breeding coins, turning paper into noodles, making peas disappear from a bowl . . . I can't recall everything. I really liked them when I was a child. I used to sneak out of the palace to watch street shows with my brother—" He stopped abruptly.

"Which brother?" I asked curiously. "Not the fourth?"

"Yes, with him," he said tersely. "But that was a long time ago."

Interesting. The two brothers hadn't always been enemies. What had changed their relationship?

"I've always loved magic tricks," I said in order to break the tense silence that had suddenly fallen upon us. "When I was in the first grade, I already knew more than ten card tricks."

"What are card tricks?"

"Tricks using cards." I explained to him what cards were, thinking that he probably didn't know.

"Oh, I played cards all the time," he said, laughing. "But I've never seen any card tricks."

"I'll get a pack of cards later and show you."

"That'll be great."

My eyes fell on his yin-yang pendant. "Where did you get that pendant? Was it a gift from the emperor?"

He shook his head. "It's from the master of the temple. He had me put it on before setting me off on the journey. He said it would guide me through."

"Guide you through? How?"

He shrugged. "I've no idea. It's probably just an amulet." He took off the pendant and let me take a closer look.

I fingered the surface of the pendant. It was as smooth as any jade, the two halves of the yin-yang symbol merging seamlessly. "It's beautiful."

I held it in my left palm and closed my hand. Then I picked up the hotel pen on the table, using my right hand. "Watch, I'm going to perform magic for you."

He smiled. "Sure."

"When I count to three, something magical will happen to the pendant," I said.

It was an old trick I'd learned in middle school. I started to tap the pen on my left hand with the pendant in it, counting "One, two, three," raising the pen high as I tapped.

On the count of three, I stuck the pen on my right ear quickly, and showed Jeng an empty right hand.

He laughed as he pointed at my right ear. "That's not a trick at all. It's so obvious."

"Yes, of course." I smiled as I opened my left hand under his eyes.

He stopped laughing, wide-eyed. "Where is my pendant?"

"It's here!" I took it out of my left jean pocket and put it into his hand.

"How? When?" He was amazed.

"When you were laughing," I said.

"This is what they call *clamor in the east and attack in the west* in The Art of the War!" he exclaimed after understanding what I had done.

His amazement flattered me. "I don't know about the Art of the War, but that's what they call *sleight of hand* nowadays."

"Whatever it's called, you're a trick master!" His eyes shone with adoration.

I blushed at the praise. "Thanks. I dreamt of becoming a magician when I was a kid."

"Why didn't you?"

"Well, I gave up because I was never confident on stage. I failed to do my tricks because of that."

He nodded. "I know what you mean. I had the same problem when I was younger. Father Emperor would have us compete in horse riding and archery every year, and I never did well during those times."

"Do you still have the same problem?"

He shook his head. "I've learned how to manage it. You just have to concentrate on what you're doing and stop worrying about the outcome."

"Easier said than done."

"You have to practice. Whenever you lose your confidence in front of an audience, just take a deep breath."

"I will." I nodded with a smile, although the chance of me performing in front of an audience was pretty small. I got up and opened the fridge, pulling out a bottle of Qingdao beer. I opened the bottle, poured half into a glass for Jeng and urged him to try it.

Reluctantly, Jeng took a sip, then he smiled. "Good stuff!" After gulping down the rest in a single breath, he asked, "What is it?"

"It's called beer," I smiled as I poured him the rest and opened another bottle for myself. "I knew you would like it. No man can resist it."

"Absolutely." Jeng nodded. "The greatest invention ever!"

I giggled after swallowing down a few mouthfuls. "You said that about the bathroom faucet!"

"I know." Jeng grinned. "There're so many nice things in this world. I'm beginning to like it!"

He looked genuinely happy, and I liked him better than the man full of rage and bitterness. "Then stay here. Don't go back!" I said to him, surprised by the huskiness in my voice.

He looked at me, cheeks flushed, eyes bright, and breaths quick.

Under his gaze, I became aware of the tingling effect the beer washed down my belly. His body, mere inches from my own, felt like a furnace, rendering the air-conditioner useless.

He held my hands and pulled me to him. His heat quickly channeled through his hands into mine. He stroked my cheeks, my neck, and my hair, sending shivers down my spine. His smoking eyes stared deeply into mine, setting my entire being on a sizzle. Three days spent with the stranger and I was unknowingly captivated by his being—his scent of sandalwood, his perfectly sculpted face and his towering size, even his quick temper. My lips parted, begging to be kissed. He bent down, grazing gently at first, but quickly turned aggressive. I felt his tongue, warm and slick, claiming every inch of my mouth with such proprietorship while his body trembled. *I don't care whether he's a prince or not, or how many wives he has. I want him.*

The ringing of my phone startled me. I broke from his embrace and glanced at the flashing name on my screen. It was my father.

"Hi Julie, where have you been? I've been calling you."

"I know, Dad. I'm sorry."

I hadn't told my dad about the events of the past three days, and I didn't know how to tell him.

"When will you be coming over for dinner?"

"Oh, I don't know."

"What about tonight?"

"Tonight?" I chewed on the inside of my cheek. Jeng had asked me to take him back to the pit tonight.

"You could bring your boyfriend along."

He meant Peter, of course, although he had never seen him. I was suddenly embarrassed. I had never introduced a boyfriend to my dad. I glanced over at my roommate, who was trying to decipher the label on the beer bottle, and imagined introducing the "time-traveler" to my dad's family. "I can't. I'm sorry, Dad. I promise I will as soon as I'm free."

"Your family is here?" Jeng asked when I hung up. "Then why are you living in a hotel?"

"Well." I pursed my lips, unsure how to explain. "My dad has a new family, you see. Besides, I came with someone at first."

"Someone?" He raised an eyebrow. "Who?"

"A boyfriend," I said reluctantly, avoiding his eyes.

"Oh." He nodded in understanding; apparently, he still remembered the meaning of the word *boyfriend*.

I felt the urge to explain. "But we're no longer together. He has another girlfriend."

He nodded again. "A man may not have more than one woman a time. Yes, you told me."

"Actually, it wasn't the real reason we broke up," I said, not sure why I wanted him to understand. "The main reason was because he lied to me and had probably never cared for me."

Before I knew it, I was telling him the whole story, and my pent-up emotions broke into vehement sobs.

Jeng wrapped his arms around me and stroked my hair. "There, there. Such a despicable character is not worth your tears."

I cried harder, burying my face in his chest. His gentle voice and soft caresses soothed and comforted me.

He kissed my neck, then whispered, "I'm sorry to have brought you trouble. I hope I'll be able to go home soon."

I was quite surprised by his humbleness. Up until now he had been quite haughty.

"I hope so, too," I said, although I didn't actually. I was starting to like him, and even with the overwhelming evidence in front of me, I still hoped he was a deluded scholar or Kung Fu fanatic of some sort, instead of a prince from the past.

I WAS LOOKING for my lipstick in my purse after dinner at a nearby restaurant when I saw the piece of paper the old street-sweeping old man had given to us. It had fallen on the ground when we were running, and I had picked it up and shoved it into my purse.

I unfolded the note, scanning the four-line poem written in traditional Chinese characters. I cleared my throat and read it aloud.

"Life is death / if you live like a ghost. Tears are nothing / but grief thrown to the winds. Amend the past / if you can't forget!"

Jeng stiffened as soon as he heard the first line, and as soon as I finished reading, he snatched the paper away.

"Priest Wang!" he cried after reading the poem one more time. His flushed face was suddenly white as ash. "I have to find him!"

"Who's Priest Wang?"

"The master of the Temple of Light and Shadow," he said. "He brought me here,"

"Are you saying that the man was the priest? How come you didn't recognize him?"

"Which man? The one in a cap? No, he couldn't be." He frowned. "Although, I didn't really see his face." He looked at the paper again before passing it back to me. "What does it say here?"

On the bottom of the note a line was written in simplified characters: "Haidian Florist, 9 p.m."

"What does it mean?"

"It looks like he wants us to meet him there at nine o'clock tonight." I looked at the clock on the wall. It was a quarter past eight.

"We must go now!" He grabbed my arm, giving it a slight shake.

I stopped a taxi outside the restaurant and asked the driver whether he knew where the Haidian Florist was. He entered the name on his GPS and found it. "It's near Peking University."

Just as I thought. "Take us there."

The taxi took us back to the university, and turned onto Haidian Road, which was on the south side of the campus. The driver dropped us off at a florist in front of what seemed to be a university dorm. It was nearly nine, but the neighborhood was still quite busy with students milling all around.

We stood under a ficus tree in front of the shop, looking around for any sign of the sweeper. As we waited, some girls in camisoles and shorts walked past us.

Jeng's jaw dropped and he scowled. "How can they be allowed to wear underwear in public?"

I chuckled, shaking my head in exasperation. "That's not underwear. Times have changed, Prince."

The girls eyed him boldly when they passed and Jeng's face reddened. The girls whispered to each other and giggled as they looked back at him.

He mumbled embarrassedly, "What're they laughing at?"

"Probably at your hair," I teased him. But deep down, I believed the girls were admiring his height and his handsomeness.

At nine twenty, there was still no sign of the sweeper. I wanted to leave—the man was probably another lunatic—but Jeng looked as if he was willing to wait forever. I leaned against the ficus tree and played mahjong on my cellphone. Jeng joined me after a while. We were in the middle of our fifth game when I noticed the flower shop was closing. I checked the time—five minutes past ten. There were few bicycles and no passersby on the street.

I straightened up and yawned. "I'm not going to wait any longer."

"Just a minute longer," he begged and looked around. "Look, someone is coming!"

I looked in the direction he was pointing. A small, hunched shadow turned out from an alley and stumbled towards us.

"He can't be," I mumbled as I stared at the figure.

The man stopped in front of us a moment later. I recognized him from his cap and glasses, but I was reluctant to admit it was him. His face was red, his eyes barely open behind his thick lenses, and he reeked of alcohol.

"I apologize, Prince," the man slurred. "I, uh, fell asleep."

Prince? I stood wide-eyed, not knowing what to think. Then I looked at Jeng, but he seemed to be elated. "Master!" he held the man's hands. "Is it really you?"

The man's smile was lopsided. "No, I'm not a master. I'm an ordinary person with no prospects."

After staring at his face in the dim street light for a moment, Jeng asked again, "You're not Priest Wang?"

"No," the man whispered. "Follow me and I'll explain."

We followed the drunk man through streets and alleys and arrived at a hutong—a traditional courtyard residence that had been a characteristic of Beijing before. It was quite rare these days. We entered through the gate of the hutong and crossed the courtyard, stopping behind the old man in front of a corner unit while he fumbled in his pockets for his keys. As he turned the knob of the wooden door, it creaked open. "Come on in," he whispered as if not wanting to disturb his neighbors.

I grasped Jeng's arm as we stepped into a dark room. The man closed the door before he flipped the light switch. It was a small room partitioned into living and bedroom areas. On the dining table stood an empty bottle of sorghum wine and a large cup.

The man quickly cleared the table and pulled out chairs for us to sit. "I had a cup too many earlier. Excuse me for a minute." He went into the bathroom and shut the door. I heard water splashing and a second later he opened the door and came out, looking fresher and soberer.

"Master Wang?" Jeng said as he stared at the man in bright light. "You do resemble him."

"No, I'm not him and he's not me," said the man in a croaky voice. "I'm his descendant. Dong Wang."

He bustled around in the kitchen and came out carrying a tray with three cups of tea. Jeng reluctantly sat down, but all the while his eyes didn't leave the man, and as soon as Wang sat down in a chair facing us, he asked, "Where is Master Wang?"

"He's not here," the man said, looking at the big man behind his thick lenses. "He lived three hundred years ago."

"But how did you know me and know that I would be here?"

Dong hesitated a moment, glancing over at me, then looking back at Jeng.

"It's okay. You can trust her. She's been helping me," Jeng assured him.

"How did you two meet?" Dong asked.

Seeing the distrust in the man's eyes, I told him about how we met, starting from how Jeng had saved me from a rogue. The story seemed to ease Dong's suspicion.

"But I don't mind waiting outside," I added.

"No!" Dong said quickly. "I don't want the neighbors get curious. It's fine. I saw how eager you were when you helped him today. I trust you. But you must promise you'll keep tonight's meeting a secret. You must not share it with anyone, not even your family."

"I promise," I said.

"I'VE BEEN WAITING for you for twenty years." Dong took a deep breath to keep himself calm, but faint flickers in his eyes betrayed his excitement.

I held my breath and waited for the man to tell us more.

"My ancestor, who you called Master Wang, kept journals to record his experiments with time traveling. Twenty years ago, when my father died, I found the journals in our old house in the suburbs. The experiments interested me, so I read everything he had written. I was especially interested in the entries he had made regarding your case, Prince Yinjeng."

Dong paused to blow on the tea in his enamel mug, a traditional item that some old folks still preferred to fancy ceramics. I could hear the thump of my own heartbeat over the man's soft blowing. It all sounded too extraordinary! Should I believe Jeng was indeed a traveler from three hundred years ago? Or was it merely a drunkard's babbling? I looked doubtfully at the man who was still struggling to sober up.

"In his journal my ancestor described how he chanced to meet you at Emperor Kangxi's cemetery, and how you came to him for help. When you arrived at the Temple of Light and Shadow, you were barely conscious,

137

beaten and bitten by wolves. And yet you refused to linger and insisted to leave after just a day's rest. My ancestor had described you as someone extremely brave, candid, and down to earth, without a pinch of aristocratic pretense."

Jeng shrugged. "I wasn't aristocratic anymore when he met me."

Dong smiled warmly. "You were. My forefather admired you. In his writings he proclaimed that you should be the one on the throne. Not your brother."

If Jeng was flattered, he didn't show it. "How did your forefather know Yongzheng wasn't fit?"

Dong paused briefly. "It was well known that Yongzheng had stolen the throne from you."

That sentence hit Jeng in the right spot. He sighed and curled his fingers into a fist.

I wanted Dong get back to his story, so I asked, "What exactly happened? How did he end up here, now, three hundred years later?"

"Well, the priest's technology was pristine."

"Technology?"

"Yes, although he called it magic." His attention turned to Jeng's pendant. "May I take a look?"

Jeng took off his pendant and passed it to Dong, who accepted it with both hands as if it was a priceless treasure. His eyes beamed as he carefully stroked its surface.

"Beautiful!" he said. "This is the magic device he designed for time travel. By adjusting the positions of the stones, a time traveler aims for his destination. But I don't want to burden you too much today. Simply put, it's like a compass that gives direction and time."

My mouth dropped open, and I stared intently at the pendant. I had thought it was either an ornament or an amulet, and certainly nothing magical. But it turned out to be a time turner!

"But it was crudely made and far from precise. He made an unforgivable mistake on Prince Yinjeng's trip. And for that mistake, I must apologize on behalf of my ancestor." Dong suddenly dropped on his knees and kowtowed to Jeng.

Jeng jumped at the man's actions. He leaned forward and helped the man up. "No need to blame anyone at this point. He had warned me that slight variation might occur."

"Slight variation indeed!" Dong sighed. "He regretted his mistake for the rest of his life. Afterwards, he never tried his magic on another person." We all became silent after that, and after a moment, Jeng took up the cup and sipped from it.

"I understand how he felt. If he had succeeded," Dong continued, looking completely sober now. "History would've been very different."

My eyes brightened. How would history have been if Jeng had become the emperor instead of his brother? Could China have escaped the humiliating Opium War, and avoided the demise of the Qing dynasty? Would China still be in the Qing dynasty?

"What's been done is done," said Jeng. "What I want to know is if you can get me back?"

Dong looked up. "I should be able to. I've been studying his magic for nearly two decades."

"Did he really come out from that dump?" I asked.

"What dump?" Dong asked back.

"Well, a pit close to the previous Temple of Light and Shadow."

"In the mountains along S32? Yes." Dong nodded. "I have visited the place a few times before. My ancestor actually called it the *time chamber*."

I tied to stifle my laugh, but seeing that Dong was laughing, I gave up my attempt.

When he fell silent, I asked the question that had been lurking in my mind. "So, were you waiting for us at Peking University? And how did you know—"

"Right," Dong smiled. "As I said earlier, I read those journals and I couldn't believe it. The fact that my ancestor had invented a time device shocked me, but what thrilled me the most was when I figured out that the prince would show up in my lifetime. The priest had spent the rest of the journal to calculate the time the prince would arrive and surmised the events afterwards. If his calculations were correct, then he would show up in late-twentieth to early twenty-first century. His estimate turned out to be pretty good. I knew that if the prince showed up, he would certainly want to visit the place his father had passed away, which was the Garden of Joyful Spring. I got myself a job at the university. I could've gotten a position inside the buildings, but I wanted to make sure to spot him when he showed up. So, I became the janitor at the west gate."

"That's incredible," I said. "What devotion. You weren't even sure you would meet him."

Dong nodded. "But it was worth a shot. My old job wasn't that great anyway. I was working in a factory—"

Before he could finish his sentence, Jeng bowed to him. "Please let me express my gratitude."

Dong backed a step first then begged the prince to get up. "I'm simply trying to correct the mistake that my ancestor made. It gnawed at him until his death. He wanted to come find you, but decided to improve his device first. He never quite fixed the problem until he became too frail to leave the temple. By then he was too frail to travel through time as well. He did leave this journal to his family, but no one took up his interest. Until I found it."

I watched the man as he talked. Dong spoke in ordinary Chinese with an impeccable northern accent. The tears he had tried to hold back now shone on his cheeks and he wiped them away with his fingers. He sounded as if he was talking to a long-lost friend, better, a long-lost family member rising from his grave—not irrational at all, considering that Jeng had in fact been in his family's records for three hundred years.

The conversation went on for another hour or so, and the tea kept all of us awake. But at the end of the evening, Dong said to us, "You two had better go back to the hotel and rest. We'll meet again tomorrow. We'll go to the time chamber. I've already asked for a few days off."

I stood up but Jeng lingered. "Do we have to wait until tomorrow?"

"Yes," I said quickly. "Because my eyelids are having a hard time staying open. Even if we could get there, I doubt we could see anything or figure anything out."

"Precisely," Dong nodded. "Don't worry, Prince, I'll do my best to send you back home in time."

Jeng thanked him and it was with reluctance that we left.

We got back to the Palace Hotel after midnight. Jeng was excited, and so was I. The tea I had in Dong's house was still in effect and I didn't want to miss a night's sleep. So, I opened another bottle of vintage wine, and offered a glass to Jeng. This time he didn't gulp it down like it was juice but sipped it slowly, letting it linger in his mouth before swallowing.

"I'm beginning to like it." He grinned.

CHAPTER 8

ALTHOUGH I HAD cringed at the thought of driving back to the nightmarish spot, the mountains weren't as eerie as I remembered. In fact, the scenery was nice along the road. Golden wild flowers dotted the green shades, and the sky was clear with occasional puffs of clouds. The suburbs felt like a paradise compared to the city choked with smog. Jeng and Dong sat in the back seat, talking about history. Dong was extremely well read in ancient texts, and he claimed that he read when he wasn't sweeping or sleeping, and apparently he wasn't boasting. The man seemed to know the Qing dynasty inside out, and it was evident that he worshipped Kangxi. He recounted an anecdote of the teenage emperor subduing the tyrant military commander Oboi with wit, his abandonment of the Great Wall in order to unite the nomads, his embrace of western medicine and foreign religions, and his contributions in science and literature.

"In my opinion, he's really the only true son of heaven in China history," Dong said in conclusion.

The praise undoubtedly pleased Jeng, and the prince treated the man he had known for less than a day with reverence.

But after a moment's pause, Dong sighed. "Emperor Kangxi had but mishandled one thing in his life."

"What's that?" Jeng replied, obviously not willing to allow even a tiny criticism about his beloved father.

"The fact that he kept the name of his chosen heir a secret until his death, giving Yongzheng the chance to revise his will."

"That evil bastard!" Jeng punched the back of my seat, startling me.

"Take it easy!" I cried, glaring at him in the rearview mirror.

But he didn't calm down. He went on to curse his brother, who, according to historical rumors, had added but one stroke on Kangxi's will, and changed history forever.

"Father probably couldn't decide who should succeed him," Jeng said, trying to defend his father's blunder. "He loved all his children. He once said every one of his sons was unique, and he wished we could merge into one body."

Sounds like his mistake was having too many sons. I kept my sarcastic remark to myself.

Dong sighed. "Well, it's not for us commoners to understand His Majesty's quandary. He had witnessed the flaws in the old system of electing the successor through voting, so he decided to name his own heir to avoid factions and bloodshed. And yet, Taizi, who he had expected so much from, failed him, thus causing more factions and putting him in a difficult position."

I recalled that Taizi, the Crown Prince, was Kangxi's second son, and the only child of his beloved first empress, who had died giving birth to Taizi. Kangxi had named the infant his successor out of grief. But Taizi turned out to be a disappointment and Kangxi had twice rescinded his title.

"Historians have mixed opinions about Taizi," Dong went on. "He was apparently a talented guy, gifted in science and literature and not lacking physical prowess. His only fault seemed to be lacking social skills. Am I right about that?"

Jeng paused for a moment before he answered. "Honestly, I still don't fully understand the reason Father Emperor changed his mind. There seemed to be some misunderstanding between them. We all thought Taizi the perfect successor. The first time Father made the announcement that Taizi wouldn't succeed him, we were all shocked."

"Is it true that Yongzheng actually pleaded for Taizi?"

"Yes, he did, but it was all an act. He pretended to be Taizi's supporter." Jeng shrugged. "So Father wouldn't suspect his ambitions. Otherwise why wouldn't he free our second brother from imprisonment after he had gained the throne?"

Dong fell silent as if to grieve the miserable ending of the once promising Crown Prince. "What would you do about Taizi, if you became the emperor?"

"I would grant him freedom and the title of a duke," Jeng said without hesitation.

"That'll be very generous of you. I can see you'll be a loving ruler just like your father."

I was listening to their conversation when I suddenly found myself lost in the mountain road. "I'm not sure where we are. It was night when I drove here last time. I don't remember being here at all. We must've passed it."

"Let's try going right at the end of the path," Dong said.

Although I wanted to turn back, I took his advice and turned right. The road looped back to the main road we had come from, and this time I went slowly and carefully, and soon I heard Jeng shouting, "There it is!"

I LET MY passengers out near the pit and parked the car, then hurried after them.

The pit looked exactly as it had been when I left it days ago. Every piece of junk was in its place—the washer and the bicycle, the broken chest of drawers and the sagging mattress. No one would ever come to this deserted spot, except perhaps semi-conscientious people who were looking for a not-so-convenient spot to dump their trash.

"The time chamber!" Dong exclaimed, looking at the dump approvingly, as if it was a spaceship launching site. "Where were you exactly when you woke from the, uh, transportation?"

"I was lying on the mattress," said Jeng.

"How fortunate!" Dong nodded. Then he stepped forward. "Let's go down to take a better look."

"I'll go first." Jeng stepped down a few steps and turned to help Dong.

I followed Dong down the stairs, less clumsy than the last time since I was wearing sneakers instead of high heels. Still, I lost my balance on the last step, which was larger than the others. Jeng caught me in his arms.

"Thank you," I mumbled embarrassedly, aware of the feel of his strong arms, even in the presence of a third party.

"Do you remember how the place looked before you were transported three hundred years ago?" Dong asked.

"Of course," Jeng said. "It was a forest with lots of trees."

"Sounds very different from now." Dong sighed.

A thought struck me. "Have you ever gone back and met your ancestor?"

He shook his head. "Not yet. But soon, I believe. I haven't been able to produce a pendant that works, although I understand the mechanism. I haven't found the right stone. What exactly happened here that night? Do you remember?"

Jeng nodded. "The master brought me down here after dark, directed me to the right spot and I waited alone. For a while nothing happened, but moments later the earth shook. A strong current soon swallowed me, and I spun. It was gentle at first and I felt light-headed and free. Then the current became intense and hot, I think I was lifted into the air but I'm not sure since I lost consciousness."

"Wonderful." Dong smiled. "That was how it worked according to the journal."

I didn't understand what he was talking about at all. "What do you mean? How does it work?"

Dong turned to me. "He got spun into the energy field, which transported him into our time."

I blinked in confusion. Dong smiled and continued. "The spinning dematerialized the passenger into an energy pattern and pushed it into the earth's active energy field, which carried it into the destined time. Once the energy current subsides, he rematerialized into a person. This pit, or garbage dump, as you call it, is very much like the transporter in Star Trek, except the pit sends a person through time while remaining at the same location."

I struggled to compare the dump with a high-tech transporter. Nonetheless, I tried to process the incredible scenario, imagining Jeng being spun, dissolved, and swallowed into some tornado-like current. "Was he also shot to space and through some wormholes?"

"Nope." Dong shook his head. "Everything took place right here on Earth. Wormholes are great but too far. These *qi* portals are right below our feet."

"*Qi* portals?" I asked incredulously.

"The priest called Earth's energy "*qi*," as a Taoist would. But it was really akin to magnetic energy. The pendant has as a dial. Depending on the time being dialed, the force of propulsion varies. The longer the timespan, the greater the force. But the dial wasn't precise at all and could make ridiculous mistakes. In the case of Prince Yinjeng, instead of three years he dialed three hundred years. My ancestor was so embarrassed of his error that he spent the rest of his life improving the dial."

My jaw dropped. I wasn't a time-travel expert but not illiterate, either. I had liked *Back to the Future* and some *Star Trek* time-travel episodes. I understood that time travel had to do with space, wormholes, and upper atmosphere etc., but didn't know it had anything to do with *qi*.

"Besides the dial, does the pendant have any other functions?" I asked, thinking the yin yang and the qi were related.

"Yes. It's an important device. The center is made of two different stones—black jade and white jade. The black jade is a lodestone, a natural magnet, and it directs the focus of the magnetic power onto the time traveler. The white jade, on the other hand, is

149

nonmagnetic. I don't fully understand its function and I don't know what stone it is. It looks like marble to me, but I'm not sure."

"Sounds incredible," I murmured, still trying to digest the information.

"Isn't it amazing?" Dong said proudly, "Modern scientists know about the earth's magnetic fields in space, but they know nothing about these *qi* portals."

And a Tao priest from three hundred years ago discovered them—was this some kind of practical joke, or a scam? I looked at Jeng and Dong, trying to understand what was happening. Were they crooks trying to trap me into some sort of investment? My dad always warned me about frauds in China, saying that they were very skillful. It could be that these two men were acting, and even the guy who tried to rob me the other night were all on it together. Worse, Peter could be orchestrating the whole thing. Otherwise, why would I have run into a robbery in this place so few people had ever visited?

My hands went cold and I didn't hear what the two men were discussing. I saw Jeng taking off his pendant again and handing it to Dong. They examined it closely.

I swallowed down my apprehension. "Will you be able to send him back?"

"I'll try," Dong said. "The priest left instructions on how to make a frame with precise scales, and I have made some already, though with stones that didn't quite work."

Jeng's eyes beamed. "Please, Master, please help me! I have to get back!"

"I know." Dong nodded. "Believe me, I'm eager to help. I'm no master but I promise I'll have it done within three days."

"Three days?" Jeng didn't seem to be assured. He looked around at the pit. "Will the portal be still open?"

Dong patted Jeng's arm. "The portal is active once every night, although the exact time varies, and the duration is as short as a few minutes."

"But what am I to do for three days?"

Dong laughed. "Relax, rest, and simply enjoy your vacation. If I were you, I wouldn't want to leave such a beautiful woman!"

Jeng blushed at that seemingly harmless humor, but to me it was a warning signal. What were they up to? Was Jeng going to seduce me?

I cleared my throat. "I don't think I can be involved in this any longer. I would like to stay out of it, if you don't mind. I actually need to get back to America soon. Besides, you've found each other, and I'm not really needed anymore, am I?"

The two men exchanged a look. "It's fine with me. I can find you a lodging near where I live," Dong said.

Jeng was silent for a good moment but he finally nodded. "Yes, sounds reasonable. I've been troubling you long enough."

The fact that they both agreed to my suggestion so easily disconcerted me. My earlier wariness seemed silly now. I was still thinking about a reply when Jeng said again, "But I need to pick up my belongings at the hotel first."

"No problem." There was a sudden lump in my throat, and I felt a twinge of regret at my decision.

AFTER A LATE lunch near Peking University, I dropped Dong off at his hutong, and then drove back to the Palace Hotel with Jeng. Dong had pointed to a hotel earlier, telling me it would be a good place to settle Jeng in later. We were silent on our way back, but all the while, I was thinking. *Is that it? I'm not going to see this crazy guy ever again?*

As we walked silently into the lobby and towards the elevator, a familiar voice called me from behind. "Julie!"

My heart raced with anger and humiliation. I turned reluctantly.

Peter had never looked worse. He had a beard, which would have made any other guy attractive, but it simply didn't belong to his chin. He looked shabby. His hair was oily, and specks of dandruff covered his head. His grin used to be cute but right now it was doleful.

He was wearing the same shirt from the day I had caught him with his fiancée. The unpleasant memories woke the pain that had gone numb in me in the past few days. The door of the elevator opened but I didn't move.

"What do you want?" I asked calmly, although I was trembling inside. From the corner of my eye, I saw Jeng watching us curiously.

Peter bit his lip. "I'm sorry, Julie."

Perhaps it was the softness of his voice, because although I didn't detect any sincerity, my eyes stung. My heart was softening already, and I wanted to say, "It's okay, baby," but I curbed my impulse. No, it wasn't okay. The bastard had deceived me long enough. I couldn't trust him anymore. I looked away.

Taking my silence as a sign of forgiveness, Peter stepped forward and took my wrist, "I've missed you, Julie. Let's forget what happened, all right?"

I narrowed my eyes and glared at him. "What do you mean? What about your fiancée?"

"She went back to Guangzhou."

"Oh," I said and stared at his suitcase, not sure what I should make of it.

"Look, can I stay here tonight? I, uh, I'm broke. She took all my cash. I didn't want to use your credit card, and I forgot to bring my own."

I rolled my eyes. He had a habit of forgetting to bring his credit card when we went out. "Don't you have any friends in Beijing?"

"I do but I haven't called them for a long time," he said. "I could call my mom in the States but you know her situation."

I sighed. He had told me about his divorced parents, and it was actually one of the few things that we had in common.

"Okay," I said, "Just for tonight. Tomorrow, I'll find you another hotel."

"Thanks, Julie!" Peter grinned happily and tried to take my hand, but I backed away from him.

The elevator door opened again, and I stepped in, followed by Peter and Jeng. Peter smiled and greeted Jeng when the three of us were inside the elevator. I thought quickly how to introduce them to each other but decided perhaps there was no need to. After all, Jeng would be leaving soon. Not knowing what to say, I kept my mouth shut for the next few seconds and got out of the elevator as soon as the door opened.

I opened the door of my room quickly and went inside. Peter followed me, and then Jeng came in. The two men looked at each other, then they looked at me.

"He's my, uh, ex-boyfriend," I told Jeng after closing the door. "And he's a friend," I said to Peter.

Peter's expression changed but he was too clever to say anything stupid, so he said "Nice to meet you" instead.

Jeng, on the other hand, frowned. "What does 'ex' mean?"

"It means before. He was my boyfriend before."

"He's the guy who deceived you!" Jeng turned hostile right away.

"Yeah, but it doesn't matter anymore," I said with a wave of my hand. "Let's not talk about it."

"It does matter!" He stepped forward, closing up distance between the two of them, and looked down at Peter menacingly. "You hurt her and put her in danger!"

Peter was unnerved. "Jeez, Julie. Where did he come from?"

That was a good question, one I didn't have an answer to.

I patted Jeng's arm and told him to pack. Seeing that he wouldn't move, I grabbed a shopping bag and put his belongings in. He didn't have many things except the set of traditional clothes he had worn the day we met, and another set of modern clothes I had bought him. Then I took the sword out of the closet and handed it to him.

As I was packing, Jeng watched Peter unpack. "Is he going to stay here with you?" he asked before we walked towards the door.

"Just for tonight," I said.

His lips formed a tight line, but he didn't say anything.

"I'm going to find a place for him," I said to Peter. "I'll be back but don't wait for me."

We walked towards the elevator in silence. Inside the elevator, I couldn't bring myself to look at Jeng. I felt him staring at me intensely, his breathing thick and quick. I could even feel the heat emitting from his body, despite the air-conditioning blowing right above me, but I didn't look up.

We were still silent in my rental car. I wanted to cry. Oh my god. Why did I tell him to leave? Did I really think that he was a crook? Why couldn't I just believe that time travel existed? Not everything in life had to make sense. In fact, a lot of things didn't. Why should I be alive, and not some other creature? Why did my mom have to meet my dad? Why . . .

We got off in front of the Yihe Hotel, the place Dong had recommended. It was a small garden hotel named after the Summer Palace. A charming garden stood between the buildings and the gate, with a man-made pond dotted with rock mountains and miniature pagodas.

I used my passport to book a single room on the third floor.

The room was small, but it had a spectacular view of the Summer Palace. We could see the Longevity Hills and Kunming Lake, as well as the bridges and the pavilions in the park.

"I guess you're on your own now," I said after hanging his clothes in the closet. "I'll call Dong and let him know that you're here."

Before I turned towards the door, he grabbed my hand and asked, "Are you sure you're okay?"

I forced a smile. "What? I should be the one asking that question."

"That ex-boyfriend of yours. I don't trust him."

"Don't worry, he isn't violent."

"But you're going to stay in the same room."

I froze. I dreaded going back to the Palace Hotel. My head knew clearly that it was foolish to stay in the same room with Peter again, but my body seemed to miss him. I recalled his haggard face and felt sorry for him. I broke free from Jeng's grasp and rushed out of the door.

I inserted the key into the ignition as soon I got in my car but couldn't make myself turn it. I looked up at the building and saw Jeng standing at a window on the third floor, waving at me.

Tears gushed from my eyes. Behind that window he was no longer a big Kung Fu master or a prince, but a helpless child. I felt like I was abandoning him. What if Dong was a swindler? What if he wasn't a street sweeper, but an employee of an asylum, in which Jeng had been confined before I met him? No, I shook my head. I no longer doubted Jeng's sanity and I knew from the way he missed Kangxi that he was his son. Yet the emergence of Dong seemed too fortuitous—even if what Dong said about his ancestor was true, what was his motive for helping the prince? And where were the ancient texts that Priest Wang, his ancestor, had left?

I pulled my keys out and got out of my car. No, I couldn't leave Jeng alone, not until I could see some sort of proof from Dong.

I walked quickly, worrying that Jeng would disappear into time. I was about to knock on his door when it swung open and Jeng took me into his arms.

"I saw you coming back," he whispered. "What made you change your mind?"

I didn't answer. Instead, I pressed my lips on his and felt him with urgency.

I SMILED CONTENDTLY in Jeng's strong arms. From the window I could see the moon hanging in the sky, filling the room with silver lights. Jeng was a passionate lover, although I wished he could've been more patient. But he convinced me that he hadn't been intimate with women for years, and simply couldn't help it. So, I forgave him. He was snoring softly now, and I got up as quietly as possible to dress. I'd barely put on my bra when he reached out and took my hand.

"Don't leave me!"

"But it's late," I said.

"So be it. Stay here tonight." He pulled me back, held me tightly in his arms.

I conceded. After all, I dreaded seeing Peter again. I cuddled against the muscular body, savoring his male scent, and enjoying his tender touch.

"Do you have to go back to your time?" I murmured, though I knew it was a stupid question.

He paused. "What would I do if I stayed here?"

"You could be my bodyguard," I said, laughing. "But with your knowledge of the Qing dynasty, you could become a curator or a researcher at the Palace Museum."

He seemed to consider it for a moment. "I don't belong here, although I love the modern luxuries, the engine-powered carriage, the shower, the ice pops, the beer, and you."

"But do you know what awaits you once you return to your world and to the Forbidden City? Your father will pass away soon, and your brother wants you dead." I buried my face in his arm so he wouldn't see my tears.

"I'm sorry." He kissed my hair. "But don't worry about me. I have a plan."

The plan, he explained, was to return to the palace just a day before Kangxi's death, and never leave his side.

"But what if the emperor won't let you?"

"I'll convince him," he said.

"Why're you so sure that your father wanted to pass you the throne? Did he tell you that?"

He shook his head. "Father would never do that. But he had told me more than once that I would be a great ruler. And he also expressed such a wish to my mother, Lady Uya."

The famous Lady Uya. I recalled instantly who she was—Kangxi's favorite consort. She had given birth to both Yongzheng and Jeng but had favored Jeng. She was so appalled by what Yongzheng had done to Jeng after he had gained power, that she refused to accept the title of Empress Dowager. Six months after Yongzheng's inauguration, she committed suicide by throwing herself against the pillar in her palace. According to historians, Lady Uya had had great expectations for her second son. Perhaps she would help Jeng, I thought drowsily.

CHAPTER 9

I WOKE BEFORE dawn. Jeng's arm circled me, and I contently wrapped my leg over his thigh without opening my eyes. If this was a dream, I wanted it to last longer. A moment later, I felt his lips on mine, and I giggled.

"Wake up, sleepyhead," Jeng whispered.

I opened my eyes, taking in the breathtakingly handsome face in front of me. He had a strong nose with a slight bump; his narrow, Mongol eyes were extremely sexy at the moment, and so were his long, thin lips.

I melted in his passionate kisses again, and we lingered in bed until daybreak. A streak of orange light peered in from the curtain. I leapt from the bed and rushed to the window.

Kunming Lake was rippling with gold. While I was lost in admiration, Jeng wrapped his arms around me from behind.

"What's the name of the pagoda? I've never seen it before."

"It's the Jade Peak Pagoda," I said, realizing it had probably been built after Kangxi's reign.

Jeng held me silently for a moment, his warm breath tickling my ear. "Have you ever seen sunrise over Forbidden City? It's most beautiful."

A thought suddenly possessed me, and I turned to face him. "No, but I've been wishing to see it."

His eyes brightened. "I know a good place."

I knew exactly where he meant. Jingshan Park. We dressed in a hurry and headed towards my car.

I sped on the still empty city street and we arrived at Jingshan Park while the sun was still climbing up the horizon. Jeng took me to a spot at the top of the hill, and away from other early birds. I fisted my hands on my hips, gasping for breath after the steep hike.

"Where is the pavilion? It used to be right here," Jeng asked.

"There was a pavilion on our way up."

"That wasn't it." He looked around for a moment, then he pointed to a rock and smiled. "Yes! The Splendid Rock! It used to be inside the pavilion and I used to sit here whenever I came."

"Splendid Rock?" I looked at the rock curiously. It didn't look splendid to me, but it appeared to be comfortable. It was shaped like a sofa, as if someone had carved a seat out of it.

He sat down on the rock and sighed with satisfaction. "Father brought me here once, when I was eight years old. And he said to me, 'Look at the palace, my child, how splendid! Wouldn't you want to embrace it?' From that moment on, the word splendid was always connected to the palace. I would come back to the spot again and again, mostly by myself, and I would sit here every time."

"I see. That's why you called it Splendid." I stood by the rock and looked down, then I gasped. It looked exactly the same as I had seen it just a few days ago in my dream. Over the green trees and white clouds, the Palace Museum veiled in the golden orange rays of morning sun.

"It's splendid indeed!"

"It hasn't changed much!" Jeng grinned.

I gazed ahead. The modern high rises beyond the palace were still buried in the gray background and not yet visible.

"It was Father Emperor's favorite view. He once wrote a poem about it: *A thousand miles of clouds embrace the dwelling of the gods. Below it lies my humble territory.*"

"Well written!" Despite his pride, the emperor put his territory below the dwelling of gods.

Jeng stayed quiet long after that. His eyes fixed on the palace and he sank into a deep rumination.

"What are you thinking?"

"This could've been mine."

I held his arm and put my cheek against his taut muscle. "It will be yours once you return."

He sighed. "Actually, I never really had the ambition to take the throne, at least not until my brother did what he did. I was so naïve. I was hoping the eighth prince Yinsi would become the emperor and I would be his general."

I nodded. I had gathered from the online source that Jeng had allied with the eighth prince, who had coveted the throne, and it was probably the reason Yongzheng gave him a hard time once he became the emperor.

JENG AND I returned to the Palace Hotel. Peter was still sleeping but I packed my suitcase and checked out, leaving him enough money for a few nights' stay in a less expensive hotel.

When we returned to the Yihe Hotel, Dong was already waiting for us in the lobby.

"Here it is." As soon as we entered our room, Dong took out an antique paperbound book from his briefcase. I had requested to see his ancestor's journal last night over the phone.

On the cover of the ancient notebook, a vertical line of neatly written calligraphy stated its title. *The Art of Light and Shadow.* The leaves of the book were all yellow, but the words were still clear.

"You can take your time and read it later," Dong said. "I'm going to leave you two alone for the rest of the day."

He asked Jeng to take off the pendant. He was going to take it to a gem appraiser at Beijing University Jewelry Appraisal Center, the most reputable agency in the city. To avoid running into trouble with the security again, he advised us not to go along and we agreed.

I sat next to Jeng as we read the opening paragraph of Priest Wang's diary together. "*Nothing in this universe is absolute and everything is relative, including time, which is the illusion created by light and shadow. I, with my narrow knowledge, have devoted my life to solving the great mystery of reversing time. Now with my life nearing its end, all I could say is I have discovered nature's secret passage and learned how to enter it to travel through time. But my understanding is still limited to how, and I regret to say I cannot explain the mystery. I leave this journal to future scholars of Tao, and may it assist you in your endeavor in pursuing the truth.*" It wasn't easy for me to understand the ancient writing, and I had to rely on Jeng's explanations.

In the first chapter, the priest described an accident that had taken place before he was a Taoist priest. Wang had been traveling one rainy night to visit a sick friend. The road was slippery and he fell into a ravine. His leg was badly injured, and he had no choice but to stay there for the night, under a tree that provided shelter. He almost fell asleep when he felt the rumbling of the earth. He woke in a great trepidation but was unable to struggle out of the "great pull of force." He soon lost consciousness, and when he woke, the rain had stopped. He went back home, only to realize that he had gone back about two years in time, since his youngest son, who had turned four the night before, was once again a toddler learning how to walk.

For days, Wang, who was about thirty at the time, was too shocked to eat or sleep. He became weak and stayed in bed. He attempted to tell his wife what had happened to him, but she took it as a madman's nonsense. After he had physically recovered, Wang built a hut near the ravine where he had fallen and left his family. It would become the Temple of Light and Shadow years later, and he stayed there for the rest of his life to study the reverse of time.

In the rest of the journal, the priest recorded his discovery and experiments in details. It would take him another decade to invent the yin-yang pendant and thus to choose the destination time.

"Wow," I said after we flipped through the journal. "He abandoned his family in order to figure out time traveling."

Jeng was as impressed as I was. "Thanks to him, otherwise, I wouldn't be here and have met you." He moved closer and stamped a kiss on my forehead.

WE MET DONG at his house after dinner.

He put the pendant on the table and couldn't wait to tell us what he had found out. "It's not marble. It is the mutton-fat jade—a rare stone. It's pure and it contains nearly no trace of metal."

Staring at the white whirl—the yang part of the symbol—I nodded with Jeng, not understanding the significance of the discovery.

"That's why it is not attracted to magnets at all. In his diary, the priest mentions that the white jade acts to balance the force received by the time traveler."

"When will you be able to make the new dial?" I asked.

"Soon," he said. "In fact, I've made a few already, in the past."

He led us into his bedroom which was also his study. A large square table stood right next to the bed, strewn with what looked like tools to make jewelry, including pliers, shears and hammers, and some silver sheets.

In one of the small plastic baskets he found some pendants with the yin-yang symbol just like the one Jeng wore, except the white stone wasn't as white. "I've made a few pendants that didn't work, because the white jade wasn't pure enough. I could simply modify one of the frames and fit the pendant into it."

I looked at the casings closely. They had various shapes, some were circles, and some were octagons or hexagons.

"The priest designed them all. The hexagon integrates the I Ching hexagram, but not the most precise. His preference was the circle." Dong pointed to a circular casing, which resembled a dial. "It's carved with 360 units, each indicating a year."

"How does it control the direction of the traveling?" I asked.

"Good question. It can't." He smiled. "You simply have to go with the direction of the energy field. It reverses every month. It travels north on odd months, and south on even months, according to the lunar calendar. And north means forward into future, south backward into the past."

He sighed. "Unfortunately, my forefather didn't know that when he put Prince Yinjeng in the time chamber. It was lunar November, so he came to the future. In fact, he hadn't known traveling to the future was possible. His prior tests had all by chance gone one direction to the south. That was why the mishap happened. But in a way it was a good mistake because what if he was sent three hundred years backwards and into the Ming dynasty?"

Jeng laughed. "Then perhaps I would have become the first Manchu ruler in Han history."

It was the first time I saw him being humorous. The hope of getting back home certainly cheered him up quite a bit.

WE SPENT THE next day at the pit, removing the trash, because Dong said they could interfere with the *qi* currents.

It wasn't until we were resting in the pit afterwards that I realized the extent of the task I was participating in. It unsettled me. What if Jeng made it and became Kangxi's successor? Then history would change, wouldn't it? Would China be different today? Would I be different, or even born?

I asked Dong the questions while Jeng snored against a rock.

Dong waved his hand. "Oh, don't worry about the consequences too much. We wouldn't be affected, not much at least."

"What do you mean?" I was taken aback by his nonchalance. Again, I wasn't a pro on the matter, but I had watched enough TV and read enough science fiction to know that the crushing of a butterfly millions of years ago could drastically change human history.

"It's not as serious as they claim in the movies." Dong sat up as if getting ready to give a long lecture. "You see, my Taoist ancestor wrote about the matter in his journal. I don't agree with him on everything but I like this particular one. According to him, the entire universe is made of *qi*, or energy, and everything in it, including human beings, is just a miniscule particle of *qi*."

I blinked as I tried to relate *qi* with time travel. I was usually dense when it came to Taoist philosophy.

"The universe of *qi* has the capacity of restoring itself to equilibrium." He smiled at my ignorance. "The death of a bug or a human being won't have any significant impact on the universe. Individuals might disrupt the *qi* temporarily, but it eventually retunes to its harmonious state."

"But we're talking about inheriting the throne," I said after blinking my eyes a few more times. "The impact would be significant, that's why the prince wants to return so badly."

"I know." Dong nodded. "If he succeeds, he could save many lives and erase many tragedies in history, which is why I'm helping him. But these changes are still infinitesimal within the big picture."

"Infinitesimal?" I cried. "He could change the history of China. Instead of Yongzheng, we will have Yinjeng for the fifth emperor of the Qing dynasty."

Wang shrugged. "History will be different for a few decades of his ruling. But in the long run, equilibrium will restore."

"What do you mean? If Prince Jeng became the emperor, then the emperors after him would also be different. Qianlong, who was the son of Yongzheng, wouldn't be able to inherit the throne, and neither would the Tsushi's husband Xianfeng, therefore Tsushi wouldn't become an Empress Dowager, and does it mean we could avoid the Opium Wars?"

Dong smiled while shaking his head. "No, this is the magic of *qi*. It's an invisible hand that directs the events in the universe. If Qianlong was destined to be the emperor, then he would be, even if his father wasn't. If the Opium Wars was a fixed event in history, then they would happen no matter who the emperor was at the time. We can change smaller events, but we can't change the significant ones."

I thought for a moment, trying to digest the philosophy. It sounded very much like fatalism, but it didn't sound passive at all. "But what about the individuals in the universe? I could end up not being born."

He laughed dismissively. "That time travel paradox again. Let me just assure you this: you, the time traveler, would remain the same biological being no matter what happened during your travel. Your parents would marry and give birth to you regardless who the emperor was. This much is certain, but the rest I cannot guarantee. You might be born in a different country, have a different job, or even live with a foster family."

His assurance offered little solace. I shuddered at the possibility of not being able to see my parents again.

DRIVEN BY A sudden fear, I made an international phone call and spoke to my mom as soon as we returned to the hotel, telling her I loved her and that I would be back home soon. Then I called my dad and told him I would be going over for dinner.

When I hung up, Jeng held me and asked, "Can I go with you?"

I laughed. "Sure. But how would I introduce you?"

"How about you tell him I'm your boyfriend?"

"And what do you do? Where do you live?"

"You'll come up with the answers," he said playfully, kissing my earlobe. "Please, I want to be with you. We don't have much time left together."

My dad lived in a condo that was not far from the hotel. It was within the community of Tsinghua University, which was right next to Peking University. On our way to my dad's house, I told Jeng my parents weren't together anymore. My mom and my dad had fallen in love when my dad was a visiting scholar at UC Berkeley back in the eighties, where my mom was a history professor specializing in East Asia. My dad returned to China when I was eight years old, after getting a teaching post at Tsinghua University. My mom had gotten her tenure at Berkeley by then and didn't want to give it up, and so the two had separated.

Jeng frowned. "Forgive me for being frank, Julie, but I think it's despicable for a man to abandon his wife for a better opportunity."

I smiled. "Actually, Dad didn't abandon Mom. It was Mom's idea that he take the job in China. She said he would be happier working in his own country. He would've stayed in the U.S. if Mom hadn't wanted him to go. They are still friends, even though my dad has a new family now."

"That's most peculiar," Jeng remarked. "In our time a woman wouldn't leave her husband unless he wanted her to."

"I know," I responded. "I feel lucky for not being born in your time."

"Do you really?" He looked confused. "Even if you wouldn't have to worry about anything other than babysitting your children?"

"Yes. And you know what, men are also responsible to look after children nowadays."

His jaw dropped. "You must be kidding!"

I shook my head in exasperation. I parked on the street outside Imperial Gardens, a gated community of high rises. Jeng's eyes widened as soon as he stepped out of the car. "They're absolutely magnificent!" He looked up admiringly, shading his eyes with a hand. "Which one belongs to your father?"

"Oh, his unit is on the fifteenth floor in Building D." I pointed to one of the buildings. "There are twenty-five floors in each one, and four units on each floor."

His shook his head. "Unbelievable!"

We took the elevator onto the fifteenth floor of Building D. As soon as I pressed the doorbell, the door was opened. My dad had obviously been waiting for me.

"Julie!" He gave me a warm hug. "You finally have time for your old man!"

He let go of me, his gaze shifting to the tall man behind me. I could see he was amused when he stared at Jeng's head.

"Dad, this is Jeng. He's an actor. He's currently in a Qing dynasty drama playing the role of a prince, thus the haircut."

"An actor? No wonder!" Dad laughed heartily as he stepped aside to let us in.

The smell of chive fried eggs reminded me that Aunt Lan, Dad's wife, was a wonderful cook. We went to the kitchen to meet the kind woman, who was doing several tasks alone—steaming buns, frying fish, boiling soup, and wrapping dumplings. I offered to help but was politely refused. Before Jeng had a chance to marvel at the gas stove, I pulled him out of the kitchen.

"These lights are so bright!" Jeng commented as soon as we entered the spacious living room, which had a fantastic view of the city in the evening. "Amazing! It feels like day within night."

My dad looked at him curiously, and I quickly explained, "He prefers dimmed lights, to conserve energy."

Dad nodded.

My sixteen-year-old half-brother Peng looked up from his iPad and said hi. Jeng sat down next to him and looked at the game he was playing. I went into my half-sister's bedroom to check her out. Not surprisingly, Yanlu was bent in front of her desk, studying. The twenty-three-year-old was a graduate student at Tsinghua University and had no time for breaks, therefore I didn't linger long after exchanging a few polite words with her. However, before I left, I couldn't help but glance at the awards she had won since elementary school. Yanlu had inherited Father's math gene, and I always envied her for that.

Dad and Jeng were in the middle of a conversation when I returned to the living room.

"You've never been abroad?" Dad was asking.

Jeng shook his head. "The farthest place I've been to is Tibet."

"You don't like traveling?"

"Not really, I prefer staying in Jing City. It's the most comfortable."

Dad laughed. "Jing City? You're quite a devoted actor. But in which part of the city do you live?"

Jeng opened his mouth to speak but I interrupted him. "He lives in the east side, near the Palace Museum. And he loves the museum, goes there all the time, knows it inside out."

"Ah, you must really like the history of Ming and Qing!"

"Oh definitely," I answered for Jeng. "He's an expert on the Kangxi era."

"No kidding?" Dad smiled. "In fact, I'm also interested in the period. The country was politically stable and prosperous, with amazing cultural and scientific achievement. Kangxi was a genius, not only a literary man, but also loved math."

Jeng nodded proudly. "It's true. Father Emperor loved learning. He memorized volumes of poetry and hired foreigners to teach him western knowledge."

I cringed at the term "Father Emperor," but my father didn't seem to notice it. He continued sharing his admiration of the emperor.

"Kangxi commissioned the compilation of many important works. For example, the *Complete Tang Poems*, The *Kangxi Dictionary*, and *Shulijingyun*—" Dad halted, as if recalling something important. He excused himself and went into his study and came back shortly with an old, dusty book. "Look, this is the first volume of Shulijingyun I got from an antique store. It contains essential principles of mathematics and has been an important math textbook for nearly three hundred years."

Jeng's hands trembled as he took the book from my father. The paper cover was wrinkled, and the pages were sewn together with a string. Inside, the pages were printed with characters handwritten neatly between vertically lined spaces. Squares, circles and triangles appeared on many pages, accompanied by math equations. "I remember this book," he said with tears in his eyes. "My third brother was working on it."

"Your third brother? Is he a mathematician, too?" Dad asked.

"Ay," Jeng nodded. "A very good one."

"I would like to meet him one day," Dad said. "Where does he teach?"

"He teaches at Shangshufang sometimes," Jeng said. "But he spends most his time to write."

"Shangshufang?" Dad looked puzzled. "What kind of school is that?"

I remembered that it was the Upper Study inside the Palace Museum, the school for the children of the imperial family.

Before Jeng could answer, I said, "It's a college prep school."

"Ah, I see!" Dad nodded, looking less interested in meeting Jeng's brother now.

Soon dinner was ready.

175

"What a sumptuous feast!" Jeng said as soon as he sat down.

Indeed, Aunt Lan had prepared so much food that the round table could hardly contain all the dishes. From cold appetizers such as soy sauce duck wings and sliced beef tongue, to main dishes such as smoked chicken and roasted lamb chops. The soup was made of deer tail, and the meat buns and dumplings were both made of lamb.

Jeng devoured the food and hardly uttered a word. But as he was about to stuff a third meat bun into his mouth, he paused. "This is the best lamb meat bun I've ever had! Aunt Lan, you should work in the palace!"

While Aunt Lan laughed demurely, Dad said, "Not to boast, but Lan's great-great-great grandfather was a palace chef. He cooked the Manchu Han Imperial Feast for Emperor Tongzhi. In fact, some of these dishes are made according to the recipes she's inherited."

"What's the Manchu Han Imperial Feast?" Jeng asked.

Dad's mouth fell open. "You don't know about it? How can you call yourself a Qing dynasty scholar? It's another great creation of Emperor Kangxi in an effort to further unite the Han and the Manchu. On his sixty-sixth birthday, a hundred-and-eight dishes were made, including all Manchu and Han dishes."

"A hundred-and-eight dishes? How extravagant!" Jeng thought deeply for a moment. "Yes, eighth brother mentioned the dinner in his letter. I missed it because I was in Tibet, gagging on blood sausages. To tell the truth, what motivated me to win the battles was the thought of the delicious food at home."

Aunt Lan and her children looked bewildered at Jeng's monologue, and Dad burst into laughter. "You're quite a good actor!"

ON THE DAY of Jeng's departure, the three of us got to the site early in the evening. The portal could be active at any time after dark. Dong checked the pendant once again and secured it on Jeng's neck.

Jeng had put on his changshan and cloak, and his sword was buckled on his waist.

Despite being shy in showing affection in public, he kissed me. "I'll miss you."

"Take care," I whispered. "And be a good emperor!"

He nodded firmly. "I will!"

I wanted to say, "Come back to visit," but swallowed my words.

Dong watched the sky and said, "The moon is up in the center, it's time to go."

I couldn't let go of Jeng's hand. My heart wrung to a painful knot, and my tears poured out like torrents. *That's it, I'm not going to see him again*. My knight-in-changshan would return to where he came from.

Dong pulled me away from the pit. "We have to get away from here, the force will destroy us," he said.

To be safe, we moved as far away as possible, but made sure we would be able to observe the pit. Finally, we stopped on a spot on the slope of a hill, among some trees.

All was quiet around us, without a single movement. Occasionally, cars on nearby highways whirred past. Not even the insects were chirping, as if they, too, were expecting Earth's great event.

I stood where I was, holding my breath. One moment I felt drowsy, another moment I felt so impatient that I was certain if I waited any longer, I would go crazy. But then it happened. At first a hissing sound came from the pit. Slowly, it turned into the sizzling of rocks, buzzing of insects, growling of animals, and finally it roared. I could feel the rumbling of earth and saw sparks of light in the darkness. A silver, spidery light suddenly appeared at the northern sky, but it vanished just as soon as it had appeared. Then the roaring on the ground stopped and the pit was quiet again.

We waited a bit longer before running towards the pit. It was dark and impassive, as if no one had been there and nothing had happened. My heart stopped beating.

Jeng was gone!

CHAPTER 10

I STARTED AT the spot where Jeng had stood, hoping that he would materialize.

"He's gone." Dong sighed and patted my shoulder. "Forget him. I know it's hard but think of it as a dream."

I nodded but my tears refused to stop.

We were silent on our way out of the mountain and onto the highway. Dong sat calmly in the passenger seat, contemplating, while I watched nervously for signs of change. Nothing seemed to have changed—the road signs were still written mostly in simplified Chinese and occasionally in English. The overview of the city looked exactly the same as I had remembered seeing it. The neon outline of the Palace Museum across the night sky reminded me of the night I had first met Jeng. He had

179

thought it was a holiday decoration and I had thought him a reclusive hermit.

"It doesn't look like he's made it," I said after we had exited the highway. "The city hasn't changed a bit."

"The changes might not be noticeable in the long run, remember what I told you?" he said calmly.

I dropped him at his hutong and drove back to the Yihe hotel.

The room was no longer as cozy as it had been just the night before. Now, it was desolate and empty. I stood by the window overlooking the Summer Palace, remembering the mornings and nights Jeng and I spent together.

"I'll build a garden for you once I return," he had whispered to me the other night. "I'll name it Julie Yuan."

"No, you won't," I had said. "You'll be too busy recruiting new consorts and you'll have trouble deciding whom you spend the night with. And your children will soon outnumber your father's—"

He had put his lips on mine, to stop me from finishing my sentence.

Tears flooded my eyes and blurred the night scene in front of me. I sighed and left the window. Regardless of the consequences on the universe, Jeng's visit had certainly changed my life. It would never be the same again. I missed his deep, rumbling voice, his narrow eyes, and his mouse tail. I buried my face in the t-shirt that he had worn, inhaling his scent. How was I going to forget this beautiful dream? Then I went to the fridge and took out the bottle of Maotai—his favorite drink—and downed two cups before I fell into oblivion.

When I opened my eyes the next day it was noon, and the first thing I saw was the brilliant sunshine outside. I got off the bed and went straight to my computer, and searched Prince Yinjeng of the Qing dynasty. A Wikipedia page pulled up slowly and I waited anxiously, expecting to see a picture of an emperor in yellow robe and red crown. But there was no picture. My heart sank, and I quickly glanced at the dates: *born Feb 10, 1688, died Dec 30, 1722, at age 34.* Wait a minute! 1722 was the year Kangxi died. Was it a mistake? Blood drained from my body and I felt a moment's blackout. Then I collected my senses and read the rest of the page to find out what had happened.

"Being the favorite son of Emperor Kangxi, Prince Jeng was extremely sad upon the death of his father. He coped with the news by excessive drinking and died of alcohol poisoning just ten days later."

"No! It can't be true!" I murmured. Jeng wouldn't drink himself to death, even though he was fond of alcohol. Besides, the Jeng who showed up at Kangxi's deathbed had an important mission to accomplish, he wouldn't be so irresponsible. No, something wasn't right!

I drove to Peking University, rushing through a series of red lights. I had to see Dong. When I saw him from a distance, he was waving his broom as usual, as if nothing had happened. But as I got closer, I saw the despondence on his face, and his bloodshot eyes.

181

"Good morning," he said. "So, you know about the bad news?"

"Yes." I nodded. "He drank himself to death. I can't believe it."

"You shouldn't." He smiled bitterly. "It's all a lie. He was murdered. Poisoned."

"Murdered?" I shivered in the warm morning sunshine. "What do you mean?"

"Contrary to what he had planned, he returned to his father three days before his death. He stood by the emperor's bedroom, preventing Prince Four from entering. They took him away by force the night before the emperor died. When he accused Yongzheng for altering Kangxi's will, he was imprisoned right away, and ten days later, ordered to drink poison."

I gasped. "That wasn't in the web article. How do you know?"

Dong paused. "I spent the night in the university library and found it in a historical record written by a credible source."

"His attempt was all a mistake, wasn't it?" I felt a lump in my throat. "I should've stopped him. He might've lived longer if he hadn't tried to change history."

Dong sighed. "You wouldn't have been able to stop him. He had made up his mind."

"No!" I shook my head in tears, recalling how close I was in my attempt. "I could've if I had tried."

Dong ignored me for a moment and concentrated on sweeping the floor. The he abruptly turned to me and said, "Instead of whining and regretting, do something useful!"

"How?" I asked in confusion. "He's dead and he died three hundred years ago. What can I do?"

He didn't answer my question, merely looked at me as if waiting for me to come to the realization.

"You're not suggesting that I go back? No, you can't mean it." I paused and shook my head. "Whatever I do, I can't change history. Look what happened to Jeng. He shouldn't even have attempted."

Dong was silent for a moment. "His mistake, or our mistake, was not to watch out for Longkodo."

"Longkodo?"

"Empress Xiaoyiren's brother and Kangxi's most trusted court official. He was the commander of both the police and the force of the capital city. Many believed he helped Yongzheng to change Kangxi's will. I warned Jeng about him. But he either didn't take my advice or couldn't do anything about it."

"Can you go back to yesterday and warn him again?"

He shook his head. "I don't think so. The priest mentioned it wasn't possible. A year seems to be the shortest interval, and it is the smallest unit on the dial. Besides, I doubt that he would listen to me."

"What makes you think he would listen to me?"

He paused for a second. "Actually, I'm not sure. But I thought you might want to take action instead of whining."

I pursed my lips. "Are you sure Longkodo was responsible?"

"I'm positive. He was with the emperor before he died. And he was promoted to the highest-ranking court official soon after Yongzheng gained the throne. I wish I had managed to convince Jeng about it, but he thought it was ungrounded conjecture only."

As I processed the information, he added, "He put Jeng in jail."

Tears stung my eyes again. I took a deep breath and said, "So all I need to do is to go back before Kangxi dies and warn Jeng about this Longkodo?"

Dong shook his head. "That wouldn't help. I already warned him. Longkodo was a very tricky guy, otherwise he wouldn't have risen to power and stayed in power for so long. He was good at earning the trust of the emperor and the princes. Jeng called him uncle and revered him."

"Then that's a real problem." I nodded. "But what can I do?"

"You can travel further back!" Dong looked at me with an encouraging smile.

"Further back? When?"

"You need a few months at the least, before he leaves for the frontier."

"He wouldn't even know me!" I was frightened by the suggestion. "It wouldn't work."

"It doesn't matter. He will get to know you."

"Sounds crazy." I shook my head. "What about my life here?"

"You'll come back as soon as it's over. And your life will still be the same."

I wasn't convinced at all, but I couldn't reject the idea, either.

"But I know next to nothing about the Qing dynasty. How am I going to survive?" I thought about how Jeng had to adapt to the modern way of living. It would be even harder to get used to the pre-industrial way of living, wouldn't it?

"I'll teach you everything you need to know. That's not a problem," Dong assured me.

My mouth felt dry. "Let me think about it."

"Of course. No hurry. And no obligation at all. After all, he's not a very important person in history," he said with a sigh.

I bit my lip. I didn't like what I had heard. From the moment that he showed up as my knight in shining armor, Jeng had been the most important person in my life. I missed him so much that I struggled to breathe.

DONG WASTED NO TIME. He took me to a reputable jeweler right away to purchase a piece of mutton-fat white jade. The price shocked me quite a bit—ten thousand USD for a tiny piece of stone that looked like plastic. But I let the jeweler convince me, after he showed me a certificate of authenticity from Beijing University Jewelry Appraisal Center.

Then, over a pot of tea and a dozen meat buns, Dong and I devised our plan. We decided I would travel to 1721, because Jeng would return from Tibet in

185

November 1721. I could warn him about the danger awaiting him, in order to prevent him from leaving in the subsequent year.

"You would get there in July, give or take a few months," Dong said.

"But how am I going to get close to him?"

"Ideally, you'll be able to become a maid in his household, or the Xunjun Mansion. If you can't, then try to become a maid in the imperial court."

I frowned. "Isn't it harder to get into the court?"

"Not necessarily. They recruited maids every February in the palace. Thus, we need to make sure you arrive before then."

After I arrived, I would go to the Temple of Light and Shadow. Priest Wang, who had helped Jeng, would be available once I was there, Dong assured me. "But if you don't see him, wait for him. He could be traveling. He did it quite often and could leave the temple a month a time."

"But will he help me?" I asked doubtfully. After all, Dong had never met his own ancestor.

"You'll have to convince him," he said. "No one in his time is supposed know about time traveling, except probably himself. So, he will believe your story."

"What will he do?"

"He could help you find Jeng. He did Tao rituals and services for imperial families, including some princes, so he had a connection."

In the following days, Dong taught me what he knew about living in the Qing dynasty, including the monetary system, how to tell status of a person by what they wore and how they spoke, how to speak to a superior without meeting his eyes, etc. In particular, I studied the rules of the court and of imperial households. I also learned how to make tea, how to serve tea and refreshments, even how to do laundry.

Dong also had me memorize important historical events and the imperial family structure, including the names of Kangxi's consorts, sons and daughters, and the complicated relationship among them.

"The court is an extremely complicated social system. Everyone—men, women, children—fights for the emperor's attention. You must be very careful with what you say and what you do. A slip of tongue could cost you your life!"

At the end, we did not have a clear plan about how to get close to Jeng in case I entered the court, and we left the details to the future, or more precisely, the past.

A FEW DAYS after Jeng had departed, I found myself in the pit again, wearing a blue Manchu cotton gown over a pleated skirt. My hair was elaborately done—two braids coiled into buns on the top of my head and two more braids resting on my shoulders. This was called the Double Bun—a popular style among young women in the Qing dynasty.

On my way here, I kept asking myself whether I was really doing the right thing. I had taken all my personal belongings to my dad's house, telling him I would be traveling to another city for a few days. I had also called YouClo and asked for a week's vacation. Although Dong assured me I would be able to return within a week, I still felt unsettled. Therefore, I scribbled a note and stuffed it in my suitcase, explaining to my dad the extraordinary circumstances, just in case I didn't make it back in time.

Dong passed me a money purse that consisted of some copper coins, or pennies, a whole silver piece and a few broken silver pieces.

"A penny can buy you a steamed bun, and a whole silver piece is enough to purchase a year's rice for a family of five," he reminded me.

I nodded, recalling that a whole silver piece was worth a thousand copper coins.

"Did you get these from antique dealers? They must've cost you a fortune!"

He shrugged. "Not really. They're from my personal collection. I got them many years ago, long before they were considered antiques."

"Thank you so much, Dong," I said, truly moved by his generosity.

"No worries. Just bring me back some valuables when you return. I'm sure Jeng will reward you a lot more than this," he joked.

"Sure!" I laughed as I tightened the purse and put it in the jacket's inside pocket.

I stood on the exact spot Jeng had left few nights before. Dong set the dial on the jade pendant and fastened it on my neck. Before he left the pit, he repeated what he had said a dozen times.

"Remember, there's a path behind the pit, and the Temple of Light and Shadow is on the top of the hill. It's behind a huge rock that looks like a gourd, which was why the locals would call it Gourd Temple. If the priest isn't there, wait for him in the temple."

I nodded and said goodbye, watching Dong climb out of the pit and his flashlight vanish into darkness. Then I waited patiently, counting sheep to calm my nerves. It seemed to be an eternity and I almost fell asleep when I felt the ground shifting under my feet. Soon, I heard a hissing sound and felt a warm current swallowing me from below. As the noise became louder, the ground turned faster, and soon I was being churned inside a strong current. I screamed as the vertigo overwhelmed me, but before I lost consciousness, I had the sensation of expanding and rising like a puff of air.

CHAPTER 11

I WOKE WITH a throbbing headache and sore body. Crickets chirped right by my ears, and the air smelled of pine. Did I make it? I opened my eyes and saw only darkness. After a while, I could make out glimpses of sky above and trees around. I was lying on the forest ground—it was quite damp, and pine needles pricked my skin as I moved my hands. I remained flat on my back, afraid my movement would stir ancient creatures around me.

Even in darkness I could tell the pit was different. Besides the canopy of trees above, I also didn't hear cars driving by on the freeways. But was I in the Qing dynasty? I couldn't tell. I touched my neck and couldn't feel the string or the pendant. I groped on the ground for a minute before giving up. There was nothing else for me to do but stare into darkness and wait for dawn.

Despite the chilly air, I fell into short intervals of sleep. But as soon as a pillar of light entered the forest, I sat up. Just as Jeng had told us, the pit was devoid of modern junk, and was instead a dense forest of trees and shrubs. I found the pendant a few steps away, its string broken. I wound the string around the pendant and carefully placed it into my pocket. Then I went to the back for the hidden path but found only dense bushes. Thinking I would go around the pit from above, I went to the front and located a way up, which was also covered with bushes. With the help of tree trunks and branches nearby, I climbed out of the pit.

Outside it was also very different from what I remembered. Trees crowded the hill, leaving little space for passing. As I had hoped, I found a way that reached the back of the pit. I went on the path and watched for the rock that looked like a gourd, which would indicate the location of Temple of Light and Shadow. But the mountain was covered with trees and shrouded with fog. After a fruitless search, I saw a steep path made of bare rocks, which led up to a skinny mountain road. I hesitated for a moment, trying to remember the last time I did rock climbing. It was at least twenty years ago during a summer camp, and I didn't do that well even with all the equipment. But I didn't seem to have any alternative at the moment, and the rock path wasn't that long. I ended up using both hands and feet to climb, which was harder than I had thought it would be. I made it to the road and followed it to the other side of the mountain, but to my frustration I found out that it was cut off by another rock path that went up. I rested for a moment to catch my breath, then I stepped onto the rocks and grabbed the rocks above. As soon as I did that, I heard a low hiss next to my ear and saw the tongue of a snake right by my hand—I screamed and lost my footing.

It was vertigo all over again as I rolled down the mountain slope, but this time I did not lose consciousness. Instead, I felt the bumping and bouncing all the way down and I thought my bones must've all fallen out of their joins, until I hit a large rock. I found myself on the bottom of a ravine next to a river. I spat out the mud and sand in my mouth as I attempted to sit up, but the slight movement caused an excruciating pain to shoot through my leg.

I lay helplessly on the ground for a moment, then I heard footsteps approaching. A man shouted, "Are you without problem, guniang?"

The ancient speech reminded me instantly of Jeng, and for a moment I thought it was him. But soon I knew I was mistaken. A short and skinny peasant man with his head shaved in the front and a braid in the back, appeared beside me. He looked twentyish, wearing a dirty side-button shirt that was probably white, over black pants, an ax inserted into his sash around the waist. The basket on his back was filled with twigs and chunks of wood. Apparently, he was gathering firewood.

The presence of the man assured me I was definitely in the Qing dynasty. "Big brother," I addressed him according to what Dong had taught me. "Please help me up. I think broke my leg."

The man put down his basket and helped me without hesitation. I stood up with his help, and I groaned from the shooting pain in my leg. Seeing that I couldn't possibly move on my own, he put on his basket again, and let me hold onto his arm. Slowly and painfully, I followed the man out of the ravine, wondering where the river had come from, since I hadn't noticed a stream near the pit before.

Still panting on the mountain slope, I caught sight of the plain in front of us and gasped. It wasn't the vast, barren plain that I had seen around highway 32 at all. It was covered with miles of lush vegetation, and houses made of mud and straw dotted the greenery.

"Let's go, that's Peach Blossom village, I live there."

"Peach Blossom?" I recalled the peach farm near Imperial Graveyard. I had been there right before I met Jeng. It must've been the same place.

I was hungry and thirsty and wanted to go with the man. But I had to look for Priest Wang. "I need to get to Temple of Light and Shadow."

Seeing that the name didn't ring a bell for him, I said, "Gourd Temple."

He nodded this time. "What for? You can't possibly get there in your condition. It's on top of the mountain. It takes a normal person half a day."

I hesitated. "But I was supposed to be there."

"Well, I have to go home, otherwise my wife will yell at me." The man scratched his head. "Why don't you go home with me now and I'll take you to the temple once you get well?"

It didn't look like I had a choice. I couldn't possibly go anywhere with the pain, and I would probably die of hunger or thirst, if not from the pain, before I got to the temple.

"It isn't far," the man continued, pointed to a particular mud house as we started to move again. "Look, right by the maize field."

"Where are we exactly, say, in relative to Beijing?" I asked once we were out of the mountain.

The man shook his head. "I don't know where Beijing is."

"Of course." I corrected myself. "Do you know where Jing City is?"

"Ay, that I know. It's southwest of us, about 200 li."

I nodded. A hundred kilometers. That was about right.

"And what year is it?" I rubbed my temple, pretending to be confused.

"Kangxi's sixtieth year." The man looked at me with pity in his eyes.

I didn't mind the look and let out of a sigh in relief. The year was 1721, just as we had planned.

"And it seems like we're in the middle of autumn?"

"No, we're in the Month of Lotus," the man said.

Love and the Forbidden City

"Month of Lotus?" I tried to recall the traditional calendar that Dong had taught me. Before the twentieth century, most of the lunar months in Chinese were named by plants or flowers. I recited silently: willow, apricot, peach, wheat, pomegranate, lotus—it was June of the lunar calendar, or July of the modern calendar. Dong's pendant had been precise.

But I was a bit disappointed because I had a long time to wait. Jeng would return from Tibet in November, five months from now. I sulked for a moment but decided to look on the bright side. I now had more time to adjust to my new life and carry out my plan.

Although I had expected a different world, my surroundings still intrigued me. Expressway 32 was nowhere in sight, neither was the wind power plant next to it. Not only that, there were no electric lines or poles at all. A river with a watermill and a bridge, seemingly the same one that ran through the ravine I had fallen into, wound through the fields and houses. Some women were doing laundry in the river, while others filled their buckets. We walked along the paths between fields. I didn't see a single piece of broken glass or any plastic bags, but the roads were strewn with dung and I had to watch my steps.

Before we reached the man's house, we ran into a few people on the road. Men wore the same waist-length shirts and black pants as the man who rescued me, and all of them had the same hairstyle. Women had their hair in buns on the back of their heads, and also wore short gowns and long pants. They looked at me with curious eyes, and asked the man, whose surname was Meng, who I was.

"A traveler, going to visit Gourd Temple, but fell on her way."

"Ah, such fair skin, must be coming from Jing City," a woman commented as she stared at my face.

"Her hair is brown. Is she a Manchu?" another woman asked.

Before I answered, a man said, "No doubt about it. Look at her big feet."

I recalled the fact that while Han women from wealthy families would bind their feet, Manchu women did not follow the brutal custom at all. Jeng had made the same conjecture that I was Manchu. In fact, the rulers of the Qing dynasty were Manchu, and the Han had resented their conqueror for many generations. I was worried for a moment, but I didn't have a better excuse for my appearance—the term Eurasian would make no sense to them. Besides, I didn't see any hostility in these villagers, so I decided not to correct them. I simply smiled and said, "How do you do?"

I was close to fainting when we stopped in front of a mud house with a coarse wooden door. Mr. Meng shouted, "Juhua, open the door!"

Soon a woman shouted back as she headed towards the door. "What's the matter? Did wolves bite off your hands?"

The door was quickly unlatched and violently flung open, and a middle-aged woman's face, red, round, and sweating, appeared in the doorway. Trailing behind

her was a sniveling child, wearing nothing but a *dudou*—
an apron that covered his torso. "Mother of kings in
heaven!" she gasped after a moment's astonishment.
"What is this?"

"It's a woman like you!" Mr. Meng said as he
dragged me into the house. "A Manchu from Jing City.
Found her in the bottom of the ravine. Probably fell off
from the mountain. Badly hurt."

"So you brought her home? Now what are we
going to do with her?" the woman shouted as she swept
the dry chili that covered the cot into a basket to make
room for me to lie down. "Heavens! Why did I marry a
pig-head like you!"

I was surprised when I heard her last comment. I
had at first thought she was Mr. Meng's mother.

"What else could I have done?" Mr. Meng
grumbled. "Let her lie there and feed the wolves?"

"Not much worse than bringing her here and
letting her starve to death," Juhua said, as she went to
fetch a bowl of water from a jar at the other end of the
room.

Mr. Meng sat down by the hearth to smoke while
his wife brought me water.

I thanked Juhua after sipping down some water.
"I won't stay long. I'll leave as soon as I can."

Juhua paused a moment before she responded,
"Let's see how bad it is."

She went out and brought a basin of water and a
clean rag. When she cleaned my face with the rag, she

said to her husband. "Get your ass out of here and let me take a look at her condition. Go split the wood."

Mr. Meng got up reluctantly, muttering inaudible words on his way out, taking the child with him. Soon, I heard the sound of splitting wood outside.

Juhua rolled up my pants and unbuttoned my gown to examine my bruises and wounds, shaking her head and flicking her tongue to indicate her pity.

"How did it happen? You just slipped off your track?"

"Yes." I nodded. "I was tired after spending a night in the mountain."

"You were in the mountain at night? Was someone with you?" The woman had an incredulous look on her face.

"No." I shook my head and told her the story that I came up with on my way to the cottage. "I was trying to get to the Gourd Temple. You see, my mother is sick, and someone recommended us the master over there."

"I wouldn't call it a temple," Juhua sneered. "They don't have any Guanyin statues there, only some incense burners. A strange wizard lives there, and he practices strange magic."

"What kind of magic?"

"Like materializing from nowhere," Juhua lowered her voice, although no one else was in the room. "My husband saw him once. He was gathering firewood, and all of a sudden the wizard was standing next to him, as if he rose from the ground."

"Really?" I feigned a scared look. The wizard must've been Priest Wang, and he must have come back from time traveling. "I'll go to check it out as soon as I can walk on my own."

"No problem." Juhua shrugged as she cleaned my wounds using the rag. Then she brought some herb-soaking spirit and massaged me over my bruises. I again groaned loudly. It seemed not only my legs were broken, but my ribs as well.

The women ignored my groans and continued to question me. "So you live with your mother in Jing City. What about your husband?"

I hesitated. I had not included any husband in my story. "I'm not married."

"Not married?" Juhua raised her eyebrow and glanced me up and down again, as if assessing my age. "How old are you?"

I couldn't help but feel offended by the woman's rudeness, but I didn't show it. I simply avoided the question. "You see, my mom has been ill all these years."

"Ah." She nodded sympathetically. "What a pity."

After she was done massaging me, Juhua said, "I could go to the doctor to get you some medicine, but we don't have the money, do you—?"

"Yes." I nodded quickly. "I have some money."

I took out my coin purse from the inner pocket of my gown. "How much will it cost?"

"Twenty wens."

It sounded a lot to me from what I had learned from Dong, but I counted twenty coins and gave them to her without hesitation. Her pupils dilated as she stared at my money purse.

I paused a moment and took out a small silver piece, approximately a hundred wens and passed it to her. "For your trouble."

She grinned happily as she accepted the silver. "You're no trouble at all."

IT TOOK ME a lot longer than expected. I had been living in Meng's house for two weeks already. I could walk without limping, but still couldn't go uphill, thus visiting the Temple of Light and Shadow was out of the question. I didn't stay in bed for long. Although I was paying for lodging and food, Juhua made sure I helped out with housework, too, and constantly complained about the extra work caused by my presence. I had to do laundry and cook, which were the lightest chores in the house according to Juhua, who had to work in the fields with her husband every day. It took me a long time to get used to making the cooking fire, and even longer to boil rice on the stove without burning it.

While I did not mind doing most of the housework, I hated babysitting the child Benben. Benben was seven years old, thus not exactly a baby, but he was mentally incapacitated and had to be watched. I had to spoon-feed him and had to take him to the outhouse when he said, "Pee-pee." I also had to play with him, otherwise, the child cried and made a fuss. The worst thing was that there wasn't anything fun to play—no toys, no chess, and of course no TV. The only game we played was hide-and-seek, and I was bored to death after playing the same game day after day, especially since there was barely any furniture in the house and the only place to hide was under the bed.

While I was shelling peanuts one day, Benben again urged me to play with him. "Hide! Hide!" he said, pointing at the bed.

"Let me finish with peanuts first, Benben."

But Benben wasn't born with patience. Barely a minute had passed before he urged me again.

I sighed. I would do anything to get away with that dreadful game. I racked my brain to come up with an idea. Then something clicked. I pushed the peanuts into a basket and cleared the table. Then I brought out a rice bowl, placed a peanut in it, and let Benben see the peanut in the bowl before putting it upside down, secretly taking the peanut in my hand. When I opened the bowl, the peanut was of course not there. The child's eyes widened, and he clapped his hands. "Do it again!"

I did it again and again. Another thing Benben wasn't born with was the ability to be bored. After doing the trick twenty times in a row, I was sick of it and let the peanut stay under the cup without any trickery, hoping the child will stop asking me to repeat. The child, however, was mad when he saw the peanut. So, because I had no choice, I said to Benben, "The peanut is tired, and it can't run fast. It needs rest."

When the child was quiet, I said to him. "If you shell the peanuts, they might run faster."

Benben sat down eagerly to shell peanuts.

After a few days the child became extremely fond of me, always tagging along wherever I went.

Juhua seemed to be pleased with me as well, and even stopped complaining when I reached for an extra bowl of rice at dinner. One day while I was playing with Benben after dinner, and Mr. Meng went out smoking, she sat next to me on my cot and said to me, "Julie, our Benben really likes you!"

I had started to like the child, too, who could be cute sometimes. I smiled and said, "He's a good child."

Juhua grinned toothily, pleased by my compliment. Then she moved closer to me and lowered her voice. "I've been looking for a wife for him, and I think you're a good candidate. Although you're a bit older than I would like, I'm not picky, neither is Ben."

I was so taken aback by the outrageous suggestion and the woman's haughty attitude that I was speechless for a few seconds.

"But Ben is a child," I finally managed to say.

The woman didn't care how I felt. "Time flies. When I married his dad, he was about the same age."

No wonder the age difference, I thought. Then I did a quick calculation in my head. When the child turned seventeen, I would be forty-three years old. I shivered at the prospect of playing hide-and-seek with Benben for ten years and becoming his wife.

"What do you say?" Juhua pressed on.

"Uh, I, I don't know really," I mumbled, not wanting to offend the woman because I was still her house guest. "I haven't thought about marrying."

The woman looked shocked for a moment, then smiled. "Well, I know why. It must have been hard for you, being so tall and with such a big nose."

I felt insulted but decided not to mind her insolence. However I was reminded of my differences. "But I'm a Manchu," I said, hoping it would deter her enthusiasm.

"Oh, we don't mind that at all!" she waved her hand.

"Thank you for your kindness," I said, doing my best not to show my rage. "But I'm not in a hurry to—"

"Not in a hurry? You're not young anymore! At least twenty, aren't you?"

"Uh." I was so flattered that I couldn't help smiling. Thanks to modern skin products, I looked ten years younger than my age to an eighteenth-century woman.

Juhua misinterpreted my smile. "Well, you can't fool me. Anyway, at your age, no one would want you for a wife, not even a concubine!"

A thirty-year-old woman then would undoubtedly have no hope for any marriage at all. I felt lucky about not being born in the eighteenth century.

"But I don't have to marry anyone, do I?"

Mrs. Meng's mouth opened widely. "What an absurd thought! Who's going to support you?"

"Myself."

She scorned. "How? With your pair of clean hands?"

Juhua didn't mention the marriage proposal for the next few days and I decided it was about time for me to look for the Temple of Light and Shadow. About a week after our last conversation, I told her that I would like to go to the mountain the next day.

She wasn't pleased. "What for? I told you it wasn't really a temple."

"My sick mom is waiting for me at home, and I have to at least see the master, I mean, the wizard."

She did not respond for a moment. "No problem. But wait until afternoon. In the morning, I need you to finish the laundry and weave the cloth."

What an unreasonable woman! I clenched my teeth but decided to give up to her request. "Sure. I will."

I MISSED THE washing machine when I headed towards the river, carrying the heavy basket of laundry and a laundry bat. Today, Juhua had added an extra load and included her bedlinen, curtains, and even maize sacks in the basket, thinking it was the last time she could use me. Even though the basket was heavy, I carried them for an extra mile or so upstream by the mountain, as instructed by her. It was less crowded over there, thus the water was cleaner.

The traditional way of doing laundry by the river was nowhere near romantic when you became the person who was doing it. First, I had to roll up my sleeves and my pants, take off my shoes before stepping into the shallow water near the shore. It was the middle of summer but the stream coming from the mountain was still a bit chilly. I soaked the clothes before laying them out one by one on a flat piece of stone and beating it with the bat.

It was pretty heavy labor. After beating a whole basket of cloths, my arms and back screeched in pain. I sat down on a rock to rest before leaving, comforting myself that soon I would be getting out of this misery. I would find Priest Wang, and he would take me to Jeng's house. The thought of Jeng brought me happiness and sorrow. I missed his gentle voice and his chivalry, his ignorance of the modern world, and even his imperial manner. I imagined the moment we met again. Would he recognize me by some magical reason?

Just then a pair of big hands grabbed me from the back and a cloth covered my eyes tightly. Before I had the chance to scream for help, my mouth was also stuffed. After that, I was lifted up and carried onto the person's shoulder. The person walked quickly, holding my two arms tightly. I kicked the person at first, but then he pressed my feet together so I couldn't move. After what seemed to be miles and miles of walk, we entered a house and I was put down on the floor. My blindfold was loosened, but not removed, and the rag in my mouth was taken away. I shouted for help right away, but the door was soon shut, and I was alone in the dark house. For hours and hours, I sat there alone, too shocked to fall asleep. Then the door opened, and I heard women's voices.

The women came, grabbed me and dragged me towards a chair.

"What're you doing? Let me go! Help!" I shouted as soon as my blindfold was removed.

"Shut up, no one will hear you," a middle-aged woman with a big mole on her chin and wore a bandana on her forehead said to me. "Don't make me drug you."

There was one more woman about the same age next to her, holding what appeared to be a make-up box with small drawers. They quickly put my hair into a bun, then they wiped my face and applied some powder on it, painted my eyebrows with a charcoal stick, and smeared my lips with a piece of red paper. After that they temporarily untied my hands, forced me out of my blue cotton gown and into a red satin robe, then they placed a crown made of cheap jewelry on my head.

It dawned on me that I was being dressed for a wedding. No! I was so horrified that I shook my head violently until the crown dropped. The woman smeared something under my nose and I passed out.

When I woke, I heard horns, drums and other traditional Chinese musical instruments being played loudly. I was blindfolded again and was being carried in some kind of vehicle.

"The bride is here!" I heard voices outside, and soon I was carried into a house again. The house smelled of rice wine and cooking. My blindfold was finally removed, but at the same time a red cloth covered my head and my face. My hands and feet were still bound and I couldn't do anything about it.

The door finally opened and I heard the familiar giggling of a Benben. "Lift my head cloth for me, Benben!"

Benben did what he was told. He was wearing a red gown as well.

"Good boy," I said, pinching the boy's cheek. "Sister will play a new game with you."

"Mom says you aren't sister anymore, you're my wife."

"You're kidding me," I said, refusing to believe. "Your mom didn't tell me that."

"She says it's a surprise."

Surprise indeed. What an evil woman. I regretted telling Juhua my plan of visiting the temple and doing her laundry. I should've simply left the house without a warning.

"Where are we?" I asked the child.

"My uncle's house."

The uncle must've been the person who kidnapped me. And judging from the distance of walking, it was quite far away from Peach Blossom Village.

That night, I lay side by side with Benben. The child managed to loosen the ropes on me, but the door of the room was shut from outside. Benben fell asleep soon but I spent the night thinking of what to do. Even if I could escape, it would be hard for me to find my way to Temple of Light and Darkness. The only thing I could do was wait. We would eventually move back to Meng's house. At least Benben was only a child and wouldn't possibly do me any physical harm.

Despite my despair, I couldn't help but see the irony in the whole debacle. Julie Bird, a college graduate and a successful career woman in the twenty-first century, but the best I could do in the eighteenth century was cook and do laundry and end up being the wife of a mentally incapacitated child! Looking back, it might be the punishment that I deserved. I had refused numerous proposals because of lack of true love and sincerity from the proposers. Would I be better off marrying Peter, or marrying Benben? I couldn't decide.

I hugged the pillow and cried as I remembered the last night Jeng stayed with me in the Yihe Hotel. I wished I had convinced him to stay with me that night. Now how was I going to find him and help him?

THE FOLLOWING DAYS, I was locked in the room with Benben. A woman who had dressed me for the wedding brought us food and water, and also emptied the chamber pot.

A week after the wedding, Juhua showed up, holding a bundle in hand. I was furious when I saw the evil woman, who had the audacity to call me daughter-in-law!

After she let Benben out, she opened the bundle and showed me my blue gown. "Here, I brought you this. I washed it for you."

I didn't touch the gown. "Why did you do this to me?"

"Tsk, tsk, you don't even look grateful," Juhua said, without any guilt. "I gave you a home. I married you to my son because he likes you. Do you think there are other reasons? You aren't pretty or young, and you can't do heavy labor."

"But I don't want to marry your son!"

She shrugged. "Want or not, you are married now."

"I'm not!" I wanted to strangle her, but I swallowed my anger. "Let me go, please! I can work for you in your house."

Juhua looked away. "It's not possible. My brother Gun is doing well here in the orchard. He was recently promoted to be the overseer. Our contract with the landlord is ending, and my husband and I will be moving here soon."

"What?"

"You have no other choice but stay here from now on. Don't even think about escaping. The peach farm is all fenced, and if you attempt to jump the fence, Gun's men and his guard dogs will go after you. From here to Peach Blossom is far, and you'll get lost for sure."

I knew she wasn't exaggerating the truth. I had surveyed the farm in the past two days from the window and saw the fences and the ubiquitous dogs. I had never seen Gun face to face, but I knew he was a beefy man. Running away from this place would be difficult indeed.

I took my blue gown from the table and fell the inside pocket. It was empty.

"Where is my money purse?" I asked.

"Well, the wedding cost a whole silver piece, and I'm keeping the rest," she said. "Another reason you can't run away."

"You scoundrel!" I took her by her collar, but she shrieked and soon the housekeeper showed up, holding a broom in hand. She beat me with the broom stick until I let go of Juhua.

"Behave!" Juhua said before she left the room with the woman. "Otherwise I'll have them tie you up again."

After the women left, I wept loudly. I couldn't believe what had happened to me, and I couldn't resign myself to the life in front of me. It sounded like a practical joke. I cried until Benben came back and demanded I play with him.

A few days after Juhua's visit, the housekeeping woman left, too, and I found myself taking over her place. I was allowed to go out of my room now, move around in the house and in the fenced yard. But at the same time, I had to clean the house, cook, and do laundry at a well in the yard. Juhua's brother Gun had a formidable look about him. His meaty face was dotted with pockmarks and looked like a layer of coarse stucco. A glance at it sent shivers down my spine.

That evening, Gun was drinking at dinner, and spoke to me for the first time since I had arrived. "You've gotten used to living here on the farm?"

I did not respond to my kidnapper.

"You're still mad," the man said and gulped down the bowl of rice spirit. "You oughtn't be. It was my sister's idea, not mine. Have pity on that son of hers. An idiot no woman wants. Wife is hard to get. I'm still looking for a wife myself."

I felt his leering and had goose bumps all over me.

Seeing no response from me, Gun grabbed my hand.

I beat his arm with chopsticks and broke free. "Watch your behavior!"

"Why should I? It's my house."

"Am I not your nephew's wife?"

He crackled. "Benben is a child. You're going to wait ten years for him? You'll dry up before that. Better have some fun with me now."

I was furious. "What would your sister think?"

"My sister?" Gun laughed. "Why do you think she had you locked up in my house?"

Horror struck me when I realized what he meant. That evil woman had made a deal with her brother. He would use her son's wife in exchange for his help in the kidnapping business.

I grabbed the kitchen knife and held it in front of me. "Don't get closer, or I'll stab you."

Benben started to wail and Gun's face went white. He put his hands up. "Okay, I won't touch you now. But you won't be holding that knife with you every minute, will you?"

I panted long after Gun had left the kitchen. When I heard the door of his bedroom shut closed, I dropped the knife on the floor and collapsed into a chair. Tears streamed my cheeks. What should I do? It looked like I should be holding that knife every minute, even when I was sleeping.

CHAPTER 12

IN THE FOLLOWING weeks, I stayed in Gun's house with Benben. Juhua visited a few times, and she talked about building a house nearby. I was angry at the woman but there wasn't much I could do. I wanted to escape but didn't have a plan. I had no idea where the farm was located, and where Peach Blossom Village or the Temple of Light and Shadow was. From dawn to dusk, Gun worked in the farm and left me and Benben in the house. A couple of times he didn't return until after midnight, apparently taking care of some business away from the farm.

I sometimes went out of the yard and wandered in the farm, which was bordered by another fence. I had checked the geography every time I was outside, but all I could see was mountains around us. There was a tiny, curvy road by the farm that went into the mountains, but I wouldn't know where it led to. One day I managed to get to the other side of the fence through an open gate and walked down the road. I got to the end of it at the base of the mountain, but a guard dog started to bark, alerting a man working nearby. He grabbed me and took me back to the house, warning me he would tell Gun if I did it again.

In the meantime, I performed magic tricks for Benben, not only to shut him up but also to keep my sanity. I used whatever props available, including utensils, vegetables, and grains; and I made everything vanish—chopsticks, chili, garlic.

Benben had the habit of waking me every night to help him to the chamber pot. One night I had forgotten to bring the chamber pot and had to go to the yard to get it. As soon as I went outside, I heard noises and saw movement on the farm. I went closer and saw a couple of men loading a donkey-drawn cart nearby. Gun was among them. They were just about finishing, and one of the men got on the driver's seat. Before he drove away, he asked, "You need any Shaoju from Jing City, Gun?"

"No, I've still got some. I'll get it when I'm there next time."

I turned quickly back into the house, my heart racing. *Jing City! They go to Jing City!*

I couldn't return to sleep afterwards because I was so excited. I thought about how I could get a ride to Jing City, or Beijing. I could simply sneak into the cart, couldn't I? But soon I became dejected: even if I could get to Jing City, how was I going to find Jeng? It would be even more impossible to get close to the palace, since it was heavily guarded. The layers of walls and gates were there to keep ordinary people out. I needed the help of Priest Wang, and I had to go to the Temple of Light and Shadow first! But I had no other choice, getting out of here was the first step.

In the following days, I observed the activities on the farm carefully, and I noticed that Gun and another guy took turns going to town. They would start loading the cart at about three o'clock in the morning and the cart would leave about an hour later. I decided I would escape the day when the other guy drove, because he wasn't as scary. But I kept postponing my escape, because I was afraid if it didn't work and I would end up being locked up again. Many nights I stepped out of the bed, dressed, and went to the yard, but I lost my courage after waiting in the dark and not finding a chance to get on the cart.

It wasn't until I noticed that the time it took them to load the cart became shorter since the peach season was nearly over, that I panicked and made up my mind.

The next night I didn't sleep at all, and I woke Benben and made him pee early. Then I grabbed my belongings, which was a bundle that contained a couple of dry corn buns that I had hidden away from the day. I had my pendant, a few coins and a bit of silver I had hidden in a secret pocket I had sewn to my underwear after noticing the greed in Juhua's eyes every time I took out my purse.

As soon as I heard Gun go out of the house, I followed suit. I hid next to the tree a few steps from the house and waited to see the cart coming into the loading zone. When Gun started to load the cart, I threw a bone to the guard dog on duty, climbed out of the fence and got to the road. I went all the way around the hill, out of the sight of the house, then I found some big rocks and piled them on the center of the road. It was an idea inspired by the highway robbery I had run into prior to meeting Jeng. I waited patiently behind a tree on roadside.

Soon, I heard the sound of hooves clomping on the road. As expected, the donkey bawled as it saw the obstacles, and the driver cursed and got off the cart. To my horror, it was Gun, not the other driver, but I had no choice but carry out my plan. While he moved the rocks, I went to the cart as quietly as I could while crouching low and climbed onto it.

The tent that covered the cart also shielded me from the driver, and fortunately there was plenty of space in the back since peaches were getting rarer. Rocking among the baskets of peaches, I soon fell asleep. When I woke, the sun was up, but we were still in the mountains. Feeling hungry, I ate the corn buns for breakfast, then I reached into a basket next to me and took a peach. It was big, juicy, and just ripe, unlike the ones Benben and I had been having in the past month, which were either too ripe or deformed. These peaches, I assumed, were to be sold to wealthy families in Beijing.

After another hour or so, the traffic became heavier. Soon, I heard the shouts of other cart drivers and the sounds of chattering in standard Mandarin. I sat up, and saw the Beijing City Wall, intact and with its watch

216

tower sitting on top. I had only seen the pictures of the original versions, since in modern times, most of the walls had been demolished. Looking around me, I saw crowds of men on foot and on horses, heading towards the gate. There were also cows, carts, and sedan chairs among the procession. Some men were in their Manchu clothes, some in long gowns and others in short jackets. Most of them were hatless, but some wore cone-shaped hats. It was a hot day, so some men had their shirts unbuttoned and pants rolled up, but no one wore short sleeves. Very few women were seen in the crowds and I assumed women didn't travel as much and some of them might be sitting in sedan chairs.

On the other side of the gate was Jing City. Shouts of other passengers greeted me. I saw no modern high rises or traffic lights, although there were two-story buildings; not a single bicycle or motor vehicle, not even rickshaws. Horse or donkey-drawn carts and sedan chairs were the main transportation tools. Street performers milled in the streets, singing operas or performing circus acts or Kung Fu. A bit chaotic and dirty, the air smelled of fried dough and rotten fruits at the same time. Although I liked it better than the exhaust fumes of modern vehicles, I also felt nostalgic. This was obviously not the Beijing I was familiar with and I felt like I was in a movie set, except that there were no actors here. A feeling of loss washed over me. Mere moments ago I had been looking forward to coming here, as if I was going home, but now I only realized how far I had gone. Jeng must have felt the same when he had found himself in the middle of the twenty-first century.

While I was musing, the cart suddenly stopped, and Gun's voice shouted, "Arrived!"

Startled, I crouched down at once. We were in front of what appeared to be a wholesale produce store, where a line of carts loaded goods. Gun found a spot to park his cart and entered the store as soon as he jumped off the vehicle. I got hold of the edge of the cart and prepared to jump, but my legs were numb from sitting and I couldn't move. I rubbed them and even beat them rapidly using my fists, and forced myself out of the cart, relying mostly my arms. But before I could start walking, Gun had come back and saw me. "Hey! What're you doing here?"

I tried to run but my legs wouldn't follow my will. I ended up stumbling and Gun grabbed my wrist. "You bitch! Trying to run away?"

He dragged me to the front of the cart and looked for ropes to tie me up. I cried loudly, "Help! Help!"

But it was all clamoring around us, and no one paid attention.

Gun put his filthy hand on my mouth to stop me from shouting. As he did that, I kicked his balls and he loosened his grasp, then I pushed him with all my strength until he fell on the ground.

I ran for my life.

"Stop!" Gun shouted and chased me.

I ran a few blocks, only slowing down once I couldn't hear Gun's shouts. Then I headed towards a crowded area and relaxed when I was among people. Even if the man was still looking for me, it wouldn't be easy for him to spot me.

After I had caught my breath, I realized that I was in a market place. It was lined with street vendors of all sorts—food, clothes, tools. Most people were gathering around in the center, where what looked like a circus show was going on. I weaved into the crowd and went all the way to the front. I gasped when I saw the man breathing fire. I had seen it on TV once and knew the trick. The performer kept a sip of alcohol or other combustible fuel in his mouth, while he held a torch between his teeth. The torch tip was wrapped with material soaked with fuel and was already slowly burned before the performer blew fuel to it. It was extremely dangerous, and my heart was in my throat until the end of the act. After a round of applause, the man came to the audience to collect coins.

I was thinking how to retrieve a coin from my underwear when another performer came, holding a fearsome sword in hand. After a bow to the audience, he pushed the tip of the sword in his mouth. My knees weakened. The man was going to swallow the sword. I had heard about the insane art before and knew that it was no magic. The man was really pushing the sword down to his gut. My stomach roiled with nausea, but I couldn't move my eyes away. Everyone in the audience seemed to be as captured as I was. No one made a sound, no one even moved. It was still and silent all around me. And that was why when a man poked his head from the crowd and looked around, he caught my attention. My heart instantly turned into a rabbit. Gun was still looking for me. I tried not to panic and quickly scanned around me to find a safe hiding place. Finding none, I bent to keep my head down and slowly moved away. I soon found myself behind the stage, where a shed with an open door looked inviting. I went inside without hesitation and saw two teenagers. A boy was practicing with swords, and the girl was pulling a thread from her mouth. Seeing me, they both stopped doing what they were doing. I put a finger on my lips to gesture them not to speak and hid behind a large water jar.

"Hey kids, did a woman in a blue gown come in here?"

My palms sweated during the silence that followed. Gun repeated his question, this time louder.

"No, no one came!" said the girl.

Another silence followed. Then I heard the steps walking around in the house.

"What're you doing?" the boy shouted. "You can't come in here! Dad! Dad!"

The footsteps quickly headed back towards the door.

After a while I heard the girl's voice, "You can come out now. He's gone!"

I crawled out of my hiding place and stood up.

"Thank you!" I smiled at the girl. "I'm Julie. Do you mind if I stay here for a while?"

"Sure. I'm Yune, and that's my brother June," the girl said. Yune was about twelve, skinny and tall. She had a bit of blood at the corner of her mouth.

"Are you all right?" I asked her.

"I'm all right. It's just my tongue." Yune stuck out her tongue for me to see. Blood oozed from more than one spot.

"Oh my god. What happened?" I was going to take a better look, but the girl wouldn't let me.

"It's done with the needles," June, who was about the same age as his sister, said. "She was swallowing needles."

"What?" I was horrified. "For real?"

Instead of explaining, the girl showed me the trick. She turned away for a moment, brought a cup of water and put some needles in. Then she drank the water and showed me the empty cup. The needles were gone.

"You swallowed them?" I grimaced.

Yune did not say anything, but swallowed a silky thread next. Then she stuck her finger in her mouth and pulled the thread back, along with the needles threaded to it.

I clapped my hands. "Well done!"

"You don't look impressed," Yune said, wiping her lips.

"I am impressed," I tried to convince her. But in fact, I knew how the trick worked.

"No, you aren't. You're not even asking how I did it." Yune pouted.

I smiled. What a perceptive girl. "Well, to tell you the truth," I said, patting her head. "I'm also a trickster, I know how it works."

"Really?" Yune raised an eyebrow. "How did I do it?"

"You placed the treaded needles in your mouth before you 'swallowed' the needles in the water."

Yune looked up at me and smiled. "Pretty good. Have you done it, too?"

I shook my head. "No. I haven't. I'm not as brave as you are."

Yune smiled proudly, but I felt sorry for her. "Do you have to practice this trick? Can't you do something else, some kind of Kung Fu, like your brother?"

The girl's smile vanished. "I can't. Dad says I'm weak like my mom, can't do Kung Fu. I can only do the needles."

I nodded and held up the needles, which were fine embroidery needles. I marveled at the blacksmith's skills for a minute. "I have an idea. We can clip the needle tips to make them blunter."

Yune looked horrified. "Dad would kill me if I did that!"

"Why?"

"He says cheating will damage my reputation. Even though it's a trick, we still perform it as authentically as possible."

I tried not to roll my eyes. "Your dad is a true artist."

At that time a voice shouted from the stage. "June, it's time!"

Picking up his swords, June ran towards the stage.

I started to tidy up the shed, which was quite messy, with weapons and costumes scattered around.

Yune put down her needles and threads and picked up a pot near a stove. "I'm going to make lunch. Are you going to stay? I can make your share of rice."

"Thank you! You're so generous!" I said. "But are you sure it's okay with your parents?"

"My dad wouldn't mind. My mom is no more." Yune's voice quivered a bit. "She died last year."

"I'm sorry," I said to the girl. "Let me help you."

I was fanning the fire in the stove when a man's loud voice shouted from the door, "Who the hell are you? What're you doing here in my house?"

I looked up. It was the man who had swallowed the sword, and apparently, the children's father.

I bowed instantly. "My name is Julie, I was on my way to look for a relative, but some ruffian kidnapped me. I've just escaped now and he's probably still looking for me nearby. Please let me stay for just a few days. I'll be gone as soon as I find my relatives."

Seeing no response, I dropped on my knees, since Wang had taught me that it was a way to show respect and would often move a person's heart.

Obviously, the man wasn't used to that kind of gesture, since he looked uncomfortable and said immediately, "Get up! I'm not the emperor. But you see,

I have trouble feeding my own family. How is it possible for me to keep you?"

"But I can work for you. I'll cook and clean."

"Yes, Dad, Julie cleaned our house earlier!" Yune said on the side.

"Shut up," the man said to his daughter. "*You* are supposed to clean the house, you lazy brat."

I said, "I can do magic tricks."

"What tricks?" the man looked me up and down. "Show me."

I looked around me for props. Off my head I knew some card tricks, but there were no cards around. I also knew the turning a glass water upside down trick, but glass hadn't been invented yet. So, I borrowed a few coins from the man and did a disappearing trick. The man wasn't impressed, but he agreed to let me stay for a couple of days.

Grateful, I went back to making lunch. My cooking had greatly improved after working for Meng's family and I was able to make a sort of Mapo Tofu, using some bean sauce and green onion, and a boiled vegetable soup. Thankfully, there weren't any complaints, and neither was there any leftover. But I wasn't that flattered, knowing how hungry the men were, and how little food they had. A total of four adults including myself, and two teenagers shared a pound of tofu and a few ounces of meat—no wonder all of them were all skin and bones.

Among the three adults in the circus, two of them were brothers, named Old Chen and Young Chen. Old Chen was the father of June and Yune. The third adult was a friend of the brothers, named Old Liu. Young Chen was single, and Old Liu had a daughter who lived on a nearby farm.

IN THE AFTERNOON, the troupe did another round of performances while I hid in the shed to do housework for them. After dinner, I cleaned the table and washed the dishes, the two kids went outside to play, and the three men sat around the dining table to smoke and drink. After they were nearly done with that, Old Chen spilled the coins from a jar and counted their earnings of the day.

"Sixty wens. That's all we got the whole day!" Old Chen sighed. "Just enough for a days' food and rent."

"We're getting less and less customers lately," Old Liu said. "Too much competition. Everyone knows how to swallow swords or needles, walk on a tightrope, or breathe fire. These aren't new anymore. East, South, West, North, every corner of the city, at least one circus group is doing these tricks."

"What're we supposed to do then?" Old Chen looked at his brother and his friend. "Any ideas?"

Old Liu seemed to be one who made decisions, but he started to smoke his pipe and wouldn't say a word.

"Maybe we can try jumping over fire," Young Chen said. "The group in the north of the city is doing it and seems to be selling. A couple of men in the audience were talking about it the other day."

"I can't jump, you know it, after that injury years ago. I'm crippled," Old Chen said.

"I can, but it'll be more of an attraction if June and Yune do it," Young Chen said. "I can teach them."

He then looked at his brother and waited for his response. Old Chen avoided his brother's eyes. "I don't know. It's such a dangerous act. Yune isn't that athletic. I've heard of plenty of accidents."

They went silent again. I was done with the dishes and sat down in a chair near them, mending a broken costume for June. Their predicament saddened me. It had always been difficult for the ordinary people to make a living in the feudal societies.

"Tell you the truth," Old Liu finally spoke, "I think it's time for me to retire from the trade. Lately my body aches everywhere, and I can't get a good night's sleep. I want to go home, get a buffalo, and an acre of land. I can at least get enough to feed myself till I die."

I glanced at the man, who was probably in his fifties, but given the life expectancy of the time, he could be called an old man.

Old Chen poured himself another drink after he heard his friend's plan. He didn't speak until he had taken a few gulps and let out a heavy sigh. "If you had your mind set that way, I wouldn't be able to keep you, would I? But you're more or less the backbone of our circus, if you left, then we wouldn't last any longer, either."

"Maybe it's for the best," Old Liu said. "The kids are already grown up. You can find Yune a husband.

She's pretty, could at least be a concubine to a well-to-do man."

"What're you talking about? The lass is only twelve," Old Chen grumbled.

Old Liu shrugged. "Old enough. And June can always try his luck in the palace. Gong-gong Yan likes him."

"My son is not going to become a eunuch!" Old Chen yelled at his friend.

What followed was a long silence, where the three of them drank and smoked more.

That night I shared a bed with Yune. The girl was exhausted and fell asleep right away. But I couldn't. The day's adventure was too much for me. I thought about my next step. How would I find Jeng? He wasn't in Jing City, but could I get to his house? From what Dong had told me, I knew that I was in the Outer City of the old Beijing, where ordinary people lived, and was not allowed to the Inner City, where the Imperial and Eight-banner families lived. The Forbidden City was the inner of the Inner City, and it would be simply impossible to approach. My only choice was to find a way back to Peach Blossom Village and look for Priest Wang.

I was grateful that I had found the circus family, but also distressed by their struggle. The prospect of Yune, still a child, becoming some old man's concubine, filled me with sadness; and June losing his manhood forever would be brutal. Even though I had known them for less than a day, these kind people were already my family. I felt sorry for them because they were risking their lives performing dangerous acts. When Old Chen swallowed the sword into his stomach, a tiny mistake could cost him his life. So was the spitting fire trick—one could easily get burned or poisoned by the fumes. I couldn't even imagine watching Yune and June jumping over fire. I'd have a heart attack just watching it.

I wished I had known some entertaining and safe tricks that could help the group. But all of the large-scale magic tricks of the twenty-first century, such as body-separation or walking through a wall, required some kind of technology or machinery that hadn't been invented in the eighteenth century. I racked my brain. Could I adopt any of these tricks without advanced technology? I tossed and turned. Then I remembered doing metamorphosis—a body swapping trick—at a Christmas party with my cousin Lydia, and I cheered up. Yes, that would work! Yune and June could do it!

The next day I told Old Chen the idea right after breakfast when they were still getting ready for the day's performance.

Old Chen shook his head after taking two long draughts from his pipe. "Won't work."

"Why not?" I asked. "All you need is a large wooden trunk with a movable back panel, and a bit a practice. It's easy and safe."

"Where am I going to get such a special trunk? It's going to cost money."

"I have a little bit silver. I was going to save it for later travel expenses, but I'll let you use it, as payment for your kindness."

He fiddled with his thumbs, not looking at me for a long moment. "Let me think about it."

After dinner that day, the three men discussed my plan and agreed to give it a try.

Early the next morning, Old Liu took me to a carpenter in the suburbs, someone he had known for years and could be trusted to keep a trade secret.

It took about three days for the wooden trunk to be ready, and I showed them how the trick worked right away. Basically, Yune's hands would be bound behind her, and she would be put into a sack, the sack would be knotted closed and then locked into the trunk. Then her brother would step on top of the trunk, holding a large piece of cloth for a curtain, and when the curtain flipped seconds later, Yune, instead of her bother would be standing on top of the trunk. She would unlock the trunk and untie the sack to show the crowd that her brother was inside.

The secret behind the trick was that Yune would be able to slip her hands out of the knots easily, and she could untie the sack from a hole. As soon as the trunk lid was closed, she would wiggle out of the sack while her brother was still locking it. Once her brother was on top of the box, she would slip out from the rear panel. And when June held up the "curtain," they would swap— Yune would jump on top of the trunk while her brother went down into the trunk and then into the sack.

Although it sounded simple, the trick had to be done quickly in order to create the stunning effect. In fact, the secret of the trick had been well known for decades in modern times, but its popularity never waned because performers were able to create new records on their speed. The fastest swapping had been done in just half a second. It took me and Lydia nearly two minutes because we didn't have much time to practice. We got applause but it was a failure. Yune and June diligently practiced hundreds of times before their debut, and made it in about two seconds, which was impressive. Within but a few days, the crowd watching their shows thickened as the circus's popularity soared. Sometimes in the audience I would spot sedan chairs, indicating the presence of wealthy people. I added body separation, using my modern magic knowledge and adapting to the current tech-free condition; and I also acquired a dove and performed the dove and scarf magic—my favorite since junior high. I convinced Chen to name the show "New Age Magic."

CHAPTER 13

❡

ABOUT A MONTH after the launch of the New Age Magic, I was collecting money after doing my dove trick, when a man in the audience approached me. He wore a navy silk changshan and a black watermelon cap—basically a baseball cap without the brim. He put a piece of silver in my jar and said, "Our master likes your performance and would like to invite you to dinner tonight."

I looked at the silver piece. It was boat-shaped, palm-sized, and the largest I had seen. I was quite dazed, and it took me a moment to respond. "Thank you. But who is your master?"

"Master Ai. You probably don't know him. But we'll pick you up at sunset."

A wave of panic attacked me. "Can I take someone with me?"

"No, Master Ai only wants you."

"But what does he, uh, Master Ai want from me?"

"He wants you to do your pigeon trick for him."

"Oh, sure!" My fear dissipated, replaced with flattery. "I'll see you soon then."

My eyes followed the man as he walked away from me. He passed the crowds and stopped in front of a sedan chair in the back, where four porters were waiting. The curtain of a window was slightly open, partially revealing a passenger inside. The man conversed with the passenger briefly, then signaled to the porters, who picked up the poles, warning the passersby to make way as they went.

I watched the sedan chair move away and the man walking along with it, wondering momentarily who the "master" was, then I quickly returned to the back of the stage to share the news with the members of circus.

"Private performance?" Everyone was thrilled. It was the first time anyone in the group ever received such invitation.

"Do any of you know this Mr. Ai?"

"It's a rare surname," Old Chen said. "But he might be Manchu."

It wasn't a surprise because at the time the Manchus were wealthier and had higher status than the Han in general.

That afternoon we finished our regular performance early so I could get ready for the event.

Old Chen offered me my pick of a suitcase, and I chose a bamboo suitcase for my props because it would allow my dove to breathe. As I packed my props, Old Liu handed me a short knife.

"Hide this in your waist belt, just in case."

I was thankful for his concern since I was a bit wary myself. I had no idea what kind of person this Mr. Ai was.

At around sunset, the same sedan chair stopped in front of the house, accompanied by the same man who had spoken to me earlier.

He lifted the curtain of the door in the front and invited me to get in. There was no one inside. I hesitated for a moment and stepped in nervously. I had seen sedan chairs hundreds of times on TV and also on the streets lately, but it was the first time I rode one. The cushioned bench was quite comfortable and was wide enough for two people to sit. I lifted the curtain and waved to Old Liu, who was seeing me off. The other members of the circus were watching me from inside the house as well. As soon as the chair started to move, I observed the interior curiously. Besides the door in the front, there was a window on each of the other sides as well, and the "walls" were all chiseled with plenty of openings, so it didn't feel confined or stuffy. The ride was extremely smooth, and I wasn't bothered by the bumpy road or noisy engines. But of course, it came at a price, and I felt sorry for the poor men who carried the weight on their shoulders.

I looked through the open space on the wall and saw that we were passing through the streets of the Outer City until we reached Chongwen Gate, a gate that led into the Inner City. Old Liu's guess was correct. Mr. Ai must've been a Manchu. The chair stopped in front of Jing Xiang Lou—Beijing Flavor House—a grand restaurant with two stories, the pillars painted red and corridors hung with lanterns. A servant helped me out of the sedan chair and carried my suitcase for me. I followed him to the second floor, where he knocked on the door of a private room and a man's voice called, "Come in!"

He opened the door for me and motioned for me to enter. I stepped in, keeping my head low, as was etiquette. From the corner of my eye, I glimpsed a man sitting at the end of the room.

"Offer your salutation to Mr. Ai!" the servant said to me as I moved slowly to the man, still keeping my head bowed.

I paused for a moment then I did my best to curtsy. "Commoner Julie Bird wishes Mr. Ai health and wellness."

"Forget the tiresome manners, come closer and you may look at me," the voice was cold and stern.

I raised my chin slowly and glanced at him, and it was all I could do to stifle my gasp. It was Jeng—or rather, the likeness of him, but skinnier and older. He had Jeng's narrow eyes and straight nose, but Jeng didn't have his mustache—a Fu Manchu without the long tendrils. Then I remembered where I had seen him. Jeng had punched a portrait of him at the Palace Museum. Ai was the shortening of Aisin Gioro, the surname of the Qing imperial family. The man in front of me was the fourth son of Kangxi, the truculent future ruler Yongzheng. Prince Yong.

My surprised reaction had unsettled him. "What? Do you know me?"

"No!" I swallowed hard and tried not to tremble under his cold gaze.

"Why are you so surprised?"

I lowered my eyes. "Forgive my offense. It's the first time I ever find myself in a nice place like this, and next to wealthy people like you."

He dismissed the servant, and said to me, "No need to be frightened. The reason I wanted you here today is because I liked your dove trick. It's quite delightful."

I couldn't believe my ears. I hadn't thought the man was capable of offering compliments. It took me a moment to realize what I was supposed to say. "Thank you, but I'm not worth your gracious attention."

"Where did you learn it?"

"Uh," I tried to think of a believable answer, instead of "from the future."

Seeing my hesitation, he said, "Don't bother if it's trade secret. Just show me the trick."

"Right now?" I hesitated. I couldn't have put the dove in my pocket beforehand because I didn't want it to be suffocated. I bowed and asked, "May I be excused for a moment first?"

He was taken aback for a second, then he nodded with understanding, and pointed to the divider screen in the corner.

I went behind the screen and did my preparation. My hand shook as I wrapped the dove in a silk scarf. I kept thinking maybe I should tell the prince that the dove wasn't feeling well, and I wouldn't be able to do any tricks. But I resisted the temptation because although Prince Yong was Jeng's rival, he was also his sibling, and he would be my chance to finding Jeng later on. I took a deep breath—the simple technique that Jeng had taught me had been helpful in easing my stage fright.

When I returned to the center of the room, the prince looked at me up and down, as if trying to detect any difference. My heart pounded and my legs started to buckle. I put the bamboo box on a table, took another deep breath and turned to face him. I ignored his keen eyes and smiled, imagining that he was Jeng and I would do my best to please him.

Slowly, I pulled out a silk handkerchief from my sleeve, twirled it between my fingers, and raised it to hide my mouth as I threw a shy smile at my imaginary audience, hoping he was dazzled. Seeing he wasn't, I slowly turned, and gave him another slightly more coquettish smile. Turning back, I twisted the handkerchief into a narrow strap as he watched my movements closely. Then I quickly pulled a hairpin from my hair, shook the handkerchief open and turned the pin into a fan. His widened eyes showed he was impressed. Again, I smiled behind the fan as if flirting with him, then I closed the fan and changed it back to a handkerchief before he had the time to breathe, I folded the scarf slowly, and let out the dove.

The prince in disguise clapped his hands. "Wonderful! Wonderful! I have no clue how you did it! Do it again!"

After doing the same trick three times, it dawned on me that the prince, like his brother, was an aficionado of magic shows. Prince Yong was more curious about how it was done, but instead of ordering me to tell him how, he liked figuring it out himself.

He had me do the same trick over and over again, as if hoping to see me make a blunder. I was so tired that I was on the verge of simply blurting out how it was done, but I had to keep it together. So, I continued. It was no longer a magic show but some sort of competition. It was difficult not to falter because he was sitting very close to me and watched me without blinking. If I had a nanosecond's delay, he could see the almost invisible silk thread that pulled the dove.

After about twenty times, the prince finally got bored. "Okay, that's it. The poor bird must be tired. And you must be hungry."

He pulled a string on the wall, which was connected to a bell outside. Soon plates of food were brought, and a singer holding a *pipa* entered the room.

I had eaten something with Cheng's family earlier, but the glazed pork belly was hard to resist. I hadn't had a proper meal in two months. Even though the circus was making money, the best Old Chen would allow was a pound of pork for the six of us every day.

I forgot my manners completely and stuffed myself with the food on the table.

"You have an interesting face, where are you from?" asked the prince as he watched me eat. I swallowed down the food and looked up at him. He had barely touched his food.

"I'm uh, from here," I said timidly.

"Doesn't sound like it," the prince said, his stern eyes staring unblinkingly at me.

I was certain he could see through my lies, but I pretended to be at ease.

"You speak in a strange manner. And you look different," the prince continued. "Your hair is more brown than black, and your nose is straight. You're not a Han and your surname is Bird. Are you a descendant of the Borgik?"

Borgik was a Manchu surname that sounded just like Bird in Chinese. I considered saying yes, but decided against it, since I was afraid he would start asking me genealogy questions. Despite feeling nervous, I picked up another piece of meat with steady hands, and before biting into it, said, "My father is a westerner."

"That's what I thought," said the prince, satisfied with my answer. "You look like one of the Jesuits. Where is your father now?"

"He, uh, left me and my mom." I lowered my eyes and stopped chewing, pretending to be sad.

Afraid that he would be asking me more questions, I put the chopsticks down even though my stomach wanted more food. As soon as I did that, the prince stood up.

WE GOT ON the same sedan chair, and I sat next to the prince with mixed feelings. I was nervous, but at the same time excited. Yongzheng, although ruthless, was quite an accomplished ruler. However reluctant I was, I had to admit that he did have a charisma that his brother lacked.

I got off a block from the circus house, because the gate of the alley that led to the market square was locked, and only people could squeeze in.

"I could just walk back to the house," I said as I stepped out of the vehicle. "Thank you very much!"

The prince looked out as if to make sure that all was safe. Then he nodded at me. "All right. I'll see you again one day."

I stood where I was, watching the sedan chair moving away. I sagged in relief. At least the ordeal was over for now. But as I walked towards the circus house, I regretted that it was over. Even though they were rivals, Prince Yong was Jeng's brother, and being close to him was like being close to Jeng. What had he meant by "one day?" It could mean never. I should've offered to perform another trick for him on another night! I stopped in the center of the road and turned to look at the shadow of the sedan chair, wondering whether I should run after it.

At that moment, a hand grabbed me from behind. I screamed but my voice was quickly muffled. My mouth was stuffed with a rag and I was lifted to a man's shoulder. I remembered this gesture too well. It had to be Gun! Horrified, I kicked hard at the man's back.

Gun carried me a few blocks through the dark alley, and onto a street where his own donkey cart was parked. He quickly tied my hands and legs with ropes. "You whore. You think I can't find you? I knew you were in that circus house. A trickster, huh?"

He threw me into the back of his cart, jumped into the front, and whipped the animal, shouting, "Go!"

But we didn't get far. Right after the donkey got on the road, two men suddenly materialized and blocked our way. One of them jumped on the donkey and dragged Gun down, while another held the reins.

They got hold of the ruffian and roped him. Another man came to me and untied me.

"Are you all right?" It was Prince Yong's voice, although it wasn't as cold as earlier.

I nodded, trembling.

"Who's he? Do you know him?"

"No, I don't know him. He's nobody to me. He kidnapped me when I was on my way to the city, and I ran away from him once." It wasn't completely a lie.

"I see," the prince said. Then he walked over and whispered something to his servants. The servants nodded and threw Gun on his own cart. One of the servants got on the donkey and drove the cart away.

"What are you going to do with him?" I asked timidly.

"He'll be taken to the magistrate."

The servant and the prince walked me back to the circus house. Before they left, the prince said, "I'll be back in a few days. Next time, I guarantee I'll see through your trick!"

"And I'll be waiting," I answered with a smile, and thanked him for rescuing me.

That night I lay awake until dawn. The meeting with Prince Yong had been completely unexpected. The prince, although cold, didn't really appear to be the hardhearted, merciless ruler that he had been portrayed to be. Perhaps, I thought, he had become crueler later. Or perhaps I hadn't had enough time to see through his true nature yet.

AS HE HAD promised, Prince Four summoned me to the same place a few nights later, and I performed the same trick for him. Only this time, he saw the silk thread. "I had guessed it last time, but you were too fast, and I couldn't catch the moment."

I bent my knees and bowed, "Mr. Ai is so talented."

In fact, I had deliberately slowed down. For one thing, I was tired of doing the same trick over and over for the same audience. For another, I couldn't stand the hawk-like eyes staring at my every movement. And I wanted to reward the prince for his persistence.

"I'll see you in a couple of days," the prince said to me before we parted that night.

"Why? You've already seen through the trick."

He laughed. "You think that's the only reason I like the show? Not at all. I like your performance."

I thanked him again. My positive feelings for the man couldn't help but increase.

In the following days, I met with Prince Yong once every couple of evenings, and I thought of some other tricks to entertain him. It wasn't easy to fool the prince. He was extremely perceptive. Out of ten coin tricks that I attempted, he saw through eight. The prince didn't care much for action shows such as the body separation and metamorphosis, but he was fascinated by sleight-of-hand tricks. True to his claim, he was more interested with the performance than the how, and his attention seemed to be even more intensified after he knew how a trick worked. My nervousness under his scrutiny lessened day after day as I got used to it, and I started to like the close-up challenge. As my meager inventory ran out, I tried to create new tricks to keep him engaged, but it was difficult because I was not a professional magician. Thus, I was delighted when I came across a card game one morning when I was on my way to get breakfast for the troupe in the market place.

Four old men sat around a table outside a tea shop, drinking tea and gambling. The cards they played were made by gluing layers of paper and seemed to be a combination of mahjong and modern playing cards. The symbols on the cards were similar to those on mahjong tiles—coins, strings, and characters—but they had four suits including the diamond and the spade, and there were also face cards. I was instantly attracted to the game and stood there watching them play, fascinated.

"What's the name of the game?" I asked one of the men.

The man looked at me as if shocked by my stupid question. "It's mahdiao. You've never seen it before?"

I shook my head. "No, but is it similar to mahjong?"

"Mahjong?" It was his turn to shake his head. "Never heard about it."

Interesting. Mahdiao was probably the grandmother of mahjong and modern playing cards.

"It is similar to Yezi. Leaf," another man added.

"Oh!" I had no idea what leaf was, either, but I was pleased mostly because playing cards existed, whatever they were called.

I acquired a set of cards right away, after ordering our soymilk and fried dough.

That night when I met with Prince Four, I showed him a relatively easy card trick using a technique called the "double lift." A card would just keep showing up on top of the deck no matter where it was supposed to be. He was stunned and couldn't figure out the trick at all. I guessed card magic didn't exist in the eighteenth-century China, even though playing cards did.

My card tricks kept Prince Four interested for a few more days. One night, about a month after our initial meeting, when the sedan chair stopped near the circus house, he told me that it would be his last meeting with me.

"Why?" My heart sank. I had not expected that we would part so soon.

"I'm busy. My father is ill, and I need to spend more time with him."

It sounded like a farewell. I sighed, looking down at my hands and desperately thought of what to say so him so he would keep in touch with me. He was my only hope of finding Jeng.

"Why don't you speak? Are you all right?"

I arranged my expression into one of sadness when I raised my head and faced him. "I'm not going to see you again?"

He looked at me intently, his cold eyes sparkling. "Not for a while, I'm afraid."

All was lost. I tried to force some tears out, but I was more frustrated than sad. He took my hand and placed a gold piece in my palm.

I gasped. A gold piece was worth ten silver pieces and a palace maid's yearly wage. Every time we met, he gave me trinkets—silver coins, earrings and bracelets. And the most I had gotten was a silver piece. While I was grateful for his generosity, I also felt sad. After all, this man had become a companion who appreciated my art of magic whether I liked him or not.

"So that's it?" I asked, now misty-eyed.

The prince didn't speak, but I could hear his heavy breath and the undulation on his chest. I waited for a moment before getting off the sedan chair.

CHAPTER 14

❻

A WEEK AFTER my last meeting with Prince Four, I told myself that it was time to look for Priest Wang. I had enough savings to hire a horse-drawn cart that could take me to the Temple of Light and Shadow, but I didn't know how to get there Although I had a vague memory of the scenery along the road near Jing City, I didn't remember the first half of the journey on Gun's cart because it had been dark. I had asked everyone in the circus, but no one knew how to get to that particular farm. There also appeared to be dozens of villages named Peach Blossom nearby and no one had heard about the Gourd Temple at all. I had been putting off my plan for the above reasons and I was also reluctant to leave the circus. They had all become my family.

It was the middle of September, about two months before Jeng would return to the palace from Tibet. Although I still had plenty of time, I was becoming more and more anxious. One day, I gathered my courage and went around town, found the fruit wholesaler, gave him some money and asked him where the peach farm was. I supposed the farm should be close to Peach Blossom Village. Not having been there himself, he managed to give me a rough location, providing some names of the villages nearby. Based on that, I hired a horse cart the next day and set off for the trip.

It wasn't an easy task. After we left Jing City, all the villages along the road looked identical. And indeed, there were multiple Peach Blossom Villages in the same area. We ended up going in a circle for half a day. It wasn't until afternoon, and after many mistakes and dead ends, that we finally reached the Peach Blossom Village where I had stayed.

I told the driver to wait for me by the foot of the mountain, and not to tell any passersby what he was doing, before going up the mountain road. After I had located the hidden pit, I wandered around it, trying to find the gourd-shaped rock that was supposed to be standing by the temple in the hill behind. Although there wasn't any fog, my vision was still obstructed by the copious trees and shrubs. Frustrated, I went down the pit, thinking maybe I could see the rock from there. I waded through the bushes and shrubs once again, trying in vain to peer through the thick canopy. After a series useless attempts, I stared down and contemplated the alternative of taking a ride back to the twenty-first century instead. A moment later I squealed with joy. There was a path hidden behind a mass of tangled shrubs. I quickly stood up and ran for the path. I had to spend considerable time to clear the shrubs, but other than that, the path was pretty smooth and it ran through a pine forest. I had a poor sense of direction but related to my prior experience of the area, I guessed the path I was treading on had been the precursor of the mountain road I had gotten lost on that fateful night, and where I had met Jeng the first time.

As soon as I was out of the forest, I looked up and saw a large rock that shaped like a gourd, or an hourglass—standing near the top of the hill like a long lost friend, although I had seen it only once before. The path uphill was slightly more trying, but not nearly as dangerous as the rocky road I had taken last time, and I was able to get to the top without much sweat.

The temple—or rather, a mud house with shingle roof and a wooden door—stood behind the rocks. A sign below the roof read "Temple of Light and Shadow." It was written in gold, although the color was fading. On two sides of the door was a couplet: *The past and the future are in unity / Morning and night are illusions of Light and Shadow*. Those were the first and the last lines of the poem written on the piece of paper that Dong had thrust into Jeng's hand the day he and I visited Peking University.

I took a steadying breath and knocked. No one answered. I knocked again, glancing around me, and noticed the cobwebs hanging on the eave. Still hearing no answer, I pushed the door and it creaked open. Gingerly, I stepped in. "Anybody home?" I called out, my voice strangely high pitched. It was dark inside and smelled of incense. Contrary to what Juhua had claimed, a Guanyin statue the size of a real person, although with peeling paint, sat in the center of the hall, flanked by figurines of a boy and a girl. A half-burned incense stick stood in the burner in front of the altar—someone had been here not long ago. I walked along a hallway on the side and into the back of the temple. Although there were a few small windows on the walls and the light of the setting sun poured in, it still felt creepy. But my curiosity compelled me to keep going. I saw another door at the end of the hallway and knocked on it. Again no one answered, so I pushed the door open. It was a simple bedroom with a cot, a table, and an oil lamp. A few books stood neatly on the table and there was a roll of paper, an ink box, and some brush pens as well. I wanted to look at those books, but it seemed an intrusion of privacy. Suddenly, a hand touched my shoulder and I nearly jumped out of my skin.

I turned with difficulty because a thick wall, or rather, the thick body of a man, blocked me. My eyes fell on his sweaty chest and ample belly under his unbuttoned shirt. As I looked up, I saw a face made of cheeks as everything else—nose, eyes and mouth—seemed to be buried under them. I stepped back in order to take a better look at him. He wore a gray shirt and pants and held a broom in his right hand. He didn't look like a priest, but I forced a smile and asked, "Priest Wang?"

The man shook his head slowly.

"Are you Priest Wang?" I asked again.

Instead of answering my question, he held the broom and made a sweeping gesture, as if telling me he was some sort of a housekeeper. He also pointed to his mouth and his ears, waving his hand.

"You can't speak? You can't hear?"

Whether he understood me or not, he shook his head again.

I nodded with sympathy. "Where is Priest Wang?"

He pointed in the direction of the window.

"He is out? When will he return?"

He shook his head again.

"Will he be back tonight? Tomorrow? In a few days?"

He shook his head again and again, either meaning he didn't know, or he wasn't sure.

"Okay, I think I'll be back in a few days to check. But can I leave a note?"

With the giant's permission, I scribbled a note. *I have something of great importance to discuss with you. I'll be back, or you can find me in Jing City at Chen's Circus.*

I waved goodbye to the giant and left the temple, found the cart driver and returned to Jing City that night.

TWO DAYS AFTER I had returned from the temple, a carriage appeared in front of the circus house in the morning, and a messenger came to speak to Old Chen outside. Old Chen dropped to his knees and kowtowed to the messenger. When he returned to the house, his face was pale, and he stammered when he announced,

249

"Everyone, listen! Big news, we're invited, invited to perform at, at—"

"At where?" Yune asked her father as he paused to breathe.

"At the House of Prince Yong!"

We were all silent for a second, then everyone shouted with joy.

"It's for the Mid-Autumn Celebration. We're famous!" Old Chen added.

The group cheered again, but only for a moment since the holiday was the very next day and we had to depart right away.

I was thrilled because I would be living in the Inner City for two days, although Prince Yong's house and Prince Jeng's house were not close—one being in the northeast and the other in the northwest corner.

The prince had provided money for new clothes, so we went on a quick shopping trip around the market. After that we packed swiftly, loaded our trunks of props onto the carriage, and set off for the Inner City.

THE HOUSE OF Prince Yong was an estate Emperor Kangxi had built and gifted to his son, and Prince Yong had lived there from 1693 to 1722. After he became the emperor, he changed its name into Yong He Gong—the Palace of Harmony and Peace. His son, Emperor Qianlong, converted the estate into a Buddhist temple, and it was the largest temple within Beijing. I remembered visiting it years ago. It was huge—sixteen acres with more than 600 rooms and 200 of them were Buddha halls. The entrance was not as ostentatious as it was in modern times, but it was still splendid. Guarded by a pair of stone lions and shaded by pagoda roofs were three red double doors, each decorated with seven rows of seven gold studs, showing the princely status of the resident.

Guided by a couple of servants, we carried our luggage through a path along the side of the property. The last time I visited it in the twenty-first century, there had been a lot more magnificent buildings, including the Pavilion of Boundless Happiness, a trio of multi-story buildings connected by bridges in the air. The bridges were called "flying attics," and they were an architectural marvel as well, being the first of its kind in China history. But presently, the estate consisted of groups of single-story buildings separated by short enclosures, and a lot of gardens. After about twenty minutes of walking from the main entrance, we stopped in front of a house at the back of the property, called Yong Hui Ge—the House of Harmony and Wisdom.

A small garden preceded the house along the path, and newly planted chrysanthemums bloomed madly. The house consisted of three rooms—a living room in the center and two bedrooms on each side. The living room reminded me of the Lama Temple I had visited years ago in Tibet. A large Buddha statue sat in a golden shrine in the center back of the living room, and in front of the shrine was a row of short tables with cushions next to them. A scroll lay on a table, and I quickly glanced at the title. *The Diamond Sutra.* It was well known that Prince Yong was a pious Buddhist, and it must've been a family prayer room. We were instructed to offer incense sticks to the Buddha as it was the ruler of the house.

After that we were led to the bedrooms on each side—one for the men and one for me and Yune. Our bedroom had a small queen-sized bed and a table. It was simple and clean, but the stuffy smell of old furniture suggested that it hadn't been occupied for a long time. Nonetheless, it was a luxury to Yune. She looked through every corner of the room, admiring the intricately carved window frames and pillars.

Once we had settled in, the servants took us to Ying An Hall, which was the main building in the front half of the property where the prince received guests and visitors. Some of the larger pieces—the trunks and jars—had been dropped off at the location when we arrived. Surrounded by a forest or dwarf pines, and dotted with mini rock hills, fountains, and fish ponds, Ying An Hall was a grand structure with upturned roofs, a wide veranda, and huge columns. The exterior was sumptuously decorated with lanterns hanging on the eaves above verandas. We gaped as we stepped into the building. The interior was spacious even with about twenty to thirty tables already set up in the center, and the stage in the front was twice as big as the stage we had in the market square.

We started rehearsing immediately. The men practiced their usual circus techniques, while I and my two little friends focused on our magic tricks. We would be performing our usual metamorphosis, body separation, and dove tricks. The highlight, however, would be a new escape show that I had taught Young Chen. The man's hands and feet would be bound, and he would be dumped upside down into a large water jar, and seconds later he would emerge from the jar, all wet, but with his hands and feet free. Obviously, the trick depended on the performer's ability to untie himself using his fingers, toes, and teeth. We practiced until dinner time since the next day's performance was extremely important to us. If we did well, the reward would be more than we had ever earned.

We had a wonderful dinner that evening. I'd had palace feasts in the modern restaurants in Beijing and hadn't been impressed by any. But the meatballs on the table were so delicious that I couldn't help but indulge myself in one after another. They were bite-sized, crispy outside and tender inside, and the sauce had a strong soy flavor. The fried dwarf Ji fish was yummy, too, and so was the sautéed pig kidney. The only vegetable dish was the stir-fried bean sprouts and I pretty much monopolized it since everyone else in the room prized the meat. Rice was brought in a wooden bucket with a ladle for self-serving. Now I understood where the expression *rice bucket* originated from. I had two bowls of rice, and the rest of my companions had at least three bowls each.

After dinner, while the men chatted over their rice wine and the two youngsters explored the back of the estate, I returned to practice my tricks. I was completely absorbed in my practicing that I only barely registered that someone was applauding me.

"Good job!" Prince Yong said.

I hurried off the stage and bowed at his feet. "Your servant Julie Bird wishes Prince Yong wellness and health."

He smiled casually. "Rise. I'm glad you came."

"Thank you for inviting me." I got up, keeping my head low.

"Show me your new tricks," he said as he sat down at a table next to the stage.

I chewed on my lip. "But I don't have any new tricks. I'm practicing the old ones."

His eyes flashed with what looked like disappointment. "I see, but that's fine, I've missed your dove trick."

That was clearly a lie, and I couldn't help but appreciate his civility. It made me feel bad that I wasn't better prepared.

"Actually, I might come up with something. Would it be too much trouble for you to find a rabbit for me?"

"A rabbit? Piece of cake," the prince said. "I'll have someone fetch it now."

"Wait." I stopped him from giving the order right away. "I can wait till tomorrow morning, and I also need a hat."

"But you can have them now."

I stifled a smile. I knew that the prince wanted to see the trick now. "Prince, I would rather not spoil your pleasure of enjoying it tomorrow, and I need to practice before presenting my humble trick."

He laughed. "Very well, you'll have them tomorrow morning. Let the servants know whatever you need, and they shall provide you."

I WOKE AT dawn the next morning. The birds were chirping on the trees and the men were talking in the yard. Yune, who was sharing a bed with me, was still snoring softly. I didn't want to wake the girl since she had been exhausted the night before, and the performance wouldn't start until the afternoon. But soon Chen's voice was at our door, "Get up, girls. We've got to practice, lest people think we're lazy."

I rolled my eyes. Typical Chinese, always worried about what others thought. I sat up, nudging Yune to wake her.

As soon as I stepped into the yard, I saw a rabbit snacking on vegetables in a cage and grinned widely. The rabbit was extremely shy, but I petted it and fed it, and earned its trust. The hat on top of the cage was a velvet sailor hat like the court officials wore. It wasn't quite ideal for the trick because it wasn't very deep, but I would have to work with what I had. I asked the servant for a piece of black silk and made a sack and a tablecloth out of it. I was going to place the rabbit in the sack and hang it inconspicuously on the edge of the table before the show. During the performance, I would show the audience nothing was in the hat, throw it up into the air and catch it, and then twirl it on my fingertip. I would then place the hat on the table, and take it up again, but at the same time take up the silk sack quickly and stuff it into the hat. Finally, I would pull the rabbit out from the hat skillfully, without showing the silk sack.

It sounded easy, but it took a lot of practice to get perfect. I waited until I was able to do it fairly quickly before showing it to Yune, who clapped her hands and said she loved it.

"I want to learn it! Could you do it with a kitten?"

"Hmm. I don't think so. They won't sit as quietly in the sack as the rabbit does."

Her bottom lip stuck out a bit. "I see."

SHORTLY AFTER LUNCH, guests arrived at the House of Harmony and Wisdom. Before the show began, I couldn't help my curiosity, so I joined Yune and June and peeked through the seam between curtains. Prince Yong sat at a center table right in front of the stage, next to a few other guests dressed in princely attire. The women and children occupied the rest of the tables. The guests chatted loudly, sipping on tea and snacking on refreshments between words. I had no idea who they were, but from their hair and fashion, I guessed some were wives and concubines of the princes, others were princesses. Just as I had seen on TV, the women in the imperial family were richly dressed in colorful silk

Manchu gowns. Their hair was wrapped around a long flat board that sat on top of their heads and was decorated with jewelry and flowers. But contrary to what was portrayed on TV dramas, most of these women weren't pretty and many were stout. Their makeup seemed to follow a trend—eyebrows plucked to two thin arcs and lips painted in the shape of a cherry.

Soon the seats were pretty much filled, and the guests started to grow impatient. Children wailed and men yawned, but everyone fell silent when Prince Yong stood up from his seat.

"Stop fooling around and get ready!" Old Chen hissed at us.

We did as we were told, waiting anxiously for a signal from the prince. But he went out instead, a servant following behind him. Women whispered to each other as soon as he left.

"What's happening?" Old Chen asked one of the servants.

"We're still waiting for Lady Uya, the prince's mother."

I quickly recalled a well-known fact—Lady Uya did not get along with her eldest son.

Prince Yong returned alone a moment later. He gave a brief speech, welcoming his guests again and wishing them a happy Mid-Autumn holiday, and announced the beginning of the show.

Yune and June started with the stacking rice bowls, a traditional circus performance that required extreme patience and calmness. With a stack of rice bowls on her head, Yune climbed to stand on her brother's shoulders. They performed a series of difficult acrobatic acts, including one where Yune stood on her hands, using June's hand as a platform. After that, Old Liu and Old Chen did their regular shows: sword swallowing and blowing fire.

The audience was mostly hushed during the performance, but occasionally I heard murmurs and gasps. Women's faces turned pale and some covered their children's eyes during the sword swallowing. But most of them couldn't take their eyes off the stage. I waited on the side, carefully hiding behind a carved wooden screen next to the stage, so I could still observe the audience.

When it was my turn, I went up slowly. My palms were clammy, my throat dry and tight, my heart galloping wildly in my chest, but I tried to appear calm by taking deep breaths. It was nothing, I kept telling myself. It was just another day on stage. I had been doing this for a month now. I would be fine. These people might dress well, but they weren't different from the spectators on the market square. In fact, they might be more impressionable, since they didn't get to see these shows regularly.

"Good afternoon," I started with a bow. "Humble magician Julie Bird wishes everyone here a happy Mid-Autumn Day." After that I did a trick that ended with scarves painted to read *Happy Mid-Autumn* and got a round of applause. I went on to do the dove trick, producing lots of silk scarves and fans apart from the dove, which made the audience cheer. Finally, I did the rabbit in a hat. The audience gasped and clapped their hands, and I bowed to them and thanked them.

"Where did the rabbit come from?" a child shouted before I could leave the stage.

I smiled, holding the rabbit in one hand and stroking it with another "It came from the moon!"

My clever answer elicited more laughter from the audience. According to the Chinese traditional legend, Goddess Chang'e lived on the moon with her pet rabbit. And Mid-Autumn Day was a celebration of the moon and the Moon Goddess.

"Are you Goddess Chang'e?"

"Yes, and now I must return to the moon." I bowed to the audience one more time before withdrawing to the back of the stage.

Young Chen did his escape trick at the end, bringing our show to its climax. The audience dispersed almost immediately as the imperial family had to get ready for the evening's celebration inside the palace.

DUE TO LACK of carriages, we stayed in the prince's residence for another night. We had our dinner soon after we packed our props and cleared the stage. Prince Yong had already rewarded us with a bag of silver pieces.

"It's more than we've ever made!" Old Chen said as he spilled the contents onto the table and counted it.

He divided the content to four equal shares, one for Old Liu, one for me, and two for his own family. I took only two pieces and returned the rest to him, telling him that the family needed the silver more than I did.

Old Liu also wanted to refuse some, but Old Chen said that it was time that he retired, and with the silver he could purchase himself a nice piece of land to cultivate and to live.

We were also awarded a bottle of expensive rice wine which the three men devoured. They were determined to finish it before they went to bed. They set a table in the yard under the moon and drank over a plate of roasted peanuts.

"I'm going to build a better stage," Old Chen said. "Put some benches for people to sit, and a roof over the seats."

"Good idea," his brother said. "We could attract more viewers for sure."

Yune and June soon got bored and went to bed, and I strolled around the estate to enjoy the moonlit gardens. In the middle of the sky, the moon was perfectly round and extraordinarily bright. The familiar sight made me nostalgic. The moon felt like my old friend at the moment. I recalled a famous line by Li Po, *"The present viewers have not seen the ancient moon / but the present moon has once shone on the ancients."* And I wondered whether I was a present or an ancient viewer.

The Garden of Harmony and Peace was right in the middle between the living quarters and the business area of the estate. When I'd passed it on my way to the main hall earlier, I had caught sight of the pink lotus on top of the green leaves. The garden was the size of a small community park, but with all the elements of a Chinese garden. Lotus pond, rock hills, bridges and pavilions. I went up the bridge to look at the moon in the pond. Everything felt surreal. Was I dreaming? Would I wake the next minute and find myself back in the modern world, in the Yihe Hotel, or better, in my own apartment in San Francisco? Would I be stuck here in the eighteenth century and be a street performer for the rest of my life? As much as I loved doing magic tricks, I could not stand the life here. I longed for a private toilet and shower, and I missed my smart phone. A wave of homesickness swept over me. What was I doing here? Where was Jeng? Would I be seeing him again?

"What are you thinking?"

I turned and saw the handsome face of the very person I was thinking about. Jeng was coming towards me from the end of the bridge, the moonlight gleaming on his skin.

I ran to him. "You're back!"

"Yes, I am. How was your evening?"

The casual way he answered my question puzzled me and I stopped in my tracks. As he got closer, I realized it was Prince Yong. He was cleanly shaven and looked much younger in the moonlight. In fact, he looked almost exactly like Jeng. I fought with my disappointment and forced a smile.

"Thank you for asking, my lord. I and others had a wonderful evening."

"Are you enjoying your stay here in my house?"

"Very much."

261

He paused and looked keenly at my face, as if to see if I was sincere. His next question took me by surprise.

"Would you like to stay here?"

I looked into his eyes. My turn to see whether he was joking. "You mean stay here for another day?"

"No, for as long as you like." His voice turned low and thick.

I shivered and looked away in a hurry. "I don't dare to wish for such luck."

"But if I wish you to?"

My heart raced, and I could hardly breathe evenly. I couldn't believe what he was saying. "Why?" I managed to steady my quavering voice.

"Because I would like to see you whenever I want to," the prince said, his voice thick and husky.

Oh my god, what did he mean? I laughed nervously and bowed my head. "Are you so addicted to my tricks?"

"Not just your tricks, *you* as well." He reached out and took my hand in his.

My breath seemed to vanish. Despite my earlier aversion and fear of the man, I couldn't help being flattered. Was the future emperor flirting with me, Julie Bird, who was far from pretty according to the traditional Chinese standard, or Manchu standard?

"What's your answer? Yes or no?" He held my chin between his fingers and lifted it. I looked up. His eyes were strangely bright, with a moon in each iris. His breaths were heavy and smelled of alcohol.

I was suddenly afraid. I did not want to have any emotional entanglement with this man, although he did look an awful lot like Jeng. "I don't know. I have to think. I mean, the circus, can they stay with me?" I asked, knowing it was a silly question.

He shook his head.

"Then I can't. They need me."

"No, they don't," he said adamantly. "They have enough to get by for a long time. And I'll make sure they don't want for spectators."

I swallowed hard. "You see, I, uh, need to find my relatives—"

"I'll help you with that."

I groaned inwardly. This man wouldn't take no for an answer. Trying to keep my voice as calm as possible, I asked, "What would I do here? Would I be your personal entertainer?"

He chuckled. "My family entertainer. In fact, Lady Nian needs a companion, and you are the perfect candidate."

"Lady Nian?"

"My *fujin*. She didn't get to see the show this afternoon because it wasn't convenient for her. She's with child."

"Oh." I quickly recalled that Nian was the prince's favorite concubine. I also recalled Jeng's emotion when he was reminded of her by the TV show.

Her Lady's companion? The family entertainer? It sounded like a great position. If I accepted the proposal, then I would be trapped here. Princes Yong and Jeng

263

were siblings but their relationship wasn't amicable. I might have little chance to get close to Jeng through his brother. But if I refused, then Prince Yong would be mad for sure, and probably wouldn't summon me again. At this point, I didn't really have a better plan in terms of getting in touch with Jeng. Priest Wang was still a phantom.

He pulled me closer to him and whispered, "Say yes."

My heart turned to a rabbit—obviously not the one who sat quietly in the hat, but one that raced around wildly. A voice in the back of my head told me to refuse him, but I was weak. Despite my better judgement, I obeyed his wish.

CHAPTER 15

AFTER BREAKFAST the next day, the circus troupe said goodbye to me. Although everyone congratulated me for my good fortune, Yune and June cried, and even Old Liu's eyes were wet. I was also sad. The five of them had been my family for the past month. I tried to look cheerful and promised I would go visit them, and assured them that they would be invited back to Prince Yong's house.

After they had left, I was alone in Yong Hui Ge. I didn't know what I was supposed to do. My rabbit and my dove were resting quietly in their cages, and I didn't want to bother them. I lay on my bed and moped for a long time, thinking I'd probably made a mistake in accepting the invitation. Would I have the chance to meet Jeng in the near future? The brothers weren't enemies yet, so there was a chance that Jeng could come to his brother's house one day. But what if he wouldn't? When should I pay Priest Wang another visit? I did not tell anyone in the circus about the Taoist monk, and I didn't know whether he would be able to find me even if he got my note.

In the midst of my brooding, a maid came in to announce that Lady Nian would like me to show her my magic tricks. I jumped up and dressed in my new clothes and did my hair and makeup. Then I carried my props, including my rabbit and dove, and followed the maid to the ladies' living quarters, located in the middle of the estate. The housing complex was impressive with its open courtyard in the middle. It was named Yong Fu Ge—Pavilion of Harmony and Happiness—and the *fujins* lived there.

Before he became the emperor, Prince Yong had four wives, and Lady Nian was believed to be his favorite. The rumor was evidently true because Lady Nian's unit not only had its own entrance but also a private garden neatly planted with orchids of varying colors. The living room was not as sumptuous as I had expected. It wasn't bright as it was designed to be—sunshine was first blocked by the low eave, and next, filtered through the paper window panes. A vase of white orchids with long slender leaves decorated a marble tea table. Chinese paintings and calligraphy hung on the walls.

Lady Nian was sitting in a recliner the size of small bed in front of the tea table. Influenced by the popular TV show *Empresses in the Palace,* I had expected to see a robust shrew, and was unprepared for the delicate and shy pretty girl. She wore a lilac brocade

266

gown and a silk peony on her hair board. She was supposed to be in her early twenties at the time, but she looked at most eighteen to me. Her protruding belly looked oddly incoherent with her young face.

I couldn't believe the person in front of me was the evil creature who would persecute every woman her husband was fond of. The innocent face showed no guile. Lady Nian's first name was Silan, meaning orchid, and indeed, I could draw resemblance between her childlike face and the pot of fresh, delicate flowers on the table. I had the urge to keep her in a safe place and protect her from harsh weather. Historian's conjecture for Prince Yong's favoritism was that Lady Nian was the sister of General Gengyao Nian, an important political ally to the prince. But I doubted any man would need any reason to love her, and I was sure that Prince Yong's devotion to her was genuine and had nothing to do with her brother at all.

I bent my knees and greeted the lady. "What can I do for you, my lady?"

Lady Nian smiled. "Call me Silan."

"Thank you." I already liked the girl. Her voice was so gentle.

"I wasn't able to see your show yesterday because of my condition. Would you like to show me your tricks?"

"It would be my pleasure," I said, and with the help of the maids, I set up the props on a table. "What would you like to see first?"

"I heard that the rabbit trick was the best. Could you do that?"

"Of course."

Although she looked physically tired, Silan watched the show with such intense concentration that I was very much flattered.

She was very smart. After only seeing the trick twice, she guessed where the rabbit came from. "You must've hidden it under the table."

Lady Nian was delighted by the dove trick as well and had me do it twice. When I offered to do it a third time she refused, saying the bird had to rest.

After I a few card tricks, the lady had the maids bring us a plate of pears for refreshment. I bit into a pear and she asked me questions.

"How long have you been a performer?"

"Since I was a child," I answered. It wasn't really a lie, because the first time I did a card trick in public was in front of my first-grade class.

"Did you perform all day?"

"No, no more than half a day."

"What else do you do when you aren't performing?"

"Well, I practice. I go to the shops and do housework," I said, wondering why she was so inquisitive.

"I wish I had the freedom you have," Lady Nian said. "Most of my time is spent here at home."

The sadness in her voice made me pity her. Most female members of wealthy families had stayed at home before the twentieth century. It was probably the reason for their poor health as well.

"I like to stay home, too," I said in an effort to comfort the girl. "There are fun things you can do, right? Like calligraphy, painting and music."

"That's true, but that's pretty much it. I would like to go shopping."

"You never go shopping?"

"Rarely. They take me to the shops in a sedan chair sometimes. But I miss roaming on the streets."

"Roaming on the streets? Have you done it?"

"Of course." She smiled sweetly. "I did it quite a few times, years ago, when I was still a child. They wouldn't let me go alone. I had to beg. Often my brother or his friends would go with me. And we watched magic shows, too."

For a moment I wondered whether Jeng had taken her out, and jealousy pierced my heart.

When I stood up to leave, I said, "We could take a walk in the garden together if you like."

"Oh no, the doctor says it's better for me not to."

"Why?"

"I shouldn't excite the baby."

"That's nonsense," I said. "Light exercise is good for babies."

"That's what I think, but the prince wants me to be really careful this time."

The girl went silent after that comment. I recalled that Lady Nian had lost her first born in January of that year, when the infant had been only seven months old, and my heart clenched for her. A mother losing a child was the worst pain imaginable.

"The prince is very considerate," I said.

Silan smiled shyly. "Yes, he is."

On my way out of the Pavilion of Harmony and Happiness, I kept thinking about Lady Nian. A delicate orchid living among luxury and loved by a future emperor, and yet she was hardly happy. The poor woman had spent most of her short, married life bearing Prince Yong's children and grieving their deaths. She had given birth to three sons and one daughter, but all of them died in infancy or early childhood. The child she was carrying at the moment would only live for seven years, and he would be her longest-surviving son. I sighed as I glanced over the grand houses and beautiful gardens around me. What use was of any of this to Lady Nian, who was confined to her room most of the time? I not only pitied Nian, but also Prince Yong—his power and wealth couldn't save his beloved woman and their children.

SINCE I WAS pretty much free for the rest of the day, I strolled into the Garden of Harmony and Peace after I had left Lady Nian. The fragrance of sweet olive permeated the air, reminding me again that it was the middle of autumn. I was admiring the various chrysanthemums on the side of the path when I heard shouts behind me, and before I knew it, a boy stumbled into me and fell.

I helped him up and saw a tearful face.

"Are you all right, child?"

The gravel had scraped the skin of his hands and he was smeared with blood, but the child stood up and went on running. He stopped and turned to me. "Please, don't tell them you saw me!"

He hid behind a large stone turtle. I hardly had time to make sense of what was happening when two adults, a maid and a man servant, came running in my direction, shouting, "Don't run!"

When they saw me, they stopped. "Where did the child go?"

I fought the urge to look at the spot where the child was hiding and pointed towards the end of the path. "That way."

The two went on down the path.

When their steps had faded, I went over to the stone turtle. The child was crouching behind it, his hands holding his knees, and his head bent low.

"They're gone. You can come out now."

When he heard it was me, he stood up. He looked quite adorable with his tearful eyes and his half-shaven head. "Thank you for helping me."

I sat down next to him and took out a handkerchief to wipe the blood off his hands. "Who are you? And why are you running away?"

The child merely sobbed, snot and tears running down his face.

My heart melted. He was probably a child eunuch who had been mistreated.

I put my arm around him and patted him.

271

"Did somebody beat you?" I asked gently.

The child shook his head.

"Did you do something bad?"

The child wouldn't respond.

"What did you do?"

"I don't know how to do math."

"What?" I was quite amused by the answer. I had thought that math was a torment of the modern times.

"Are you a eunuch?"

The child darted a look at me, as if I had insulted him. "I'm not!"

"Who are you, then?"

He was about to speak when a man suddenly materialized in front of us, he was no other than Prince Yong.

Seeing the man, the boy dropped on his knees immediately. "Father Prince!"

I bent my right knee and curtsied.

Without a word the prince lifted his hand and slapped the boy across the cheek, instantly leaving a red handprint. More tears rolled down his little face.

I couldn't stand it. Such a violent person wasn't fit to be a father! I went over to the boy and hugged him. Then I spoke to the prince with indignation, "How can you treat a child like this?"

The prince reared back, apparently unaccustomed to having a woman question him. Then he said to me coldly, "He ran away from his duty."

"Duty? What duty? He's just a little boy!"

"His duty is to acquire knowledge by studying."

"But I don't want to learn math, Father," the child entreated. "I promise I'll recite the Four Books and Five Classics and copy the entire collection of Tang Poetry. But please, spare me from math! I can't do it! My head hurts!"

"Shut up! How dare you bargain with me? Every child of the imperial family has to learn math. It's an order from His Majesty."

He grabbed the boy's arm and dragged him away. I was horrified by what I saw, even though I knew it was usual for a father to treat a disobedient child like that in this time period.

"Wait, please!" I ran after them. "Perhaps I can help."

Prince Yong turned. "What do you mean you can help?"

"I know some math," I said. "And I have tutored children before."

"That's quite unnecessary," the prince said. "Hongli has the best tutor in Jing city."

"Hongli?" I murmured. Hongli was the name of Emperor Qianlong. I stood in awe, staring at the back of the little child stumbling behind his father. Although I didn't have good opinions about the father, like most of the Chinese, I adored the son, who would become not only a loving emperor, but also an accomplished artist and poet.

THAT EVENING, I returned to Yong Hui Ge after having had dinner with the servants. I was thinking about how to spend the night alone, having neither TV nor the internet, when I heard a tap on my window. It was Prince Yong.

I opened the door and saluted him, keeping my head low so I didn't have to face him. I felt uneasy being alone with him, knowing his actions were indeed as unpredictable as Kangxi had once commented.

"Do you have a moment?" He sounded gentle and agreeable, very different from the stern father from earlier.

"Sure," I said tersely, wondering how I could refuse to let him into my room.

"What's the matter?" he asked. "Don't tell me you're mad because of Hongli."

"Not at all," I lied and avoided the subject. "Do you wish to see tricks?"

He smiled. "You're a worm in my stomach."

I cringed at the expression, which meant "you read my mind." Then I gathered my props and followed him to the prayer room next door.

He told me to leave my props alone, then he pulled out a palm-sized, gold-inlaid lacquer box from his sleeve and gave it to me.

"What is it?" I asked nervously.

He smiled. "Open it and you'll see."

I untied the ribbon and opened the lid reluctantly, afraid that the box would contain a ring of some sort.

When I saw the contents in the box, I let out a sigh of relief. It was a deck of cards—silly me!

I spread the cards on the table, delight and astonishment spreading through me. They weren't the coarsely made cards I had acquired from the market place. These cards were made of finer paper, painted with beautiful portraits and written with elegant poems. I looked at them carefully and realized that they were characters from the classical legend *Outlaws of the Marsh*. I read the familiar names of the heroes aloud. *Leopard Head Lin Chong, Tattooed Dragon Shi Jin, Black Tornado Li Kui, Rowdy Monk Lu Zhishen* . . . On top of each card, it stated the monetary value in coins and on the side was a line of poem.

"How exquisite!" I exclaimed.

"These are hand-drawn by Mr. Hongshou Chen."

My jaw dropped. "The Hongshou Chen from the Ming dynasty?" His paintings were worth millions a piece in the modern time.

He nodded proudly.

"How did you get hold of this?" As soon as I asked the question, I realized it was silly. I had forgotten that I was speaking to a prince.

He shrugged. "Someone gave it to me."

He let me indulge in the art of Hongshou Chen for a moment longer, then he reminded me of his purpose.

My hands actually shook now that I was aware of the value of these cards. Not only that, the size of the cards was a bit different. They were longer and narrower than the cards I was used to. But I managed to pull off some tricks.

The prince clapped his hands at the end of a trick. "I love it! Can you teach me how to do it?"

"Sure," I said, impressed by his passion for magic. "Are you going to show it to the emperor?"

"No," he said, his cheeks reddening. "Actually, I want to show it to my mother."

"You mean Lady Uya?"

He nodded. "Yes, she likes magic tricks."

"Really? Why didn't she come the other day?" I asked, a malicious bite in my tone.

"Oh, uh," he stammered, looking embarrassed. "She wasn't feeling well."

I glanced down at the cards, unsure if I should comfort him. The prince had not been raised by Lady Uya, which was the main reason for their estranged relationship.

I began the lesson by teaching him the basics—holding, flipping, and spinning cards.

IT WAS QUITE a surprise when a couple days after I had encountered the little child, I received a letter from him.

Thank you for your help the other day. Would you care to meet me at the same place again at four hours past noon?

The handwriting was elegant, almost too good to be written by a child, and it was signed by Hongli.

When I showed up at the same spot where I had met the little prince, he was already waiting. This time, he had a parcel next to him. He beckoned me to sit and opened the parcel. Inside was a stack of paper with drawings of geometry.

"I need help with these," he pleaded, his small face schooled in a frown.

I took the paper and looked at the problems. Most of them were simple proofs from high-school geometry, but I hadn't encountered them for at least ten years. Math wasn't my favorite subject, either, but I had gotten decent grades on it, thanks to my father.

"Let me see," I sat down on a bench, picked a problem that looked familiar, and tackled it.

It was a simple problem that was based on the fact that an exterior angle of a triangle was equal to the sum of the opposite interior angles. After I was done, the little prince was very impressed.

"I have to go. Otherwise they'll be looking for me again. But do the rest for me, okay?"

"What? You want me to *do* it for you, instead of teaching you?" I looked at him, my mouth agape. "That's cheating. And what if your dad finds out?"

"Shh." He put two fingers on his lips. "He won't. He's too busy to check my homework anyway."

"But—" I said doubtfully. "Don't you wish to learn?"

"No!" The child wrinkled his nose. "I would rather compose a hundred poems than do a math problem."

I stifled a laugh. The future emperor sounded no different from an average child in the twenty-first century. "Look, it's easier for me to do your homework than to teach you how to do it, but I don't want you to get in trouble."

He looked up at me with pleading eyes. "I promise I'll study the solutions later and make sure I understand them."

At the end I yielded to the child's stubbornness, although I knew I wasn't doing the right thing. "When do you need them?"

The little prince grinned. "Tomorrow."

My mouth fell open again. "You expect me to finish all of these in one day?"

"But you said you were a tutor before!"

"I was a tutor, not a genius! I need at least three days."

"All right. But no more than that. I'm already late on these."

He turned and walked away but returned after a few steps. "Here, this is for you." He took out an object wrapped neatly in a piece of paper and put it into my hands.

"What is it?" I asked, guessing it was some sort of pastry from the scent.

"A mooncake," he said. "Father gave it to me. It's a gift from Grandfather Emperor."

"Then you should keep it!"

"It's okay. I had it last year. Thanks for your help."

He was such a sweet, yet beguiling, child. I grinned as he darted away like a squirrel.

CHAPTER 16

THE DAYS PASSED quickly during my stay in Prince Yong's house. I spent most of my mornings with Lady Nian, and in the evenings, Prince Yong would sometimes come by to learn magic tricks. My friendship with the lady grew. Since the day we met, she treated me as her own sister. She was not particularly interested in my magic tricks, but she was lonely and craved my companionship. Every time we met, she did her best to keep me from leaving. She taught me the Go chess game, so I could play with her. Knowing that my handwriting wasn't that good, she also taught me calligraphy. And when she had enough energy, she even played the *zheng*—Chinese zither—and sang for me.

One day after playing the classical piece *High Mountain and Flowing Water*, she asked me, "Do you know why the piece was named so?"

I shook my head.

"The musician Boya from 700BC was playing the zheng in the wilderness one day, when a woodcutter came to listen, telling him the music made him see a lofty mountain and flowing water. Boya and the woodcutter instantly became friends. When the woodcutter died, Boya smashed his zheng, proclaiming that it would be pointless to play it anymore since no one would be able to truly understand his music." She seemed pensive for a moment. "A soulmate is hard to find."

"I'm sure Prince Yong appreciates your talents."

Lady Nian blushed at my comment.

"Did you know him since you were a child?"

Lady Nian shook her head. "Not really. I met him a few years back, when I was fifteen. He invited my brother and I to the Garden of Perfect Brightness, and he proposed to me soon after that."

"Wow. Sounds like love at first sight!"

Her face turned crimson again. "Honestly, I barely looked at him that day, and really don't think he had the chance to look at me, either."

"Why didn't you look at him? Were you afraid of him?"

She nodded with a smile. "Quite so. He was so serious all the time. Unlike his brother Jeng, who—" She stopped abruptly.

I couldn't help my curiosity. "What about Prince Jeng?"

She hesitated for a moment, then she lowered her voice as if not wanting the maids to overhear her. "Jeng is more easygoing."

"Do you know him well?"

"Yes. He used to practice archery with my brother."

It was true then, Jeng and Lady Nian were friends before. My heart raced. Perhaps Lady Nian could help me meet Jeng?

"I heard he was not only smart, but fearless as well."

She smiled at the compliment. "It's true. He's good at so many things. A poet and a fighter."

A poet? I didn't know Jeng had that talent. Did he compose poems for her? I wanted to ask but Silan had become pensive after that, as if dwelling on her memories of Jeng. Her eyes were so bright and her face so genuinely happy that I had very little doubt that she was fond of him. Despite our friendship, I was suddenly intensely jealous towards her. She was a rare beauty and had certainly occupied Jeng's heart for quite some time.

But I quickly repressed my irrational feeling. "I would love to meet him one day. Does he come here often?"

The smile disappeared from her face. "He seldom does."

"Can't you invite him to dinner or something?"

She shook her head. "He's not in Jing City and probably won't be back until winter."

I was going to suggest she invite Jeng to a dinner once he returned, but I resisted, not wanting to appear too eager and arouse any suspicion.

ONE AFTERNOON, I was taking a nap when I heard an urgent knocking on my door. It was a servant in the house. "You're wanted by Prince Yong."

I quickly dressed, wondering why I was wanted at this time of the day, and wondering whether I needed to take my magic box with me. I decided not to take it since the servant said he had received no instructions regarding it.

I followed the servant into the Hall of Harmony and Peace, where I had performed with the circus but a couple weeks ago. The prince's study was right next to the main hall.

As soon as I entered the study, I knew I was in trouble, for there was Hongli, kneeling in front of his father. Prince Yong's face was absolutely wooden the moment I walked in. He gave me a cold glance and continued to look at the stack of paper in front of him.

I went next to the little prince and saluted the master of the house. "Your servant Julie wishes the prince wellness and health."

The prince looked up from his desk. "Do you know why I summoned you here?"

I shook my head slowly, doing my best to pretend. "Would Your Excellency wish to see tricks? I should've brought my props—"

The prince slammed on the desktop. "Stop playing dumb! And stop playing tricks on me!"

I took a deep breath and reminded myself to stay calm. "I beg your forgiveness, Your Excellency. But your servant hasn't played any tricks on you."

"Oh, really? Then what are these?" He threw the papers on the floor in front of me.

I bent slowly and picked them up, knowing that they were the homework that I had done for Hongli.

My heart beat frantically, but I forced a smile and said as calmly as possible, "Ah, these. I see. I helped the little prince with a few problems."

The prince sneered. "Helped? You did them for him. And not just a few problems!"

"I beg your pardon. I was only trying to help!"

He ignored me. "What you did was unforgivable. The master at the Imperial School was impressed with Hongli's improvement on his math skills, and he reported it to the emperor. The emperor was impressed, too. He summoned me to the palace today and told me he would like to give Hongli some advanced math problems to do. And guess what? The little rascal can't do any of them! If you hadn't done those problems for him, then he wouldn't have gotten into this mess!"

He stopped talking in order to catch his breath.

I kowtowed one after another, asking for forgiveness. My head hurt even though I did my best not to hit the floor. Finally, the prince stopped me.

"Only the emperor and some math masters could solve these problems, and Hongli has to finish them in three days. Oh heavens, we're in trouble!"

"Perhaps his majesty would forgive Hongli. After all, he's just a little child."

He looked at me sharply. "The emperor hates being deceived. And even if he would forgive Hongli, he would not forgive me. He'll blame me for not instructing my child properly. My title of prince could be forever removed!"

I gasped. That was the equivalent of a death sentence to a prince. Would the consequences really be so serious? Was he being paranoid?

"Hongli hasn't had the honor of meeting his Grandfather Emperor yet, and I was hoping he would have the chance soon," Prince Four continued. "But look what you've done to us!"

I apologized again. "I'm sorry, Prince. I deserve to be punished!"

"Punish? What's the point of punishing you?" he said with a derisive smile. "Just pack and go! Don't let me see you again. I should've known better than to keep a street performer, a trickster, on my property."

Tears poured out of my eyes. I didn't care much what the Fourth Prince thought of me, but the fact that I had gotten him and his family in trouble unsettled me. "Please don't dismiss me like this, Prince! Let me amend my fault! Let me help!"

The prince slammed his palm on the desk again. "Enough! You and your help. Who do you think you are? You think your bag of tricks will work this time?"

He then stood up and walked in front of his son, who was still kneeling on the side. "You may get up now, but you are not allowed to leave this room until you solve the problems!"

After that, he stomped out of the room.

I pitied the boy. Although he was reluctant to learn math, he was quite intelligent. His handwriting was ten times better than mine, and he could indeed recite the entire collection of Tang poetry.

I went to him and patted him on the head. "Little prince, I'm sorry. You take care of yourself!"

Hongli looked up with tearful eyes. "Are you really leaving me?"

I sighed. "You heard your father."

"But if you go, then we're dead for sure!"

I paused. "What do you want me to do?"

"I'm sure Father wants you to help me, too. Otherwise, he wouldn't have summoned you here. He would just order you leave his house."

"Good point." I nodded, impressed by the boy's logical reasoning. "What do you want me to do then?"

"You must solve those problems!" He pointed to the desk, where a sheet of paper was placed in the center under a marble paperweight.

I hesitated. Should I walk away, or should I stay? If what Prince Yong had said was true, that his title of prince would be removed, then it would be good for Jeng, wouldn't it? But what about Hongli? I had grown fond of him. Despite his aversion to math, he was a good child. He always brought me little presents, usually his favorite sweets or fruits, to thank me for my help. I sighed as I met the child's pleading eyes, then I sat down and looked at his assignment.

There was a total of twelve problems, including algebra and geometry. A few solving equations and word problems were relatively easy, but some of the geometric and trigonometric problems were pretty advanced. I explained to Hongli how to solve the first few problems, and thankfully, the child wasn't as ignorant in math as he appeared to be. And apparently, he did study because he was able to understand my explanations quickly. I groaned when I saw the last problem—prove the Gogoo (Pythagorean) Theorem using three different ways. Did the emperor really expect a ten-year-old child to be able to do this?

Proofs were not my strong point, but I remembered learning the Pythagorean Theorem in high school and had liked it. I recalled a right triangle with three sides—legs were a and b, and c was the hypotenuse. The square of a plus the square of b equaled the square of c. I also remembered reading the history of the theorem. It was published by Pythagoras in Greek around 500 BC, although it had been recorded in the Chinese math texts 1000 BC and had been known to the Babylonians in 1900 BC. My high-school textbook had mentioned that there were about five hundred different proofs in the world, and the earliest was by Euclid around 300 BC.

My high-school textbook had shown the three easiest proofs, one by the Chinese scholar Zhao, another by the Indian scholar Bhaskara, and the third one by U.S. president James Garfield. I had memorized them at the time for the exam but couldn't recall anything at the moment.

"You don't know how to do it?" Hongli asked, looking disappointed.

"Oh, I've got it," I forced a smile. "Don't worry. I just need time to think."

"You'd better hurry because we don't have much time."

"Okay," I said, feeling annoyed by his demanding tone. "You have to participate, too. Don't just wait for me. Did your master ever show you how to prove the Gogoo Theorem?"

He shook his head. "I don't remember."

"Can I take a look at your math textbook?"

"I don't have any. The master has it."

"Do you have any math books at all in this house?"

"Father Prince might have some," the child said, and looked through the books on Prince Yong's bookshelf.

Soon he found a couple of books related to math. One was a translation of *Synopsis Mathematica,* written and brought to China by the Belgian scholar Antoine Thomas. It was as thick as an encyclopedia and contained geometric figures and algebra equations. Emperor Kangxi had scribes copy them for his subordinates and children to study. Another one was *Essence of Mathematics*, mainly a summary of some mathematical findings in China and in the western countries, compiled by Emperor

Kangxi himself, who was obviously a mathematical zealot.

"You don't have anything that is old, like, written a thousand years ago?"

Hongli thought about it, went to another bookshelf where his father kept classical texts, and picked some books. "Father says these were written by Ancient Han Chinese mathematicians."

One was titled *Zhou Bi Mathematical Scripts*. A book written by the fourth son of the King of the Zhou dynasty, at around 1000 BC. The other one titled *Commentaries on Zhou Bi Mathematical Scripts* written by a Zhao Shuang from the Three Kingdoms dynasty, which was around 300 AD. *Zhao Shuang*. I read the name aloud several times and something clicked. He was the guy who had the earliest proof of the theorem.

I quickly looked at Zhao's proof. It was actually quite easy to follow. I explained to the little prince and, driven not by curiosity but by fear and worry, he learned it fairly quickly as well. I flipped through the other books for more proofs but didn't find any.

"I have to go," I said to Hongli. "Your father will return, and I don't think he wants to see me here. But I'll come back as soon as I figure out two more ways. Keep thinking. Do the other problems, I'll help you when I come back."

The child nodded reluctantly, without a smile.

As soon as I returned to my room, I sat down at my table and drew some triangles. I reproduced Zhao Shuang's proof of the theorem over and over again, trying to remember other methods I had seen. Most of the proofs involved rearranging the triangles and making a new figure such as the square, parallelogram, and trapezoid. Then you would write an equation. On one side of the equation you would find the area of the new figure using the known formulas, while on the other side, sum up the areas of the smaller figures that made up the large one, which usually contained right triangles. The ingenuity lay on how to construct these larger figures so that the final equation would have squares of all sides. I racked my brain while drawing one picture after another. But none worked. I gave up when my oil lamp burned out around midnight.

The next day, Lady Nian summoned me to her unit again. I did not tell the kind woman what had happened since I didn't want to distress her. But I told her that I would be leaving the estate soon. She was quite disappointed by the news, and I had to comfort her by promising to come back to see her.

It wasn't until the night before the due date when I finally remembered more proofs, including Bhaskara's, Garfield's, and Euclid's. I went to Prince Yong's study, and there I found Hongli sitting at his father's desk, his head resting on top of a pile of paper, snoring softly.

I picked up a sheet among the pile, and saw the solutions written neatly below each problem. The child had been studying, I smiled. And to my surprise, the little prince had also figured out a new way of proving the Pythagorean Theorem. Within a large right triangle, he added a line from the vertex of the right angle and the line was perpendicular to the hypotenuse, or the side opposite to the angle. I remembered seeing this method. Pleased, I patted gently on the child's shoulder, waking him.

Hongli started. "Yes, Your Majesty!"

"It's only me, little prince." I smiled at the child, who looked a lot thinner than he had three days ago. His eyes also had visible dark rings around them, proving his lack of sleep.

"You're finally here!" He broke into a smile. "I've got one proof besides Zhao's. Still need one more!"

"Did you figure this out by yourself?" I asked, pointing at the proof.

"Yes, but I don't even know how I came up with the idea." The little prince smiled. "I must've seen it in a dream."

"No, it wasn't a dream. It's inspiration." I pinched his pale cheek. "It happens when you keep thinking about something for a long time."

I sat down and showed Hongli the three methods—Euclid, Bhaskara, and Garfield. The prince listened attentively, and this time, he was obviously more interested in the problem than he had been three days before. He grinned up at me when he understood each proof, showing his appreciation.

"You're a genius!" the child said to me after I had finished.

I laughed. "No, I'm not. To tell the truth, I didn't invent any of these."

"Who did?"

"Mathematicians from foreign countries," I said.

"Foreigners? Where are they? How do you know them?"

"Oh." I pondered on that for a moment. "I don't know them. But I learned it from—"

"From whom?"

"From my father."

"Your father? Is he a foreigner?"

"Uh, yeah, sort of." I avoided the child's eyes.

"Where is he? Is he in the Jing city?"

"He used to be, but he isn't now."

"No wonder you're so smart."

I was flattered by the compliment but pretended to be nonchalant. "It has nothing to do with being smart or not, little prince. If you spend more time on the subject, you'll do well. It isn't half as hard as . . ."

I wanted to say "as ruling a country" but stopped short. Voices came from outside.

"Well, I'd better go, little prince. And I wish you luck!"

The child looked as if he would cry, but he held his tears and stood up. I went to him and hugged him before I left.

CHAPTER 17

I LEFT THE House of Prince Yong the following morning. I didn't think saying goodbye to the prince was necessary since he was angry with me and probably didn't want to see me again. But I did leave a note on the table, thanking him for being a generous host in the past month, and apologizing for the trouble I had caused.

My only choice at the moment was to go back to the circus. The market square looked the same, but the stage in the center was hardly recognizable. It was now fenced, with shades above the seating area. The place looked like a small open theater. A teenage boy stood at the entrance, holding a jar for coins. They were charging for admission now! I grinned. I had made the suggestion to Old Liu, but he had been reluctant to adopt it.

"I'm here to see Mr. Chen," I told the boy.

"No free shows," he said, looking at me skeptically.

What a shrewd boy! I took a coin out of my purse.

But before I gave it to the child, Yune had spotted me and squealed with delight. "Julie!"

The child apologized and let me in.

"How nice of you to come back and visit!" Yune took my hands and looked at me, all smiling.

"No, I'm not here to visit," I said. "I was banned from the prince's estate."

"Why?" Yune pulled me into the house, which had also been remodeled.

I didn't feel the need to explain the whole situation to the girl, so I said, "He thinks it's a bad influence on his children to have a street performer in his house."

"That's outrageous!"

"That's how rich people are," I said. "They have the power to make you their guest or enemy depending on how they feel."

"Don't worry, sister, you're always welcome here!"

I WAS GLAD to be on stage again, doing my magic tricks. Based on the techniques of Harry Houdini, the famous magician of the twentieth century, I also developed my own version of walking through a wall. It was a fairly simple illusion that required the help of divider screens and a trapdoor beneath a rug.

In order to have more privacy and convenience, I also rented a room in a nearby *hutong*, although I still ate at the circus. After a long day's hard work, the troupe enjoyed their short evenings. Old Chen and Young Chen would normally drink in the house or visit some local taverns. June and Yune sometimes watched opera performed on the streets. I didn't care for the opera and preferred staying home or taking walks along the alleys. I liked seeing the capital city in its still original state— streets without any motor vehicles and less crowds than in modern times. When I walked past a residential area, I didn't hear the noise of radio or TV. I heard music from playing erhu and the flute and voices of real people. Chatter and quarrels filled the air, along with clinking of rice bowls and clanking of pots.

I had stayed in Beijing on and off for many years, but it was the first time I ever lived in a hutong as it was pretty rare in modern times. Hutong was a Manchu word for water well, although the form of residential area had existed long before the Manchus ruled China. Each hutong was an alley formed by joined *siheyuan*—a community of four buildings and a courtyard. I couldn't say I loved living in a siheyuan, but the experience was quite interesting. You didn't have as much privacy living in a hutong as you did living in a condominium, and the sense of community was much greater. You didn't have to guess what your neighbors were having for dinner by the smell in their kitchens, because they often ate in the courtyard and you could see the food on their tables. Men and children even bathed in the courtyard since that was where the well was located.

I hadn't had a bath since I had left the prince's house three days before. All I could do was take a basin of water to my room and clean myself with a damp towel. It was the perfect time to do it since no one else was using the well. I was about fetch my basin when the neighboring kids ran towards me. "Julie, show us some tricks!"

I couldn't refuse. These kids couldn't afford to go to the shows, not since Old Chen had fenced up his theater. So, I did some coin tricks to satisfy their curiosity. They had seen the tricks before, and some of them even guessed how I did them, but they still liked them, and clapped their hands at the end. I guessed it was because at the time entertainment was so scarce. After that, they went back to where they had been before seeing me, which was in front of Mr. Yang's house across the courtyard.

I closed the window and the door but could still hear Mr. Yang's voice. Mr. Yang, the old man who had been a clerk at the town hall in his early years, was telling the tale of *Wushong Beats the Tiger* from the classic literature *Outlaws of the Marsh*. Even though I had heard him telling it a dozen times already, and could pretty much predict his next sentence, his audience—some of them adults—still gasped when he got to the part where "suddenly a roar came from the dark bushes next to him, and he was confronted by a giant beast—a tiger with eyes as large and bright as lanterns, and teeth the size of daggers." Of course, the reaction was partly credited to Mr. Yang's story-telling skills, his deliberate alternation of tones, masterful delivery of the sense of danger, and vivid descriptions of the tiger. The audience listened to the story over and over again, knowing every detail of the plot, but still responded to it with laughter and sighs.

It wasn't completely dark yet, but I had nothing else to do. Since it was too early to go to bed, I sat down at my desk to practice calligraphy. I had brought home with me a roll of rice paper, some brush pens, and an ink box—gifts from Lady Nian. I had barely finished a line when I heard an old man singing. I didn't pay attention to it since it was usual to hear men sing in the evenings, especially when they got drunk. The singing became louder and louder, presumably the man had come into our siheyuan. Soon, it was right next to my window and I heard the words distinctly. *"Light is shadow / shadow is light."* I stopped writing and listened attentively for his next line. Then I heard Mr. Yang telling the singer to go away. "We don't have money, can't afford your service." I lifted the curtain to a tiny gap and saw an old man in a beige robe and black hat, holding a sword in one hand and a wine gourd in another. It was just a drunk man. But the man turned at the same moment I let go of the curtain. I recognized the hat that looked like a sloping roof, and the yin-yang emblem on it. A Taoist priest? As my heart started to race, the man sang again, *"The past and the future are in unity / Yin and Yang are two halves of the same circle / Today was tomorrow and tomorrow will be yesterday / Morning and night are illusions of Light and Shadow!"*

I opened the door and ran after him. "Hey Mister, I mean, Master, please wait!"

The moment he turned to look at me, I gasped. Despite his white goatee and white eyebrows, this old man bore a striking resemblance to Dong. He had the same height and the same build. But I looked again and saw the differences. The priest's eye sockets were darker and deeper, and his forehead and cheeks were thinner and full of wrinkles.

"What is wanted from an old monk?" His voice was thin and squeaky, and his archaic way of speaking was very different from Dong's.

"Are you Priest Wang from the Temple of Light and Shadow?" I asked, lowering my voice.

"I sure am." He nodded slightly.

I was so happy that I almost hugged him, but I controlled my impulse. "Did you get my note?"

"What note?"

"I went to the temple a month ago, looking for you."

The priest nodded. "I did indeed receive a note. Are you the visitor?"

"Yes, I'm Julie Bird, I've come a long way to meet you!" I could hardly stifle my excitement. "Could you please, please come inside my room? I have something important to tell you!"

He shook his head. "I'm afraid I can't. It's improper for me to be in the same room with a young woman. Why can't you speak to me right here?"

I looked around me, the crowd in front of Mr. Yang's house had dispersed, but there were still people sitting in the courtyard, and some of them were already watching me curiously. The woman whose unit was closest to where I stood poked her head from the door.

I thought quickly of a place where we would get more privacy, and the first thing came up was the circus's theater. There would be plenty of space there, even if the occupants were back.

We headed towards the theater, which was only a few hutongs away. I opened the gate of the seating area and we went inside. We sat down on a bench before I started to tell him the whole story, starting from how I met Prince Jeng, to how we met Dong, his own descendant, and how I ended up being where I was.

Although he looked skeptical, the priest was undoubtedly astonished by my story.

"Are you saying that you're from the future?" He squinted as he looked me over. "That indeed explains your strange accent and manner."

It wasn't a compliment, but I was glad that he seemed to believe me.

He looked around once again to make sure no one was nearby before asking me, "So the fourth prince will inherit the throne?"

I nodded, realizing that it was quite a piece of information. No one was supposed to know about it.

"And he will kill and imprison many of his brothers who oppose him, including Prince Jeng, his full sibling."

"That's unimaginable." He looked concerned and fearful. "Did you tell anyone else about it?"

"Well, it's no secret in the future, but I haven't told anyone other than you in the present time."

"Good, good." He nodded. "How long have you been here in this century?"

"About three months already."

"That long? Why didn't you contact me right away?"

"It's a long story." I went on to tell him about my days living with Meng's family, how Juhua forced me to be the bride of her mentally incapacitated child, and how I escaped and ended up with the circus. I also told him that I lived in the House of Prince Yong for a month.

I must've sounded regretful about being dismissed by the prince, since the priest said, "It's good that you left his house. You wouldn't have had a chance to leave otherwise."

I felt much better about the experience hearing that. "Actually, I could've avoided it altogether. Before he invited me, I went to the Temple of Light and Shadow to look for you. But you weren't there."

"Yes, I was traveling to beg for donation," the priest said. "That's how I make my living. Not entirely begging but doing some magic shows in exchange for money."

Tao priests originated from wizards. Their magic was more like sorcery—expelling evil spirits, making longevity pills, developing inner strength that led to eternal youth, and turning metal into gold, etc.

"But I'm glad we finally met," I said.

He nodded solemnly. "My descendent will be working on my unfinished business three hundred years later?"

"Yes, and he's doing a darn good job. He knows how to control the direction and precision of the travel. This time for example, I was off by only three months."

I was hoping he would smile at Dong's accomplishment, but he sighed instead. "I was off by three hundred years, and the wrong direction? Unbelievable! Shameful!"

"Well, failure is the mother of success," I mumbled the Chinese adage in order to comfort the priest, who probably didn't like being reminded of his mistake, whether he made it in the past or in the future.

"Really?" The priest thought for a moment. "But since you're here before I make the mistake, I can avoid it all together."

I blinked as I realized the paradox. That was very true.

Before he dwelled on the paradox, I added quickly. "I don't have much time and really need to get in touch with Prince Jeng when he returns. Could you find me employment in his house or the palace?"

The priest shot a glance at me. "What makes you think that I have the power or means to do that? I'm just a commoner."

His answer was completely unexpected. Dong had convinced me that his ancestor would be able to help me, and for months he had been my only hope.

"Are you saying that you don't know how? Dong said you had connections with the imperial families!"

"I do not know how my descendant gets that idea." He paused.

What was going on? Could it be that Dong had mistaken the time frame? Why had he made such a mistake? "Then you must think of a way. Can you go to Xunjun Mansion to beg donation and perform magic? You could make acquaintances with his household members."

He shook his head. "Like his father, Prince Jeng only believes in Buddhism."

My heart sank. What was I supposed to do? How was I supposed to carry out my task?

Perhaps he was sorry to see my distress, because the priest said the next moment, "I could try to send you back if you wish."

I couldn't believe what he was saying. I had regretted coming to the eighteenth century, but not once did I wish to return without even seeing Jeng. Failure or success, I had to at least see him.

My gut warred at the priest's passivity. "You have to think of way to help me. You are the reason that I'm here. If you hadn't made that mistake, I wouldn't have come! And if you sent me back, you would be making that mistake again, because I am not going to tell you how to fix it."

The priest looked at me as if stunned by my anger. He sighed. "Can you wait until February?"

February was when the annual palace maid selection took place. "That will be my last resort. I really don't want to wait so long."

He nodded. "Give me some time then. I'll think of something."

I wasn't convinced, but I thanked him and told him I looked forward to hearing from him again, and I would look for him at the temple if I didn't see him within a month. He disappeared into the night, and I returned to my siheyuan.

CHAPTER 18

TEN DAYS PASSED before I saw the priest again. He came around noon on a day in the middle of October and we spoke outside the theater. He had contacted an old patron who was a relative of Lady Uya, and the lady happened to be looking for a maid.

"Lady Uya?" I couldn't believe my luck. "Prince Jeng's mother?"

"Yes, the mother of Prince Fourteen and Prince Four."

I smiled. I would have plenty of chances to see Jeng if I worked for his mother.

"Don't celebrate yet. I'm not promising anything. I'll recommend you, but it's up to them. They have high standards for maids in the palace."

I needed to learn lots of etiquette and manners. But that wasn't a problem because I had seen plenty of palace dramas and had practiced quite a bit with Dong. Besides, after living in Prince Four's house for a month, I'd observed the authentic way the maids behaved in imperial families.

"No problem," I said, feeling confident about myself.

The next day, the priest took me to House of Uya in the Inner City for the job interview. Uya was a prestigious Manchu surname, and Lady Uya's family belonged to the Plain Yellow Banner, an upper banner within the eight-banner military caste. Her grandfather had been the supervisor of the imperial kitchens, and her father had been the commander of the guard and held the title of first-class duke.

The entrance of the house wasn't as stately as the House of Prince Yong, but grand nonetheless—red pillars, red lanterns, and red doors with bronze studs. An elderly maid from the court was in the living room when we arrived. A servant introduced her as "*Momo* Shu." She was tall and stout, her eyebrows arched high, and her lips pressed into a thin line. As her sharp, narrow eyes looked me up and down, the momo frowned slightly. "Not the type I'm looking for," she said, looking eager to get rid of me.

I knew I wasn't supposed to speak, but it was my only chance and I couldn't just let it go without trying. "Please." I knelt on the floor. "Momo, I really need this job. My mother is ill, and I'm the only family she has. I'll do anything. Give me a chance. I learn fast. I promise!"

The momo hesitated.

305

"Aren't you making a living in the circus?" she asked.

"Not really." The lie felt thick on my tongue. "I've spent all I have on Mother's medical expenses. I've found her a good doctor but he's very expensive."

"Ah, a filial child," she looked at me, with a bit sympathy in her eyes. Then she sighed. "Okay, I'll train you for three days and see how much you progress before I consider others."

I kowtowed to her and thanked her.

The training started the next day. Momo Shu taught me everything from how to stand, sit and walk, to how to speak and how to kowtow. Even a maid had to walk with graceful steps, and when she spoke to her master, she shouldn't look up at all. There were other rules as well, such as whose orders I should take, and the proper answers to certain questions. I would always address myself as *nucai,* meaning slave or servant, in front of any imperial family member. I learned fairly quickly not only because I knew some basics, but also because Momo Shu held a bamboo stick in her hands and would use it liberally on me if I didn't follow her instructions.

Three days later, after my entire body ached, I passed the scrutiny of the momo, and she would take me to the palace the next day.

"You're going to be a maid in the living quarters of Lady Uya, and you will be working in her kitchen."

Oh great, I chucked inwardly. A CPA working as a kitchen maid for the emperor's concubine. What irony.

But I smiled and bowed to her. "I'm grateful for Momo's kindness."

I SAID GOODBYE to the circus family once again, telling them I had found my relatives, and would be living with them. Old Chen kindly asked me for the location of my destination, saying they would visit me one day, but I told them vaguely that it was one of the Peach Blossom Villages north of Jing City.

Momo Shu was waiting for me at the Inner City gate and we got in a horse carriage.

Through the flimsy curtain of the window I could see the Gate of Divine Might, the north gate of the Forbidden City, as we got close to it. The guards at the side entrance stopped us, but as soon as Momo Shu lifted the curtain and waved at them, they let us pass. As soon we were on the other side of the gate, the momo and I got off the carriage and walked to the Palace of Eternal Harmony, Lady Uya's living quarters. It was one of the six Eastern Palaces in the Inner Court. I was curious and nervous when I followed the momo and treaded along the high-walled alleys in the Inner Court. For a moment, the red walls and yellow roofs brought me back my memories of the past—or the future—and it felt like I was in a dream, or in a movie. Although it was the middle of October, I could still smell sweet olive in the air. The place wasn't exactly quiet; I could hear bouts of laughter and chatter from behind the walls. Eunuchs and maids scurried past as if in a great hurry, holding parcels or trays in hand. Sedan chairs also appeared often, and whenever they did, Momo gestured at me to retreat to the side and bow.

"Here it is." Momo Shu pointed to a splendid gateway flanked by two red walls and covered with yellow, ceramic, roof tiles. Under the roof, gold lettering on a blue plaque announced the name of the palace. We entered the courtyard through a double red gate, each with nine rows of nine gold studs, symbolizing the emperor's long-lasting status.

She led me to the maids' quarters so I could drop off my parcel, which contained some clothes and a few strings of silver coins and a couple of silver pieces. I had given most of my gold pieces to Old Chen, to thank him for helping me again. I wouldn't be needing money as much since room and board were both provided, but I kept some silver because according to Priest Wang, bribery was quite common in the court, and money was the best way to get things done.

As soon as I had changed into a maid's outfit, I was led to the kitchen. My rank was a level-two palace maid and my job was to wash everything from vegetables to cooking utensils. For the next two days, I either stood or squatted next to the well outside the kitchen and cleaned stuff. I wondered why I'd had to go through all the training at all since I seldom even talked to anyone. The third day around noon, when I was washing the pots, the maid who oversaw the household told me to take off my apron because one of the maids was ill and I needed to serve the lady. I took up a tray and followed the other maid to set the lunch table for Lady Uya.

A veranda connected the rooms in the complex, and in the center a garden with flowerbeds and potted plants brightened the area. I glanced at the garden, taking in as much as I could with my head bowed. A tall and somewhat plump woman wearing a turquoise gown embroidered with golden floral patterns and a black hat decorated with golden brooches fed fish in a pond, accompanied by maids. That must've been Lady Uya, the Fourth Empress of Kangxi, and the most favored out of his hundred-and-something imperial consorts. At the moment, Lady Uya held the rank of Imperial Noble Consort, the highest after Empress. She had born the emperor three sons and three daughters—more than a tenth of Kangxi's fifty-five children.

I didn't get a close look at the lady, but even from a distance, I could feel her regal beauty and charm. She was about sixty, but looked no more than forty, which was quite extraordinary at a time when beauty products weren't readily available.

My heart pounded with excitement but I took deep breaths to keep calm as I followed the head maid into Lady Uya's living room, holding a tray of food in hand. The living room was spacious but dark, a characteristic of all rooms in the palace due to the wide overhangs of the roof and the push-out windows that tended to block light. Rosewood curio shelves displaying vases, miniature statues and other ceramic arts covered all the walls. We placed the food on the large marble-top table in the center of the room—a total of eight dishes and a pot of soup, all for the lady herself.

I stood on the side with the other maids while Lady Uya came in and sat down at the table. Whenever the lady needed something—a cup of water, or a clean napkin—Furong, her personal maid took care of it. The rest of us weren't really needed. But we still had to stand there, our head bowed, so we could be regarded as furniture and the lady could eat at ease.

Lady Uya didn't seem to have much appetite since she put down her chopsticks after perfunctorily tasting the food on the table.

"What's wrong, my lady? Is the food not to your liking?" Furong asked.

The lady sighed. "The food is fine. It's just me. I wonder how the emperor is feeling today."

No one seemed to dare to breathe for a moment as we were reminded of the emperor's health. Kangxi was afflicted by various illnesses in his later years.

"Don't worry," the maid said. "His Majesty is doing fine. Little Yuan said he was up most of the day yesterday."

"I hope so. But where is Little Yuan? I sent him to the emperor a while ago."

"He will be back soon," Furong comforted her. "Would you like some more soup, my lady?"

Lady Uya nodded and Furong scooped some soup into her bowl.

Just then a eunuch came in and knelt in front of the lady.

"How's the emperor?" Lady Uya asked.

"My lady, the emperor is feeling better today. He took a walk in the Imperial Garden."

Lady Uya smiled. "Ah, that's good."

She spooned some soup and had some more rice. Evidently the news had enhanced her appetite. "Any news of the fourteenth prince?"

My ears twitched as I heard the name.

"I'm sorry, my lady, but we still haven't heard from the western borders yet."

She sighed again.

"One more thing, my lady," the eunuch said, still bowing.

"Yes?"

"Lady Nian has given birth to a boy."

I couldn't help but glance up at Lady Uya, who was still frowning at her earlier distress. It took her a moment to respond to the good news.

"Oh, good, good," she said without a smile. "Send gifts."

The eunuch acknowledged the order, but didn't get up right away, as if waiting for more instructions. After a moment without Lady Uya speaking to him, he got up.

A FEW DAYS later, after breaking too many bowls in the kitchen sink and injuring myself with the kitchen knife multiple times, I was demoted to be a gardener, which was the lowest rank among the palace maids. My duties now included cleaning the garden and the yard, and trimming plants. I didn't really mind it. In fact, I enjoyed the outdoor work much more. Besides, I finally got to use the skills I'd learned from a floral art class I had taken a few summers back at a community college. Since I was also responsible for making sure that the lady's flower vases were filled with fresh flowers every day, I took the liberty to show off my creative flower arrangements. I boldly mixed flowers and plants that didn't seem belong together according to traditional aesthetics. Not surprisingly, the lady was pleased and not only watched me when I worked with the flowers but also gave me her opinions.

It was the end of October and I was arranging the chrysanthemums with some maple branches in the living room with Lady Uya, when the eunuch announced that Prince Yong had arrived. Oh no, I thought, I can't let him see me. "My lady, nucai will take leave now."

"Don't go," her ladyship said with a gesture of her hand. "Stay and finish your work."

She didn't move, either, remaining where she was, which wasn't the usual seat to receive a guest.

Soon Prince Four came in. My heart thumped in my chest as I bowed and greeted him in unison with the other maids, keeping my head as low as possible.

Fortunately, he didn't pay much attention to the maids. He knelt in front of his mother and greeted her.

Lady Uya gestured for her son to get up and sit. I changed my position, so I wouldn't face him.

"Mother, we're having a celebration for the newborn in a few days, would you please attend?" Prince Four asked.

"Oh, I don't know," Lady Uya said. "It depends. My back hurts lately, and I can't sit for long."

I knew that was a lie. The lady hadn't made any complaints about her back in the time I spent with her every day.

"I see. What does the imperial doctor say?"

"Well, I don't need a doctor to tell me I'm getting old," the lady said curtly.

Silence fell on the room.

I glanced at the prince. He appeared to be such an obedient child in front of his somewhat callous mother. I couldn't help pitying him. Lady Uya was both Prince Yong and Prince Jeng's mother, but she cared more about her younger son, probably because she had raised him. Lady Tonggiya, the empress of the time, had adopted Prince Four right after his birth. Still, Lady Uya's lack of enthusiasm for her eldest son was a mystery to the historians. And her refusal to take the title of Empress Dowager that the future emperor wanted her to have was the grounds for the conjecture that the fourth prince wasn't the rightful heir.

"How're you going to celebrate?" Lady Uya finally spoke.

"I invited an Anhui Opera troupe."

The predecessor of Peking Opera, Anhui Opera originated in the Ming dynasty and matured in the late Kangxi era.

"Oh, I don't know how anyone can stand their howling."

I stifled a laugh. I quite agreed with her. But seeing the prince's pale cheeks made me feel sorry for him again.

The atmosphere became quite stiff, but the prince didn't seem to mind his mother's rude response. He chuckled. "What does Mother wish to see then?"

"The fujin of the thirteenth prince told me the other day that the magic show at your house last month was quite magnificent."

My scissors dropped to the floor at the mention of the magic show, and they turned to look at me. I apologized and bent down immediately to pick them up. When I straightened up, I felt the prince's gaze on me and hurriedly lowered my head even more.

After a moment, Prince Yong spoke again. "I will hire the circus troupe then. Would you really come, Mother?"

The lady was quiet for a moment, then she mumbled, "It'll depend on my back."

I marveled at her tough treatment of her son. She was civil to her servants, including me, but she didn't seem to be fair to Prince Yong. He hadn't chosen to be separated from her as an infant, the emperor had ordered it.

I wished the prince would just take leave in order to avoid more humiliation from his own mother, but he lingered, sipping silently on his tea. When the lady asked what other business he had in mind, he took out a small wooden box from his sleeve pocket. I almost gasped. It was the box that contained cards painted by Hongshou Chen. My curiosity piqued, and I stopped clipping the flowers as the prince cleared his throat. "Uh, in fact, Mother, your son would like to show you a card trick."

The lady frowned. "I don't play cards."

The prince was again undaunted by his mother's disinterest. "It's a magic trick, Mother."

Lady Uya raised an eyebrow but didn't say anything.

Prince Yong took out the cards, shuffled them and divided them into two stacks. He passed one stack to his mother. "Please pick any card, Mother, give it to me and don't let me see its face."

The lady paused and reluctantly took the stack. She then followed the instructions of her son, picked a card, looked at it, and passed it to him, ensuring he couldn't see the face. Prince Yong put the card on top of Lady Uya's stack, and then put his stack on top of it. Then he spread the cards, face up, on the table, and picked out a card. "Black Tornado Li Kui with ninety million coins. Is this the one you picked, mother?

Lady Uya's hand flew to her mouth, then her astonished look turned into a smile. "Yes, it is indeed! How did you do it?"

"It's magic, Mother," the prince said proudly. "I'll tell you how I did it if you promise to come to the party."

"I see! Playing tricks on me, huh?" she chided her son, but she was still smiling. "Okay, I'll go. And what's the child's name?"

The conversation went on amicably, as the prince told his mother about the child. Every now and then, my gaze went over to the prince. He was such a conundrum. Would such a filial son really become a merciless ruler in the future?

CHAPTER 19

☯

IT BECAME GRADUALLY colder as winter approached. November had started with a light sprinkle of snow, which was unexpected. I had seen snow in Beijing, usually during December, but I guessed the climate was different in the eighteenth century. The garden looked sublime with a light dusting of snowflakes on the eaves and tree branches. Buds appeared on the branches of the plum tree, which would bloom in December, the coldest month of the year.

I swept the snow off the path, and started to trim the plum branches, since Lady Uya was impatient for an early plum in her living room. *"Plum, plum, you're everywhere. The colder it gets, the madder you bloom."* I was humming a modern song by the future Taiwanese singer Teresa Ting, when I heard a voice, "That's a beautiful song!" I froze at the voice as fear washed over me. It sounded like Prince Yong! I didn't want him to find me here. I pretended not to have heard him, and continued to sing, only louder this time. But he came over and stood in front of me, blocking the sunlight. I took a deep breath and slowly looked up. I squealed as I recognized him, and the branches I gathered fell from my arms. I stared at him just to make sure I wasn't mistaken. Yes, tall and handsome, straight nose and square chin. It was Jeng, the fourteenth prince.

"What's wrong with you? Why are you staring at me like that? Why aren't you saluting me? Are you new here?" he asked with a smile.

His words reminded me of my status, and I immediately bowed. "Your humble servant Julie Bird wishes the fourteenth prince health and wellness."

"All right. Get up," he said and studied my face for a second. "Julie Bird? Have we met before?"

My heart raced. Could it be possible that he remembered seeing me? But no, our encounter in the future hadn't happened yet.

I hesitated, and said, "Yes and no."

He laughed. "What a strange answer. It's either yes or no."

"I know Prince, but Prince doesn't know me."

He nodded. "There are too many maids in the palace. But I wonder why. If I'd seen you once, I wouldn't have forgotten your exquisite face."

I blushed at his flirtation. That wasn't the Jeng I had known at all. "Actually, you haven't seen me, my lord. I am indeed new here."

"You are? Then how do you know me?"

I shrugged. "I've heard about you. You're the hero of the nation. Everyone talks about you in the palace."

"Oh? What do they say?"

"That the frontier general had accomplished his mission. He conquered the Dzungars and pacified the western borders."

He raised his eyebrows. "Sounds like I'm famous. What else do you know about me?"

I was about to list his other merits, but he looked away and smiled. "Mother!"

Lady Uya appeared at the door of her room. She must have been informed of her son's arrival.

I quickly bowed to the lady although she was still yards away.

Prince Fourteen left me and rushed towards his mother. He knelt on the ground in front of her, while she put her hands on his shoulders and then on his cheeks.

"Get up, son! Come inside," she said, her voice quivering with joy.

THAT NIGHT, the imperial family celebrated the return of Prince Jeng inside the Palace of Heavenly Purity. Only the imperial family members were permitted to attend the dinner party. I wasn't Lady Uya's personal maid, so I didn't get to go. But the atmosphere at home was just as lively. The Palace of Eternal Harmony was decorated with more lanterns, and the servants were treated with a sumptuous dinner. All they talked about over and after the dinner was the fourteenth prince.

"He's so handsome!" Ling, the maid who normally tidied up the rooms, said as the three of us cleaned the dishes after the others had left.

"Absolutely, handsomer than last time I saw him, two years ago." Hua was the kitchen maid.

"Life in the western frontiers must've been harsh. He's lost some weight, he's darker and thinner!"

"I know. Poor Prince Jeng. I'm going to ask Lady Uya to let me make some tonic for him," said Hua.

"Tsk, tsk," Ling shook her head. "Making tonic? You're not his fujin!"

Hua blushed. "I don't have to be his fujin to make soup for him. Didn't you make a pillow case for him last time?"

"How did you know?" It was Ling's turn to be embarrassed.

"I just know," Hua said smugly.

"You spy!" They went on hitting each other with their sleeves and laughed.

I got a bit jealous by the two maids' blatant display of infatuation for Jeng, and I wondered whether he was a womanizer. "Is the fourteenth prince a philanderer?"

They gasped simultaneously.

"Not at all!" Hua spoke first. "He's a gentleman, decent and noble."

"And he never flirts with maids."

I thought about our earlier encounter and thought maybe it wasn't flirting after all, at least not according to the maid's definition.

"Isn't it strange that the prince hasn't had a new fujin for all these years?" Ling said a moment later.

Hua giggled. "Maybe he has his heart set on you!"

"No, seriously, he's only thirty-four, but none of his fujins have been pregnant for the past fifteen years. What is his problem?"

They went silent for a while, and Hua whispered, "Maybe he's . . . you know what?"

Ling shook her head vehemently, "No way! He can't be."

"But many men are. I've heard that," Hua lowered her voice. "Including the second prince. He used to summon eunuchs every night, said he preferred men because they wouldn't get pregnant."

"Shut up! I don't want to hear it! Prince Jeng isn't like that!" Ling squealed, covering her ears with her hands.

I stifled a laugh. These silly maids. Jeng was everything but gay. I remembered his ardent kisses and I missed his warmth. Yet his lack of progeny was indeed a puzzle to historians. Contraceptives weren't a norm and as a prince he was expected to reproduce. Jeng had produced the last of his nine children at age nineteen, which was fifteen years ago. It did look like he had married simply to fulfill his duties.

After I left the kitchen, I was too excited to return to the maids' quarters and decided to take a walk in the

Imperial Garden. I had accompanied Lady Uya there a couple times already, so I knew my way. It was but a few blocks away from the Palace of Eternal Harmony. Lanterns illuminated the garden, but still there were dark corners. Even though I was holding a lantern, it felt a bit eerie from time to time. I lingered in front of the lake. Although it was night, it reminded me of the day I'd visited the Palace Museum with Jeng. Our brief encounter earlier brought back those memories into my mind, and they were so vivid it was as if it was yesterday. It had been five months since I'd last seen him, or had it been three hundred years?

I stopped in front of a cluster of rock hills. It was the spot where he had proved his identity to me. Where was his secret storage? I had wanted to locate it during my previous visits but didn't get a chance. I scanned the rocks and tried to remember the location. The rocks looked identical and I didn't pay much attention that day when he was looking for the hole. Nonetheless, I raised the lantern in front of every potential spot, even gingerly poked my hand into a couple of them.

My hand was still down in a crack when a voice startled me from behind. "Who's there? What're you doing?"

I immediately withdrew my hand and turned. It was a palace night guard.

I stayed calm and explained. "I'm Lady Uya's maid. I'm just taking a walk, and I heard noises in the hole, so I became curious."

The guard rolled his eyes. "You have nothing better to do? I order you return to your quarters. It might be a snake!"

"I apologize for my stupidity," I said, bending my head as I retreated from the area.

Just then I bumped into another person, who seemed to have been standing nearby for a while.

"Wait a minute," he said in a low voice, right by my ear.

I shuddered as I recognized Prince Yong's voice. Realizing I had no way out, I turned to face him.

The guard greeted him right away, "Your servant wishes Prince Yong wellness."

I followed suit.

The prince dismissed the guard, took over my lantern and stared at me silently and intently.

"I wasn't sure the last time, but it is you. How long have you been in the palace?"

"About a month, Prince."

"And why? Why are you working here?"

I kept my head low and tried to keep calm. "I, uh, wanted a secure life. Being a lady's maid is better than being a street performer."

"I didn't know you had that wish. I could've kept you for a maid. I've been looking all over town for you!"

That was unexpected. Hadn't he kicked me off of his property? "Why? I left because, because—"

"I know, I know," he interrupted. "I was an idiot. I made too big a deal out of it. I regretted it very much later. But you see, Father Emperor was ill during the time and I didn't want to further upset him."

He looked at me as if begging me to understand. I nodded.

"I later went looking for you, but you were just gone. The circus people said you left to look for your relatives. I sent people to search all the Peach Blossom Villages near the city but couldn't find you."

"I'm sorry," I stammered. "My relatives moved away. I was looking for a job at the House of Uya, and by chance met Momo Shu, who was recruiting a maid."

He held my chin up with his fingers and scrutinized my face, as if to see whether I was speaking the truth. I shivered at the sparks in his eyes. His attention flattered me for a moment. Was he sincere in his apology? But I quickly reminded myself that this man was supposed to be sharp and cruel, and I shouldn't let his apparent kindness fool me.

My trembling must've sent the wrong signal, for he suddenly pulled me close to him, and held me tightly. "I've missed you!" he whispered.

I was so astonished that I didn't know what to do. I squirmed a bit, but it was useless because Prince Yong was strong. I could feel his throbbing heartbeat, a phenomenon quite contrary to his usual cold countenance. Since resistance was futile, I let him hold me and waited for his next move. If he dared to kiss me, I would scream. There were guards around and I was pretty sure with his discretion, he wouldn't. And I was right. The prince let go of me and said, "I'm glad I found you again."

I decided formality was the best way to get out of my dilemma, so I bowed and said, "Your humble servant apologizes for all the trouble."

He held my shoulders and pulled me to face him. "You were forgiven long ago."

The sparks in his eyes made me nervous again. "How are Lady Nian and her newborn?"

He composed promptly at the mention of his family. "They're doing fine."

"I'm glad." I smiled.

"And Prince Hongli is doing well, too," he said.

I apologized again for helping Hongli to do his homework.

"Oh, don't mention it," he said. "In fact, I want to thank you."

I looked up, surprised.

"You see, the emperor has rewarded Hongli for what he had done, although I had informed him of your help."

"Really?" I grinned. "That's good to hear. I knew he would be fine."

"But it was your effort." He smiled warmly. "He couldn't have done it without your help."

I was moved by his compliment, which sounded sincere enough. "Don't forget I got him in trouble in the first place."

"No, it wasn't your fault at all. The rascal asked for it. You were trying to help."

"Still, I didn't do it right." I insisted, afraid that he would hire me back.

But my effort failed.

"Would you like to be his tutor?"

The invitation was flattering but I knew the answer had to be no. I couldn't leave Lady Uya and I had to hold on to my chance to see Jeng now that he was finally here.

"Well, I . . ." I stammered. "You see, I quite enjoy working with Lady Uya."

"Why? What's so enjoyable about putting flowers in a vase?"

"Oh, uh, you see." I thought quickly. "It's not just putting flowers in a vase, it's an art. It's called flower arrangement."

He shrugged. "I don't care what it's called. I'll speak to Lady Uya."

"Don't!" I said quickly. "Please. Give me some time. Besides, you don't want Lady Uya to be mad at you. She enjoys my company."

That certainly cooled him off quite a bit since he had tried hard to win the affections of his own mother. He nodded slightly. "All right. I'll wait, but I'll think of a way."

Prince Yong saw me to the gate of the Palace of Eternal Harmony. As soon as he left, I sighed in relief. He really made me nervous! I was certain that he had seen through my lies, but he pretended he hadn't. What disturbed me the most was the hug. Could he have really missed me? And why did I care? I shouldn't. I pushed the thought aside and concentrated on Jeng instead. Jeng would stay in the palace for five months before he left for the western borders again. Somehow, I had to convince him not to leave the emperor's side.

CHAPTER 20

SINCE THE PLUMS were blooming madly now, I became quite busy. Gardening could be tough since it snowed every day and was very cold outdoors. At first, I was thrilled to see snow falling and covering the palaces so completely, but after a few days of continuous snow, it became less exciting. I had experienced snow storms when I traveled to the east coast in the US, but I stayed indoors most of the time and had never worked in the snow. Now, under a wool cloak, I not only wore a cotton-padded jacket, but also put on wool scarf, wool gloves and leather boots. I was as stiff as a doll, but still I preferred being in the garden instead of staying indoors—the way they kept warm here was by closing all the windows and burning coal furnaces. I couldn't stand the carbon monoxide.

I saw Jeng almost every day since he had returned two weeks before, but I didn't get a chance to speak to him. He came to see his mother often. Exactly as the other maids had said, the prince didn't flirt with the maids. In fact, he seldom even looked at us. In order to attract his attention, I spent an hour doing my hair and makeup every morning. Like the other maids, I now twined my hair around a black frame that stood on top of my head, and inserted flowers and jewelry onto it. The hairstyle was called *big wings*. While I'd gotten used to the weight, I tended to forget its presence and couldn't stop my *wings* from bumping into the walls and the doorframes. I also tried to be creative with my flower arrangements, hoping he would take notice of them.

Finally, my chance came when the head maid told me that Lady Uya wanted some fresh branches in her bedroom. Jeng was still inside. I was thrilled! I quickly tried out my newest creation—a plum branch with an unusual shape in a shallow fruit bowl that contained pebbles and water.

The lady was delighted when she saw the arrangement. "How exquisite!"

Prince Jeng turned his attention to the flowers. "A bowl for a vase? How did you come up with that idea? And how do the long branches stay upright?"

I bent my knees humbly and thanked them for their compliments. Then I showed them my secret weapon buried inside the pebbles—a flower frog. Although flower frogs had a long history in China, I had not seen any in Lady Uya's house, so I made one out of a piece of eggplant and toothpicks.

"Elegant!" Lady Uya's eyes were transfixed on the flowers.

"I see Mother has a talented maid!" The prince grinned at me.

That smile sent shivers down my spine, and I had the impulse to hold him and kiss him. But I took hold of myself and smiled coyly.

"It's stylish no doubt, but it also seems to be lonely by itself," the lady said after a close examination.

"You're absolutely right, my lady," I said. "I was going to find some bamboo and pine to make a combination but didn't know where I could find them."

"There're lots of pine in Jingshan Park," Prince Fourteen said quickly. "I'll take you there later."

I flushed as I remembered watching the sunrise with him at Jingshan Park and I wanted to shout, "Yes, let's go there again!" But I bowed my head immediately to hide my excitement. "Thank you for your kindness, but nucai wouldn't dare to trouble you. Prince could simply tell nucai where to find them."

"It's no trouble at all. And I enjoy—" Jeng didn't get to finish his sentence.

"Decree from the emperor," called a man from the courtyard.

We scurried towards the front door and knelt to receive the decree.

"It is the emperor's order that Julie Bird, maid in the Palace of Eternal Harmony, report to the Palace of Heavenly Purity immediately!"

I was so astonished that I forgot how to breathe. What had happened?

Lady Uya's voice brought me out of my near trance. "Hurry up and accept the decree."

"Yes. Nucai accepts His Majesty's order most gratefully." I was too shocked to remember the proper language, but thankfully the others knew what to say so I followed suit. "Long live the emperor! Long live His Majesty!" We then all kowtowed three more times before the eunuchs that had come along with the messenger helped me up, and I followed them out of the palace.

What would the emperor want to see me for? And how did he even know about my presence? I kept guessing the possible reasons while walking between the walls of the palaces, then it dawned on me that it must have had something to do with Prince Yong. Instead of speaking to his mother, he must've spoken to the emperor, and had his permission to remove me from Lady Uya's household, so I could tutor Hongli. But why would I have to see the emperor himself? Whatever the reason, I knew I was in trouble. If the emperor agreed to grant his son's wish, then I would be out of Lady Uya's house, and I wouldn't see Jeng again. I sighed—I had almost gotten a date with him.

The Palace of Heavenly Purity wasn't far, but it was the longest walk of my life, as I was tortured by the sorrow of possible separation from Jeng and the anxiety of seeing the emperor for the first time. We arrived at the palace at last. It looked very different from the tourist site that I had visited. There was virtually no one around except the guards, and the square in front of the building looked vast. I followed the eunuchs onto the long passage bordered by alabaster railings that led to the main hall. At the entrance of the hall, I paused with my head bowed until an elderly eunuch came for me. His gentle voice and courteous manner ought to have set me at ease, but my legs couldn't stop trembling as I followed him into the main hall. I had been here twice before as a twenty-first century tourist, but this time, I was a commoner and a slave, and I was about to be interviewed by the greatest emperor in Chinese history.

My heart was in my throat and I was about to pass out when we finally entered the hall. My head was down, but I could still see shapes of people and objects around me. I knew there was a dragon chair in the center of the room, and the emperor was sitting right there in his dragon robe. Following the instructions of the eunuch, I knelt and kowtowed to Emperor Kangxi.

"Nucai Julie Bird wishes Your Majesty longevity and health!"

"You may rise and raise your head," the emperor murmured.

I rose slowly and looked up at the man in the golden seat. He didn't look that different from the portrait of Kangxi I had seen—his cheeks were hollow, and his eyes were sunken. I was reminded again that the emperor had been struggling with health problems in the last decade of his life. But there was something the portrait failed to capture. Although old and frail, the emperor maintained a regal look. It might've been the rigid dragon seat, or the grandeur of the Palace of Heavenly Purity itself but I couldn't help but being impressed by his exalted continence.

"So, you are the famous Julie Bird?" He looked at me with amusement in his eyes.

"Nucai doesn't dare to claim such fame."

"Tell me, who taught you mathematics?"

Mathematics? So, it did have something to do with Prince Yong!

"Your Majesty, I learned it from my father." My heart pounded frantically as soon as I said it. Lying to the emperor would result in death. But I wasn't lying. I had learned math from my dad.

"Your father?"

"Yes, Your Majesty," I said, lowering my eyes again, out of fear.

"And who might he be?"

I panicked. Great. What should I say next? Professor Liu of Tsinghua University? No, it wouldn't do. Make up a name? The emperor would know every scholar in the city, wouldn't he? I tried to remember what I had said to Prince Yong, because he must have told the emperor about me already.

"Ignorant nucai!" the eunuch shouted at me. "Answer the emperor's question!"

I trembled and feigned sorrow. "Forgive me, Your Majesty. He is a foreigner."

"Very well. I can tell your father is a foreigner. Is he a priest?"

Yes or no? "I believe so, Your Majesty. He left me and my mother when I was eight years old."

"Eight years old? And you learned all that math before that?" the emperor looked incredulous.

Obviously, the old emperor's mind was quite sharp. "My father left me some books and notes, and I studied them afterwards."

"I see. Self-taught!" The emperor sounded impressed.

I heard murmurs rise instantly in the room, and boldly looked around. As soon as I did it, I noticed the presence of the fourth prince. It was him indeed!

Kangxi then pointed to a pile of paper on his desk. "Your proofs of the Gogoo theorem are impressive!"

I blushed and said quickly, "Your Majesty, nucai doesn't have the intelligence to prove it. Nucai merely remembers it from books."

"I like your honesty. But even so, it is incredible," the emperor said, smiling. "Father Bouvet, my tutor, said he hadn't even seen one of the proofs."

Of course, I thought, President Garfield wasn't born until a hundred years from now. In fact, the United States wouldn't exist for another fifty years.

"Now," the emperor continued. "I wish to show you another way of proving it. My way."

"It would be nucai's honor," I said quickly, flattered by the emperor's wish.

"Not yet. I started it, but couldn't quite finish it, which is why I summoned you here today."

My legs trembled in an instant. The emperor needed my help with a math problem? Oh no, what had I gotten myself into? My mind blanked out for a second as I saw the expectant looks of the eunuch and Prince Yong. Then I quickly bowed and answered, "Nucai doesn't deserve such honor."

"Go over there, and take a look," the emperor said gently.

I followed the eunuch to a table and watched him unroll a scroll of paper, all the while clasping my hands tightly in front of me. The paper was filled with math equations and numerous drawings of triangles. I stared at the paper, my mind still frozen. I felt like I was taking an exam—the most difficult exam in my life, since it was given by Emperor Kangxi. Then I reminded myself what Jeng had told me. I had to focus on the task itself and not worry about the outcome. Slowly, I took a deep breath and focused on the drawings in front of me. I saw a large square divided into four small right triangles by two pairs of parallel lines that ran diagonally across. Each pair of the parallel lines also divided the square into two larger right triangles, and one of the legs of these larger triangles were the sides of the overall square. The emperor had shown that the area of the square was the sum of two large right triangles and the area enclosed by the two parallel lines between them, which was a parallelogram, but the problem was that he ended up with an identity $b^2 = b^2$ instead of the equation of the theorem $a^2 + b^2 = c^2$.

"Do you see the problem?" The emperor had moved into a chair next to mine.

"Yes, I do," I said. "You don't have enough squares."

"Exactly," the emperor nodded. "But the question is, how do I get more?"

Again, my heart fluttered, but I forced myself to think quickly. "Perhaps, instead of using the most obvious way to find the sum of the large square, you could take a different route so the small square in the center could be included in the equation."

"How do you know it's a square?" the emperor asked after looking at his own drawing. "It looks like a square, but remember, pictures can be deceptive."

"That's true," I said. The emperor surely knew what he was doing. "Maybe we can prove it with similar triangles."

"Wonderful!"

I was flattered but also nervous because I had no idea what to do next.

I tried various ways, but the task wasn't easy. Although I had a fairly good mathematical comprehension, proving a theorem from scratch required ingenuity and solid background knowledge. What I had reviewed or learned in the past months or so wasn't enough to render a quick solution.

Thankfully, the emperor had other, more important business to take care for the day. After I scribbled two pages, he stopped me. "It'll do for now. You think about it when you have time."

"Nucai thanks Your Majesty's kindness." I bowed.

"One more thing," he said. "I'll confer you the title of Master of Learning, and tomorrow you'll report to Shangshufang."

"Master of Learning?" I had no idea what kind of rank it was, but I remembered visiting Shangshufang with Jeng that day. The Upper Study was the school for children, mostly sons, of the imperial family.

"Yes. You'll be the math tutor of the princes."

Robotically, I knelt again and thanked the emperor, although deep down I wanted to cry. Math tutor? I knew Kangxi was open-minded but hiring a woman to tutor his sons seemed way too progressive. Although anxious of the job, on my way out I was filled with admiration for the wise emperor.

As if it weren't enough of a shock for me, after getting out of the Palace of Heavenly Purity, a eunuch informed me that I would be moving into scholars' quarters near the Imperial School, which was also near the Palace of Heavenly Purity, as the emperor might wish to discuss mathematics with me in the afternoons.

My excitement soon waned, and sorrow replaced it as I sat in the sedan chair on my way back to Lady Uya's house. The position was an enviable one, but it ruined my chance of seeing Prince Jeng, who had already graduated from the Imperial School years ago. I had waited all these months for him to return, and now—it was all because of Prince Yong! I ground my teeth. Why did he keep interfering with my plan? And what was I going to do? If I moved away from the Palace of Eternal Harmony, then I wouldn't have many chances to see Jeng.

I was summoned to see Lady Uya as soon as I returned. I told her what had happened and cried when I told her I had to move. The lady chided me, "You silly girl! Many would envy your luck of being noticed by the emperor. And here you're crying."

"But I don't want to leave, my lady! I would rather arrange flowers for you for the rest of my life!" That was a bit of an exaggeration, but then, between tutoring math and arranging flowers, I would indeed choose the latter.

Touched by my emotion, Lady Uya took out her handkerchief to wipe my eyes for me.

"All right, good girl, stand up, stop crying. I'll speak to His Majesty and let you stay here, if you don't mind walking a longer distance."

"Not at all!" I thanked her profusely and kowtowed multiple times.

"Okay, that's enough." Lady Uya stopped me. She let me sit down in a chair next to her and placed a jewelry box in my hand. "And here, it's not much, but it is my gift."

I thanked her and opened the box. I gasped at the pair of earrings made of pink quartz and carved into the shape of plum flowers.

"So pretty." I said. "Pin quartz is a rare stone, and plum flowers are Lady's favorite. I can't take these!"

"Oh, I have more jewelry than I can ever wear. But you, Julie, really need some." Lady Uya was glad that I knew the value of her gift. "Put them on!"

I obeyed and put on the earrings right away. She examined me and nodded with satisfaction. "Becoming!"

That night, I moved out of maids' quarters and into a small room in the back of the Palace of Eternal Harmony.

THE IMPERIAL SCHOOL—the Upper Study—was located on the east side of the Gate of Heavenly Purity. I remembered the look in Prince Jeng's eyes the day we had visited it together. Far from being deserted as I had last seen it, the school was in its best days. I heard the sound of poem recitation as soon as I neared it. Kangxi had over a hundred grandchildren but not all of them had the chance to come here. In fact, most of them would be homeschooled, under private tutors. When I approached the classroom, about a dozen students, all grandsons of Emperor Kangxi, were sitting inside with a book in front of them on the desk. They all looked up when I entered, although I tried to be as quiet as I could. One of them even waved at me, and he was none other than Hongli. I smiled and nodded at the child.

As far as I knew, the children who had the privilege to come to the Imperial School had to come every day during the year, except a few holidays, and from dawn to evening. They studied Han and Manchu languages, mathematics, and astronomy in the mornings. In the afternoons they practiced riding, fencing, and archery. I was a bit earlier than I was expected and the princes were still studying Han Chinese literature. I stood aside to watch them read and write. Shortly after they were done with Han literature, they studied Manchu language, which was the mother tongue of the Qing rulers, who had come from north of Great Wall and conquered the Han less than a hundred years before.

A man showed up shortly after I had arrived and introduced himself as Master Wen, the math teacher. He was in his forties, skinny and short. He bowed to me as he spoke and made me quite uncomfortable. Lady Uya had congratulated me for my new title of Master of Learning, saying that it was the fourth official rank from the top. Except for the Grand Masters, most of the teachers who worked at the Upper Study were only Masters, which was a lower rank. I could almost feel the resentment in Master Wen's eyes, even though he was smiling, and I wished I hadn't been given any rank at all.

"What is the Master of Learning going to lecture today?" he asked me.

"Uh," I was taken aback by the question. "I'm sorry but I wasn't prepared to lecture. The emperor only told me to come help out."

"Very well," Master Wen nodded. "Please have a seat then."

I sat down in a corner in order to make myself invisible. Master Wen began his lesson with some simple algebra equations. He hung a scroll of paper on the wall with a problem and its solution written on it. I realized that the chalkboard hadn't been invented yet and presentations were done using the paper only. It wasn't bad at all except the master couldn't do any spontaneous teaching, since he couldn't erase any mistakes. This kind of lecturing, similar to a PowerPoint presentation, could really put students to sleep. I looked around and saw a couple of nodding heads. As the master rambled on, I thought about the possibility of making a chalkboard. While a board wasn't hard to make, I had no idea how chalk was made or what it was made of. Then I remembered the whiteboard—perhaps I could use that, and markers could be substituted easily with a brush. Ink was readily available and all I would need was a glossy white surface. I could use marble or ceramic—it shouldn't be hard, should it? I was so excited by the idea that I didn't hear when the master called me. When I heard him, all heads had turned to look at me.

"Master of Learning, could you please teach the princes geometry?"

"Of course!" I eagerly stood up and walked to the front, thinking the master wanted me to explain a particular topic.

But that was not the case. He picked up his notes and left the podium. Pairs of curious eyes stared at me and I flushed from head to toe. What was I supposed to do? Although there was paper and ink on the desk, I had no idea what I would teach. I glanced over the students as calmly as possible and did my best to turn the gears in my brain. When my eyes met Hongli's, I remembered

341

helping him with a problem of solving similar triangles. Then I got an idea. I would have them do an activity.

"Let me ask you a question, princes," I said with a smile. "Do you know the height of the Gate of Heavenly Purity?"

As expected, no one did.

"Don't worry, we'll find out. I want everyone to grab some paper, ink and a pen, and follow me."

While they packed, I also borrowed a yardstick and a rope from Master Wen, who watched me with suspicion. "What does it have to do with geometry?"

"You'll see. You can come along if you want," I said as I led the students out of the classroom.

We stopped in front of the gate, which was right next to the Upper Study. Then I had the boys measure the length of the shadow of the gate, which was pretty short since it was near noon. After that, I measured Hongli's height and the length of his shadow. As they wondered what I was going to do, I spread some paper on the floor, and drew two triangles on the paper. "Look, these two triangles are similar because all the matching angles are equal. The height of the large triangle is the height of the gate, and the height of the small triangle is Hongli's height. The bases are the shadows. Does anyone know how to find the height of the gate?"

"Oh!" the children exclaimed and started to work eagerly. It didn't take them long to compute the answer.

After they were done, they asked me, "But how do we know it is the right answer?"

"Well, you can check with palace records, or you can measure it. Who's a good climber?"

Half of them raised their hands. Most of these children practiced Kung Fu, so climbing the wall should be a piece of cake. However, I didn't want any accidents to happen on my first day, so I passed the rope to a palace guard and asked him to measure it for us. Needless to say, the result turned out to be the same as we had found.

After we returned to the classroom, the children explained excitedly to Master Wen what we had done. Master Wen said, "Well, I showed you a problem like this just a few days ago. The only difference was I used the Meridian Gate, remember?"

The imperial children scratched their heads.

I wanted to tell the old master that there was another difference—he'd presented the problem and its solution, while I had them do it.

A FEW WEEKS later, I was again summoned to see the emperor. But this time, I was shown into the South Study, a room on the west side of the Palace of Heavenly Purity. I was told to wait for His Majesty. It looked like a private study with books all over the shelves. I recalled the legend of the young Kangxi capturing his arrogant subordinate Aobai in this room, with the help of a dozen teenage eunuchs.

The emperor came in shortly, in a casual beige cotton gown without the emblem of a ruler, looking like a commoner, or a learned commoner.

"Have you made any progress?" he asked me after I had curtsied and saluted him.

"Yes," I said. In the past weeks I had practically squeezed my brain in order to carry out the proof. "Nucai has figured out how."

"Oh?" Kangxi was delighted. "So, it worked, after all?"

"Yes." I smiled. "Should nucai show you?"

"No!" the emperor stopped me quickly. "I would like to work on it myself. You only need to give me some hints, make sure I'm not too far off. Come sit down."

I hesitated. "Nucai doesn't dare to." A servant wasn't supposed to sit in the presence of the emperor.

"If you don't sit down, I won't be able to think," he said, smiling.

I took the order and sat down.

It only took me a few words to point the emperor towards the right direction, which was to sum up the area of the triangles, parallelogram, and a small square within the large square. Once he understood what he had to do, he didn't speak to me again and buried himself into the process. He did get stuck later on, in the process of eliminating variables other than a, b, and c, which were in the theorem, but he only allowed me to give him a minimum amount of help. The path he had chosen was long, and many times harder than the classic proof by Shuang Zhao or Bhaskara, since it required not only finding areas of three different geometric figures but also using similar triangles to eliminate variables, and at the end, long and tedious algebraic operations. But the emperor liked the challenge. He was perseverant and wouldn't give up easily. He stayed in his study until ten that night, until he was able to finish the proof. He proudly wrote down QED after the last line.

"Father Verbiest, my science mentor, taught me that, but I forgot what it meant," he said.

I wasn't sure the original meaning in Latin, but remembered my high school teacher's explanation, "Quite Easily Done."

The emperor laughed at the joke. "It wasn't easy in my case. I think it's unnecessarily hard. Compared to Shuang Zhao's, this is a monster!"

He counted the pages the proof took, a total of five sheets of paper, including pictures.

"Your Majesty," I said. "Your proof is more sophisticated."

"Sophisticated is not the equivalence of good," he said, shaking his head. "A good proof is supposed to be simple."

I thought he was right about it, but I was afraid to agree with him. It was one thing for an emperor to point out his own imperfections, and quite another for a servant to do so. If I weren't careful, I might lose my head. "Your Majesty can find a simpler way, too."

"True." He nodded. "There seems to be endless possibilities to this beautiful theorem. That's why math fascinates me."

Despite of his self-criticism, he ordered some dessert to reward his success, and invited me to share it with him.

"Do you enjoy working at the Upper Study?" the emperor asked me after savoring a spoonful of the sweet soup made of snow fungus, red dates, lotus seeds, and goji.

"Yes, very much so. Thank you for asking."

"Be strict on those rascals," he said. "I know how lazy they are. Some of them don't want to learn, only want to play. Many of them hate math. But don't be afraid to punish them."

I told him my idea of making an ink-board for teaching. "With it, it'll be easier for the students to learn and for the masters to teach. I can show them how to solve a problem step by step."

"Great idea!" The emperor stopped eating and smiled. "What should the board be made of?"

"That's the part I haven't figured out. I think ceramic, or any stone with a glossy surface will do, as long as the ink can be easily erased."

The emperor nodded. "Not a problem. I'll have someone take care of it. You shall have it in a few days."

I took leave after the sweet soup, and since it was late at night, the emperor insisted that a couple of palace guards escort me back to the Palace of Eternal Harmony.

Although it was nearly eleven when I returned to my room, and I was exhausted, I couldn't fall asleep. It was cold even though the room was heated by a fire pan. I still couldn't quite process my extraordinary experiences. I, Julie Bird, who failed Advanced Calculus in college, was now the math tutor in China's Imperial School, and Emperor Kangxi's math buddy. My father would've been so proud of me. The emperor was impressed by my practical teaching method. His sons and grandsons liked it much more than memorizing the digits of pi. My interest in the subject soared as I was trying hard to make it interesting to my imperial students and to please His Majesty.

While I did enjoy my new job and new life, I also worried about my mission. I didn't forget for a second that I was here to help Prince Jeng, but how was I going to help him without seeing him? It had been about two weeks since I had last seen him.

AS HE HAD promised, the emperor had someone deliver a piece of white marble to the classroom few days later. It was framed in wood and looked like a piece of art. I leaned it against the wall in the front of the classroom.

"What's this?" The imperial kids were all curious.

"It's a divider, isn't it?"

True, it looked like a divider.

Master Wen waited patiently for me to explain its function.

I demonstrated it right away—taking up the brush and writing a word on it, then erasing it with a cloth. It was far from being perfect—the ink tended to drip on the board, and it couldn't be erased as easily, but it would do. With a damp cloth it was just as good.

I went on and showed them how to solve an equation on the marble board. The class, including Master Wen, was very impressed.

I was having my students solve a word problem I had created when I saw a tall man standing at the door of the classroom. It was none other than Jeng! I could hardly hold my excitement and went to him right away.

"What brings you here? Do you miss school?" I asked after I greeted him.

"Yes, I do," he said humoredly. "I heard that the master here was beautiful and smart."

I blushed. He knew how to flirt after all. "Since you're here, you must join us for the challenge," I said, pointing to the board.

"Oh no, please, I'm done with math!" He frowned. "I only came to say hi."

"Chicken!" I taunted, hoping he would stay.

He took the bait and turned to look at the board. "'The hare can run thirty li per hour, and the tortoise can run three li per hour. If the hare wants to take a nap in the beginning and catches up with the tortoise at fifteen li from the starting point, how long should his nap be?' Interesting."

While he was thinking, I said, "Do you want to sit down? You're supposed to solve it with a one-variable equation."

"No," he said. "The answer is four-and-a-half hours."

I gasped. "How did you know?"

"Well," he said smugly. "It takes the tortoise five hours to run fifteen li, and it takes the hare half an hour, so five minus half is four-and-a-half."

I slapped his arm. "I didn't know you were so good at math."

"I'm not!" He laughed. "I had no idea how to solve the equations."

He then turned to leave.

I followed him out of the classroom. "Where are you heading to?"

"I'm on my way to see Father Emperor. He summoned all the princes for a meeting."

"I see. When are you going to take me to gather pine branches?"

He smiled. "Still remember that, huh?"

"Of course."

"What about this afternoon?"

"Perfect!" I was so thrilled I clapped my hands like a silly school girl.

Just then Prince Yong showed up. The two brothers exchanged a few words and Prince Yong said to his brother, "It's my birthday today, and I would like to invite you to dinner in my house this afternoon."

My heart sank, and I cursed Prince Yong silently. The rogue ruined my plan again!

Prince Jeng looked at me, and then back to his brother. "I'm afraid I can't. You see, I've just promised Julie to take her to the Imperial Garden to—"

Although I was thankful that he was declining, I interrupted him quickly. "Please, Prince, it hardly matters. We can go another day."

"But a promise is a promise!" Jeng insisted.

It suddenly dawned on me that he didn't want to go to the dinner in his brother's house and was using me as an excuse.

I was in a difficult position now. Although I wanted to be with Jeng, I didn't want to come between the two brothers, even though they weren't on good terms.

After an awkward moment, during which Prince Yong silently observed the two of us with his sharp eyes, he said shrewdly, "I have a simply solution to your dilemma, Prince Brother, I will invite Julie to the dinner as well."

It was hardly a solution at all, and I tried to refuse it right away. "But that's not necessary. Nucai doesn't deserve such an invitation."

Prince Four paused for a second and said firmly. "Lady Nian would like to see your magic tricks again."

The mention of Lady Nian silenced me. I missed her, and I was curious about the newborn.

"In that case, I . . ." I curtsied again. "Nucai accepts the invitation."

Then I looked up apologetically at Jeng.

He didn't seem to mind, though. Instead, he looked amused. "You know how to do magic tricks?"

I nodded.

"I can't wait to scc them!"

Despite the cold and watchful eyes of Prince Yong, I blushed and smiled.

The two of them moved on and headed towards the Palace of Heavenly Purity. I stood where I was for a moment, feeling the challenge of the mission I had brought onto myself. Helping Jeng to win the battle against his brother wouldn't be an easy task.

CHAPTER 21

LADY NIAN LOOKED cheerful when I saw her in the afternoon. She was doting on her two-month-old baby Fuhui, who was clearly the center of her universe. The baby looked healthy and adorable with his wide forehead, pink cheeks, and round face. His eyes were a pair of glistening jewels. She let me hold him and he smiled at me when I clicked my tongue at him. The child would become Prince Yong's favorite, although he wouldn't survive to adulthood, either, like Nian's other children. I wished I hadn't known the fate of the baby because it made me sad and I had to try hard not to show my pity.

Lady Nian congratulated me about my new post in the palace.

"You're so talented, Julie." She smiled warmly at me. "I didn't know women could do math. I, for example, barely know my multiplication table."

"But you have many other talents, my lady," I said humbly. "Music, poetry, painting, and chess. These are the must-learns for a good woman."

When the servant announced that the fourteenth prince had arrived, my heart skipped a beat, and I looked up eagerly. I wanted to see Jeng's family, but he appeared alone at the door.

Jeng was wearing a silk brocade Manchu gown, without any official insignia but embroidered with characters of luck in gold. He was cleanly shaven. Although he had been reluctant to come, he still did his best to look good. I couldn't take my eyes off him and when he came towards me, my heart pounded although I knew he was coming to see the baby.

Lady Nian grinned when he stood in front of her. "It's good to see you, Jeng! But where are your fujins?"

"I didn't bring them," Prince Jeng said. "They would fight if I brought more than one, and if I brought one, the others would burn the house down."

Lady Nian stifled a laugh. "You should've brought all of them. They could sit separately."

"Good idea. Why didn't I think of it?" the prince said amicably to his sister-in-law. "I should let you manage my household."

I caught just a fleeting glow in Lady Nian's eyes when she heard the comment, and an unmistakable pink flushed her face.

Since I wasn't a member of the royal family, I left Lady Nian and sat at a table among respected guests, including tutors of the children and scholars whose literary talents Prince Yong admired. Soon the table was filled with sumptuous dishes. My mouth watered at the roasted suckling pig and I was eager to touch my chopsticks.

But I looked around and saw that although everything was ready, no one touched the food. I soon realized we were waiting for the arrival of Lady Uya, who had been invited but hadn't promised to come. The emperor had also been invited, although he most likely wouldn't come. If the prolific emperor had to attend every of his children's birthday parties, then he would be very busy indeed! A carriage was sent twice to the Palace of Eternal Harmony, and finally, just before Prince Yong was about to stop waiting for his mother, the lady arrived. In spite of her tardiness, the fourth prince was delighted at her presence. He bowed and saluted her at the entrance of the dining hall. As soon as she settled down, the wine cups clinked, and chopsticks clapped.

Needless to say, my eyes followed Jeng throughout the dinner. He was sitting among the men, next to the thirteenth and the seventeenth princes, who were Prince Yong's loyal friends and would be promoted once he succeeded the throne. Jeng was talking and drinking with his half siblings, but his attention wasn't with them. Even when he was smiling and nodding at their speeches, he was looking across the room at someone. It didn't take me long to figure out who had his attention. It was Lady Nian. They weren't casual glances, but intense stares. There were moments where he seemed to be lost in thought when he looked at her, and his eyes were full of longing and pity. Could there have been more than friendship between them? The possibility pained me and puzzled me. None of the history books even hinted at the love interest between Prince Jeng and his brother's wife. But the realization haunted me and pretty much ruined my appetite.

Somewhere during the dinner, after the performance of an opera troupe, I did my dove and rabbit tricks. I hadn't had time to come up with any new tricks, but I had practiced my old tricks regularly. Since I had moved into my own room, I also kept a dove and a rabbit.

"Bravo!" Lady Uya clapped her hands. It was the first time she'd seen my show. She was so proud of me that she beckoned me to sit down next to her.

"I didn't know you had such skills, Julie! That was the best performance I've seen."

"Thank you, my lady."

"You know what?" she said to me. "You should perform at the Ice Play."

"The Ice Play?" I asked curiously. "What is it?"

"It's our winter celebration." She explained the Manchu tradition. During the first month of the year, when the lakes at the West Park—an imperial garden to the west of Forbidden City—were frozen, soldiers performed martial arts while skating on ice.

I was fascinated and recalled a scene in a historical TV drama where a consort, desperate for the emperor's attention, performed a court dance while skating. I had thought it was all made up by the imaginative producer. Yes, it would be great if I could do a magic show on ice.

"What do you think?" Lady Uya went on, "I'll make the suggestion to the emperor and I'm sure he'll like it."

"But I don't know how to skate."

"Oh, it's easy. I used to skate when I was young. Jeng can teach you. He's good at it. And he'll be overseeing the training anyway."

"Jeng!" she called her son before I could decline the offer.

"Yes, Mother," Jeng answered and promptly came over.

"Would you teach Julie to skate, so she could perform her magic during the Ice Play?"

Jeng's smile vanished. "Uh, Mother, the Ice Play is about two weeks away."

"So?" Lady Uya shrugged. "You'll teach her quickly. All she needs to learn is how to walk on ice. I could do it if I were young."

"It isn't as easy as you imagine, Mother. I can teach her quickly, but she—" Jeng hesitated.

I knew what he wanted to say, and I didn't want to cause him trouble. Besides, I still remembered the pain and humiliation I had suffered after falling over and over on the skating rink back in middle school. "My lady, thank you for your kind suggestion, but I'm afraid I won't be able to learn so fast. I do not wish to make a fool of myself and ruin the important event."

The kind lady didn't insist but she didn't give up, either. "Well, maybe you can do it next year. I'm sure it would be sensational."

I promised her I would try, knowing very well I wouldn't be in the palace this time next year.

Before Jeng walked away from us, Lady Nian said to her mother-in-law from the other side of the table, "What a fantastic idea, my lady! We'll call it Ice Magic!"

Then she said to me, "Promise us you'll do it, Julie. I'm looking forward to see it!"

Jeng stopped where he was and turned to look at her. "Are you serious? You never cared for the Ice Play."

"True," said Lady Nian. "It is just too cold out there. And frankly, every year it's the same thing. Shooting arrows and fighting with swords. But if Julie does her magic, I promise I'll go!"

Jeng's expression changed somewhat as he looked at me. He opened his mouth for a moment but didn't say anything.

LADY UYA LEFT the dinner without seeing the dance that followed. I stayed until the end and accepted Jeng's offer of a ride. But instead of telling the driver of the carriage to head for the Palace of Eternal Harmony, he ordered him to go to the Imperial Garden instead.

"I'll be busy for the next few days," he said. "But I want to fulfill my promise before I go away."

I was glad to hear that, although I was drowsy after the rich dinner and really wanted my pillow at the moment. "But I thought we would go to Jingshan Park?"

"It's too late. There are pine trees in the garden, too."

We got off the carriage at the garden.

Jeng took a lantern from the carriage and dismissed the driver.

It was my second time being in the Imperial Garden at night. This time because of the snow, the garden was hardly recognizable, and illuminated by the lantern lights, the scenery was all white and not much else. But I thought it was the most beautiful garden I had seen in my life, because Jeng was next to me. I had waited for him for months, and he was finally within my reach. I wanted so much to hold him, but I knew it would be impossible at the moment. The memories that I cherished and the passion between us were absent from his mind.

"What are you thinking?" he asked me suddenly.

"Oh nothing." I quickly pushed my sorrows aside. "I'm just enjoying the moment."

"I love the tranquility, too," he said.

"Do you come here often, at night?"

"Not really," he said. "Gardens are mostly for ladies. But when I was a child I used to love playing here."

I nodded and said without thinking, "And you liked to hide stuff here."

He stopped walking and turned to look at me. "How did you know?"

I realized my blunder. "Oh, uh, I guess I heard about it from Lady Uya."

He paused to think. "How did she know?"

I laughed nervously. "Well, a mother knows everything about her child."

He didn't look convinced but didn't make further inquiry. I secretly let out a sigh of relief.

We passed the center of the park and entered the forest where some very old trees stood. With the help of the lantern, we found our path, stepping on the snowy ground, the ground crunching beneath our feet. I could hardly discern one tree from another because they were all covered with snow. But Jeng seemed to be able to see through the covers. "There it is," he pointed to a tree at least thirty feet tall, reaching to the blackness of the sky.

He then held the tree trunk and shook off some snow. He raised the lantern high enough for me to see the branches. "Which one do you want?"

I squinted in the dim light. "Any branch would be fine. I could trim it later."

"Sure," he said and motioned me to step back.

He drew his sword, and with one strike, brought down a huge branch.

A memory flashed in my mind's eye. Jeng drawing his sword and slicing the rock into halves. He did it to scare the villain who had attempted to rob me. Again, I wanted to hold him—my hero and my knight in shining armor.

"Here you go," he said when he placed the branch into my hands. "Is it enough?"

I nodded. "It could fill many vases."

"We can come back if you need more," he said. "After the Ice Play."

The Ice Play again. I wasn't happy about it because it took Jeng away from me. "Will you be performing?"

"No. But I'll be there every day to monitor the training."

"Are you going to live in West Park?"

"Oh no, I'll go home. It isn't that far from my house."

But I wouldn't be seeing him for another two weeks. I had been over the moon after seeing him this morning and had been looking forward to being with him. But the moment was so short. I didn't really know when I would see him again. I slowed down voluntarily, trying to prolong our time together.

"And after the Ice Play, will you be staying in Jing City for a while?"

"Ay, until April."

Four months. And then he would go back to the western boarders, and wouldn't return until his father's death in December next year.

I suddenly felt anxious. This was my chance to convince him not to go. If Jeng stayed by Kangxi's deathbed, then perhaps his brother wouldn't have a chance to seize the throne.

"Do you have to go to the front again?" I started.

"Of course," he said. "I have to fight with the Dzungars. I've chased them out of Tibet but they're still looming along the borders."

Ah, the Dzungars—the last nomads left from the Mongol Empire. They had been the Manchu's toughest enemies and had been resisting the control of the Qing government since the beginning of Kangxi's reign.

"Why do you have to go? There are other generals, aren't there?"

"But I'm the son of the emperor. The soldiers fight harder in my presence."

"Aren't you afraid of death?"

"Of course not!" He looked insulted. "Only cowards are afraid of death."

I sighed. Jeng was brave, honorable and duty-bound. His merits were the reason for his tragic end. How could I convince him to stay in Jing City? If he wasn't afraid of death, then what else could stop him?

"Lady Uya would be sad if you go away again."

"She would also understand I was doing it for Father Emperor and the Great Qing Empire."

I sulked at my inept persuasion. My frustration made me inattentive and I slipped on our way out of the forest. He caught me, wrapping his strong arms around me.

"Be careful!" he murmured. I froze in his arms for a moment, meeting his warm eyes, and feeling his warm breath. The alcohol on his breath smelled awfully enticing.

I struggled out of his embrace as soon as I regained balance, and we both fell silent.

Once we were out of the Imperial Garden, I said, "Nucai knows how to go home from here. Prince may leave as you wish."

"I can't leave you here," he said. "I must see you to your door."

"But it's late, and your fujins might worry."

He scoffed. "They won't. They're probably praying I drop dead and never go home again."

"Why?" I asked curiously.

"I don't know." He sighed. "When I'm home there's simply no peace. Strangely, when I'm not home they get along fine."

"How do you know?"

"The children told me."

It isn't strange at all, I wanted to say. They must've been all vying for his attention when he was home.

When we reached my unit, I bowed to him and wished him good night. "You still owe me a trip to Jingshan Park. I want to see sunrise at the Splendid Rock."

He paused, grabbed my hand and stared into my eyes. "How did you know about the Splendid Rock?"

I realized my blunder again. "I, uh, I don't remember. Lady Uya probably told me about it, or was it Lady Nian?"

He shook his head. "I don't think I told anyone about the place."

I shrugged. But he wouldn't let me off easily. "I have the feeling I know you from somewhere. But I can't pinpoint it."

I could hardly stop myself from falling into his arms and crying. I wanted to tell him how much I'd missed him and why I was here in front of him. But I knew if I did, he would think I was crazy. I trembled and held my tears instead.

"Nucai was a street performer before. I did magic shows with a circus. Perhaps Prince saw me there."

He shook his head. "I've never cared for street shows."

"It isn't true," I blurted out. "You loved them when you were a child. You and your brother used to sneak out of the palace together to see them."

His grasp tightened on my hand and he pulled me closer. "And how do you know that?"

"He told me," I lied, struggling out of his grip. He wasn't really hurting me since I had thick layers of clothes on, but he made me nervous. "Is it true?"

He paused and said, "Yes. It was one of the few common interests I shared with my . . . with the fourth prince."

I added boldly, eager to test my suspicion. "Lady Nian likes magic tricks, too. She said Prince Yong used to take her out to see them before they married."

His face instantly hardened. "That wasn't true. They had never even seen each other before they married. It was I who—"

He stopped short, but I already understood the meaning of the unfinished sentence.

A long silence followed. I wanted to say something but was afraid I would agitate him further. I could hear his heavy breathing in the silent night.

After a long pause, he said with a sigh, "I used to go to Nian's house often because Silan's brother was training me in archery. She was still a little girl at the time, very smart and curious, but not that happy staying home all the time. She always begged her brother and I to take her out."

His voice was low and nostalgic. His emotion clearly spoke his love for Lady Nian. She was probably the love of his life and the reason he neglected his own wives. I had suspected it, but now that it was confirmed, I could not bear the pain in my heart.

"Why didn't you marry her?" I asked.

He was taken aback by my insolent question. He glared at me, looking as if he was about to behead me. Then all of a sudden, his anger deflated, and regret filled his eyes.

"I wanted to. But she was too young, and wasn't healthy." He sighed. "She really shouldn't be . . . well, never mind."

His last comment reminded me of my own pity for Lady Nian, and my jealousy vanished. I felt sorry for the poor man instead. He had waited for the girl to grow up and to become healthy enough for a wife, but he lost his chance during the wait. And the fact that it was his own brother who took her! He must've hated Prince Yong already.

After a moment's silence he wagged his finger at me. "Don't let anyone know what I've spoken about tonight. Especially not Prince Yong. Do you hear me?"

I nodded. "Are you saying Prince Yong doesn't know about your feelings for her?"

"I don't know, and I don't care. But I don't want to get her in trouble because of any rumors."

"I promise I won't gossip." His concern for Nian made me envious again. "Although anyone with eyes could see you care about her. Your eyes never left her this evening."

He stared into my eyes with an expression that was hard to read. A moment later, he smiled and held me close to him. "Actually, I had my eyes on you all the time, at least when you were doing your tricks. Tell me, where did we meet?"

His low and sensuous voice made my knees weak, the proximity of his lips dazed me, and the warmth of his body threatened to melt me on the snowy ground. I knew I should break free from his embrace, but I couldn't. "Prince must've mistaken me for someone else," I whispered.

He pulled me closer. "I had the urge to hold you the moment I met you."

My knees wobbled and my heart beat frantically. "Why didn't you?" I whispered.

"You had a pair of scissors in your hand."

I laughed. "I wouldn't dare stab a prince."

Then my eyes fell on his lips and I waited. I wanted to feel them again.

I did promptly. The next moment, he set the lantern on the ground and I dropped my pine branches. He cupped my face in his hands and bent to kiss me. I forgot all the etiquette expected from a woman living in the eighteenth century and moaned.

He let go of me and stared at me, breathing heavily. "I'm sorry," he said.

"Not at all," I mumbled, feeling disappointed. I must've disgusted him with my wantonness.

"Come with me tomorrow," he said with urgency. "To the West Park."

"For the Ice Play training?" I was thrilled that he wanted to be with me and couldn't contain my excitement. "But I can't learn how to skate in two weeks."

"You can learn it in one day. Mother is right, you don't need to learn any fancy moves."

What had happened? I wondered as I looked at his eager face. At the dinner earlier he didn't think it was possible for me to learn skating in two weeks, now he thought I could do it in a day? It must be because of Silan.

"Why are you doing this?" I asked after taking a deep breath to calm my jealousy. "Is it to please Lady Nian?"

His face turned red and he squeezed my hands until they hurt. "You're very smart, aren't you?"

I had guessed it right, but it didn't make me feel good. I wanted to refuse him right on the spot, but I couldn't let go of the chance of being with him, either.

"I'll go," I said as calmly as possible, despite the tears that threatened to flood my face.

"Are you sure?"

"Yes, I'm sure. I want to learn how to skate." And perhaps I also wanted to please Lady Uya and Lady Nian.

"Wonderful!" He smiled.

He saw me enter my room and left. I stood at the door and watched his body vanish into the night. Hot tears rolled down my cheeks as I could no longer control my sadness and disappointment. Jeng was in love with another woman, very deeply. How could I have not taken the hints when we were together? I remembered his comments when we were watching *Empresses at the Palace*.

"This is ridiculous. Silan is the sweetest creature on earth!"

After a good cry that night, I reminded myself my wish was to save Jeng from his cruel fate. Whether he was in love with another woman or not was of no importance. I smiled as I imagined spending the coming two weeks with him.

CHAPTER 22

JENG SENT A messenger the next day to inform me that he would be taking me to West Park the morning after. And he also sent me a parcel containing a training outfit—loose fitting, side-button, cotton-padded jacket and pants.

I got up before dawn that day, ate a quick breakfast and walked to the Gate of Divine Might, where his carriage was waiting.

Located west of the Forbidden City, West Park consisted of three lakes—North, Middle, and South. In modern days, the north lake would turn into Beihai Park, while the other two together would merge into Middle South Sea—Zhongnanhai—and become the central government headquarters.

Inside the carriage, Jeng filled me in on the history of the Manchu Ice Play tradition. Living north of the Great Wall, the Manchus frequently fought on icy ground, and skating was a crucial military technique. Aguda, Emperor Taizu of Jin who founded the Jurchen Jin dynasty in the twelfth century, had efficiently used ice shoes and sleds during winter battles. In early times, they simply fastened animal bones on the bottom of their shoes. Later on the bones were replaced with wooden and metal pieces. Nurhaci, the Manchu king who laid the foundations of conquering the Ming and establishing the Qing dynasty, was besieged during a battle with the Barga Mongols. The Bargas had been defeated days before but unexpectedly returned and attacked them by surprise. Nurhaci's troops had left after an earlier victory and were miles away. Bargas thought Nurhaci was doomed to die because it was during the month of December, and the river that separated him from his soldiers was frozen. Yet hundreds of Manchu soldiers showed up just in time, flying across the frozen river, an incredible sight enough to shock the Mongols into dropping their weapons. Since then, Nurhaci celebrated the historical event by honoring the tradition of skating. The celebration usually took place in January.

The carriage stopped at the gate of West Park. Guards saluted the prince as they let us in. Soon I saw the White Stupa Temple, the landmark of Beihai Park, erected on top of the Jade Island in the center. I remembered the last time I had visited the Imperial Garden. It was but a couple years ago and I had come in the summer. The lake had been as blue as a sapphire and had been covered with acres of lotus flowers. Right now, the water looked like a solid piece of marble-like ice, and there was no sight of any plants. Some soldiers were already moving about on ice. Some were gliding across, some were jumping, and others were actually doing martial arts—standing on one foot, spinning and somersaulting, etc. I hadn't expected such advanced techniques and was stunned by what I saw. At the farther end of the rink, a group of soldiers were tossing and catching a ball while skating, very much like a playing handball, or water polo on ice.

"The Ice Play used to serve the purpose of military training only. Archery, martial arts, running and jumping, but lately, Father Emperor has encouraged more entertaining items. That's why we now have dancing and ball games," Jeng explained.

Jeng took me to one of the pavilions by the lake to get skates.

"Your feet are so tiny," he said with amusement after measuring my foot with his palm. "Don't tell me your mother had your feet bound when you were little?"

"Of course not!" I defended myself, knowing that the Manchus derided the Han custom. "Actually, I'm size six, about average!"

"What's size six?" he asked curiously.

The modern shoe sizing hadn't been developed yet. "It's, uh, never mind."

With the help of a soldier who worked at the stand, he found me a pair that was the smallest. The soldier showed me to a stool, so I could sit down to put them on.

I examined the skates curiously before putting them on. Each was made of a wooden piece with two thin metal blades inserted into the two sides of the bottom. Jeng explained that the double-blade skates were much more stable and made for beginners.

Jeng put on his single-blade skates and helped me fasten my straps. We left our coats at the pavilion, and he held my hand in his as he led me out slowly to the ice rink. I stumbled along, trying to balance myself the best I could, but it was hard. For one thing, it was the first time in twenty years that I tried the sport; and for another, the warmth of his hand was quite a distraction, and it caused a serious fluttering in my heart. For the first hour, I basically did nothing but learn how to balance on the ice, and how to fall skillfully so it would hurt less. I spent the rest of the day practicing how to walk forward and backward. It wasn't as easy as Lady Uya had said it would be, but it wasn't as hard as I remembered either. Jeng held my hands most of the time and I was surprised at how gentle and patient he was as a coach. He steadied me as soon as I threatened to fall. Nonetheless, I ended up falling a lot, fortunately without serious injuries.

Jeng wasn't with me every moment of the day, since he had to oversee the training, but he was mostly within my sight. When I took my breaks, I watched him and the soldiers practice. Some soldiers wore heavy armor and helmets, while waving the Qing flag or shooting arrows at targets. Jeng demonstrated how to shoot a target after doing a double loop—gracefully and smoothly—all done in a cumbersome changshan and primitive skates. I clapped my hands and shouted praise along with others.

That night, I returned to the Palace of Eternal Harmony with my body sore all over and headed straight to bed after dinner. But I was content since I had spent the whole day with Jeng.

IT TOOK ME about two days to be confident enough to walk on ice alone, with Jeng about two feet away. After that he taught me how to swizzle, glide and turn. It took me another week to master those skills. Finally, I learned how to spin slowly because I thought it would add some dazzling effects on my performance. After that, I practiced the magic tricks. I decided not to do the rabbit trick for a simple reason: I couldn't carry the hat with me. So, I would perform a variety of production tricks—the scarves, flowers, and of course, doves. I had acquired a dozen doves and a few cages with the help of Lady Uya. And I had sewed multiple pockets inside a gown that I planned to wear. I practiced how to pull out my doves smoothly so they wouldn't fly out of concealment. That turned out to be the hardest part since I had to put most of my effort into keeping myself balanced, and as soon as I paid attention to the tricks, I tended to sway right away. It took me days to train myself not to think about balance, but to trust my body. Only then could I freely focus my mind on the tricks.

The day before the Ice Play, I returned home a bit early. A maid intercepted me at Lady Uya's courtyard and told me I was wanted in the lady's living room.

"Are you ready for tomorrow?" Lady Uya asked me from where she sat on her recliner.

I nodded. "I think so."

"Great. I have something for you." She motioned to her maid, who then picked up a bundle from a table and presented it to me.

I saw the beautiful fabric before the maid unfolded its contents—a cloak made of green silk brocade with golden threads.

I gasped with delight. "Beautiful! Is it really for me?"

"Yes, it is. It's for you to wear tomorrow. It's padded with silk cotton, so it's warm although light. Do you like it?"

"Of course. I love it!" I said with appreciation as I caressed the smooth fabric. To my delight, I saw that inside was sewn with four large pockets, two on each side—perfect for hiding props.

I promptly put it on as expected, walking and turning to satisfy the kind lady, who couldn't stop complimenting me. "You look beautiful, my girl. I'm glad the color works for you. You know why I ordered a green one? All of the performers will be wearing prime colors—white, blue, red, yellow. You'll for sure stand out!"

"Do you mean you had this cloak made especially for me?" I said in astonishment. I had thought it was an old gown of the lady's, although it looked new.

"Yes," Lady Uya said with a smile. "I want you to look good for the emperor, Julie. It's an important event."

That explained the handy pockets as well. I immediately dropped my knees on the ground and thanked the lady profusely. Although part of her enthusiasm stemmed from her wish to please the emperor, I still felt indebted to her kindness.

That evening I had a sumptuous dinner with Lady Uya before returning to my room. I added a pocket in each sleeve of the gown and practiced my tricks one more time before going to bed. When I was in bed, I tossed and turned for a long time. I had agreed to do the Ice Play because I lost my head over Jeng, but now I realized how much my success meant to others. Lady Uya would be embarrassed if I faltered, and Jeng would be disappointed.

EARLY NEXT MORNING, a cannonball was fired to announce the opening of the Ice Play. It was no less grand than any Winter Olympics I had seen on TV. I stood in amazement when Lady Uya's carriage rolled into West Park. The whole palace was already here. There must've been thousands of people and hundreds of sedan chairs. Soldiers on skates stood by the ice ground, some in Manchu gowns tailored for easy movement and others wore stiff armors. Some held Eight Banner flags, others held bows.

Everyone was ready for the event to begin, but the most important person hadn't arrived yet. The emperor, as a rule, would appear the last. We waited patiently. Finally, murmurs filled the crowd and I turned to see a carriage moving slowly at the edge of the ice ground. After it had halted, Emperor Kangxi stepped out of his carriage and entered another vehicle that had been waiting for him. It was a sedan chair that looked like a dragon boat. Instead of carrying the sedan chair, men on skates slowly pushed it onto the ice. The vehicle stopped in the center of the ground, and brilliant fireworks lit up the gloomy sky. Group by group, soldiers glided through the ground in choreography patterns. They stopped in front of the emperor's sedan chair to salute him, then retreated to the edge of the ground.

After a second firing of a cannonball, a line of soldiers dressed in blue and white gowns rushed onto the ice and started the first item on the agenda—speed skating. After that, ice handball, archery, martial arts, and figure skating. Most of the performers were men, since the tradition was for military training. Although the figure skating wasn't as sophisticated as it was in the twenty-first century, the other performances, such as sword-fighting and boxing on ice, were spectacular. I was so enraptured by the brilliant performances that I almost forgot about my role. I was in Lady Uya's carriage, and my turn wouldn't come until near the end since Lady Uya wanted me to leave an impression on the emperor.

My pockets were stuffed with ribbons, scarves, and a bag of plum petals that I would be throwing into the air. My six doves stood quietly inside the cages.

"Will I be the only female performer?" I asked during a break, after watching the show for nearly two hours.

"I don't think so," Lady Uya said. "Last year some court dancers participated."

The dances turned out to be pretty ordinary and didn't look much different from the court dances I had seen on TV. But what came after surprised me and the lady herself—a woman doing a sword dance. She held two swords in hand, tossed them up in the air and caught them steadily, causing quite a lot of murmurs. The emperor seemed impressed, because he summoned her to his dragon boat and rewarded her with a bag of coins, presumably gold.

"Who is she?" Lady Uya asked her eunuch.

"My lady, she was hired by Consort Shunyimi."

Shunyimi was one of the few Han consorts of Kangxi, and he favored her very much. I glanced at Lady Uya, who's eyebrow was slightly raised. "Oh? No wonder."

She turned to look at me, as if saying, "You'll do better than her, won't you?"

I forced a smile to assure her, but inside, I was trembling.

"Are you ready, Julie?" Jeng's voice came from outside, and it soothed my nerves quite a bit.

"Yes." I responded quickly as I put the doves into my pockets with quivering hands. Then I took the empty cages with me.

Lady Uya gave my hand a tiny squeeze and told me she would pray for me.

I shivered as I stepped out of the carriage. It was freezing outside. But the sight of Jeng made me forget the cold right away. He wore a silver armor and looked divine. He took my hand, helping me steady myself.

"Your hand is so cold!" He looked at me with concern in his eyes.

I smiled nervously. "I guess it's because it's snowing."

"Let me warm you up." He grabbed my hands and rubbed his hands over mine.

My heart pounded even harder.

"Calm down," he said, looking deeply into my eyes. "Don't worry about the outcome. Just focus on the performance."

My blood started to heat at his words, which had appeared in my head hundreds of times already after he had first said them to me that night at the Palace Hotel. I nodded, smiling cheerfully.

I SWIZZLED SMOOTHLY onto the ice, clutching the cages to me. The audience hushed with my entrance, and I could feel their curious eyes. After saluting to the emperor, who expressed his surprise of seeing me with a loud gasp, I twirled around and glided on ice for a moment. Then I looked up at the sky, whistling, as if calling my lost birds. The audience laughed. After a seemingly futile attempt, I placed the cages on the ground and attempted a spin. Alas, it turned out to be as awkward as it could be. I got stuck at first, then I fell on my bottom. My cheeks burned. My first thought was Lady Uya. She must've been very embarrassed of me. I dared not imagine her reaction, but the audience's laughter somehow cheered me up. On the spot, I decided to turn the act into a comedy. I sat on the ice and hammered the ground with my fists. I paused a moment before extending a hand with a handkerchief on my palm. The audience murmured at the unexpected production. Then I stood up, wiped my eyes with the handkerchief, halted suddenly and looked above me. The audience followed my eyes and looked up, and at the precise moment, I pulled out my first dove from my sleeve and let out a whistle as I petted it. The audience gasped as I placed the dove in the cage. I walked backward, as if admiring the dove, then made another clumsy spin, this time not falling, and within the motion, I produced another pair of doves. The audience applauded this time. After that, I brought out the ribbons and scarves, threw the petals into the air, and produced the remaining doves after I cracked some eggs. The popping of firecrackers echoed the applause from the audience.

Imperial soldiers flew to me and helped me gather my props.

The emperor summoned me to the front of the dragon boat. "Julie, is that really you?"

"Yes, Your Imperial Majesty."

"Where did you learn such amazing trickeries?"

"Online, Your Majesty," I blurted out.

"What line?"

I quickly corrected myself. "I mean, I learned these while watching the street performers in a line."

Kangxi laughed. "Great performance! Reward!"

One of the emperor's servants handed me a heavy bag, and I kowtowed to the emperor before leaving him.

"You did great!" Jeng told me as he escorted me back to Lady Uya's carriage. He was holding my arm to lend me support, and I could hardly stop my urge to lean on him.

"Father Emperor was no doubt impressed," he continued after feeling the weight of the reward bag.

"I hope Lady Nian was impressed, too," I said.

He blinked. "I'm sure everyone is."

"Oh, Julie, you were such a great actor!" Lady Uya said to me once I returned to her carriage. "You had me fooled. I thought you really fell."

"My lady, I really did." I said solemnly, but she didn't believe me.

She had me open the reward bag in front of her and Jeng. Glittering gold coins dazzled me in an instant.

"This is a first-class reward!" Jeng said. "My archers only got silver coins."

I grinned. "Well, perhaps there were too many archers."

"I HAVE A reward for you, too, Julie," Lady Uya said as we returned to the Palace of Eternal Harmony in the afternoon.

She presented me with a trunk of silk fabrics and gowns, and embroidered slippers.

"Wear these to dinner with me tonight," she said, pointing at the shoes.

"Sure," I said as I picked up an embroidered silk slipper dotted with pearls with a thick, wooden piece on the bottom.

"Try them on!" she urged me.

I tried to detach the slipper from the wooden piece it was on, but it was stuck. Then I realized they were meant to be stuck—the wood was the shoe's sole. These weren't just slippers—they were the famous Manchu Flower Pot shoes—or Horse Hoof shoes!

I put them on and stood, holding onto the back of a chair for support. I was about four inches taller, but I could barely balance.

"Take a few steps!" Lady Uya encouraged me.

"Uh, I'm afraid I'll fall," I said embarrassedly.

She laughed. "Fall for real?"

I smiled at her humor. If I could skate on ice, then perhaps I could walk in these shoes. I let go of the chair and moved forward. Sure as hell, I fell on my bottom again.

Lady Uya laughed as the maids helped me up. She stood up and demonstrated. "Rule number one: you can't hurry. You must take your time, step by step. Rule number two: keep your back straight. A tiny slouch will result in the loss of balance. Rule number three: throw your hips. It helps you maintain balance and nice figure."

I spent the rest of the day learning how to walk on the Manchu shoes. It was much harder than walking on modern high heels. I felt like a robot with stiff joints. And I wondered how Lady Uya and other court ladies managed to walk with such grace. Or did their shoes force them to be graceful? I hadn't really mastered the art before dinner, but thankfully the lady found me a pair that wasn't as high.

The dinner was at the Palace of Heavenly Purity. Lady Uya let me sit next to her since she was proud of me. I wasn't sure whether all the princes and princesses were present, but the hall was full. I spotted Jeng sitting with a few other princes at a table nearby. He looked extremely handsome tonight in his light-blue brocade gown with a python emblem and golden belt. His tanned face glowed as he drank the toast proposed by the princes next to him, and he laughed without restraint as he shared anecdotes with them. Having tasted a few cups of palace wine myself, I was restless inside and could hardly resist the pull I felt towards him. I must've stared at him for too long because he looked my way and smiled, and his bright eyes seemed to be speaking to me. I quickly averted my eyes and involuntarily unbuttoned the top button on my gown to cool down the surge of heat that nearly smothered me.

"Don't be silly," I told myself. "He's in love with Silan, and no one else."

The thought of Silan reminded me of Prince Yong. I looked around and saw him at the table near the front among some court officials. I nearly gasped when I realized the man sitting next to him was Longkodo, Kangxi's right-hand man, who was said to have helped Prince Yong seize the throne. Prince Yong must've been cultivating their friendship already. The two seemed to be engaged in a formal conversation. The old man did most of the talking, while the prince nodded in agreement.

At the request of the emperor, I improvised a magic trick during the dinner, using a handful of red dates from the dessert plate, and making them appear and disappear under some rice bowls.

The emperor was impressed again, telling me that I was to become his personal entertainer as well.

After the dinner, we watched singing, dancing, and other performances. Once the emperor left, the family members lingered at the palace to socialize. When Lady Uya spoke to other consorts, Prince Yong came to me.

"Your performance was amazing today," he said, smiling. "Congratulations. I'm proud of you."

"Thank you!" I curtsied. "Nucai must thank Prince."

"For what?"

"For the opportunities you brought nucai. If it weren't for your recommendations—"

"You deserve it." He reached out and brushed a crumb off my jacket.

I blushed at the intimate gesture and hoped that no one else had noticed it.

"But I regret it often," Prince Yong said, in a voice so soft that I was afraid to look at him. "I wish I hadn't made the recommendation. You're a rare treasure, and I should've kept you in my house instead."

I laughed nervously. "Prince drank too much. Nucai doesn't deserve such praise."

He was standing very close to me and I could feel his breath on my skin. I stepped back, afraid he would grab me. "How's Lady Nian? Did she enjoy the show?"

The mention of his favorite fujin seemed to have reminded him of himself. "Lady Nian is well. Actually, she didn't make it to the Ice Play today, but she wants to congratulate you in person. Will you come to my house again sometime?"

"Of course, nucai will be honored to," I said with a bow.

When I straightened, I saw Jeng striding toward us, his displeasure clear on his face.

Prince Four's eyes flickered with something unreadable and he took leave right away, after wishing us good night.

"What were you talking about?" Jeng demanded.

"Nothing. He congratulated me, that's all," I answered, bewildered by his rudeness.

383

"Didn't he also invite you to his house again?" His face was dark.

"Yes," I said, wondering how long he had been watching us and what else he had overheard.

"What's your relationship with him?" he asked tersely.

"Nucai used to work in his house and tutor his son."

"That's it?" He looked unconvinced.

"That's it. Nucai accepts his invitation because of Lady Nian," I said quickly, hoping desperately that he wouldn't misinterpret anything between me and his brother.

But he didn't seem to be satisfied, and he left, his face schooled in a grimace.

That night I went to bed as soon as I had returned home from the dinner celebration. In my fragments of dreams, I kept chasing Jeng on ice, as if we were figure skating, except he was forever out of reach.

CHAPTER 23

☯

DURING THE MONTH that followed the Ice Play, I took on the duty of a court entertainer as well as being the Master of Learning. Even in school, the imperial children frequently requested magic tricks. I did my best to please them, making it an incentive for them to learn math.

Jeng was an infrequent presence in my life. He came at around noon when I got ready to leave school and walked me home. But that was it. He never went any further than walking side by side with me. When we reached the gate of the Palace of Eternal Harmony, I asked whether he wanted to come to my garden for a cup of tea, but he refused and went to see Lady Uya instead. When I reminded him his promise of taking me to Jingshan Park, he made excuses. It confused and irritated me. If he wanted to keep a distance between us, why would he even bother to come see me? While his coldness hurt me very much, what worried me the most

385

was not having a chance to warn him about his future. How could I help him prevent the upheaval that would ruin him and others? Constrained by decorum, all I could do was to wait patiently.

My opportunity finally came one day in March when Jeng suggested we go hiking in Jingshan Park. I was overjoyed because I had given up bringing up his promise again.

I met him at the Gate of Divine Might—the north entrance of the Forbidden City—one afternoon. We crossed a bridge above the palace moat and made our way to the park.

I remembered the crowds here the day we had come here early in the morning in the twenty-first century. In the Qing dynasty, the park was imperial property and commoners weren't allowed. We were the only visitors. The park in front of me looked very different—peach trees blossomed madly and billows of pink covered the hills. Following Jeng, I climbed uphill among the sea of flirtatious petals, letting them caress my cheeks and sniffing their light but sweet fragrance. There weren't any rails or benches around but there was a pavilion right at the vista point, and Splendid Rock was in the center.

Jeng settled on the rock when we reached the pavilion. He looked around at the scenery below us and sighed with satisfaction. "Splendid!"

I smiled and sat down on a bench next to him. "Did someone bring the rock here for a chair?"

"No!" Jeng smiled. "The pavilion was built around it. See? It goes below the floor. I guess the builder thought the rock made a perfect seat."

The sun was behind us, but its rays were spreading in front. The Forbidden City looked no less gorgeous in sunset than in sunrise, but the orange hue was gloomier. I remembered Jeng's sadness last time we were here. The Jeng next to me, however, looked content although reticent. He gazed at the view in front of us, as if mesmerized. I sat quietly, afraid of disturbing his meditation.

He spoke at last. "I never grow tired of it. Coming here always brings me joy."

I nodded. "It is a nice spot."

"I'm glad you like it." He smiled. "I've never brought anyone along."

"Nucai is honored." I stood up and bowed.

He got up from his seat and held my hands. "We're alone, Julie. There's no need to stick to the rules."

The warm gesture was quite unexpected after nearly a month's aloofness. I looked up and trembled under his gaze.

He caressed my face and smoothed away a strand of hair from my cheek, then he held me and whispered in my ear, "I've thought about you every day and night."

His soft voice and warm breath made me tremble more. I could feel his violent heartbeat against my own, and I wrapped my arms around him to enjoy the moment, unable to speak. Then I remembered his coldness that had tortured me. "Why did you keep your distance from me all these days?"

He stroked my cheek. "Because I thought you were Yong's."

"What gave you that idea?"

"You were very friendly with each other. He doesn't smile often, but he does when he's with you."

I wasn't aware of the fact, and I denied it instantly. "You've only seen us together a couple of times, and he happened to be happy during those few occasions. It had nothing to do with me."

He was unconvinced. "No, I can tell you're special to him."

I shrugged. "He likes my magic tricks."

"No, he likes you!" Jeng hissed.

"Stop it!" I tried to break free of his grip on my shoulders. "Did you bring me here to talk about Prince Yong?"

"No," he said, loosening his grasp. His eyes were still filled with heat. "But I want to know. Are you his?"

"You!" I punched his arm and turned away from him. Here I was, hoping to help him to escape his dreadful fate, but he was acting like a silly, jealous schoolboy.

"I'm sorry," he murmured, hugging me from behind. "He just has the habit of taking away what should be mine."

I forgave him and let him pull me onto his lap as he settled into the rock seat again. Then he kissed me, first my forehead, then my nose, and my lips. I tasted him hungrily, closing my eyes to enjoy the moment. I grabbed him tightly, afraid he would disappear like the ghost in my dreams. His powerful arms twined around me and crushed me, as if he wanted to meld my body into his. The passion we had stifled in the past month burst like a rampant wildfire, consuming us until we were out of breath.

"I haven't seen the emperor for days," I said when I snuggled in his arms a moment later. "How's his health?"

"He's all right. I played the chess with him yesterday."

"Did his hands shake?" I asked. I had noticed that symptom from time to time.

He paused for a moment. "Not when I was there. Don't worry. He's had that problem for years. The imperial doctors will take care of him."

His optimism upset me. "But I do worry."

"Why?" he looked at me with surprise.

"What if His Majesty—" I paused, knowing such inference was considered blasphemous.

Jeng understood my unfinished sentence, but he didn't blame me. "How long we live is all determined by the gods in heaven."

That was Jeng's problem. He believed in fate. I took a deep breath. "But you at least have to be prepared."

"Be prepared, how?"

"If the emperor passes away then everything will be different."

He didn't seem concerned at all. He pulled me to him, brushed his lips against my cheek, and said, "Don't worry your pretty, smart head about it. I'll be fine."

His confidence puzzled me. I lowered my voice even though there was no one else around. "What do you mean you'll be fine? Do you mean you'll become, uh, the emperor?"

He shrugged. "That would be nice, but I don't care. What I mean is, I'll be the same as I am now. If one of my brothers became the emperor, then I'll still be a duke."

"What if Prince Yong ascends the throne? Would you still be fine?"

He paused for a second. "He will not! I assure you."

"How could you be so sure? What if—" I was so frustrated that my tears streamed down my cheeks.

He smiled and kissed my tears away. "Among us, he's the least favored by Father Emperor. Father said years ago that his fourth son was reckless and moody, thus wouldn't be fit to rule. Yong knows he doesn't have a chance, either. That's why he's made friends with the Crown Prince, and then Prince Eight. He thinks they'll be the successors. He even tried to win me over, but I didn't give him the time of day."

I shook my head. "That's his strategy. He is the most ambitious of you all, but pretends he doesn't care, so the emperor doesn't think he's a threat."

Jeng laughed. "That's absurd. Yong isn't such a clever guy."

Another tear slid down my cheek, and Jeng brushed it away with his thumb. "I'll tell you a secret, but you absolutely have to keep it to yourself."

He looked around as if to make sure no one was eavesdropping, then he whispered in my ear, "Not that I care, but I have a pretty good chance."

His earnest face almost convinced me, even though I knew he was wrong. "Are you sure?"

He nodded. "Mother told me."

"What did Lady Uya say?"

"Father told her just recently that I was the best candidate."

"You see," I said. "He didn't say you would be his successor. Candidate and successor are different."

"But it isn't his style to be straightforward."

"That is precisely the cause of all the tragedy."

"What tragedy?"

"The fourth prince will rule, and you will be banned from the court. You'll be confined in the Imperial Graveyard."

He chuckled. "What a horrid story you're making up!"

"It's true! It's not a story. It's the future!"

"When did you become a fortune teller?"

I grabbed his arms and stared into his eyes. "I'm not kidding! I come from the future."

He gazed at me as if trying to decide whether I was sane. Then he grinned. "I see. You're trying to scare me, so I'll stay here in Jing City. I knew you liked me but didn't know you liked me that much!"

Under normal circumstances I would roll my eyes at his smugness, but at the moment I felt nothing but frustration. I took a deep breath. "I'm serious!"

"Okay! Okay!" He pulled me to him again, and whispered, "I promise I'll come back soon. Wait for me, all right?"

Then he pressed his lips on mine.

"SINCE WE'RE ALREADY out of the palace," Jeng said as we exited the park. "I want to take you to the Inner City to see someone."

"Who?"

"The eighth prince. He's been wanting to meet you."

"Great! I want to meet him as well."

Prince Eight—Yinsi—was the son of a beautiful palace maid, thus he was of lower rank among the princes. But he was very talented and had not only been Kangxi's most favored son at an early age, but also well-liked by his brothers. Soon after the emperor had annulled the Crown Prince, Yinsi became ambitious, and took a series of actions to compete for the future throne, including forming the Eighth Prince Clique. His ambition, however, only earned him adverse feelings from the insecure emperor, who felt his son was challenging him. After a series of misunderstandings, the emperor not only took away Yinsi's title and punished him with confinement, but also called him "the son of a low-born hussy," in front of other princes. Yinsi never recovered from the blow and had lived a secluded life ever since.

As soon as we entered the courtyard of the eighth prince's mansion, I heard the music of the flute. It was *Wild Geese Descending on Sandbank*, a famous piece from the Ming dynasty. I soon saw a man in a plain navy gown holding the vertical bamboo flute and sitting by a pond under a pear tree of snowy blossoms.

"That's him," Jeng whispered.

I glanced at the man whose mind seemed to be carried away by the music and was oblivious of his surroundings. He had pallid, hollow cheeks and a sharp chin, and he looked forlorn. I tried to reconcile him with the portrait of the eighth prince I had seen before—a man with a sanguine complexion and kingly countenance, square chin and straight nose, and a benevolent smile. I had thought him the most handsome among Kangxi's sons, and he was supposed to be cheerful and charismatic, but I guessed years of seclusion and his father's neglect had worn down his spirit.

We stood quietly at a rock a few feet from the man and listened to him play. The classical piece was melancholic and beautiful. It was meant to express the disappointment the artist felt about the world around him, which was full of power struggles, and his wish to fly away from this sinister world, like a carefree wild goose. The melody was smooth and not at all monotonous, sorrowful and yet playful at the same time. Some notes even mimicked the sounds of the wild geese. In the murmuring low tones, I could hear the geese cooing and imagined them playing peacefully on the sand in the sunset, and when the tone rose it sounded like the geese's joyful calls when they soared high into the sky.

Prince Eight held the flute and kept the same posture long after he had finished playing the last note, as if he was deeply immersed in the music and unable to detach himself from it.

Jeng clapped his hands. "Brother's skills have improved."

Yinsi started. He turned and smiled as he saw us. "Jeng! It's good to see you! And is this the famous—?"

I curtsied right away. "Your servant Julie wishes the eighth prince well."

"No need for formalities. Ah, let me see. Jeng wouldn't stop talking about you when he was last here. I know so much about you already, you're a math genius, a trick master, and an accomplished skater. But he concealed your beauty from me. Why?"

The eighth prince was indeed as amiable as legend said. No wonder he had many friends. My cheeks burned at his compliment, and after chiding Jeng with a quick glance, I looked down.

Yinsi laughed. "Come, let's go inside. Have you two eaten?"

Soon, dinner was brought into the cozy living room.

The eighth prince's fujin Guoluoluo came out to meet us. The glamorous Manchu princess sat with us for a while and played the zheng to entertain us. It was well known that the eighth prince had loved dearly and even feared his wife, but the woman in front of me was not at all formidable. She was rather graceful. She played *Plum Blossoms in Three Movements* for us, a delightful piece that praised plum blossom's fearless, enduring character that enabled it to survive frost and snow. Although she never looked up even once from the instrument, I couldn't help but feel that the princess was playing it with her husband in mind. The couple had been through much hardship in the last decade, but had supported each other with love, and perhaps music. I could not imagine the loneliness and grief that Yinsi would have to bear five years from now, when he would receive a decree from his half-brother, Emperor Yongzheng, ordering him to divorce Guoluoluo and forbidding him to even write to her. Shortly after that cruel, final strike, the dejected prince would die inside the Imperial Clan Court.

But at the moment, unaware of their future, the two brothers chatted and laughed over rice wine.

"Frontier general. I knew my little brother would grow into a big man." Yinsi gazed at Jeng after having finished a few cups of wine. "I still remember the first time I took you hunting. You were only ten years old but hunted more rabbits than anyone else."

"Thanks to you, brother. You taught me well."

"Don't be humble. You're a natural."

"Did you go autumn hunting last year?" Jeng said.

Yinsi stopped smiling and sighed. "No. Father didn't ask me to."

"That's ridiculous. It's been so many years!" Jeng exclaimed. "Let me speak to him."

"No!" Yinsi said. "Please don't. I don't want you to lose his trust in you because of me. Did you forget that last time you almost lost your head when you tried to help me?"

Jeng fell silent. Yinsi was referring to an incident that had taken place about eight years ago. Yinsi had excused himself from accompanying his father to the Summer Palace in order to attend the death anniversary of his mother. He sent a pair of gyrfalcons—the fastest flying birds and regarded as God of Falcons by the Manchus—to his father to apologize for his absence, but the prized birds had become ill by the time they reached Kangxi. The superstitious emperor was outraged, saying that his son was cursing him by using dying birds. He had been about to execute Yinsi, but Jeng and other princes begged him to reconsider. However, the timing was bad, and the emperor not only didn't forgive Yinsi, but he also nearly sentenced Jeng to death at the moment.

"But that was such a long time ago." Jeng laughed. "I'm sure Father has forgiven you. I just want to remind him that you liked hunting."

"I'm not sure if that's a good idea," Yinsi said after downing another cup of wine. "To tell the truth, I'm afraid of being with Father. He hasn't been the same since that incident. I can't face him without remembering what he said about my mother. Those words hurt me more than blades."

Jeng put his hand on his brother's shoulder. "Forget them and forgive him. He wasn't himself. Remember the days when he doted on you."

"Those days are gone for good." Yinsi smiled bitterly. "I forgave him long ago. I feel sorry for him. I know he loves all of us deep down, but he's also wary of us. Especially after what Taizi did to him. He can't help but be distrustful of his own sons. But you're different, Jeng. He still treats you well. Don't ruin your chance because of me."

Jeng Shrugged. "I don't care for the throne."

"But you must!" Yinsi said. "You're our only hope. You know how much Prince Yong hates us and our ninth brother. If he became the emperor, he would treat us all like he treated my gyrfalcons, and we'll all die."

I gulped. I didn't know Prince Yong had been responsible for the death of the gyrfalcons.

"No way!" Jeng said, looking horrified. Apparently, he hadn't known it, either. "He couldn't be such a monster. He didn't poison the falcons. Someone else did it."

"It was him. I spent years investigating the matter. The falcons were tough birds and they could survive with no food or water for days. Why would they die in just half a day? I had someone watch the messenger for years and found out that he was related to Yong's second fujin. He had always been jealous of me, I finally realized it. He never shows off in front of Father, but behind our backs, he's doing a lot of sordid business. He's dangerous, Jeng, you have to watch out!" Prince Yinsi grabbed Jeng's arm when he shouted the last sentence.

Jeng's jaw fell. "That's not possible. You've drunk too much, brother. And you think too much. You should get out of your house more often."

A string broke on the zheng, and Guoluoluo stopped playing. She stood up. "Let me take him to his bedroom."

Jeng helped her with the task, and I waited alone in the living room. I glanced around me. The prince's lack of favor from the emperor was evident from the simple furniture and display items in the house. On the wall, however, hung scrolls of calligraphy written by Yinsi himself from years ago. When the eighth prince had been little, Kangxi had hired the famous calligraphy master Chao He to teach Yinsi and ordered him to turn in ten scrolls of practice per day for the emperor to inspect. It showed Kangxi's care for his son. How could that much love vanish into the winds just like that?

A FEW DAYS after my visit to the Jingshan Park, the emperor summoned me to his study.

"Julie, what do you think of Jeng?"

I was taken aback at that question. I stammered, "Your Majesty, I do not know the fourteenth prince well enough, except that he, uh, seems to not like math."

Kangxi laughed. "That's true. He hated it. I remember him crying when I forced him to solve equations. He was eight at the time. He was the naughtiest of my sons. Loved fighting and nothing else.

Whipping him wouldn't help, so I punished him by making him do math. It worked!"

I couldn't help but laugh. "No wonder he hated it so much. On the other hand, his math probably improved because of the punishments."

I told the emperor about how Jeng had figured out the hare and the tortoise problem in his head and he was impressed.

"You see, I know he's smart. If only he would spend some time to learn it!"

I was surprised again. The emperor seldom expressed his opinions about his sons in front of me. I didn't know how to respond.

After he had dwelled on his thoughts for a moment, he looked at me again. "You've known him for months, and he taught you to skate, didn't he? What do you really think of him?"

Seeing I couldn't avoid it, I said, "I think Prince Jeng is honest, brave, and kind. He's also a filial son. He often speaks of his Father Emperor."

Kangxi nodded. "I know, I know. He's a good son, and he's a good husband, too. He never mistreats his fujins, although I've been told they are a handful."

I clasped my hands tightly in front of me, not knowing what to make of that piece of information.

"To tell the truth," Kangxi went on, smiling at me. "Jeng has asked me for your hand."

I gasped, realizing the emperor had the authority to marrying his servants off. "What? Nucai, uh, dares not to—"

The emperor laughed. "Stop it, Julie. I'm an emperor but I'm also a human being. I know how you feel about each other. I see the glances between you two when you are together."

I blushed and tried to recall the few occasions we were together in front of the emperor. He had to be referring to the dinner after the Ice Play. But there were so many people around, and I wasn't really looking at Jeng that often, was I? "Nucai—"

"That's fine." He waved my concern away. "Do you wish to become his fujin?"

"I, uh," I thought quickly what to say. I had no plans of marrying Jeng, although I loved him dearly. I didn't plan to stay here in the Qing dynasty for long and would have to leave him sooner or later. But the emperor's wishes were not to be disobeyed. "Can nucai think about it first?"

Kangxi's smile disappeared briefly. "Of course. I'm not giving you an order. But I don't see why you need to think. Jeng is to become my—" The emperor paused, and I waited eagerly for him to finish his sentence, but he didn't. "I have great expectations for him," he said instead. "And with your talents and your prescience, I think you'll provide him tremendous help."

I bowed and thanked the emperor for his praise.

From the emperor's words, I had no doubt that he indeed favored Jeng and intended to make him his successor. The fact only saddened me more as it lent support to the conjecture that Prince Yong had seized the throne from his brother.

I had a sleepless night and kept thinking what I could do to change Jeng's stubborn mind.

APRIL ARRIVED AT the Forbidden City, bringing with her warmer weather and colorful gardens. Pear blossoms and peonies added liveliness to the austere walls and the lofty buildings. But the sight did not cheer me. Jeng could be leaving any day. I still hadn't been able to convince him to take my request seriously.

I was with the emperor in the South Study when the very object of my vexation showed up, asking to speak to his Father Emperor. The emperor was glad to see him, and he did not dismiss me.

"Do you have enough supplies for the trip?" Kangxi asked warmly after Jeng sat down.

"Yes, I do. Thank you for asking."

"What's the purpose of your visit? Not because you miss me?"

Jeng bowed when spoke to his father. "Your Majesty, please forgive your son's bluntness, but I think it's time to restore the eighth prince his title."

The smile disappeared from Kangxi's face. "Didn't I already give him back his Beile?"

"Yes, you did. But he deserves to be a duke, at least."

"How dare you?" Kangxi smacked his hand on the desk, giving me quite a start. "Helping that conceited good-for-nothing again!"

Jeng knelt and kowtowed. "Father Emperor! Please allow your son to speak! My eighth brother deeply regrets his wrongdoings, and often expresses his wish for Your Majesty's forgiveness. He is the most capable among us. Please give him a chance to use his talents!"

I kept my eyes on the book I was reading, afraid to make a sound. The subject of discussion was very sensitive, and I wished I wasn't present.

"I know who is the most capable and who is not," Kangxi said. "And I don't need you to tell me what to do. Who do you think you are? I can take away your title just as easily as I took away his. Now get lost!"

For a moment, Jeng didn't move but stared at his father with a dazed look. He was shocked. But soon he took hold of himself, kowtowed, and excused himself.

After Jeng left, Kangxi was in no mood to study math, and he soon dismissed me as well.

THAT EVENING, I was practicing embroidery in my room when I heard a knock. Jeng stumbled in, smelling of alcohol. I helped him onto the couch.

"I don't understand, Julie," he mumbled. "Father is a great emperor, and yet he can be so unreasonable from time to time."

"Well, he's also a human being," I consoled him, passing him a cup of hot water. "I think he must love Prince Yinsi a lot, otherwise he wouldn't have been so hurt by what he'd done."

He drank the water silently and held my hand. "I'm leaving in a few days."

I had expected it, but unstoppable tears gushed from my eyes nonetheless.

He wiped my tears and kissed me. "Don't cry. I'll be back soon."

"Why can't you stay?"

"I can't, Julie. It's my duty to make sure the borders are free of invaders."

"Didn't you already expel the Dzungars from Tibet?"

"Yeah but they could come back. That's why I have to eradicate them. They've retreated to Xinjiang, and that's where I'm going next."

"Why is it necessary?" I said, looking away.

"The Dzungars are a constant threat to the Qing Empire," he said with a sigh. "They never cease their attempts to invade our land. They are the reason for Father Emperor's anxiety and worries. We've had a great victory, and I want to annihilate them before they can recover their strength."

He was indeed a filial son and he was doing it for his father. I squeezed his hand. It would be hard to change his mind, but I had to try. "But giving them a little break wouldn't hurt much, would it?"

"Why? If I took care of it now, then I wouldn't have to go again. I could spend all my future days and years with you!"

I was touched for a moment by the prospect but came to my senses right away. "No, you couldn't!

You'll—" I couldn't finish the sentence. Instead, I put my face in my hands and cried again.

He held me close. "You worry too much. I promise you I'll come back."

His gentle words made me weak, and I melted into his embrace. I stopped speaking and let him caress me. I tasted his lips and then his tongue. He unbuttoned my Manchu shirt and kissed my neck. I unfastened his belt and helped him remove his jacket. Then I let him carry me to my bed.

Although he was only three years younger, this Jeng felt a bit different from the Jeng I remembered. He was a lot more vigorous due to the constant military training. But he was gentle and considerate all the same, making sure he didn't hurt me during our love-making.

I nestled in his arms afterwards, enjoying the precious moment of being close to him.

"I've already asked the emperor to give you to me. Has he spoken to you yet?" he said, kissing my forehead.

"He did."

"Have you agreed?"

I hesitated, not sure what to say. I did not want to disappoint him, but the matter was the least important on my mind. "I haven't yet, but I will, if you promise not to leave me."

"Come on, Julie!" He sighed heavily. "Why are you being so unreasonable?"

"On the contrary, I'm being very reasonable," I said. "If you left me this time, you would never be able to marry me at all. I would probably be Prince Yong's possession by the time you came back."

"I see! So, he's the reason? Has he also proposed to you?"

"No! That's not what I mean!" I said desperately. "He's going to become the emperor."

He fell silent for a moment, then he said, "I don't know why you and Yinsi think it's possible. But even if Yong did indeed become the emperor, it wouldn't matter much. He wouldn't do anything to harm me."

"He would. Like I said the other day, he will take away your titles and you'll become a caretaker of the imperial tombs. He will also order the eighth prince Yinsi to divorce his beloved wife Guoluoluo, imprison him along with the ninth prince, and starved them to death." I concealed the part about Lady Uya committing suicide, simply because I couldn't bear to speak of it. I buried my face in his arm and tried to prevent my tears from flowing again.

He kissed me gently. "Stop predicting the future."

"Not predicting. Revealing." I took a deep breath and told him how we met in the future. "You time traveled in order to change history but ended up three hundred years in the future instead of three years in the past. I helped you find your way home. But apparently, you failed again when you returned, and got killed by your brother. That's why I'm here. To help you."

He raised an eyebrow. "That sounds incredible."

"I know, and I didn't believe it when you told me you were from the past and you were the son of Emperor Kangxi. I thought you were a lunatic."

He didn't respond, as if wanting to hear more. "I took you to the Forbidden City, which will become a tourist attraction in the future, and there you proved your identity to me. You showed me your secret storage in the Imperial Garden, and you found the sling you had hidden inside the rocks. You told me when you were a child you hurt someone using the sling and Lady Uya ordered you to throw it away, but you hid it instead. We also went to Jingshan Park to watch the sunrise, and you looked for Splendid Rock, which was no longer there. You recited the poem His Majesty had written: *A thousand miles of clouds embrace the dwelling of the gods. Below it is my humble territory . . .*"

Jeng's eyes widened as he listened, then he squeezed them shut as if he was thinking hard. I waited anxiously for him to respond. When he opened his eyes again, he asked. "What could you do to help me if I died even after time traveling once?"

I let out a sigh of relief. Whether he believed my story or not, he was willing to listen. I then told him the role Longkodo played in Prince Yong's scheme. "He'll be responsible for forging the emperor's will."

"Uncle Longkodo?" he cried in disbelief. "But he's Father Emperor's most trusted court officer! Why on earth would he do it?"

"That's a mystery to historians. But it doesn't matter why he did it. The important thing is that you must do something to stop it from happening."

"How?"

"You have to get rid of him," I said. "I don't mean you have to kill him, but you have to get him away from the emperor."

"That'll be very difficult." He frowned. "Father trusts him more than any of his sons."

"I know. But you'll have to try, for the sake of not just you, but your other brothers."

"But how exactly would I try? Do you have a plan?"

I hesitated. The truth was, I didn't. I was hoping he would come up with one. "Maybe you could tell the emperor to watch out for him, because there are rumors that he has ulterior motives?"

He shook his head. "It won't work. There isn't any proof of wrongdoing and Father hates slander without proof."

True, Longkodo hadn't committed the crime yet, and he had been the emperor's dedicated right-hand man.

"What about gathering evidence? Longkodo seems to have a close relationship with Prince Yong."

"You mean, conduct a secret investigation?" Jeng's brow furrowed, then he sighed. "Finding others' faults is not one of my strong points."

"But you have to do something!" I flapped my hands in agitation. How could he be so passive?

Jeng held me again and stroked my cheek. "Don't worry, let me think of another way. I can't do anything now because Father is still mad. But he will forgive me once I'm out of his sight. I'll write to him in a month and warn him about uncle. It's probably better than saying it in person. And I promise I'll come home before he falls ill. When will that be?"

"Beginning of December."

"Then I'll come back early November."

JENG LEFT JING CITY a few days later in the middle of April. It drizzled the morning he and his troops set off for the journey. I stood on the veranda of the Hall of Supreme Harmony and watched him among the soldiers lined up in a square in front. He sat erect on horseback in a set of dazzling silvery blue armor. His face was half hidden under his helmet, but I knew he was glancing at me as well. I held my tears and waved at him before he turned away.

CHAPTER 24

FOR DAYS AFTER Jeng had left, I excused myself from my duties and stayed in my room, feeling depressed and confused. I felt that I had failed my mission and wasn't sure what I was supposed to do next. Should I wait another six months for him to return? What other choice did I have? I thought about going back to the Temple of Light and Shadow, and returning to the future, but I quickly dismissed the idea. *I have to help Jeng. He will return.* I kept telling myself that over and over, but I was exhausted. The palace with its high walls felt like a prison sometimes, and I didn't really have the freedom to go out. I wasn't sure whether I could wait that long.

Lady Uya came to see me and commiserated with my feeling of loss. Jeng had told his mother about his plans to marry me, and the lady treated me like her daughter, even sending maids to bring me food and to sing to me. Thanks to her care, I regained my strength soon enough.

ONE MORNING IN May, as I was on my way to the Upper Study, I saw eunuchs scurrying around in the narrow alleys, which was an unusual sight in the peaceful palace. One of them was in such a hurry that he nearly bumped into me. When he looked up, I recognized the eunuch who worked for Lady Uya. "Little Yuan, what's going on? Did something happen?"

"Yes," he lowered his voice. "Someone broke into the Palace of Heavenly Purity last night!"

I gasped. The palace was normally heavily guarded day and night. "That's not possible! Is His Majesty all right?"

"Yes. He didn't stay there last night. The guards were all drugged with incense."

"What did the thief steal?"

"So far, they haven't found anything missing, but all the drawers have been looked through. And the official documents are scattered everywhere."

"What about the emperor's collection of antiques and treasure?"

"Intact."

"That's strange."

"Exactly. I have to go. Lady Uya is waiting for my report."

I found myself wondering about the incident throughout the morning. What had the thief wanted?

I wasn't summoned in the afternoon, but I went to South Study anyway, hoping to find out more about the break in. I waited outside for nearly an hour since the emperor was taking an unusually long nap.

Although clearly suffering from after-nap gloom, the emperor smiled when he saw me. "Ah, just the person I want to see. Perhaps you can help me solve the mystery."

"Is it about last night?" I asked.

"Yes." He then told me what I had already heard from Little Yuan. What troubled me also troubled him. "What could the thief be interested in among my papers?"

"Couldn't Your Majesty simply check to see what document has been stolen?"

He paused and laughed. "I see. You have no idea how many memos and proposals I have to read per day, and how many unread documents I have on my desk!"

I shook my head and apologized for my ignorance.

"On average I have to read about two hundred memos each day," he said, still smiling. "I read them from four o'clock in the morning to noon. Eight hours, thirty per hour. And I have to comment on them, too. Although most of the time I just write 'noted'. Quite often I have to write down reasons why I disapprove the proposals."

"Nucai appreciates Your Majesty's hard work," I said sincerely. I didn't know the emperor was so busy.

And after all that work, how could he have the energy to study math? No wonder his health deteriorated so soon.

"Including the ones I haven't read, I have thousands of memos on my desk. How am I supposed to know which one is missing?"

"Nucai's suggestion is silly," I muttered.

"That's okay. You're forgiven. Now think of a better suggestion."

I groaned inwardly and regretted my curiosity. *Why did I come?* "What did the palace inspectors say?"

"They told me to try to remember what I had been reading." He rolled his eyes.

I had been about to say the same thing, but I swallowed it back and thought hard for a better suggestion. I recalled all the mysteries that I had read in the past. "Perhaps we should think of the motives of the crime, Your Majesty."

"What do you mean? We don't even know what has been stolen, how could we guess the motive?"

I wasn't entirely sure what I had in mind, but I went on, "Yes, we'll reverse the procedure. You see, someone risked his life to break in the central government of the Qing Empire. So, it must be something that's very important. Perhaps Your Majesty can remember the most important memos you've read lately? For example, have you approved the death penalty of someone?"

The emperor fell silent, his face a mask of concentration. Then he said, "Yes, there was a case regarding a corrupted county magistrate. Let me go check."

He stood up and I accompanied him to the Palace of Heavenly Purity.

"They tidied it up," the emperor said as we stepped into his study in the back of the main hall. "But it was a mess this morning when the maid came in. There were papers all over the floor."

He checked the piles of papers on his desk and found the memo regarding the county magistrate. "I did indeed approve his death penalty. But the paper is still here."

After that, he recalled a few more cases similar to the above, but all of them were intact. Finally, he gave up, and called for refreshment and tea.

"Another thing that troubles me is this," he said, taking a sip of his red date and goji tea. "The lock was open, and yet the keys were intact at the Imperial Household Affairs."

All the palaces were locked at about eight o'clock in the evening, and all the keys were submitted to Imperial Household Affairs. Anyone who wished to use a key must make a request and the request would be recorded on a log.

"That's strange," I said. "Where is the lock?"

He pointed at a miniature bronze statue on the table. I stared at it and realized it was a lock. It was made in the shape of a *qilin*, a Chinese mystical creature with the embodiment of lion, dragon, deer, and tiger. A bar ran from the lion's head and the dragon's tail of the creature, and the key hold was inside its mouth.

"Are there spare keys?"

He nodded as he fumbled in his pocket for the spared key. "Yes, but I have it."

Obviously, the thief must've picked the lock. But the emperor's next words explained his doubts. "It can't be picked because of its unique mechanism."

He took out a string of keys, and pointed to a particular one, which looked surprisingly similar to modern keys with its serrated edge. "It's highly secure. I have had skillful locksmiths in the city try to open it with various tools, and all of them failed. There is a row of pins in the mouth of the qilin, and unless the teeth of the key matches the shape of the teeth under those pins, the lock won't turn." He demonstrated by inserting the key into the mouth of the qilin. As soon as he turned the key, the shackle sprang open.

I realized I was looking at an early version of modern pin tumbler lock, which wouldn't be invented by Linus Yale until the nineteenth century and wouldn't be adopted in China until the twentieth century.

"How is it possible?" I blinked.

The emperor mistook my perplexity for awe. "It's designed by my late science tutor Father Verbiest. A genius and a great man," he said proudly.

I recalled reading about the man during my preparation for the time travel. The Jesuit had actually invented the world's first steam-powered, self-propelled vehicle, although as a toy for the emperor.

"Someone probably figured out a way," I said, knowing that the modern lock was not pick resistant and could be opened easily using a bobby pin or a paper clip, although none of them had been invented yet.

The emperor sighed. "That is possible. After all, it has been more than thirty years."

"Are there any suspects at all?"

"A palace guard reported seeing a eunuch around the palace shortly after nine. He didn't recognize the face, only remembered he wasn't young. He claimed he was from Consort Nala's palace and had been sent to get an imperial doctor. But the consort didn't verify the story, and she doesn't have a eunuch that fits the description."

We didn't speak a word until we finished our tea. After the maid had cleared the table, I asked, "Are you sure that nothing valuable has been stolen?"

"I am. Nothing is missing."

"What about books?" I asked. Rare books could be treasure, too.

He shook his head.

"Nucai has a thought, but nucai dares not to speak."

"Go on!"

"Where does Your Majesty keep your will?"

Kangxi raised his eyebrow. "You're right!"

He went promptly towards the mahogany cabinets against the wall. "Here. It's no secret to everyone in the palace. For generations, the testaments of the emperors have been kept here. And mine is right here." He pointed to one with a lock in the shape of a fish.

"It is locked," I said. "So, I guess nothing has been stolen."

He sighed. "I'm not sure. You see, Father Verbiest designed it, too."

He chose another serrated key from his string of keys and opened the lock. Then he took out a carved wooden box, also locked. He opened it as well, and it was empty.

I gasped. "Does that mean—?"

"No." The emperor smiled. "It's been empty for years. I haven't written one yet."

He put back the box and closed the cabinet door, then he opened it again, and looked inside. "Strange."

"What is it?"

"Actually, I put a scroll of paper right next to the box a few days ago. I was going to draft my will."

He reached his hands inside the cabinet. "Ah, there it is. It's been pushed all the way in." The emperor's face turned white and he was silent for a moment. "Was it what he wanted? Who could it be?"

My heart pounded. Relating to the fact that the crime took place only days after the emperor had attempted to write a will, I had very little doubt it was the motive.

"Who was present when Your Majesty wanted to draft your will?"

"Oh, the usual people. Eunuch Li and the maids."

"Are you sure? Did anyway drop in, even for a brief second?"

The emperor paused. "I believe Prince Three had come by, and Longkodo."

"Longkodo!" I repeated the name. It must've been him. He must've been curious about who had been named the successor. Once he knew, he could devote his attention to the future emperor before everyone else. It would certainly be an advantage in his future.

"No," the emperor said. "It couldn't be the reason. I might have pushed the scroll inside myself. You see, if the person was here for the will, then he wouldn't be looking through the pile of memos."

"But he might be trying to fool us," I said. "He created a mess on your desk on purpose, in order to mislead Your Majesty into thinking he was after the official memos.

Kangxi's mouth opened. "Clever indeed!"

I had no idea whether he meant the thief or me, and I didn't ask.

He locked the cabinet and turned to leave, but only turned back as if stopped by a thought. He took out his keys again and opened another cabinet, which contained three boxes.

"These are the testaments of my ancestors," he explained as he brought the boxes down one by one and set them side by side on the desk. "Nurhaci, Hong Taiji, and Shunzhi."

He opened those boxes, in the same order of the succession, and he froze as he opened the last one. It was empty.

"What's the meaning of this?" The emperor knitted his eyebrows.

I stood silent, not knowing what to make of it, either. What could anyone do with the will of the last emperor?

"When was the last time you opened the box?" I asked, trying to be helpful.

"The same day I was trying to write my own testament," he said. "I wanted to see the format."

"I see." I nodded gravely. Did the thief have the same purpose in mind?

"Could I have misplaced it afterwards?" he said, squeezing his eyes shut in concentration. When he opened his eyes again, he said affirmatively, "No, I'm not that old. I remember putting it back into the right place."

We were both silent as he closed the boxes and placed them back in the cabinet.

After he had locked the cabinet, he turned to me and sighed heavily. "I can't trust anyone. That was the reason I was reluctant to write the will. I seemed to have a premonition. I somehow knew someone was watching me."

Kangxi, like any other emperor, was neurotic and distrustful, especially towards his sons. One couldn't blame him, really, because he had what they coveted— the throne.

"Your Majesty," I said cautiously. "May nucai dare to ask why you must keep the name of the successor a secret? If you made it known, then such crime and unnecessary fights could be avoided."

"True," he said. "That was why I made the second prince my successor as soon as he was born. While my decision stopped my other sons from hankering after the throne, it made the Crown Prince forget himself. He waited impatiently for me to die!"

His sorrowful eyes confirmed the reason why he'd annulled Taizi. Among his sons, he had cared the most about the second prince, but his love was never reciprocated.

"I chose to not name any successor because that way, at least I can enjoy a few years' illusion of being loved," he continued. "But the problem is, what if I died suddenly?"

Seeing the emperor's distress, I got an idea. Actually, it wasn't my idea, but the idea of Emperor Yongzheng—Prince Yong. Yongzheng solved the problem with naming a successor by hiding his will in a box behind the sign "Fair and Square" above the dragon seat.

"Your Majesty, you can hide it in a secret place and let your most trusted person know."

He nodded slowly. "Not a bad idea. But then, who should this person be?"

Anyone but Longkodo, I wanted to shout but held my urge. "That, Your Majesty, nucai has no idea."

"You see, Julie, there is no simple way to solve the problem."

The emperor went on to laugh wholeheartedly, but I could feel his agony and bitterness.

He dismissed me shortly, but before letting me go, he said to me, "You must not breathe a word about what you've witnessed today and our conversation."

I bowed. "Nucai wouldn't dare to."

On my way home I considered the incident. Was Longkodo responsible? I secretly wished he was, because such a crime would lead him to the gallows for sure, and he wouldn't be able to commit the more heinous crime later that would destroy many people's lives. Even if he wouldn't be caught, his reckless act had undoubtedly put the emperor on guard, and he might be even more vigilant against his few trusted subordinates.

CHAPTER 25

☯

SUMMER WAS UNBEARABLY hot in the palace. Neither AC nor electric fan was available, and the only tools for cooling off were handheld fans. There were fans made of all sorts of materials—feather, bamboo, straw, palm leaves, paper, and fabric; in shapes of squares, circles, hexagons, plum blossoms, and ellipses; and most of them were painted with beautiful pictures and often written with poems. Fancy they might be, they didn't seem to be useful even three hundred years before global warming, mainly because I was used to better, modern cooling methods, and also because short-sleeves hadn't seemed to be invented yet. Lady Uya had given me some shirts made of light gauze, but I could only wear them indoors and when I was alone. When I went out, I still had to wear long gowns with long sleeves. I was all sweaty when I arrived at the Upper Study, and by the time I went home, my shirts were usually drenched. Thankfully, the lady also gave me some perfumed powder, otherwise I wouldn't have been able to stand my own body odor.

The emperors seldom stayed in the Forbidden City during the summers, which was why I hadn't seen Kangxi for nearly two months. There were numerous summer palaces near Jing City, and he would stay in different places depending on the season. His preferred location was Chengde Summer Resort, which he had built about twenty years ago, and he spent every summer there. Thus, when the eunuch summoned me one day in the middle of August, saying I was wanted by the emperor, I was quite surprised.

When I entered the South Study, two other men wearing imperial robes and cone hats were bending in front of a desk, reading and writing. The ruby beads on the tips of their hats indicated they were high-ranking court officials. They looked up when I stepped in. One of them was a foreigner in his sixties, with a plump figure and an amicable smile. The crane emblem on his black court robe indicated he was a scholar. The other was a Manchu in a blue robe, about forty-five, tall and skinny, with high cheekbones. His four-clawed dragon emblem and his strong resemblance to the emperor suggested he was a prince.

"Julie," the emperor, who looked well rested after a long vacation, said to me. "Come here, meet Father Bouvet and the third prince."

I curtsied to each of them. While it was the first time I had the honor of meeting Father Bouvet, Kangxi's science tutor, he felt like an old friend because the emperor mentioned him quite often. I had also wanted to meet the third prince, since he was the most scholarly among Kangxi's twenty-four sons. He was devoted to erudition instead of striving for power and was notorious for his lack of attention about rules and taboos. Indeed, he didn't have a bit of imperial arrogance about him, and instead looked very much like a nutty professor. I stifled the urge to laugh when I recalled the anecdote about the prince being demoted from a duke to a Beile because he had disregarded the taboo and washed his hair on the hundredth-day death anniversary of his father's late consort.

I waited for the emperor to introduce his son, but he turned to the foreigner first. "Father Bouvet is a French Jesuit, sent by His Majesty Louis XIV to deliver the gifts of the western culture and science. He has done quite a marvelous contribution to the Qing Empire."

Father Bouvet bowed to the emperor and responded in fluent Mandarin, "Imperial Majesty flatters me. Your servant is underserving of such wonderful praises."

"Not at all," said the emperor, promptly pointing to a map hanging on the wall of the study. "This is the Kangxi Atlas of the Qing Empire. It couldn't have been made without Father Bouvet's dedication."

I glanced at the map, stunned by how similar it was to the map of China that I had seen in modern times. The rooster shape was clearly delineated, except it was not all, but only part of the map. Besides the current China territory, the map also included the land of Central Asia to the north of it, namely Mongolia, Kazakhstan, Korea, and Russia.

The emperor went on to inform me that the map had taken nearly fifteen years to complete, and was not only the most comprehensive, accurate map of the Qing Empire, but also the first map done with scientific surveys and scientific methods, and the first map that showed longitude and latitude lines. It was quite an impressive accomplishment. As he spoke, the emperor looked at the map with pride in his eyes, then turned to Father Bouvet and smiled. The priest said humbly, "It is an honor to serve the Qing Empire." I liked him immediately.

Now the emperor turned to his son. "Out of all my sons, Yinzhi is the only one who likes math as much as I do."

"Math isn't that important to ruling a country." Prince Yinzhi looked up from the geometry problem he was working on. "Not as much as literary or military talents."

"I beg to differ, my lord," Father Bouvet said. "Math disciplines your mind. A great ruler has to have a logical mind."

"Well said!" Kangxi nodded and looked at me, as if waiting for my opinion.

"Of course," I agreed quickly while trying to think of other rulers or leaders who were good at math. The only one I came up with was President James Garfield.

"Besides," Kangxi continued. "Math is the foundation for any science—astronomy, physics, medicine, and sciences make a nation strong."

I listened quietly, impressed by the emperor's insight.

"Although I do wish you were as passionate about politics as you are about math," the emperor said to his son.

Prince Yinzhi bowed. "I'm sorry to disappoint you, Father Emperor. But we don't lack political talents among my brothers."

"True," the emperor nodded with a smile. "Although I often wish I had only one son who embodied all the talents, instead of twenty-four sons."

The emperor was troubled by the matter of passing the throne. He loved each son for their uniqueness but could only pick one as his successor. If only he could find one single son who was multitalented as himself, then it would be so much easier for him.

The third prince understood his father's dilemma, too, for he said promptly, "Father, we could always help each other and complement each other's imperfections."

The emperor smiled. "I like that! And I hope it'll be so."

I was touched by the prince's good will. But it also saddened me that I knew what would happen to him. Although he didn't join any factions among his brothers, he did have a close relationship with the annulled Crown Prince and held animosity towards Prince Yong. After the fourth prince claimed the throne, he was demoted to a grave guard as well, and died in confinement years later.

I wished I could help him escape the future awaiting him, and I took solace in the hope that I could still change history. If Prince Yong didn't become the next emperor, then Prince Three would survive. My thoughts turned to Jeng. Would he return home early, as he had promised?

"Tomorrow," the emperor interrupted my contemplation. "You'll go with me to the Garden of Joyful Spring. You'll be working with Yinzhi at the Office of Mathematics over there. He's compiling a book on mathematics. We're putting mathematical discoveries all together, Eastern and Western. It will be an encyclopedia of mathematics that includes subjects in arithmetic, algebra, geometry, and trigonometry. And you'll help him with that."

I was so surprised that it took me a moment to remember I had to thank His Majesty for such an honorable position.

THE MORNING I got off the horse carriage at the entrance of the Garden of Joyful Spring, I understood Jeng's rage the day we'd visited Peking University. The sheer size amazed me. It wasn't just a garden, it was a town embraced by lakes and hills. Although it lacked the magnificence of the Forbidden City, it surpassed the former with its natural beauty and idyllic peace. The air was fresh and moist. Just the sight of willows and other trees made me feel cool. I was dropped off in front of a large house with a courtyard and a group of maids and eunuchs received me. When I found out that the entire complex—including a living room, a bedroom, a study and a garden—was for me to use, I nearly squealed with joy. I spent the rest of the morning wandering along the lakeshores and enjoying the scenery. I crossed numerous stone bridges just to feel them before they were gone; I prayed in the garden temple, I even lay down in the shade by the creek to enjoy the coolness.

After lunch, I followed a eunuch to Mengyangzhai, where the Office of Mathematics located.

The third prince was already there, speaking with a group of young men in imperial robes. The prince quickly introduced me to them—the fifteenth prince Yinxu, the sixteenth prince Yinlu, and a couple of scholars, including mathematician Juecheng Mei, who was the grandson of the late mathematician Wending Mei. These men were surprisingly friendly to me, the only female in the room at the moment. Juecheng Mei even complimented on "my" proofs of the Pythagorean Theorem.

On the wall facing the entrance was a picture of a European. He was a bearded man in a cassock and Manchu winter hat, standing next to a telescope and an armillary sphere. Seeing me looking at the picture, the prince explained, "Jesuit Ferdinand Verbiest, Father Emperor's science teacher."

I nodded in awe. So, this was the famous scientist Kangxi revered so much.

"Using his math and astronomy knowledge, he convinced my father the old calendar was inaccurate, resulting from an error in construction. After that, Father appointed him to be his personal tutor and the head of Mathematical Board and Director of the Royal Observatory. He translated many western texts into Chinese and Manchu."

"Manchu?" I was further impressed. It was the mother tongue of the Qing royal family, and a Tungusic language that would be endangered in the twenty-first century.

The Jesuit was also responsible for building an aqueduct and designing more advanced canons and guns.

The prince went on, obviously respected the man very much.

Prince Yinzhi then showed me around the office. It wasn't simply a math office, and it actually consisted of five departments—math, astronomy, medicine, music, and literature. Then he took me to a room next to the main hall. It was a small study piled with books and paper. A scribe was writing at a desk.

He pointed to a stack of paper filled with math equations. "Your job is to read through these and make sure the computation contains no errors. Leave the language part to Mr. Wu. Refer to the original texts if necessary."

In other words, I was to be a math editor. I couldn't imagine a more boring job on earth. But I bowed and thanked him. When I sat down and looked at the ancient text of mathematics, I heard a buzz in my head. I gazed at the scenery outside and sighed. How could anyone concentrate on math in such a beautiful setting?

I gasped when I noticed the title of the book Prince Yinzhi was compiling. It was *Shulijingyun*, the *Essential Principles of Mathematics*, the very book my father had showed Jeng the day we had dinner at his house. It was an encyclopedia of mathematical knowledge that was known in China at the time, containing fifty-two chapters in three parts—math notations, theories and techniques, and tables. I was reading chapters from the second part, which contained mostly elementary algebra and geometry. I was fairly interested in the topics, but I still had difficulty to stay awake after two hours of deciphering not just math but the archaic Chinese language. It was midmorning when I finally got permission to take a walk outside.

I couldn't contain my surprise when I saw Priest Wang walking towards the office a moment later. He was wearing his usual black cap, and strands of fine white hair stuck out of it, flapping as he moved.

"What a surprise," I said as I hurried towards him. "What're you doing here?"

"The third prince summoned me to discuss astrology with him. What about you?"

"I work here now." I told him about my experiences in the palace, including how I became a tutor at the Upper Study and sometimes even the emperor's study companion.

"Good for you," he congratulated me and looked around to check for privacy. Then he gestured me to a spot farther away from the building. "Making any progress?" he asked in a low voice.

I shook my head in despair. "Prince Jeng wouldn't take my warning seriously. He left for Xinjiang in April. It doesn't look like I will be able to change the course of history."

The priest knitted his eyebrows. "Did he not believe you?"

"Actually, he did. But he said he couldn't neglect his duty of frontier general."

"That's understandable. He's a responsible young man and a valiant soldier. That's why the emperor favors him."

"But I don't know what I'm supposed to do now. He said he would return at the beginning of November."

After pacing back and forth, he said, "There isn't much we can do other than being patient. But in the meantime, you should keep an eye on the fourth prince. We still have a chance to prevent what he's about to do."

"I don't see how I can do that, either, since I don't see him often."

The priest smiled. "From what I know, he visits the garden very often. You should be seeing him soon."

"Oh?" I wasn't sure whether it was good news or not.

"Prince Yong seems to like you," the priest said with a sly smile. "Otherwise he wouldn't have recommended you to the emperor. I would take advantage of it."

"Do you mean I should befriend the wolf?" I blurted out a Chinese idiom.

He nodded. "If doing so you can protect the lambs."

After the priest parted with me, I thought about the implication of his words. Although it was true that Prince Yong had been good to me, I was reluctant to being close to him again. Jeng wouldn't like it, would he?

AS PRIEST WANG had predicted, I met Prince Yong soon after my arrival at the Garden of Joyful Spring. It was an early morning and I was on my way to the office when I heard someone calling my name. I turned and saw Prince Yong getting out of a sedan chair.

I curtsied in a hurry, explaining to him I was on my way to the Office of Mathematics.

"I see you've been promoted again." The prince smiled. "Good job!"

I bowed and thanked him. "Are you here to see His Majesty?"

"I am."

"So early? Did something happen at the palace?"

"No." He shook his head. "But Father invited me to breakfast with him."

"Oh." What a long way to travel for breakfast.

"You see, the Garden of Perfect Brightness is right next door."

"That's right!" I said, remembering that Kangxi had gifted one of the imperial gardens to his son years ago. "Garden of Perfect Brightness—how marvelous! I always wonder how it looked before—"

I stopped before I blurted out "it was burned down."

The prince smiled. "You're welcome anytime!"

"Is Lady Nian there?"

"She is. She will be delighted to see you."

He walked me to the Office of Mathematics. I hesitated at the entrance of the building, remembering that the third and the fourth princes weren't on good terms. But Prince Yong quickened his pace, saying he was looking forward to seeing his brother. Prince Yinzhi came to welcome his brother, although without much enthusiasm.

"What brings you here, Prince Yong?" he said rather perfunctorily.

"Good to see you, Prince Yinzhi, I escorted Julie."

"Oh, that's right. I forgot you two were acquainted. You recommended her to the emperor." Yinzhi glanced at me.

I looked down, feeling somewhat guilty at being acquainted with a man who would persecute most of his brothers.

"Julie was Hongli's tutor. If it weren't for her, the little rogue wouldn't be so serious about math now!"

The brothers went on to chat, politely, without any brotherly affection at all. Prince Yong took leave shortly after.

I was worried that the third prince would be mean to me because of my past relationship with Prince Yong, but thankfully, Yinzhi was a true scholar and didn't treat me differently because of his brother.

PRINCE YONG'S INVITATION came a month after our last encounter, a few days before the Mid-Autumn Festival. He invited the emperor and the entire staff of the Office of Mathematics to a celebration at the Garden of Perfect Brightness.

I arrived at the garden shortly after sunset in a sedan chair the prince had sent. The scenery made me gasp. Lanterns hanging along bridges and verandas illuminated the garden, and lights reflected in the lakes. I followed the servants onto a narrow bridge that led to a pavilion in the center of a lake. As I crossed the bridge, I glanced at the moon that was climbing up the western sky on the edge of the lake.

The emperor and other members of the imperial family were already sitting at the tables inside the pavilion, enjoying fruits and desserts. I was led to the tables occupied by the ladies and children. Lady Nian waved at me as soon as she saw me, and I went to her. She was looking quite well, and the eleven-month-old Prince Fuhui sat next to her in her maid's arms. Although Fuhui had grown bigger, he was just as cute as when I had last seen him. Wrapped in a maroon gown, he was sucking his thumb, babbling and laughing. With his mother's permission, I took the baby onto my lap, and played with him.

While I played with the baby, a child's voice called, "Master Julie!" I looked up and saw Hongli's smiling face at the next table. He sat next to a tall, stout woman in her early thirties. Her strong figure and healthy complexion fit the description of Lady Nyuhulu, Hongli's mother. I bowed to her. Lady Nyuhulu's healthy genes had been widely credited for Hongli's success—the future Emperor Qianlong. I couldn't help but steal another glance at her. Indeed, she had what Chinese face-reading regarded as prosperity—a full forehead, plump cheeks, square chin, rounded nose, and long earlobes. Despite her unquestionable fecundity, Prince Yong hadn't favored her, and she had born him only one son. But Hongli would live to nearly ninety and would be the longest living son out of his father's eleven children, of which only three lived to adulthood.

While indulging us with food, the hosts had also prepared entertainment. The prince had hired a musical band and an opera troupe. I didn't know that bands had existed in the Qing dynasty and I was quite amazed by their performance. The band consisted of a family of three—a middle-aged couple and their young son. The father played the erhu, the mother played the pipa, and the son played the flute. The musical pieces they played were all classics, and I had heard them over and over in modern times, but never heard them played so well. As I enjoyed the music, lines from Juyi Bai's poem *Pipa Song* echoed in my mind. *Pearls falling onto a jade plate / oriole singing among flowers / a sudden storm turns into a murmuring stream.*

After the band took leave, the moon was full and bright in the center of the sky. The emperor suggested a poetry contest among his sons. "Seven-word or five-word *jueju* poems, but you have to include the moon and Moon Goddess Chang'e in it," he said. "And I'll be the judge. The winner will be handsomely rewarded."

Kangxi's sons were famous for their poetic talents, and the suggestion instantly caused excitement.

"Yinzhi," the emperor said to the third prince. "You're the eldest here, you go first."

The prince got up right away. *"Night throws its curtain / and darkness swallows earth / Yet the brilliant pearl pedant of Chang'e / illumines the lake and turns the lotus blossoms to radiant jewels."*

I clapped my hands loudly along with the rest of the audience. I didn't know it was possible to be a poet and a mathematician at the same time.

Prince Yong rose slowly and took his time in the composition. *"The moon is unusually inviting through branches of the sweet olive / what a blessing it is to enjoy flowers and the moon at the same time. And how generous is the Moon Goddess—she sends each of us a moon to our cups."*

The emperor nodded in approval, clearly impressed. I liked the poem and clapped my hands again, meeting the prince's gaze. His bright eyes fixed on mine for a moment and I recalled what the priest had said to me. I blushed and looked away instantly.

"Very well, very well!" the emperor said after all his sons had composed a poem. "Now, they're all so good! I'll need a moment to decide who gets the prize."

He barely finished his sentence when Hongli stood up. "But, Grandpa, I haven't read mine!"

All eyes fell on the child. Prince Yong chided his son for his lack of manners, and Lady Nyuhulu bowed to the emperor right away, asking for forgiveness.

But the emperor smiled. "You must be Hongli! I've meant to see you but haven't gotten a chance. So, let me hear it, are you better at poetry than mathematics?"

"Thank you, Your Majesty!" Hongli bowed to the emperor and read aloud with a confidence that was unusual in a twelve-year-old. *"Chang'e flaunts her moon in the sky—dazzling and unreachable / The lake holds another moon in her bosom—no less bright but seemingly accessible / The invincible Monkey King falls for the trap—and wastes his effort / The moon is for appreciation only—not for possession."*

The air was still for a moment, but promptly a wave of low murmurs swept through the audience. I vaguely recollected the Buddhism fable of the Monkey King who ordered his monkeys to scoop up the moon that had fallen into the well. The first monkey held on to a tree branch, and the next one grasped his tail, and so on. At the end, the branch broke and the hoard of monkeys fell into the well. Although I didn't remember the original moral of the fable, Hongli's interpretation was thoughtful and inspiring.

"Brilliant!" the emperor said as he gazed at his grandson warmly. "You know what, child? You've just won the competition!"

Hongli happily knelt to thank the emperor and to receive the prize—a set of exquisite inkstone and inkstick. The lid of the inkstone was chiseled with a dragon with stunning details.

"It's the work of the late ink artist Sugong Cao," the emperor informed his grandchild as Hongli fingered the smooth surface of the body of inkstone.

While the child didn't seem to be impressed by the name, Prince Yong bowed to his father again. "Father Emperor ought to keep the rare treasure for your own use. Hongli does not deserve it."

"He surely does," the emperor said as he glanced warmly at the child. "He'll compose hundreds and thousands great poems in the future."

His prediction was correct. Emperor Qianlong had indeed composed a vast amount of poems during his lifetime, besides being an accomplished painter and the ruler of the country.

The night deepened although the moon was still bright. The baby prince had fallen asleep, and Hongli also started to rub his eyes. Kangxi looked tired, too, but seemed reluctant to end the party. He raised his cup again, but before he drank from it, he recited a couplet while gazing at the sky, *"The moon is perfectly round in the immense sky / And my family stays untied on my boundless territory."* After emptying the cup, he sighed. "I've received a letter from Jeng, wishing us a happy holiday."

My heart jumped to my throat, and I battled with my urge of making inquiries. Fortunately, the third prince was ahead of me.

"When will he come back?"

"He didn't mention it in his letter." The emperor paused. "The Dzungars are quite evasive."

My heart dropped.

"Father Emperor, forgive your son for speaking boldly," the fourth prince's voice distracted me from my sorrow. "Eradicating the Dzungars isn't easy. May I suggest we postpone it for now, until we come up with a better strategy? Besides, the fourteenth prince has been on the mission for nearly three years and has achieved impressive results."

The considerate remark surprised me. What had happened to this man? Was he sincere?

Kangxi, however, seemed quite touched. "I see you're worried about your brother. That's very good. I quite agree with you. In fact, I was going to tell him that."

My mood lightened. Please do! I shouted in my heart and I smiled as if Jeng had already gotten his father's letter.

Finally, the emperor decided it was time for him to rest. But before he left, he told Hongli he would come back to see him soon. I realized I had just witnessed a historical moment—the first encounter between the two greatest emperors of the Qing dynasty. Kangxi had been not only impressed, but smitten by his grandson, who was not only endowed with literary talents but also athletic prowess as well. In the last months of Kangxi's life, the two would seldom be separated.

AFTER THE EMPEROR had left, the men set up a table to play the chess, and the women played cards until midnight. Lady Nian asked me to stay the night in the garden and I agreed.

"Let me take you to your dwelling," Prince Yong said when I was about to cross the bridge with a servant.

I agreed reluctantly as he took over the lantern from the servant. But soon I forgot my concerns as the night was beautiful beyond words and I reminded myself I was inside the historical Old Summer Palace, which would be gone in the next century. I looked at the sky as we walked and paused in the center of the bridge, to appreciate the moment as much as I could. The moon was brilliant in the sky, and even its reflection in the water was glaring.

"So beautiful," I said, mumbling a line that entered my head from nowhere. "*A perfectly bright moon rises in the Garden of Perfect Brightness.*"

"I like it!" Prince Yong smiled. After a moment's pause, he turned my line into a couplet, "*A fair lady enters a fairyland.*"

"Nice!" I was impressed by the well-matched line.

"I'm glad you came, Julie." He stepped closer to me. "The Mid-Autumn Day has become my favorite holiday, you know why?"

"Because you like writing moon poems?"

"That's one reason, but there's another one, more important." His eyes glowed. "You."

"Me?" I forced a smile and lowered my gaze, but he lifted my chin to face him. "You moved into my house on Moon Day last year, remember?"

"That's right! A year has passed!" I exclaimed. *And I haven't accomplished anything.*

He probably mistook my exclamation for something else because he pulled me into his arms without warning, letting the lantern drop on the ground. "I wanted to celebrate the day with you, alone!"

439

"Let go of me, please," I pleaded. "Someone will see us."

"No, this is the most secluded place in the garden."

He was right. I looked around and saw nothing but the shadows of willow trees on the shore, shielding us like curtains.

"But it's inappropriate," I said as I struggled against him.

"Why?" He pushed me slightly away and looked into my eyes again. "You know how I feel about you. And I know the feeling is mutual."

I couldn't deny it. I had indeed had feelings for him in the past, although I had none at the moment. I stood in silence.

He brushed my cheek with a finger and said, "Don't worry. We're on my property. Even if someone sees it, it's all right." Then he bent towards me and was about to kiss me.

I pushed him away. "Prince Jeng has proposed to me."

He froze at the mention of Jeng. "He did? When? Have you agreed?"

"Not yet, but I will," I said quickly, eager to free myself from his embrace.

He let go of me right away. "Why does he always take away what's mine?"

I recalled that Jeng had said the exact same thing about his brother. "I'm sorry but I'm not yours."

Hurt flashed over his face and he turned and faced the lake. "Everyone is in love with Jeng. Mother, Father, Silan, and now you, too."

So, he knew about Silan and Jeng? "Silan? What do you mean?"

"I didn't know they had feelings for each other when I married her. But it wasn't hard for me to find out. My heart broke when I realized it. I loved her so, and yet she would never forget him!"

He smashed his fist onto the stone railing, and I winced. Then he buried his face in his own arm and his shoulders shook.

Despite the crime that he would commit in the future, at the moment, the man was pitiful. I went to him and held him.

We walked in silence towards an individual cottage on the lakeshore. Lanterns lit the path and I could see the orange light of the oil lamp through the windows.

"What a charming house!" I exclaimed.

He smiled. "I hope you'll like it. It was Princess Huaige's favorite place."

"Princess Huaige?" I didn't recall the name.

"My daughter. She passed away five years ago." He sighed. "She was a very smart girl. You know what? She had a talent for math, just like you."

"I'm sorry," I said. My sympathy for him deepened.

A maid opened the door and greeted us.

Prince Yong went in and checked to make sure everything was ready, including the bedroom. Then he nodded. 'Very well, good night."

I WAS TOO excited to sleep, knowing I was inside a historical garden that would no longer exist three hundred years from now. The night's events replayed in my head. Though I was glad that Jeng could return sooner, I also wondered about Prince Yong's gesture. Why was he doing Jeng such a favor? Knowing his ambition, I simply couldn't make sense of it. Was he pretending to be nice to win his father's favor? Or did he really care about his brother? Was it possible that he wasn't the monster historians had conjectured? Once again, his agonizing words rang in my ears. *Why does he always take away what's mine?* And once again I felt his pain. After a restless night, I rose early in the morning.

I walked along the lakeshore, still shrouded in a light fog. The place felt immense with endless lakes surrounding me. Willows and gingko trees lined the lakeshores, and houses dotted the islands and hills.

"Why didn't you sleep in?" I was started by a voice. Prince Yong stood a few feet away, in a gray changshan and a black cap.

I curtsied in a hurry. "Just wanted to see the morning scenery before it passes."

"Dawn is my favorite moment of the day," he said. "And that's why I always rise early."

442

"You're so lucky," I said. "Having such a marvelous place for yourself."

He nodded. "But sometimes I wish I were not as lucky."

"Why is that?"

"The more you have, the more you'll lose," he said with a sight.

"How would you lose it?"

"Father Emperor often does things on impulse. He can take it away just as easily as he gives it."

"I see." I nodded with sympathy. The impact of Kangxi's whim was felt by every son of his, at least he was consistent on that. "But would it be that terrible if you ceased to own this garden?"

He paused. "Not at all. But the problem is, if I lost the garden, I would probably lose everything else."

I didn't fully understand the meaning of his words. Could he be worrying that he would end up having nothing at the end? Was that why he contrived to seize the throne? I forced a laugh. "Why? That's so pessimistic of you!"

"I have no choice," he said, looking at me with melancholic eyes.

Despite my reluctance, I felt his pain and had the urge to comfort him. "You worry too much, my lord," I said. "Everything will end well for you."

He smiled as if consoled by my words. "I hope so."

We passed a sweet olive tree, and enticed by its fragrance, I went close to it and sniffed. "Smells wonderful!"

The prince didn't answer, but he picked one and inserted it in my hair.

"Now you smell the same."

I felt embarrassed and didn't know what to say. The sparkles in his eyes made my cheeks flush.

"Come back any time you want," he said warmly. "Lady Nian will be delighted to have your company."

"Thank you," I said. "But I'm very much needed at the Office of Mathematics."

I was going to move on when he said to me, "Do you love Jeng?"

My heart did a flip-flop and my impulse was to say yes, but I paused. If I did so then no doubt his animosity towards Jeng would increase.

"I . . ." I stuttered. "I can't answer that question."

He stared at me suspiciously. Then he smiled. "No, you don't love him. If you did, you would've already accepted his offer of marriage."

I remained silent. I wanted to tell him he was mistaken and that I loved Jeng with all my heart, but I again curbed my urge and bowed my head instead. What did he want from me? Why was he being so insistent, even after knowing that Jeng had proposed to me? Was it simply sibling rivalry?

He lifted my chin, forcing me to look at him, and spoke in a low voice next to my ear. "Julie, give me a chance. After all, I've known you longer."

The urgency in his voice made me shiver. I had never taken his affection seriously, thinking he was merely being impulsive. But at the moment it felt different. He sounded sincere and his doleful eyes begged for affection. I could hear his heart thumping through the silk gown and I couldn't flat out refuse him. Besides, I was grateful that he had asked the emperor to let Jeng return home last night, regardless of his motives. As I searched desperately for a solution, I remembered Priest Wang's words. If I couldn't stop Prince Yong from seizing the throne, then perhaps I could at least negotiate with him, so he would spare the lives of his brothers in the future? It seemed to be a better alternative than waiting for Jeng's possible early return.

I nodded and reached out to touch his cheek.

He trembled at my touch, and he drew a deep breath. Smiling, he took my hand, and pressed it onto his lips.

CHAPTER 26

❦

IN THE MONTH after the Mid-Autumn celebration, I frequently saw Hongli in the Garden of Joyful Spring, accompanying his grandfather. The two read, wrote, or played chess together in Kangxi's study, the Bookhouse of Clear Stream. Sometimes Prince Yong would be with them, too. Whenever we met, I would pretend nothing had happened between us, but I could feel his eyes following me from time to time, making me uneasy. Another figure frequently seen in the garden during these days was Longkodo, who, against my wishes, was apparently still Kangxi's most trusted official. I had gathered from bits of conversation with the emperor that the palace inspectors hadn't found the person who had broken into the Palace of Heavenly Purity, and the case seemed to have been closed since nothing important had been lost.

Prince Yong invited me to the Garden of Perfect Brightness in the middle of October. The garden was gorgeous in the afternoon, as the supple branches of willow trees hung above the lake like golden draperies. The gingko trees had turned golden, too, and they stood like towering torches under the blue sky. Leaves of gold paved the paths in the garden.

Prince Yong was waiting for me in his study. When the maid announced my arrival, he was holding a brush pen, and writing at his desk.

"Are you practicing calligraphy?" I asked.

"No," he said as he stopped writing and looked up. "I'm helping Father Emperor with his memos."

"Oh." I raised an eyebrow. This showed how much the emperor trusted him. "Congratulations."

He smiled bitterly. "If only you knew how much work it takes. I've been up since four this morning, it's now four in the afternoon and I haven't finished half of it. I don't know how Father has done this every day for sixty years."

"You're too serious," I said as I got closer to his desk and glanced at the document he was working on. He had written a paragraph of comments and was signing when I approached. "The emperor told me most of the time he simply wrote 'noted.'"

He chuckled, pushing the document aside. "That's because he's been doing it all his life, he knows what's important and what isn't from a quick glance. But I'm still learning and can't afford to be sloppy."

I laughed as I was reminded an online article about Yongzheng, who would spend most of his ruling life going over memos. "Even if you do it all your life, you still won't be sloppy."

"You're probably right." He stood up from his desk and held my hands. "How do you know me so well? Are you a fairy?"

"I guess so." I shrugged and looked away.

He pulled me closer and bent towards me. Before his lips could touch mine, I turned, and he kissed my cheek instead. But he wouldn't give up and went on to kiss my earlobe and my neck. I wanted to break free, but he held me firmly. Remembering the priest's advice and my own plan, I surrendered to his affection. But when he reached the buttons of my gown, I whispered into his ear, "Would you enjoy such a life? Reading memos all day long?"

My question cooled him off and he shook his head. "I don't think so."

My heart raced at the question I was about to ask. "Does that mean you don't want to be the next emperor?"

His grasp on my shoulders tightened, and his eyes bored into mine. I waited eagerly for a painfully long moment, until his hands relaxed and slid down to my arms. "I would prefer spending my days to write poems and paint pictures, but then I would be living at the mercy of one of my brothers, whichever it would be. All I have now will be taken away from me, including this beautiful garden we're in."

It wasn't a straight answer, but I didn't press him further. "Why are you so certain?"

"I know because of the envy in their eyes whenever they speak of it. I'm the only prince who received a garden of such size from the emperor."

It was true, and the fact led historians in favor of Prince Yong to argue that Kangxi had set his mind on passing his throne to his fourth son long before his death.

"I see, but is the garden worth so much trouble? You would be mainly reading memos most of time, even if you lived here as an emperor."

He smiled at the irony. "Yes, I would rather work myself to death in this rich garden, than live a carefree life as a pauper."

I raised an eyebrow. How similar he was to modern workaholics who would compromise leisure for luxury!

After serving me some refreshments, he asked me to show him some card tricks. I obeyed his wishes, and did some of my latest creations, although clumsily. He wasn't impressed. "You haven't practiced lately," he said, shaking his head.

It was true. During the days I didn't have much free time and I spent most of my evenings reading classic Chinese literature instead.

"I have no time. There's too much work at the Office."

"I see. The third prince is overusing you."

"I'm not complaining."

"Do you enjoy your work?"

I hesitated before I spoke. I didn't want to sound ungrateful. "It gets tedious sometimes. But in the words of Prince Yinzhi, it's rewarding to be working on such a significant project."

He scoffed. "What's so significant about compiling an encyclopedia? If I were him, I would devote time to inventing some new theories."

I knew it was sibling rivalry again. "It'll enhance the math education of the future generations, and the book will be the treasure of the nation. The emperor is looking forward to its completion."

The mention of the emperor humbled him. "Okay. Let's talk about something else," he said, changing the topic. "I've got an idea of a card trick for you."

"Idea? You mean you created it?" I was puzzled.

"No, I have an idea, but you would need to make it work."

"Sure," I said, and passed him the deck of cards.

He waved. "I don't need them."

He took two pieces of paper on his desk, folded them into the size of cards, and wrote the character "sun" on one and "moon" on another. Then he brought a wooden box and placed the card with "sun" in it, the side with the character facing down.

He waved the "moon" card at me. "You see, I would like you to switch the two, without me noticing it," he said. "Can you do it?"

"Sure." I paused and thought about how to do it. There were two ways I could think of. One way was placing the "moon" card in the beginning skillfully, so the audience thought it was "sun" instead. But the prince made it clear that it wasn't an option. The "sun" card had to be inside initially.

My second option was to use a box with a movable bottom, so I could switch the cards from below it. But again, it wasn't an option.

"Perhaps I should make it clear," he said after seeing my inability of producing a method. "I want you to reach in to take the 'sun' card but when you pass it to me, it becomes the 'moon' card."

"Oh, that's much easier." I smiled. All I needed was a large sleeve pocket.

"Take them home and practice it. Once you're good at it, I would like you to teach me how to do it," he said.

"Why? Are you going show it to someone?"

He didn't answer my question right away. "You don't need to know at the moment, but I'll tell you later. And don't tell anyone about it or let anyone see you doing it."

"Sure." I shrugged, feeling all the more puzzled.

I thought about the warning on my way home later. Why practice such a trick? Why keep it a secret? Then it dawned on me that the prince was scheming on switching the emperor's will. It was a historical conjecture that he had changed the word "fourteenth" to "fourth" in the original will and thus seized the throne from the fourteenth prince, the rightful successor. The ingenuity of the crime no doubt fascinated the public for generations. However, historians had pointed out the flaw of the conjecture by analyzing the psychology of the assumed usurper. If Prince Yong was determined to seize the throne, he would choose a way that worked in case any other prince was designated. It was easy to change the word "fourteenth" to "fourth," but not so easy to change from "third" to "fourth." In other words, his method would have to be versatile, and switching, not editing the original will, would make more sense. The only chance he had to carry out the scheme was when the will was revealed right after the emperor's death, during which the prince wasn't likely to be alone.

My heart pounded as I realized the plan and my role in it. I wondered how he knew the emperor wouldn't name him as his successor. Had he found out from Longkodo, or did he simply guess it? In any case, he wanted to switch the will without anyone noticing it. That was why he was so interested in my magic tricks. And that was why he was interested in me as well. The *chance* he had asked from me that night at the Garden of Perfect Brightness, was not a chance to love him, but a chance to help him seize the throne. What was I supposed to do?

CHAPTER 27

❦

IN NOVEMBER, the air gradually turned cold. It snowed in the middle of the month, and the plum trees in the Garden of Joyful Spring blossomed, reminding me of the time in the previous year, when I met Jeng at Lady Uya's house after his return from the western borders. I hadn't heard any news of him lately. The emperor hadn't mentioned him since the Mid-Autumn Day. As the days in November passed one by one, my hope also vanished bit by bit. Kangxi would die in December and my time was running out. I visited the garden temple frequently, praying for Jeng's return, the health of the emperor, and that history would turn out different from I had known.

I was summoned to the Bookhouse of Clear Stream one morning, to help the emperor tutor Hongli. When I arrived, Kangxi was practicing calligraphy on a roll of rice paper, and Hongli was rubbing an inkstick on an inkstone containing water, a traditional way of producing ink.

I waited quietly on the side and watched the emperor write. Kangxi was an accomplished calligraphic artist and his work would be priceless in modern days. He was writing a seven-word couplet in Xingshu, a semi-cursive Chinese script. As he was writing, the emperor patiently explained the differences between Xingshu and Caoshu to his grandson. "In Caoshu, the characters are connected, and many strokes were reduced into curves and dots, but in Xingshu, characters aren't linked but the strokes in each character run smoothly together."

Hongli nodded. "I like Xingshu, Grandpa. It's elegant and fluent. Can you teach me that?"

Kangxi put down the brush pen and smiled. "Very well, that's why I like the style, too. But you must practice Lishu first. You can't write cursive well without a good foundation of standard strokes."

Seeing me, the emperor said, "Julie, you should join Hongli in practicing. Your writing needs improvement."

I blushed. True. I had been practicing in the past year, but I was just not good at holding the brush. "Your Majesty, your humble servant believes that she has passed the age of training."

"Not at all!" Kangxi chided. "It's never too late to improve. Come here, sit down next to Hongli."

I had no choice but sit down next to the little prince, and scrawl on a piece of paper like a school girl.

The emperor paced next to us, making comments, and even adjusting our postures, like a patient master.

Calligraphy was frequently compared to martial arts, as one had to use the right force on the strokes, and also paired with breathing to control one's arm movements. Soon my shoulders, neck, and arm ached. When the emperor told us to take a break, I was grateful.

"Time for some exercises, Hongli," Kangxi said to his grandson when we were out in the garden.

Hongli obeyed the emperor's wish without any hesitation. After some stretching, he practiced sword and archery. The emperor sat down on a stone bench and watched the child, nodding and mumbling his approval.

"This child is a godsend," he said to me. "Full of talents!"

I could see the pride in the emperor's eyes, and I could easily believe his intention of passing the throne to his grandson directly, skipping a generation of sons. Rumor also said that the emperor had already checked the child's birth characters, or horoscope, and had been impressed by them.

After Hongli was done with his martial arts, the emperor let him play in the garden. The child immediately ran around, chasing birds and catching dragonflies. When he saw a squirrel, he shouted with delight. He picked up the bow and the arrow and went after the poor animal.

The emperor got excited, too, and he followed the child quickly, giving him advice on how to catch it.

The squirrel froze behind a rock, thinking it couldn't be spotted, but Hongli saw it. He snuck on it from behind, but just as he raised the bow, the animal dashed towards a tree trunk by the lake. Hongli wouldn't let it go, he followed it closely towards the lake.

"Be careful, child!" the emperor shouted, his face full of apprehension.

I had never seen Kangxi so worried. At the moment he was no longer an emperor, but an ordinary grandfather.

Hongli came back empty-handed. "I almost got it!"

The emperor laughed. "It's hard to catch prey in a garden. But on a hunting ground, it'll be much easier. I'll take you with me next year when we go hunting at the pampas."

Hongli's eyes beamed. "Really? Thank you, Grandpa! But why must we wait till next year?"

Kangxi paused. "Because that's the tradition. Mulan Paddock in August. But perhaps we can go to a Nanyuan to hunt for deer. It's not late at all. We can leave in a few days."

Hongli clapped his hands and hugged his grandpa.

What a lucky boy, he has the sole favor of the emperor. As we stood up to return to the study, a sudden revelation came across my mind. *Nanyuan Hunting.* Kangxi got sick because of that trip, and he would die soon after he returned.

My heart almost stopped beating at the realization. I looked at the aged emperor and the youthful child walking hand-in-hand before me, laughing as they chatted. This kind of blissful life would soon end for the emperor, and so would the harmonious lives of many of the princes. Anxiety hit me. *I cannot let it happen. I have to stop his plan.*

I ran past the emperor and knelt in front of him. "Your Majesty, please don't go hunting!"

Kangxi's eyes widened. "Why? Julie, what's gotten into you?"

I paused. I hadn't had time to think of a good reason. "It's too cold."

"Too cold? Not at all. It's the best season to hunt for deer. The meat won't spoil."

I thought quickly and ventured another attempt. "But the deer, don't they hibernate in winter?"

The emperor laughed. "Not at all! Julie, you need to go with us and see. The deer are most active in winter. They don't sleep day or night. It's called the rut."

"The rut?" I blushed at my limited knowledge about deer's behavior.

"What's the rut, Grandpa?" Hongli asked innocently.

The emperor laughed again. "You don't need to know it now, child. But I'll let you know when you grow up."

But you won't be around when he grows up, I thought with despair.

"What about your health, Your Majesty?" I tried again.

Kangxi looked displeased. "I'm perfectly healthy! I might be old but I'm strong. You'll see, I can easily hunt a bear."

After saying that, he quickened his steps as if to prove that he was still agile, and soon left me far behind.

I had to do something. This might be my last chance to change history.

I HAD DEVISED a way to switch cards according to Prince Yong's wish. I put a card in my sleeve pocket and practiced how to pull it out and swap it with another card in a box. Basically, I would have to pull out the card in my sleeve in advance and hold both cards in my hand momentarily as if they were one card, then slide the card from the box into my sleeve. Of course, it was easier said than done. But having wide sleeves certainly helped. Not only could they be used to hide objects, but also as screens to shield actions. The Qing dynasty court robes had no pockets in the sleeves, but they could easily be added.

Prince Yong had been visiting me in the Garden of Joyful Spring frequently, nearly every day in the past few weeks, to practice the trick with me. He was a diligent student, but magic wasn't something that anyone could accomplish quickly. It took years of practice to achieve coordination and agility. Not surprisingly, after two weeks, he was still clumsy.

458

"It's harder than I thought," he said after about ten trials of practice one afternoon.

I comforted him. "Don't worry, keep practicing and you'll get it eventually."

He nodded. "You're a patient teacher."

Deep down, of course, I hoped he would not master the skill any time soon and wouldn't be able to switch the will if the emperor died in the near future. I intentionally slowed him down, telling him he needed time.

"Let's take a break," I suggested as he tried again. Seeing his lack of intention to stop, I went to him and held him.

Surprised by my affection, he put down the cards, and wrapped his arms around me.

I nodded and put my head against his chest, so he wouldn't be able to see my face.

He kissed my hair and caressed my back. Then he whispered to me, "Shall I ask Father Emperor's permission to marry you?"

"No!" I pushed him away. "You can't do it."

"Why not?"

"It's not the right time," I said. "It hasn't been long since the emperor tried to convince me to marry Prince Jeng."

His face hardened at the mention of his brother. "But you haven't agreed, so what's the problem?"

"The emperor would think I was a seductress, fooling both you and your brother."

He smiled. "But you are a seductress."

"What?" I struggled out of his embrace.

He pulled me back. "Wait, Julie, you're not a coquette, but you simply attract me. I don't know why or how. It must be your magic power."

Although I distrusted the man, I couldn't help being pleased. I let him kiss me.

When we sat down to rest, I mentioned the emperor's plan for the hunting trip.

"We must stop him," I said. "It might be too arduous for him."

He paused a moment and sighed. "I agree. But you need to know something about Father. He does not believe he's old, especially when it comes to hunting. He's stubborn. You can't blame him. He's been the emperor, the Son of Heaven, since he was eight years old. He simply won't take anyone's advice, especially if it's something that's supposed to be good for him."

"But there must be something we can do," I said.

He shook his head. "He's already making arrangements. He sent someone to Nanyuan Palace two days ago, and he ordered me to take care all court affairs during his absence. If I told him to cancel the trip now, he would simply ignore me, and even get mad at me."

November 26th, 1722.

A LIGHT SPRINKLE of snow added the color of winter into the Garden of Joyful Spring. I sat on a bench by the lake despite the cold, hoping to be frozen into numbness. But my brain wouldn't cease working, and my anxiety continued to attack me. It was the day before the emperor's departure for Nanyuan, and yet I hadn't come up with any plan to prevent it.

"Good day, Julie," an old man's voice startled me out of my stupor.

It was Priest Wang. I smiled. I had been hoping to see him since Prince Yong had revealed his scheme to me. "It's so good to see you," I said, truly glad. "I need your help. So much has happened."

I first informed him of Prince Yong's scheme. "He's practicing hard," I said. "And might be ready soon. What should I do?"

The priest's eyes widened but he didn't say a word. Instead, he paced up and down, keeping his head low as if he was thinking hard.

I offered my opinion. "Perhaps I should also tell Prince Yinzhi, so he could catch him in the act?"

"Good thought, but what if the third prince isn't able to catch him?"

I thought for a moment. "I can show him how the trick works. It shouldn't be hard."

He paused again. "Prince Yong is very cunning. We have to be very careful."

"What should we do?"

He sighed. "To tell you the truth, I really can't think of any way. Let me think about it first, and in the meantime, let's see how it goes. There's a chance he'll give up his plan. But if he carries it out, then we'll think of a way to alarm the third prince."

I nodded. "The emperor is going to Nanyuan to hunt tomorrow and I need to stop him."

The priest frowned. "Why?"

I told him the significance of the trip. "It'll be the beginning of the end of Kangxi's reign."

He took the information calmly, like a Tao master would. And unexpectedly, he said, "It's better to leave it alone."

"What?"

"It's not up to us to interfere with the emperor's actions."

"I know that. But it shouldn't be a reason not to try. I've spent more than a year of my life in order to change history, and now it's the pivotal moment!"

He fell silent. "The only thing I could think of is to perhaps to convince Hongli, because the trip is for him."

"Hongli?" I hesitated. "The child was eager to go."

"But you will probably have a better chance to convince him."

A bell rang in my head, and I smiled. "Of course! I'll speak to the child instead!"

For the rest of the morning, my eyes were on the paper, but my mind was outside the office. My ears were vigilant, waiting for the sound of the child's voice, and my anxiety built up when I hadn't heard anything at the expected time of emperor's routine walk. Could they have altered their routine because of the trip tomorrow?

But soon my worries proved to be unnecessary. There they were, the emperor and his grandson, again passing the garden path in front of the Office of Mathematics.

I made an excuse and went out, following them at a distance, waiting for my chance to be alone with the child. Soon, my chance came when the emperor sat down on a bench to rest and let Hongli roam around in the rock garden. I hid behind a rock, and when Hongli neared me, I pulled him to me, and put my finger on my lip to shush him.

"Listen, child, I need to ask you for a favor," I whispered.

"What is it?" The child's eyes beamed with curiosity.

"Are you a good child? Do you care about your grandfather's wellbeing?"

He nodded and smiled. "I see, it's about Nanyuan, isn't it?"

"You're smart," I said. "It is indeed. I want you to tell the emperor that you don't want to go Nanyuan tomorrow."

The child's eyes widened. "No way! I won't do that."

"Why not? Listen. If you don't, then the emperor might get sick during the trip."

"How do you know?"

"I just do," I said. "Will you help me or not?"

He shook his head. "I already tried. My dad told me to."

"You did?" Prince Yong did help me after all. That was unexpected.

"I told him the other day that I wasn't ready for a real hunt yet and I would like to wait until next year. But he insisted I try."

My heart sank. Now what was I supposed to do?

Seeing my distress, the child shook me and whispered, "I've got an idea."

"What is it?"

"We can play hide-and-seek with Grandfather."

"How?"

"You can hide me in your room and pretend I've disappeared. Without me they won't go tomorrow."

It sounded childish. I rolled my eyes. "They'll search every corner in the garden, including my room."

"You need to hide me in a secure place."

I shook my head at the insane idea. "Do you know what kind of crime it would be? Kidnapping the emperor's favorite grandchild?"

"But if you cared about his health so much, then you wouldn't mind being punished for helping him, would you?"

The child's wisdom amazed me. He was right. It would be worth a try and I could think of ways to avoid punishment later. "You are absolutely right." I kissed him on his cheek and he smiled embarrassedly.

Together, the two of us thought about where to hide him. At first, I thought I would take him to my room, as he had suggested, but with the eyes of all the servants, it would be hard to keep it a secret. I had a better idea. I would ask help from the priest. I told Hongli to wait for me where he was, and I ran back to the Office of Mathematics.

The priest was still with the third prince, but he freed himself soon to speak to me.

"I need your help. The child has agreed to come with me. Get us out of here."

The priest's face went pale, although he still tried to remain calm. "Do you realize what consequences your action will have?"

"Of course, I do," I said. "And I don't care."

He paced up and down again, with his hands on his back. Then he stopped and nodded. "Okay, I'll get us a horse carriage and I'll wait for you at the gate in an hour."

AS PROMISED, the priest waited us in a carriage by the gate of the garden at the said time, and the three of us set off for the temple.

"I know you!" Hongli said to the priest as soon as we entered the carriage. "You're the astrologist."

"Your humble servant is flattered by Prince's attention," the priest said respectfully.

Hongli laughed. "You don't have to be so formal with me. Thank you for helping us. And I like your eyebrows. It's so cool. Can I touch it?"

The priest hesitated and said, "Sure, go ahead."

Hongli reached out right away. He not only touched the eyebrow that was as long as the priest's mustache but plucked it gently as well. A strand of hair fell instantly.

"Ouch," the priest groaned as he grabbed the child's hand. "Please, little prince, this is not an imperial gesture."

Hongli giggled like a naughty child. I stifled a laugh. In fact, the priest's eyebrows looked so unnatural that I always had the urge to pluck them.

The Temple of Light and Shadow looked the same as the last time I had seen it. The big man nodded at me as if we were old acquaintances. Hongli was delighted with the place. The priest left for Peach Blossom Village to purchase meat for Hongli's dinner, and during his absence Hongli and I explored every corner of the property.

The temple was larger than I had thought. During my last visit I had only seen half of the building. There were many more rooms along the hallway in the back of the main hall. Most of them were empty, and some of them had simple furniture such as desks and chairs. In the room at the end of the hallway, Hongli even discovered a trapdoor on the floor. We opened it and saw stairs that led to a basement. It was dark and smelled of overripe fruit.

Hongli was excited. "A secret room!"

He went down the stairs before I could stop him. I didn't follow him, but said anxiously, "Come back!"

"It's dark in here!" he shouted from downstairs. "Can you bring a candlestick, please?"

Knowing the child wouldn't obey my wish, I went to the front of the temple and took a candlestick from the altar, then I went down to the basement.

It was spacious and cold. And the air was permeated with a fruity, alcoholic scent. Some broken chairs and desks were scattered in the center of the room, and a few ceramic containers lined the wall.

"Rice wine jars!" Hongli exclaimed. The curious child went to one of them and lifted the lid.

A pungent and sweet smell attacked us, and we backed off.

"The priest is an alcoholic!" Hongli whispered.

It was precisely my thought, but I chided him. "How do you know? It might be for the other guy."

That evening, after a simple dinner, the priest had the big man, whose name was Big Dumb, tidy up two of the empty rooms for us.

"Will you be all right?" I asked the little prince after I had tucked him in bed. "Are you warm enough?"

The priest had placed a small furnace in the room, but the building had poor insulation. I had placed two layers of blankets on the child.

"Yes, I am!" he said. "Don't worry about me. I've stayed in cottages before."

"When?"

"When my mom took me to my grandparents' farm."

I WOKE IN the middle of the night to the sound of a commotion. I heard shouting, banging on the door, and then the floor creaking. I got up right away, put on my jacket and went to the front of the temple. Through the windows, I saw torches illuminating the sky outside, and imperial soldiers surrounding the premises.

I knocked on the priest's door right away and told him what had happened. "They must've come to get Hongli."

The priest lost his calm for the first time since I had known him. "How could it be? Someone must've seen us leaving the garden. Take Hongli to hide in the basement. I'll take care of it."

I woke Hongli and took him to the basement. For a while it was all quiet, but soon we heard footsteps trampling above. Loud crashing sounds followed and voices of strange men roared. I started to pray that they wouldn't notice the trapdoor.

We huddled together as the noise moved closer to us. Hongli whispered in my ear, "I'm afraid they'll find us. But don't worry. I will tell Grandpa I begged you to take me here, and that we had planned to return in the morning."

I nodded. "Thank you. You're a good child. Tell him it was my idea. I don't want you to get in trouble because of me."

As we spoke, the trapdoor opened and torchlight flooded the entrance.

An imperial guard dragged me out of the basement, while another carried Hongli.

468

The priest and Big Dumb were kneeling outside on the ground, heads hanging low. Imperial guards holding broadswords stood next to them. An older man in a court robe stood afar with his hands locked behind his back. He was none other than Longkodo. He walked quickly towards us as soon as he saw us.

"Good morning, Grand-uncle!" Hongli called out sheepishly.

The old man chided without a smile. "You little rascal. Do you realize what you've done? His Majesty and your father are all worried sick!"

"I'm sorry," Hongli said. "But I was curious about this temple."

"Curious? Humph." The old man's lips twisted but he did not smile. "Come here, let me whip your bottom!"

Seeing that he was reaching to get hold of the child, I dropped on my knees. "Commander! Please forgive the child. It's all my fault. I enticed him to come with me."

He drew back his hands and stared at me. After a moment's pause, he said, "Very well, I'll let the emperor decide what to do with you two."

On our way back to the Garden of Joyful Spring, I thought about how futile my actions were. No matter what I did, it seemed I wouldn't be able to change history.

Hongli did as he had promised and begged the emperor not to punish me. The emperor took the whole thing as a child's whim and forgave him as well. In fact, he was only too happy for his grandson's return. The hunting trip commenced as it had been planned. Emperor Kangxi, Hongli, and the imperial attendants left at noon. I stayed in bed for the next few days. The garden looked empty, since the princes all returned to their houses during the emperor's absences. The Office of Mathematics was closed. I had the choice of going back to Lady Uya's house, too, but I decided to stay in the garden. For one thing, I felt more independent here, for another, I wanted to wait for the emperor to return.

THE EMPEROR AND his hunting group returned two weeks later, on the fourteenth of December. Snow covered the garden when I saw a group of eunuchs carrying a sedan chair, heading towards the Bookhouse of Clear Stream. I went to them and inquired about the emperor. A eunuch at the end of the procession told me he wasn't feeling well.

For the rest of the afternoon I was unsettled. I knew very well what would happen from now on. A new emperor will ascend the throne within seven days—and who would he be? I tried to convince myself that it was yet to be determined, but I couldn't.

That night, Prince Yong came to my room, his face solemn.

"It's just as you've predicted," he said with a sigh.

For a moment, I feared he was accusing me of cursing the emperor, as the ancient people would, but that didn't seem to be his intent. I suspected that he had also had the premonition, which explained why he had attempted to stop the emperor as well. At the moment, he looked really concerned and I again thought he wasn't cold-blooded.

"Hongli said Father caught a cold the second day, but he insisted he was all right."

I wasn't surprised to hear that. "How is he now?"

"I don't know." He shook his head. "I've never seen him so beaten. He wouldn't even open his eyes to speak to me. In the past, he would smile no matter how sick he was, and assured me he was all right."

I wanted to say something to console him, but instead tears rolled down my cheeks.

That night, he did not practice switching cards.

On the third night after the emperor had returned, I heard a knock on my door. I thought it was Prince Yong, but when I opened it, I saw a man in a black cloak and a black sailor hat, a scarf covering half of his face. I thought it was a eunuch at first, but when he pulled off his scarf, I saw the white mustache and eyebrows of Priest Wang. He hadn't been to the garden lately because the third prince wasn't in and I was glad to see him.

"How did you get in?" I asked after letting him in. The garden was heavily guarded during the nights.

"I know a secret passage, and this hat is very useful." he said. "Listen, I won't stay long, but I want to tell you my plan. You'll go ahead and do the switch, except using a different will."

"I don't understand."

"I'll bring you a will, and it'll name the fourteenth prince instead."

"I still don't understand. Why is it necessary? Can't we just prevent the act?"

"No," the priest said patiently. "How do you know whom the emperor has named in his will? What if it isn't Prince Jeng?"

I felt cold from head to toe. "Then we will be committing the same treason as Prince Yong will!"

He tilted his head. "Isn't that the reason you're here? You've traveled three hundred years to help Prince Jeng, haven't you? Didn't you tell me that Prince Four would be a merciless ruler? From what you've told me, many tragedies could be prevented if the fourteenth prince became the emperor."

I was confused. Did I really come to make sure that Prince Jeng would become the next emperor? I stuttered, "I came to make sure that he wouldn't be killed by his brother."

"Yes. But that's the best way to ensure it."

My mouth felt dry. What did it mean? Would I have to do what Prince Yong was about to do?

Priest Wang patted on my shoulder as if to soothe me. "The fourteenth prince is loving and generous. He will become a great emperor. You know that, don't you?"

I wasn't sure, although I loved him.

"What you can do is to make sure the new will is to benefit the right person," he went on. "Think about it. You don't want to regret not doing the right thing later."

I fell silent after that.

"I'll be back in a couple of days," the priest said before leaving. "And you'd better make up your mind."

KANGXI HAD BEEN in bed for five days already, and there were no signs of recovery. Prince Yong had spent most of his past few days in the Garden of Joyful Spring. Occasionally, Longkodo would be here as well. Perhaps sensing his father's days were numbered, the prince again practiced switching cards. He had not said a word about Kangxi's will, and I was careful not to mention it.

On the sixth day after Kangxi had returned from the hunting trip, Priest Wang came see me again at dusk, passing me a piece of folded paper. I unfolded it and read its content. It started with the line, "*Since ancient times, a ruler of the country must obey the wills of gods and respect the laws of nature,*" which was the form of all testaments of emperors. It went on to state the emperor's accomplishments as well as providing justifications for the ruling of the Great Qing Empire. It was written neatly in regular script, but the language was hard for me to fully understand every line. At the very last paragraph was the line "the fourteenth prince shall succeed the throne . . ."

"How do you know it looks authentic?" I asked the priest.

"I had a chance to look at copies of some old testaments of emperors," the priest said. "And I have witnessed plenty of documents handwritten by the emperor at the third prince's office."

Given his relationship with the third prince, I had little doubt about his claim. But I still felt unsettled.

"The emperor's days are limited," the priest said. "You have to act fast. In fact, tonight is your last chance."

"Tonight?" I gasped. He was right. Kangxi would die on December 20th, which was today's date. I knew it was approaching but I was reluctant to accept the fact. "Maybe it would be different this time," I mumbled with a lump in my throat.

The priest shook his head as he sighed. "I calculated the emperor's fate using his birth time this morning. It showed that a fatal disaster would befall him within a day."

I had never been a believer of Taoist astrology, but I believed the priest at the moment. "What should I do?"

"If I were you, I would keep Prince Yong here for the night, then you would have plenty of chances."

"Keep him here for the night?" I frowned at his suggestion.

He smiled. "I know what it means. But you wouldn't mind a little sacrifice for Prince Jeng, would you?"

He folded the paper carefully and calmly, but when he passed me the paper, his trembling hands betrayed his nervousness. The paper fell to the ground and he stooped to pick it up, then gave it to me. "Put it in a secure place. Remember tonight is your last chance."

He hurried away.

I held the forged will in my hand and my hand sweated. Tonight was my last chance? Kangxi would pass away tonight? Although I had been expecting this, I still wished it wouldn't happen so soon.

I was pacing up and down in my room when Prince Yong came in, wearing his court robe. He was probably expecting the death of his father as well, otherwise he wouldn't be dressed so formally. When he embraced me, I deliberately felt his sleeves, and confirmed the existence of a piece of folded paper in his left sleeve.

"How is the emperor?" I asked, knowing well what to expect.

He shook his head. "He didn't recognize me."

"Shall we practice?" I asked, looking at the folded paper on my desk that had been his prop lately. He had not told me his purpose for practicing the trick yet.

He paused for a moment. "No, I'm tired."

I was taken aback. What was he up to? Was he confident about his skills, or had he had a change of mind? But then I understood. He had the forged will in his sleeve, and if he practiced now, he might drop it accidentally.

"It's getting late. I should get going." He stood up to take leave, but I took his arm. He looked at me with surprise.

I forced a smile as I said, "Perhaps you should stay here tonight, just in case."

He hesitated for a moment, then he grinned. "I'll let the porters know."

When he returned, I had already blown out most of the candles, leaving only one burning. I had also removed my Manchu dress and wore only a silk nightgown.

I helped him remove his official robe and hung it in the wardrobe next to my own dress. I squeezed the left sleeve just to confirm my earlier suspicion.

I had barely reached the bed when he pulled me to him and undid the buttons of my nightgown. I shivered as the cold air kissed my bare shoulders. I discerned the lust in his eyes when he stared at my body.

"You're beautiful, Julie!" he murmured. As we lay in bed side by side, he lifted my dudou camisole, and kissed me.

Memories of Jeng flashed in my mind. I shivered and attempted to break free. But Prince Yong held me tight and whispered, "It's too late to change your mind."

I took a deep breath and closed my eyes. Jeng's face wouldn't go away from my mind, so I pretended I was making love to him.

I lay quietly next to Prince Yong and waited until he started to snore. Then I carefully disentangled myself from his arm and got out of bed. I tiptoes to the wardrobe, afraid I'd make the floor creak. I reached into the sleeve pocket in his court robe, and took the paper out. I again moved in slow motion towards the candle in the corner of the room and unfolded the letter. "*Since ancient times, a ruler of the country must obey the wills of gods and respect the laws of nature.*" The will looked exactly the same as the one Priest Wang made, not only the format, the handwriting, and the stamp signature, but also the content as well. Both included the emperor's reflections on his long reign and his content on his accomplishment. I quickly skimmed through and spotted the line at the end, "The fourth prince shall succeed the throne."

I went back to the wardrobe. The will made by the priest was in the pocket of my jacket, and all I needed to do was an easy switch. I put Prince Yong's paper in my pocket and pulled out Priest Wang's paper, but I paused the moment before I put it in Prince Yong's sleeve. What if Priest Wang's calculation was incorrect? What if Prince Yong checked the will tomorrow before he left? My heart pounded in my ears and I gasped for air.

I jumped when I felt a hand on my arm. "What are you doing?"

I cried in fear and started to tremble.

Prince Yong took the paper from my hand. "You've known about my plan all along, haven't you?"

I nodded, waiting for him to strike me.

But he didn't. "And yet you pretended you didn't know."

I sobbed. "I couldn't believe it."

He sighed. "I can't believe it myself."

He held my hand and led me to the bed. He put the folded paper on the nightstand and sat down next to me. "But this is the only way I can ensure my loved ones enjoy the life they're used to. And Hongli, he is destined to rule. I have to make sure it'll happen."

"Don't do it, please!" I said. "If it's his destiny, then you don't have to do anything."

He paused as if willing to be convinced by my words, but only for a second. "No, I can't take the chance. I don't see how my son will have a chance if my brother will be the next emperor."

"How do you know it won't be you?"

He took a long pause as if to decide whether he should tell me more. "I accidentally saw the will. A few days after Mid-Autumn, Hongli was playing with Father in the garden. Father told me to get a book from his study. I couldn't find the book on his desk, so I started to look into his drawers. And there was the will box which I had seen once in the Hall of Heavenly Purity. I couldn't resist my curiosity, so I opened it."   He buried his face in his hands, then he looked up. "I wish I hadn't seen it! It was like a curse. Prior to that day, I had no ambition for the throne. I might have hoped for it, but I never had the ambition. But since then, every word stuck in my mind. The word *fourteenth prince* is a whip that slashes me every time I remember it."

So, Jeng was right, the emperor had indeed wanted to pass him the throne! In the middle of misery, I felt happy for Jeng. Priest Wang's forged will was unnecessary and I should destroy it. But Prince Four wouldn't give me the chance to touch the paper, and even if I were able to, he might still have the time to compose another one, one with his name on it. How was I going to prevent him from carrying out his plan?

In desperation, the words rolled off my tongue. "I've always thought Prince a pious Buddhist."

"I am," he said with a sigh.

"And I remember reading the Diamond Sutra in your house. But what you're about to do is against Buddha's teachings."

The prince raised an eyebrow and waited silently for more.

I went on. "'Living without attachment and cultivating without attainment.' And yet, you're being a slave of your ambition for power, which is but a delusion."

The prince's head hung low for a moment, then he took a deep breath. "Wrong. I'm not driven by ambition, I'm simply doing my duty as a father and the head of a household. I'm simply trying to survive, and there is nothing in the Diamond Sutra against that."

I was going to speak again, but he put his finger on my lips. "No, this is not the time to hesitate. I've been passive long enough. I have to change my fate. It's my only chance."

He picked up the paper and started to unfold it. My heart caught in my throat and I said urgently, "Are you sure it'll work?"

Still holding the paper, he stroked my cheek with his free hand. "I will succeed. Per Father Emperor's order, no one except Longkodo is allowed in the Bookhouse. If something happens, none of my brothers will get here as fast as I can. And I will find a way to get to the will first. Longkodo isn't hard to deal with."

479

I paused for a moment, wondering whether Longkodo was in it with him. But I had no time to indulge my curiosity. "What if they found out it was fake?"

"Don't worry about that," he said. "It's as good as the real one. I memorized every line. If I have no other talents, I have my skill of memory. Hongli got that from me, too."

"What about your handwriting?" I asked, trying to divert his attention from the paper.

"Father Emperor taught me calligraphy himself. Since I was a child, I copied his writings when I practiced. That's the reason why he prefers me to mark his documents for him."

He was about to read the forged will, but I grabbed his wrist. "Please, destroy it. What if you failed?"

He stared at me for a moment, then he smiled. "I didn't know you cared for me so much. The chance is small, but if I failed, I would be hanged for sure."

How could he still smile? I almost felt sorry for him, knowing whether he succeeded or failed, Jeng would be the emperor.

He pulled me closer to him. "But if I succeed, I will make you a noble lady."

I kissed his lips. The paper fell onto the floor.

He reached to pick up the paper when we heard a knock on the door. "Is Prince Yong here?" It was the head eunuch's voice. Prince Yong answered right away.

He opened the door to a slit. "Is the emperor all right?"

"That's what I'm here for. You've got to hurry."

"I'll be right there."

He put on his robe right away. I picked up the paper on the floor and folded it with trembling hands, then I gave it to him. He stuffed it into his sleeve pocket.

Before he left, he stamped a kiss on my forehead. "Don't worry. I'll succeed. Go back to sleep."

I collapsed onto the bed after the prince had left, but I could not return to sleep after that. Was history about to change, after all? Would Jeng really become the emperor? As much I had wished for it, it seemed too good to be true. Instead, anxiety and fear seized me. I thought about what I should do next. A logical thing to do would be to leave the garden right away and return to Lady Uya's palace, so I would avoid seeing Prince Yong. But I couldn't do it because I felt guilty tricking him and felt sorry for him. He had tried hard to win the love of his own mother and his favored concubine, who had both preferred his younger brother. I could understand his rage when he found out that his father would give Jeng the throne. Besides, I wanted to make sure that Jeng was indeed named the successor.

I quickly washed and had breakfast before going out for a walk in the garden.

I GOT AS close as I could to the Bookhouse and watched at a distance. I saw the arrival of some court officials first, then the princes.

It was freezing cold, but I stood where I was, afraid that if I moved even for a second, I would miss something important.

Finally, at around noon, I saw people walking out of the building. The princes chatted with one another. I caught the sight of Prince Yong in the crowd. He looked at ease, as if nothing had happened. For a moment, I couldn't decide how to feel. I was unsure what it actually meant. Who would become the emperor?

Prince Yong spotted me and walked towards me. As he neared, he said calmly, "I didn't make it."

Instead of happiness, I was possessed by a surge of pity. I held his hand silently.

"Your hands are cold," he said, trying to warm me. "Let me take you home."

After we had returned to my room, we sat on the couch and I waited nervously for him to speak. He sat silently for a long moment, then he started to laugh.

"What's wrong?" I asked worriedly. "Are you all right?"

He paused from laughing and said, "Father Emperor had us all fooled!"

"What do you mean?"

"It's Yinreng—can you believe that?"

Yinreng was the twice-annulled Crown Prince. "What about him?"

"He's gotten the throne after all."

"What?" I gasped. "I thought it was Prince Jeng."

"I thought so, too." He laughed again. "But Father revised his will. He must've done it just two days ago, when Longkodo visited him."

I felt the blood draining from my body. "Did you not get a chance to switch them?"

"I did," he said. "I thought I did. But I blundered. It was harder than I thought. I didn't know news would travel so quickly. By the time Longkodo opened the box and let me see the will, the room was full of people. My hand was shaking. I must've put my own paper back in my pocket."

"I see." I was disappointed. Jeng was not named, and the Crown Prince . . . the historians had mixed opinions about him.

He cheered up soon. "Don't worry. At least no one saw me doing it. Yinreng isn't my enemy, so I shouldn't be too worse off. He can have the Garden of Perfect Brightness if he wants."

I felt sorry for him since I knew how much he loved the garden. I patted his arm. I also wanted to take Priest Wang's forged paper from his sleeve before he read it. I couldn't imagine what he would do to me once he found out I had switched the paper.

"Would you like to rest for a while?" I asked gently, trying to help him out of his robe.

"Sure." He let me do it, but before letting me take the robe, he took the piece of paper from the sleeve and opened it.

My heart plunged.

After glancing over it, he crumpled the paper and threw it on the floor.

I embraced myself for a blow, but he didn't even look at me.

Curiously, I picked up the paper, and quickly looked over it. Instead of *fourteenth prince*, I saw the words *fourth prince*. My mind went blank in an instant. Had I not been able to switch them the night before? I threw the paper into the waste basket and quickly went to my wardrobe. Then I checked the paper in the pocket of the jacket I wore the day before. On the paper it also stated the fourth prince to be the successor.

I was totally confused. What had happened? I remembered distinctly the word *fourteenth* on Priest Wang's forged will. Whether I had switched the two wills or not, one of them should have *fourteenth prince* on it, right?

As I was still thinking, I heard the prince shout, "Impossible!"

I hurried out to the living room. He had picked up the crumpled paper again and was standing near the window in order to take a better look. He was staring at a particular spot for a long time. "This is Father Emperor's handwriting!"

I didn't understand what he meant. "What do you mean? You wrote it, didn't you?"

"No." He pointed to *ren,* the character for human. "Truth is, my imitation is not perfect. Look at this second stroke, Father's is very smooth, but I can't imitate it because I have the habit of pausing too long before lifting the pen at the end." To demonstrate, he quickly rubbed some ink in the inkstone, and took the brush pen on my desk. "Other people might not be able to detect the difference, but I can."

With my heart pounding in my chest, I compared the stroke he wrote with the one on the document. He was right, there was a subtle difference. Prince Yong's was less smooth.

I swallowed as I realized the implication of the fact. If the document in front of us was the authentic will, then Prince Yong must've switched it with the one that Priest Wang had forged. But how was it possible?

While I was struggling to make sense of the situation, Prince Yong spoke, "Which means I succeeded in the switching!"

I must've turned very pale when he turned sharply to look at me, his eyes like blades.

"What did you do?" He grabbed the collar of my shirt with one hand and balled his right hand into a fist.

"I'm sorry." Tears flooded my face. Although I still didn't fully comprehend what had happened, I knew I was to be blamed.

"Father had named me . . . and yet I . . . How foolish! But why did you help Yinreng?"

I shook my head vehemently. "I didn't."

He loosened his grasp on me, then roared in agony.

I watched him pounding his fist on the wall again and again, and finally dashing out of the room. Then I dropped onto the floor and sobbed. *What have I done!*

The unexpected outcome of the event shocked me, and I stayed in my room for the rest of the day, trying to make sense of it. Prince Yong had seen the previous will with Jeng's name in it shortly after Mid-Autumn Day. The emperor must have written it during the holiday, when he missed his son who was away from home fighting for his empire. But he changed his mind and revised the will since then. Why? The only reason I could come up with was Hongli. The child had brought enormous joy to Kangxi's life in the past months, and he was multi-talented—the perfect heir that the emperor had hoped for. Naming Prince Yong his successor was the only way to ensure Hongli would be the emperor one day. Despite its political intention, the testament was a loving gift to his grandson. Pictures of Kangxi and Hongli practicing calligraphy and taking walks together flashed in my mind, and once again tears trickled down my face.

Reluctantly, my thoughts turned to Prince Yong and I couldn't imagine what he was going through. Regret and remorse filled me, and I spent the whole night wishing I had not taught him any magic trick. I wanted to see him and ask for forgiveness, although he was also responsible for the disappointing and ironical ending. I thought about what he had done for me in the past year. He might have the potential of being a merciless emperor, but up to this point, he hadn't really done anything condemnable. He had been a loving husband to his wives and a caring father to his children. And he had been nothing but kind to me.

CHAPTER 28

THE NEXT MORNING, I rose before dawn and picked out a green silk qipao from my closet. Lady Uya had a palace seamstress make it for me after the Ice Play, saying the color fit me, and it had become my favorite ever since. But I had picked it out for another reason. I had sewn the necklace with the yin-yang pendant onto the inside of the wide sleeve for safekeeping. Last night I had realized reluctantly that perhaps it was time for me to stop messing around and go home.

But first, I hired a carriage to take me to the House of Prince Yong. I felt the need to explain everything to him, although I did not know how. It was still early when I saw the familiar entrance of the grand estate. But the traffic around it was heavy. At least three horse carriages were parked in front of the gate, and servants were going in and out, carrying trunks and crates. What was going on?

I spotted Jade, a maid I had been acquainted with during my stay the previous year and made inquiries.

"Oh, it's terrible." Jade's voice trembled. "I can't believe it happened just like that."

"What happened?"

"The prince received decree from the new emperor last night. His property has been confiscated. We all have to move out."

"Heavens," I murmured. Didn't Prince Yong say Yinreng was not his enemy?

"And that's not it," Jade's voice broke as she went on. "The prince has been taken away to the Imperial Clan Court."

"What? What about the ladies? Is Lady Nian still here?"

"She should be. You can go check."

I wasted no time and ran towards the Pavilion of Harmony and Happiness. Lady Nian was sitting on the couch, passively watching her maids packing. Her eyes were red and swollen.

Tears streamed down her cheeks as soon as she saw me. "Julie! Tell me what I'm supposed to do?"

I took her trembling hands and tried hard not to cry, too. "Are you going to return to your parents' house?"

She shook her head. "I was going to, but they were ordered to evacuate, too."

"What?"

"Yes, everyone who's closely related to the prince must move out of Jing City."

"So where are you going?"

"My family will be moving to a village near the Imperial Mausoleum. The fourteenth and the eighth princes' families will be there as well."

My mouth fell open. This Yinreng was no better!

I observed the chaos that filled the space around me as I exited the property. Servants shouted at one another, and children were crying. Elegantly carved vanity tables, chests of drawers, tables and chairs that had belonged to the imperial house crowded the square between the gate and Ying An Hall, some with contents spilling next to them, waiting to be transported to their new demoted home. Some maids were saying goodbye to each other since many of them had been dismissed.

In the midst of clamor, I heard the clear voice of a child, calling me. "Master Julie!"

I turned and saw Hongli, who was standing hand-in-hand with his mother Lady Nyuhulu, among the servants. He ran towards me and hugged me. I squatted down and held his shoulders. "Where will you go?"

"We'll be going to Grandpa's farm!" he answered cheerfully.

I remembered him saying that he liked the farm, but I still felt sorry. I must've looked like crying because the child asked me, "Are you sad about Papa and Grandpa?"

I nodded. "I'm very sorry."

"But it isn't your fault," he said in an adult-like manner. "You tried to save Grandpa. You foresaw this. I wish I had tried harder to help you. I wish I had feigned illness."

I stroked his cheek that was red from the cold. "Don't blame yourself, child. You did your best. Just remember, your grandpa expected greatness from you. Don't let him down."

The child pressed his lips together and nodded with determination.

It had started to snow, and I wandered aimlessly inside the Inner City. Where should I go? I thought about going to the Palace of Eternal Harmony, but I couldn't face Lady Uya—she must've been devastated by the sudden turmoil following her husband's death. Soon, I found myself crossing the city gate. In the Outer City, the commoners went on about their lives as usual, oblivious of the turmoil within the imperial families.

Near the front gate of the city wall, a woman holding some handkerchiefs in her hands shouted at the passersby, "Embroidered handkerchiefs!"

I was going to pass her by, but she spotted me. As she approached me, a man who was pushing his way through bumped into her, and a white handkerchief in her hand dropped on the ground in front of me.

She picked it up quickly and waved it at me as soon as she stood up. "Take a look. It matches your dress!"

It took me a second to realize the handkerchief I was looking at was green and was not the one dropped on the ground earlier.

A sudden revelation struck me. Since yesterday, I had been thinking about how the priest's forged will had changed and couldn't figure it out. Now I knew. He must've switched it the moment he dropped it on the ground and picked it up. I had thought he was nervous, but it had all been an act. I drew a breath: The priest was a trickster! But why did he trick me? Why did he want to help Yinreng? Could the third prince be responsible since the two princes were friends? I gave the woman a copper coin without taking her handkerchief. Then I went to the next carriage cab I saw on the street, gave the driver enough silver and told him to take me to the Temple of Light and Shadow. I had to find out the truth and try to clean up the mess I had made.

When I got off the carriage at the foot of the hill, it was late afternoon. I ran up the snow-covered path and past the hourglass rock. The door was open, and incense was burning, but no one was inside. "Priest Wang, are you in?" I called out as I walked through the creepy, semi-dark front hall, then I heard a rhythmic rustling sound. Through the window I saw a hunched figure sweeping snow in the backyard. It had to be Priest Wang. Why was he sweeping snow in the midst of snowing? I quickened my steps and walked towards the back door, but before I could reach it, I heard a thump, and felt an excruciating pain on the back of my head before everything turned dark around me.

WHE I WOKE, the first thing I felt was the weird taste in my mouth—something salty, most likely a rag, was stuffed in my mouth. I wanted to spit it out but couldn't move my tongue. I had difficulty moving my hands and feet as well since they were all bound. It was dark around me, and it was cold. I made muffled cries as I wriggled my body around. I hit the leg of a table, and with all my might I managed to kick the table and a huge crashing sound broke the silence of the night. Soon after, a door creaked, and dim lights moved through and illuminated the room.

I heard footsteps thumping on the floor above me right before I saw the candlelight and the man holding it. His frail stature told me it was Priest Wang. But as he came close, I gasped. It was Dong Wang in black-rimmed glasses and pajamas.

As soon as he removed the rag in my mouth I cried, "Dong! Am I back in twentieth century?"

"No, Julie, you're still in the Qing dynasty, 1722." It was Dong's croaky voice.

"Why are you here then?" I asked confusedly. "Are you not Dong? "

"It is I indeed!" His laugher chilled me. "I'm Dong Wang."

"Where is Priest Wang then?" I asked with faltering voice, staring at the man.

"He's here. I am Priest Wang, too."

I shivered. "Is that so?" Somehow, I wasn't that surprised. In fact, I had been troubled by the striking similarities between the two. The priest's white goatee and eyebrows were all fake, and he must've painted his eye sockets and wrinkles as well. "So, you were Priest Wang all along?"

"No, I was Dong Wang all along. I came from the future." He switched to the priest's high-pitched voice, as if to mock my stupidity.

His words chilled me to the bone. The priest I'd met in the hutong, who had pretended he didn't know me, and who had tricked me into switching the emperor's will, was actually the man who swept the campus of Peking University. But why? Why did he trick me?

He told me the answer before I even asked. "I was born into the family of a farmer, but I loved science as a child. I came to Beijing when I was fifteen, entered Peking University, but quit because my father became ill and I had to work to support my family. I worked as a mechanical engineer at a car plant in Hebei, worked my butt off but couldn't get to the top, because I didn't have a college degree, and because I wasn't born into the right family."

He paused and took a deep breath, as if shake off the resentment that still possessed him. Then he went on again, "When my father died twenty years ago, he passed our genealogy to me. Based on that and some research, I found out our family was Manchu, and our real surname had been Ai. Not only so, I was the descendant of

Yinreng, the second son of Emperor Kangxi, who had died shortly after Prince Yong had ascended the throne."

My mouth fell open at the incredible story. For a moment, I refused to believe it, thinking he could be lying. But the look on his face when he spoke again somehow convinced me that he was speaking the truth. "It's one thing to be born into a poor family, quite another to know that it shouldn't have been so."

When he paused, I spoke. "So you decided to change history?"

"Yes. But it wasn't until I realized I had the power. At first, I merely became interested in everything about the Qing dynasty—politics, culture, science and religion. I spent most of my spare time at Peking University's library. Then by chance, I discovered the book *Taoist Spells of the Qing dynasty*. Among them, was a time-traveling spell. It was basically how to utilize the earth's yin and yang energies to time travel. Combining that and my knowledge in physics and engineering, I spent nearly twenty years to find the qi portals, and to make the pendant."

So, all the stories about his ancestor were made up, and so was the diary. What a liar. I had been completely fooled. "I see, you never intended to help Jeng, you only wanted to use him to get the second prince's crown back."

"Wrong. In the beginning when I sought Prince Fourteen at the cemetery, all I wanted was to help him get back his throne. If he succeeded, I would ask him to make Taizi a duke. I believed Jeng would be a benevolent ruler, and I had no other choice. But then, as luck had it, I had a bit too much to drink the night he came to me, and not only messed up with the dial on the pendant but also got confused about the direction."

"Why didn't you go back to correct your mistake, then?"

He chuckled. "Didn't I tell you time traveling sucked up your energy? By the time I met him, I'd already done about ten trials. I was simply tired of it."

I couldn't repress my rage. "Are you saying you were going to abandon him in the twenty-first century? He was all alone, and badly injured. If I hadn't run into him, he might've died in the pit!"

He shrugged. "Well, he didn't, did he? I was planning to meet him there and send him back. Anyway, it was fortuitous that you came along. At first, I didn't think you could be much help. I racked my brain to come up a plan regarding the will, I befriended the third prince, and I even broke into the Palace of Heavenly Purity—"

"It was you!" I suddenly recalled the priest in a eunuch's hat. Why had I been so dense?

He ignored my interruption and went on. "It was me. I had the thought of forging the will in the beginning of the year, when Prince Three told me about your promotion in the palace, and I started to practice Kangxi's handwriting. The other day when we met at the Garden of Joyful Spring, I was going to convince you to take on the mission, since you were close to the emperor. You cannot imagine the moment you told me about Prince Yong's plan! I was absolutely thrilled!"

I recalled the moment. The priest's pupils had dilated, but nothing more. He had hidden his emotions well. "You evil bastard!" I spat at him. It dawned on me that he must've revealed the whereabouts of Hongli and I to the third prince the day before the emperor's Nanyuan hunt.

He stared at me with angry eyes, his jaw hard, looking as if he would lose his composure. It was the first time I had ever seen any expression on his face, and I waited excitedly to see what he was about to do. But he relaxed with a chuckle, wiped the spittle off his face and sat back in his chair. "I used wit instead of violence. And indeed, my success is a proof that the former is more effective."

I, on the other hand, wished I could use violence at the moment. But all I could do was talk. "Why didn't you simply travel to the past and warn Taizi of his impending fate instead? Why go through all this and drag Prince Jeng into it?"

"How do you know I haven't tried? The first time I spoke to him he called me a swindler and chased me out of his palace. The second time he almost killed me before even speaking to me." The priest sighed. "The problem with Yinreng is that he's too self-confident. He took his title of Crown Prince for granted and never doubted that he would be the next emperor. Who can blame him? He's almost born with the right. He didn't lose the confidence after being annulled the first time, neither did he change the second time. You know what he said to me when I brought him the news of his succession to the throne the other day? He said, 'I can't believe it took so long.'"

What a conceited jerk, I cursed silently. True, if Taizi had had the humility of taking any advice, he wouldn't have lost his title twice.

"So, are you happy with the result?" I asked bitterly.

"No, I'm abhorred." Dong shook his head. "I didn't expect Taizi to be atrocious as well vain. I thought he would make a good emperor with all his talents and training in politics."

I detected a hint of remorse in his voice. "We could start it over and give Prince Jeng a chance."

He said adamantly, "No, I'm not going to change it. It isn't bad at all to me personally."

"How do you know you won't become a commoner again in the twenty-first century? A lot could happen in three hundred years."

"I don't care," Dong shrugged. "I don't plan to go back at all."

"But you're nobody here."

"Wrong! The third prince believes it's my magic that helped restore the second prince. And with his words and my knowledge of future, I'll become His Majesty's right-hand man in no time."

It took me a second to realize by 'His Majesty' he meant Yinreng, and that it was against Kangxi's will to have the scoundrel son to inherit his title. I squeezed my eyes shut with regret, knowing I had taken part in the treachery. I thought about Prince Yong and Prince Jeng, and their families.

Inhaling deeply, I looked up. "What's going to happen to Hongli? Will he still become an emperor?"

"That is not for me to say." Dong shook his head. "But he'll live."

"You liar! That wasn't what you told me. You said he would be the emperor even if his father wasn't."

"Yes, and I also said *if he was destined to be so*," he said with an evil smile.

I felt sick to my stomach. The possibility that China would lose a great emperor was simply too much for me. "What're you going to do with me then? Are you going to send me back to the future?"

He chuckled, shaking his head. "Julie, you're intelligent, but not smart. Do you think I'll give you a chance to come back and ruin my work? No, you'll stay here in the Qing dynasty, specifically inside the Temple of Light and Shadow. Not a soul will come up here, except Big Dumb. But don't worry, you won't be starved. You'll even have books to read if you wish."

"You monster!" I screamed. "Why don't you just kill me?"

"Oh no," he said. "Killing is not my nature. I do not take lives."

"Maybe not with your own hands, but you do. You're a murderer. Prince Yong, Prince Jeng, and many others will die because of the treason you committed."

"Ah, with your help, Julie. You switched the papers for me, didn't you?"

"You!" I was so mad and frustrated since I couldn't move my hands to strike him.

He stood up and took the candle. "Anyway, I hope I've answered your questions. Now I have a new life ahead of me. The temple is your home now, Julie, and soon will be your grave!"

Fear replaced my anger. "No, wait! Stay! You can't just leave me here!"

He ignored my curses and went up the stairs. The candlelight vanished as he closed the door behind him, and so did my hope.

FOR MONTHS I lived in the basement of the temple. The priest hadn't shown up again. But Big Dumb came every day, bringing me food and drink, and occasionally a basin of water for me to wash myself. My hands and feet were no longer tied, but there wasn't a chance for me to escape the dungeon-like room with no windows. I tried but couldn't lift the trapdoor, which was locked from above. The big man never moved a foot past the staircase and his huge body left no room for me to squeeze through.

Days passed without seeing another soul, although there were mice and roaches crawling around me at night. It was cold, although counting the days, I knew winter had long passed and it should be March. I missed Jeng terribly and I was afraid to think what had happened to him. I had cried so much that I had no more tears left. In the absolute silence of my confinement, interrupted only by the squeaking of mice and Big Dumb's footsteps, I dwelled on reflections day and night. I regretted what I had done. If only I had not switched the paper in Prince Yong's pocket. If only I had not come to meddle with history at all! But I also realized one thing—history could be changed after all. I believed the reason Kangxi had changed his mind and named Prince Yong his successor was because of his love for Hongli, who was the multi-talented son that he had wished for, and obviously I played a role in the child's mathematical talent. Had Dong Wang not intervened, I would've talked Prince Yong out of attempting to switch the will, and he would still have become the emperor just as in the original version. But the fact that it had been his father's intention and no treason was involved might have prevented any cruel treatment of his siblings.

After a while, I stopped reflecting. It didn't ease my regrets. I became numb and I accepted my punishment. I ate, drank and waited passively for death to summon me.

One night, I woke to the sound of heavy thump. I opened my eyes and saw a huge shadow moving slowly towards the wall of the basement. It had to be Big Dumb, but what was he doing? I stared at him without stirring. He was holding something in his arms—a vine jar. He bent and put it down next to the other jars, then he picked up another jar and headed back up the stairs. I was curious because it was the first time I'd seen him coming farther than the base of the staircase. After he had left and closed the trapdoor, I went to the jars and opened the lids.

All of them were full. The jar that had been brought down earlier must've been new since its alcoholic scent wasn't as strong. Big Dumb had been periodically adding new jars and removing them as well. He must've been fond of drinking and thus needed a constant supply. Or he might be doing it for Dong Wang, who had confessed his love for alcohol. But why did he have to sneak in at night, when I was asleep, to do the work? It didn't take me long to get it. He didn't want to create an opportunity for me to escape!

The realization sparked hope in me right away and I started to make plans. I began to do exercises every day—yoga, pushups, and jump squats. I also practiced running the stairs in an agile manner. But mostly I thought about how I would plan the timing. I had to take action at the precise moment when Big Dumb bent and put the jar down, otherwise, he could easily drop the jar and run after me. Even so, I had less than a minute. In order to make sure I was awake when he showed up, I had to adjust my sleeping cycle as well. He had come with the same purpose a few more times and I had a pretty good idea of the time and frequency. He would come every five days, about two hours after he cleared my dinner tray.

I'd been tracking the time and I was pretty sure it was middle of April, where the energy field would carry me south into the past. I had contemplated the idea of going back in time again, but I couldn't be sure what I could accomplish. If I prevented Prince Yong from carrying out his scheme, then he would become the emperor, but would it be good for Jeng and his other brothers? And how would I know things wouldn't turn out differently? What if I only ended up making a bigger mess? I had already spent a year and a half on the impossible mission. It was time for me to go home.

After another month's patient waiting, I was ready and eager to carry out my plan. It had been five days after Big Dumb had carried away a wine jar, and I went to bed right after he had removed my dinner plates, with all my clothes on. I lay in my cot, pretending to snore evenly, and waiting for the trapdoor to open. I almost fell asleep, but I pinched my thigh to stay awake. Then the floor above creaked and a faint shred of light entered the basement. The big man descended the stairs carefully and slowly, hugging a jar in his arms. I was so excited that I forgot to breathe for a second. He stopped at the base of the staircase, putting the jar on the table as if checking on me. I snored and he moved on. Still snoring, I moved out of bed slowly, and towards the stairs. But I didn't even get to the stairs when a broken chair fell into my way. The big man must've moved it earlier. I nearly tripped and Big Dumb ran to me in an instant, letting the jar fall onto the ground. He was about to seize me, but I lifted the broken chair and hit him right in the face. He yelped, covering his eyes. I ran up the stairs within a single breath, closed and locked the trapdoor, and pushed a table on top of it. Before going out of the temple, I took the stick that was used to bolt the door and stuck it through the handles on the outside of the door.

It was cold and wet outside, but I had no time to shiver. Thanks to the stars in the sky, it wasn't pitch dark and I had enough light to help me discern the path that led down the hill. After tripping and falling numerous times, I reached the forest where the time chamber was. I took the pendant out from my sleeve and fastened the string on my neck. I waited impatiently. What if the current had already come and past for the night? My heart beat frantically and I could hear my heavy breathing in the quietness of the night. I closed my eyes and prayed. Then the hissing sound came, and I felt the current sweeping me off my feet.

To be continued.

Thank You

Thank you so much for reading Love and the Forbidden City. I hope you enjoyed it! Please stay tuned for Book Two, where Julie Bird will return to her unfinished mission. If you're interested in historical backgrounds that the story is based on, please visit my website at bijouli.net.

I would also like to ask you a favor: If you like Book One, please leave a review on Amazon! If you have comments and suggestions, please feel free to contact me at bijouli.net.

Acknowledgments

Love and the Forbidden City turned out to be a project bigger that I had imagined. I couldn't have completed the book without the support of friends and family. I would like to thank the authors in my writing group for listening and commenting on my early drafts. I also want to thank my Facebook friends for their advice on writing as well as publishing. My biggest thanks goes to my editor Monique Fischer, for not just correcting grammatical errors, but also smoothing my sentences and providing better word choices. My book is more enjoyable to read thanks to her professional competencies. Last but not least, I would like to thank my husband Ryu, who is a firm believer of "Do what you love, and the money will follow," for his patience and encouragement.

About the Author

Bijou Li grew up in China and came to the U.S. in her late teens. She received her BA in English literature from University of California, Berkeley. Her short story, The Big Banyan Tree, won the Shrout Prize in UCB's 2000 literary contests. Since then, she's written volumes of short stories, and many of them were published in school journals. While doing her MA thesis, Bijou lived with the Mosuo, an ethnic group living in China who practiced "walking marriage." The hard-working Mosuo women inspired her to write The Chief's Runaway Bride, Country of Daughters and other novels based on the Mosuo culture. Please visit Bijou Li at bijouli.net.

Made in the USA
Las Vegas, NV
22 October 2023

79496435R00298